Last Exit to Montauk

Phillip Vega

First edition 2017
Published in the USA by *thewordverve inc.* (www.thewordverve.com)

eBook ISBN: 978-1-941251-88-1
Paperback ISBN: 978-1-941251-89-8

Library of Congress Control Number: 2017930872

~~~~~

Last Exit to Montauk

A Book with Verve by *thewordverve inc.*

Cover design by Robin Kraus
http://www.bookformatters.com

Interior design and eBook formatting by Bob Houston
http://facebook.com/eBookFormatting/info

To my Immortal Beloved

What People Are Saying About *Last Exit to Montauk*

"A romance that begins in the heat of a Long Island summer bares two young souls to new love, intimacy, and tragedy. Highly recommended!"
> *– Lawrence Kelter, bestselling author of* BACK TO BROOKLYN, *the sequel to* My Cousin Vinny

"Raw, real, and packed with heartfelt emotion, *Last Exit to Montauk* is a sentimental love story of a whirlwind romance that stands the test of time, spinning the perfect tale of the challenges and awkwardness of love at first sight. One minute you'll laugh, the next you'll reach for a tissue. Full of twists and turns, the unforeseen twist at the end wrenches your heart, leaving you breathless, and reminding us all just how precious life truly is. We all have but one life. The magic is found in living it."
> *– Cheryl Bradshaw,* New York Times *and* USA Today *bestselling author of the Sloane Monroe mysteries*

"Vega's account of first love is so authentic it's hard to believe he wasn't seventeen when he wrote it. *Last Exit to Montauk* will have you reminiscing about summers as a teenager and all the foibles and joys of those times. With references to the 1980s that ground you and an ending that doesn't pull any emotional punches, this books keeps you turning the pages."
> *– Elena Stowell, author of* Flowing with the Go *and co-founder of the Carly Stowell Foundation*
> *(www.carlystowellfoundation.countmein.com)*

"I loved the book and cried at the end. It was a wonderful heartwarming tale of an adolescent boy and his heart. I loved the characters and could relate, as I am a fellow Long Islander. The references to the 1980s are great."
> *– Nancy O'Hara, early reviewer*

"It brought back some great memories of high school. I felt very 'seventeen,' which was a fun way to feel during the week of my fiftieth birthday. I can't even guess how many times I literally laughed out loud. I was expecting a great book and was definitely not disappointed."

– Karen Nelson, early reviewer

"I loved the '80s memories of Friendly's fribbles, Spencer's Gifts, the music, movies, etc. I have lots of family in Long Island and grew up going there all my life, and I feel like he nailed the Long Island '80s vibe of malls and beach days. The book has great nostalgia for me, especially given the world we live in today with constant social media and everyone on their phones. It was a great escape!"

– Danielle Boniauto, early reviewer

Table of Contents

Prologue

W ho knew that going into Whole Foods with my wife of twenty-five years, on a rainy Saturday afternoon in Florida, would bring me back to the summer of '87? It happened right there in the bulk section among the garbanzos and Forbidden Rice. Yep, *Forbidden Rice*, which kind of made sense considering the direction of my thoughts at that moment.

There she was—the catalyst for my memory. I hadn't thought about her in years, but there she stood. It was her honey-colored hair and the way it flowed down past her shoulders that first caught my attention. I couldn't help but do a double take and stare for moment . . . at her hair, among other things. But mostly her hair. She was a carbon copy. It was uncanny.

She wore a pair of blue shorts, white Keds, a white T-shirt, and a beige cardigan sweater. Her legs were sun-kissed and athletically toned too. From ten yards away, I could feel the glow of the sun radiating off her body, even on this rainy day. And her body language was just so similar, her movements, the way she carried herself.

The only thing missing from the scenario was a piece of fruit that she would hold up to her nose for a whiff of the yummy freshness (more on that later).

My wife and I hit the dairy section next, stocking up on yogurt for a couple of weeks. After that, we made our way through the middle sections of the store. My mind continued to wander as we meandered, and . . .

Man, there she is again, down the ethnic food aisle. Damn, is she following me? I'm old enough to be her father . . . er, really cool uncle. What did she just pick up? Why is she furrowing her brow? What gluten-free, locally grown ethnic food from the exotic land of Or-land-o has her stumped?

I wonder what she smells like. Is that too creepy? Yeah, it's too creepy. But still, I wonder if she smells like rain. After all, it is raining. Why is she shopping here today? Surely, she has better things to do on this rainy summer afternoon in Florida.

Let's just avoid that aisle, shall we?

I manipulated the shopping cart, and my wife, to keep moving to the next aisle, feigning interest in an item—any item really—stocked there. Ah, pasta sauces. It was an aisle full of non-ethnic pastas, sauces, soups, and other canned goods, including Italian food and spices. *I guess Italian is not ethnic. Who knew?* As we walked up the aisle, the blonde came down from the other side.

Shit, did our eyes just meet? Did she just look at me? Am I sparking some distant memory for her too? Did she just smile at me? Focus, man, focus. You're here for pasta, not for the blonde. You're married, for Christ's sake!

My wife placed a jar of spaghetti sauce in the cart and then flipped around to the other side of the aisle to examine the latest in pasta design: the hollow spaghetti noodle.

She held up the box and asked, "Should we try it? It's gluten-free, and no GMO."

"Sure, why not? Let's throw caution to the wind," I teased.

Throwing the box in the cart, my wife snorted at my wit, which made me snort too. Then I held my breath because . . .

Man, she's right here, practically in my lap. Okay, not that close, but across the aisle, looking at the sauces. Wow, I can smell her from here. She smells like, I don't know, sunshine, the beach . . . and sex? Is "sex" even a scent? Do they bottle that scent?

"Hey, babe," my wife said, touching my arm as she scanned the shelves for other meal possibilities, "why don't you go pick out a bottle of wine to go with dinner?"

Jolted out of my aromatherapy moment, I nodded. "Sure thing. I'll go see what they have."

"I plan on putting center-cuts in with the sauce, so pick out something nice, okay?"

"Yep, sure thing. Center-cuts in the sauce over hollow spaghetti and get something nice. Got it."

I hurried off, maybe a little too quickly, but I seriously needed a breather. I homed in on the vino aisle and tried to focus on my task. I found a nice cab-merlot blend. Blackberry flavor profile, grown by some guy named Javier on his family-owned vineyard in Napa. Good for Javier. Living the American Dream. Pleased with my selection, I headed down the aisle to find my wife, and oh . . .

There she is again at the premade salad section. I swear she's following me.

I tried my damnedest to be cool and nonchalant, which I was sure I was. Fairly sure. But crazy thoughts kept shooting randomly through my head.

She looks like a tennis player, but she's not built like Serena or Venus. She's more like Anna Kournikova or Caroline Wozniacki. I bet she plays tennis, and I bet she's good too. She's probably real competitive and hates losing, but does so with grace. She probably bounces on the balls of her feet, going back and forth while waiting for the serve.

Just keep walking, champ.

"Did you pick a good one?" Ah, the wife.

I held up the bottle and smiled. "Hmm, oh yeah, I think you'll like it."

She took it and read the label, nodding. "Looks like a great choice," she said as she read.

Her eyes were on the bottle, but mine . . . well, mine had wandered again. To the gluten-free baked goods section. Where my blond doppelganger was selecting a loaf of Italian bread.

I wonder if she's having pasta for dinner too. No, I picture her more of a free-range salmon and wild rice kind of girl, with a sprig of rosemary. She'll probably serve it with a glass of chardonnay, mirroring her wavy, golden hair and skin tone.

I bet for dessert she'll serve a mix of fresh berries topped with real whipped cream. She and her young lover will have dessert outside next to a fire pit, even though it's summertime. The fire pit will crackle and pop, while various berries burst in her perfect mouth. They'll sit there staring into each other's eyes, smiling and sipping wine as the fire crackles in the background.

My wife and I were now at the checkout line. I didn't remember moving in that direction.

Was it really close to thirty years ago?

"That'll be $114.73," the cashier said, and my wife stepped aside so I could run the card.

"What the hell did we buy?" I said to my wife under my breath. "We just came for yogurt and some people-watching, to get out of the rain."

"And that's what we did," she said, popping my shoulder playfully. "And then some."

Boy, she can say that again.

~ ~ ~

As I lay in bed, the clock helpfully pointing out it was way too early for anyone to be awake at 4:17 a.m., I realized my recurring shoulder pain and my evil, aging bladder were not going to let me return to dreamland anytime soon.

I flipped on the bathroom light and got down to business. As I washed my hands and popped a few Advil, I got to thinking about my grocery store adventure . . .

I wonder if that blonde is getting any sleep. I bet she is. She probably has some dog curled up against her too. She probably has one arm under her pillow, while the other rests at her side, as she's curled in the fetal position. When she rolls over, I bet her wavy, blond hair slightly covers her face. You can still make out her nose and mouth, but her hair is partially blocking her blond eyebrows and blue eyes. I bet when she rolls over and wakes up, her smile lights up the room as she stretches her gorgeous body.

Many years ago, she lit up my world when she smiled at me—my blonde, not the one from Whole Foods. There she had stood, shopping for some fresh fruit at a local market. That was where it all started, back in the summer of 1987.

1 - My Blonde

It was the summer between my junior and senior year of high school. Summer camp was over and, as a result, so was my day job. I still had a solid three weeks before school started, so this gave me time to enjoy the rest of the summer.

It helped that Ma had bought me a car a few months before that, so I was able to get around without having to rely on rides so much anymore. I hit the beach with friends, walked the mall, swam in my pool, and played tennis with my best friend, Jean Paul. He and I were day students at a local boarding school. This meant that sports camps wouldn't start until after all the students came back to school after Labor Day. I played football, and Jean Paul played soccer. Anyway, we were both pretty good tennis players and usually got in a couple of sets before calling it a day.

One morning, Ma asked me to drop off some mail at the local post office.

I was low on gas, so I rode my ten-speed bike that day. On the way home after tennis, I rode to the post office, located in the middle of a hamlet. Not Shakespeare's *Hamlet,* a normal hamlet. Across from the post office was a local grocery store. Not one of the big chains, like A&P or Publix. It was just a local grocer in a world before gluten-free and non-GMO food. After dropping off the mail, I stopped in to buy something to drink.

And there she was, standing in the produce section, *my blonde*. I can still see it today. She was checking out the peaches and nectarines. Or maybe they were apples.

Hell, I can't remember what fruit it was. All I remember is she was standing there in the produce section, smelling fruit.

She'd pick up a piece of fruit, sniff it, decide if she liked it, and then place it in her hand basket or return it back to the pile. There was something so sophisticated and funny about it.

It was the first time I'd seen anyone do that. Sure, I'd seen people handle fruit before. Was it firm? Ripe? Too ripe? Does it *sound* ripe? *Have you every knocked on a watermelon to test for ripeness, or is that just me? Of course, I have no idea what the perfect watermelon sounds like, but that never stopped me from knocking on one.* Anyway, there she stood, smelling the fruit.

She had honey-blond hair tied back into a ponytail with a black scrunchie. Her skin was sun-kissed, perfect, and blemish-free. She wore a polo shirt and a pair of shorts. She was definitely pretty, but in an unassuming way. I imagined she was the type of girl who was pretty but didn't know it, or at least she didn't walk around like she was God's gift. Although to me, she would become a most precious gift from God.

She went to my school, and we were in the same grade, so I'd seen her before. I even knew her nickname: B. She started attending our school in the tenth grade. I just didn't realize she lived nearby. She had the reputation of being exceptionally smart, which to me translated as someone being aloof or stuck up.

Boy, was I wrong. She took all AP classes and was on track to be our class valedictorian. I, on the other hand, only took a couple of AP classes and was nowhere near the top of my class.

We only had about five hundred kids in our entire school, ranging from seventh grade to twelfth grade, and she and I didn't really travel in the same circle. Our senior class consisted of just over a hundred kids—the most in three decades. My children today, on the other hand, hosted their graduation ceremonies in a local football stadium, and there were still limits to attendance numbers.

She must have felt me staring, because she looked up and caught me watching her smell fruit. She turned red from embarrassment, shook her head, and smiled at me. I guessed that she recognized me from school, so I smiled back and walked over to introduce myself.

"Smell anything good?" I asked, trying to sound clever.

"Yeah, I've smelled a lot of good stuff today actually. I love the smell and feel of fresh fruit, don't you?" she asked.

I shrugged. "I never really thought about it, I guess."

"What do you mean, you've never really thought about it?" She motioned for me to come closer as she held up an orange. "Now close your eyes and tell me what you smell."

The hell with the fruit—that was the first time I caught a whiff of her natural scent. She smelled like summer, sunshine, and citrus. Okay, maybe the citrus scent came from the orange, but she definitely smelled like summer and sunshine. I closed my eyes and sniffed the fruit she held to my nose.

"Hmm, nice. I smell oranges and sunshine." I opened my eyes and grinned. "I've never done that before."

"You've never smelled an orange before?" she replied and raised an eyebrow.

"What? No, no, closing my eyes and smelling an orange like that before. You know, on purpose."

I remember she furrowed her perfectly shaped, blond eyebrows, as if she didn't believe me. When she realized I was being honest, she laughed. Normally, I was self-conscious of people laughing at me, but she didn't make me feel that way. She made me feel comfortable. There we were, two teens standing in the middle of the produce section, laughing and smelling the fruit.

We walked around the market while she continued her shopping, like a pair of old friends. She asked me if I played a lot of tennis, since I had my racquet with me—I couldn't just leave it with my bike outside. I told her I played a bit with Jean Paul over the summer. Then we talked about what we'd done that summer. She was a lifeguard at a local swim and racquet club.

This gave her the advantage of swimming during off hours and playing tennis for free, when she wasn't lifeguarding. She was in great shape, toned and athletic, standing about five six or so, maybe a hundred fifteen to twenty pounds. In my eyes, she was perfect from head to toe.

Why haven't I noticed you at school before? How is it possible that this is the first time we've ever had a conversation?

She paid for her stuff, and I paid for my drink, which I almost forgot. *If you saw her, you'd forget too.*

As we walked out of the store, she went her way, toward the parking lot, and I walked over to the bike rack. As I hopped on my bike, she pulled up next to me in her car and waved me over.

"So what are you doing the rest of the afternoon?" she asked.

"I have nothing planned. Why?"

"Are you up for a quick round of tennis? I know you just played, so if you don't want to, that's okay. But if you're up for it, we can play, and the loser buys pizza."

Well, I wasn't about to miss out on this opportunity. "Sure, I'm up for another set."

"Great. I'll drop my groceries off at home, grab my tennis gear, and meet you at the school's courts in twenty minutes. Cool?"

Notice, she didn't say I'll meet you in *a half hour, in fifteen minutes,* or even *a few minutes.* She said *twenty minutes* specifically, and wouldn't you know it . . . twenty minutes on the dot, she rode up on her bike wearing the same outfit she had on in the store. Her hair was still pulled back in a perfect ponytail. She had her tennis racquet in hand and Ray-Bans on—ready for action. I grabbed the tennis balls from the back of my bike, and we warmed up for a few minutes, hitting tennis balls back and forth.

After a few minutes, she was ready to get to it. "Okay, remember our agreement. We play one set and the loser buys pizza," she said.

"Yep, I've got it." I spun my racquet. The W was up, so I served first. I tried taking it easy on her and gave her a really weak first serve, which she slammed down my throat.

"That's love-15!"

Clearly, she's here to play! Okay, I wasn't expecting that, but again, she did mention she's been swimming and playing tennis for free all summer.

From then on, I didn't pull any punches. We had a good match. As she waited for my serves, she would bounce on the balls of her feet, like she was dancing on hot coals. It was very cute and sort of distracted me.

"That's game, set, and match! I win!" she yelled as she hit the winning shot by me an hour later. Much to my chagrin, and slightly wounded male ego, she won. She beat me fair and square. I was a man of my word, so we rode over to a local pizza parlor near school, and I bought us a couple of slices of pizza and Cokes.

I guess since I was on my bike, she had decided to ride hers as well. She was like that; I would learn—considerate. She was so different than I thought she'd be. Again, we had never spent time together before, but she was one of the smart kids, not to mention really pretty. That combination of individual usually turned out to be stuck-up and standoffish, at least in my limited experience. She became another example of not judging a book by its cover.

She teased me that I let her win so that she wouldn't have to pay for the pizza. "I guess chivalry isn't dead," she said.

I just laughed it off and admitted that she had won fair and square, which was true. To this day, I have no idea if she believed me or not. We passed the time there at the pizza parlor like any other teenage pair, talking and laughing. After finishing our slices and Cokes, we headed for our bikes.

Before hopping on hers, she stretched, and I damn near fainted. There was something so, I don't know, sensual and graceful about it. The funny thing was that she wasn't being inappropriate or trying to convey a message. She was just stretching before getting on her bike, totally unaware of the effect she had on me. There was something special about this girl. I knew it the moment we spoke at the market.

"I had no idea you were this much fun. Had I known, we would have played years ago," she said in a matter-of-fact manner, as if I had no choice in the matter. Had *she* known, *we* would have played years ago, period.

I grinned. "Yeah, I feel the same way."

"What are you doing tomorrow? I have to work the morning session, but I'm free in the afternoon. Want to play a couple of sets tomorrow?"

Of course I did. "Sure," I said.

"Great. Let's meet at school at two. We don't have to play for pizza. I don't want you to lose all your money," she joked.

I laughed. Then we both jumped on our bikes and rode to the end of the parking lot.

"I'm going this way," she said, pointing left.

"And I'm heading this way," I replied, pointing right. *Damn it, Ma. Why do we have to live THAT way? I'm sure she lives in a nice neighborhood too. Would it have killed you and Dad to move there seventeen years ago?*

We did the "Okay, I'll see you tomorrow" thing, and I watched her ride off until she turned the corner.

I was home in about a half hour and wanted to call Jean Paul right away to tell him what happened. It was what you did with your best friend—you experienced something and told him or her immediately! Plus, this was the eighties, remember. It was before cell phones, Facebook, Instagram, and Twitter, so I would have to wait until I got home before telling him

The thing is . . . I didn't call him. I didn't call or tell anyone. Ma was still at work, my kid brother was off with his friends or something, and my older brother worked and lived in Boston. So I wouldn't have to explain my smile to anyone. What a great day!

The next day, however, was completely different. It rained. *Seriously? Rain! But I had a tennis date! Al Roker, you fat-bastard-son-*

of-a-bitch, you're screwing me! Again, this was the eighties, when Al was not his sleeker, current-day version. *Sorry, Al, it's true, but you look great today, and I still love you!*

Sigh! Do I call? More importantly, *how* do I call? I don't have her number. *If only Al Gore had invented the Internet, I could Google her number and then Face Time with her. This sucks!*

While I stewed over this conundrum, the phone rang, and since we didn't have caller ID back then, I blindly answered the phone.

"Hello?" I answered, sounding like an annoyed teenager.

"Hey."

It was her!

"How 'bout this rain, huh? So much for tennis, I guess."

"I know it sucks, right? Hey, how'd you get my number?" I asked.

"I looked it up in the White Pages."

Brilliant! The White Pages!! Again, she's *valedictorian* smart.

She explained she just got home from work, and since it was raining, she wanted to know if I was up for bowling instead.

"Sure, bowling sounds like fun," I said.

"Great, I'll pick you up in thirty-five minutes."

Not a half hour, not forty-five minutes, but *thirty-five* minutes.

Ding, thirty-five minutes later on the dot, there she was, pulling into the driveway of our four-bedroom, two-and-a-half-bath house. How did she know where I lived? GPS wasn't available in 1987, at least not for us civilians. It would forever remain a mystery, because I never asked and she never told me.

2 - Bowling

B knocked on the front door, holding an umbrella. My younger brother answered it as I walked down the stairs from my bedroom. He was all sweaty from playing his drums, a passion he developed very young in life, along with playing other instruments like piano and guitar. He eventually took it up professionally and has been playing in bands his whole adult life.

He invited her in, and she closed her umbrella and placed it against the wall. They stood in the foyer as I reached the bottom of the stairs. To her left was our living room, which we hardly ever used. It had your standard '80s furniture: sofas along the wall, coffee tables, a bar, and a grand piano that my mother and I played periodically.

To her right was our formal dining room, which led to my younger brother's drum room and also had an open doorway leading to our family room and kitchen.

"Hey, do you want something to drink?" I asked.

She declined, so we walked through the family room to the kitchen, where I grabbed my house keys and wallet off the counter. As we walked through the house, B noticed the artwork Ma had hanging on the walls. Ma enjoyed the arts—classical music, ballet, opera, and artwork—and it showed in her decorating style.

I guess this was why she had allowed my brother to convert her former office into his music studio when he turned twelve. I would have preferred a comic book room, but quickly lost that battle.

"This is real pretty. Who painted it?" she asked from the family room.

"Have no idea," I replied as I joined her.

"What do you mean you don't know? You live here, don't you?" She laughed while trying to make out the artist's signature.

I shrugged my shoulders. "I guess I never thought about it."

She just raised her blond eyebrows at me and laughed. "You're such a typical male."

Man, what a great laugh.

Then she turned and looked through our glass patio door into our back yard and noticed our in-ground pool. We had a roomy back yard. It was about a quarter acre, with a nice-sized lawn, a couple of large shade trees, and a red brick patio with a couple of picnic tables, umbrellas, and a built-in barbecue grill off to the side that separated the back of our house from the pool.

I followed her gaze and asked her if she had a pool.

"No we don't. It must be nice."

"It's cool, but I hate vacuuming it."

"Oh, you *poor* thing," she replied sarcastically, which I ignored.

I invited her to come over for a swim any time; after all, it was one of the house rules: all friends welcome, at least most of the time.

My brother returned to his drum room and started his afternoon session, which was our cue to leave. As we walked to the front door, B punched me in the arm for no particular reason as she grabbed her umbrella.

The bowling alley was located at a strip mall near my house. We checked in with the guy behind the counter, who assigned us a lane, then gave us each a score sheet and a pair of really fashionable bowling shoes. You know the ones. Red and black separated with a white stripe down the middle, white soles, shoe size emblazoned on the back. To this day, they still remind me of clown shoes.

We found a couple of black bowling balls and put them in the ball return area. I placed the scoresheet on our bowling desk and wrote our names down.

Back then we didn't have electronic scoreboards, so you had to know how to keep score. You had to know the difference between a strike and a spare, how to score it properly, and what happened in the last frame if you threw one. Of course, each table had the rules written down, so if you didn't know how to keep score, you could read the directions and learn the rules. It was bowling, not rocket science.

We were playing the best of three. Like tennis, the loser would buy pizza. "And don't take it easy on me. I plan on winning again," she warned me, grinning.

I laughed. "Oh don't worry; I don't plan on losing two days in a row. I hope you brought your wallet."

I wasn't much of a bowler and only played now and again. I was lucky if I broke a hundred, but don't judge. How many famous Hispanic bowlers do you know? I bet you could rattle off a few hundred Hispanic baseball or soccer players though, right?

Besides, most kids in the neighborhood didn't come to the bowling alley to bowl. We came to play video games. I remember when they got Ms. Pac-Man. Adults and kids would put their quarters down on the lip of the machine and patiently wait their turn. While you waited, you could play another video game, like Asteroids, or play pinball.

They had the classic pinball games like Kiss and Pinball Wizard. Today, it's all about X-Box, iPads, Sony PlayStation, and online computer games. Man, times have changed. But that day, we were there to bowl.

She bowled first. She did a quick stretch, blew into her right hand, and picked up her ball. Before making her approach, she bent over and stared down the bowling pins as if to say, *"You're mine."*

What a view.

She inhaled, held it, and exhaled. Then in a very fluid motion, she took a few steps and released the ball, knocking down nine pins. She twirled around, smiling, and looked over at me, raising her eyebrows. "I hope you brought your A game!"

Oh, crap!

I just smiled back. Her ball returned, and she picked it up. She went right back to her previous spot and picked up her spare. She yelped and did a fist pump. She then turned around and bounced back to the bowling table as if it were no big deal. So, she can bowl. Who knew?

Maybe she got lucky. Yeah, that's what it was—luck. Just like tennis yesterday. Luck.

"Do you know how to keep score?" she asked.

"Yeah, I know how to keep score. This isn't my first time bowling," I replied. *It'll only look like it.*

We spent the rest of the afternoon bowling without a care in the world. Strike! Spare! Gutter ball! Seven/ten split! Spare! We laughed. We high-fived. Most importantly, we had fun. We only played two of our best of three games. Yes, Charlie Brown lost again . . . *sigh!*

I just laughed it off. Besides, she had distracted me with her awesomeness.

"So where do you want to go for pizza?" she asked.

"I know a joint," I joked.

Like most Long Island strip malls, this one had a grocery store, liquor store, card store, record store, Carvel ice cream parlor, drugstore, dry cleaner, Chinese food, and, of course, a neighborhood pizza joint.

On Long Island, every neighborhood has a locally-owned Italian pizzeria in every shopping center. You had Tony's, Vinnie's, Mario's, Johnny's, and an assortment of other places that were names ending in a vowel. The very best pizza on the planet, in my opinion, was our neighborhood's local pizzeria—Giuseppe's.

If you want to get into a pissing contest, make the mistake of saying your pizza place was better than someone else's. You know the expression about never discussing religion and politics? Well, when you're on Long Island, add pizzerias to the list. You will argue for hours.

When the pizza chains started to open up, people would order from them only if they didn't feel like driving, or were in a jam; otherwise, people looked down their noses at those places. You never admitted to ordering from Domino's, or being seen in Pizza Hut.

It wasn't raining very hard, so we walked a few stores down to Giuseppe's Pizzeria. We ordered a couple of slices each and Cokes and found a booth toward the back. And that was how you ordered it: "Let me get a couple of slices and a Coke."

Back then, you didn't have a great selection. You couldn't order a Hawaiian slice or a Meat Lovers slice. Gourmet slices like goat cheese and truffles or escargot pizza were not yet *in vogue*.

For those of you wondering, *yes*, I was the one who once had eaten escargot pizza. *Yes*, it was *awful*, and *yes*, there was a girl involved. Fortunately, the girl I was trying to impress that day, still agreed to marry me the in the mid-'90s. The lesson I learned *that* day? Don't be a *shmuck!* When in doubt, go with pepperoni. Okay, back to the story . . .

"Did you let me win again?" B teased.

"You were there. Did it look like I let you beat me? Besides, you only beat me the last game by two pins. And I do recall *someone* coughing real loud as I threw my last ball. I'm not making any accusations or excuses, mind you, I'm just saying."

She tried to hide her smirk.

We spent the better part of an hour eating pizza and laughing about our tennis and bowling adventures.

After we finished our slices, we threw away our paper plates and made our way toward the door, sipping what was left of our sodas. Tony, the guy dressed in his pizza whites behind the counter, asked if we wanted to top off our sodas, so I told him, "Sure." While he did this, B stared out the front window, taking in the rain, seemingly lost in thought.

That was when Tony gave me a subtle wink and a smile of approval. I just nodded in response as he handed the cups back.

"See ya later, Tony!" I said as we exited.

"Yeah, see ya later, Tony!" B said, popping her head back in the door, which made him laugh and wave goodbye.

She's funny. Who knew?

"Were you serious about me coming over any time to swim?" she asked as we left the parking lot.

"Sure, why?"

"I don't know," she replied.

"Tell you what, if it's not raining tomorrow, do you want to go swimming?"

"Really, you're serious?"

This confused me—what was the big deal? "Yeah, why are you being so weird about it?"

She arched her eyebrows and laughed. "*You're* being weird," she said. And then she punched me in the arm again. *What's with the punching?*

"Ow! And yeah, as long as it's not raining, come on over and we'll go swimming, okay?"

She said she didn't have to work tomorrow, so we made plans for her to arrive at two before she drove off.

Did I really just invite her over tomorrow to go swimming and did she actually say yes? Oh God, please don't let it rain tomorrow!

3 - The Movies and the Twins

Just before dinner, Jean Paul called to see if I wanted to go see *The Lost Boys* with him and his twin sister, Hannah. It was playing at the triplex movie theater near my house. *The Lost Boys* was a teenage vampire love story. It was our version of *Twilight*, only not a trilogy and with a much better soundtrack. The soundtrack actually introduced me to INXS. The band followed it up with their multi-platinum album *Kick*. Jean Paul and I made plans to meet later for the seven-thirty show.

To this day, I love going to the movies. The smell of fresh popcorn calls to me like a siren, even if I've just had dinner. That night was no different. We stood in line, waiting to order our popcorn and sodas. Suddenly, I felt a slight kick in the pants as someone walked by me. I turned around and saw B smiling innocently and sipping on her soda. She was there with a few friends, heading into a different theater.

Before entering, she gave me her version of Robert De Niro's *"I'm watching you"* move, using her index and middle fingers to point at her beautiful blue eyes, then at me, and back again. Then she mouthed, "two o'clock," and held up two fingers before entering the theater with her friends. I just smiled to myself and shook my head, lost in the moment and forgetting I wasn't alone. That was my mistake. Jean Paul and Hannah had witnessed the whole thing.

Oh, shit. Here we go! Let the grilling begin!

What can I tell you about the twins? Jean Paul and Hannah were my best friends. We'd known each other since the seventh grade, back when our class was twenty-three students strong. We practically went everywhere together. They were "fac brats," a.k.a. "faculty kids." I loved calling them that. Of course, they hated it, which was why I loved it. Their parents taught at my school.

"So what was that all about?" Jean Paul asked as we made our way into the theater to find seats.

"Yeah, since when do you talk with B?" Hannah chimed in.

"I didn't know you knew her," Jean Paul said.

"Of course I know her. Everybody at school knows her, dude. You guys know her, don't you?" I replied defensively.

"Okay, you *know* what he meant," Hannah said, choosing our seats.

"Guys, what's with the third degree? Jeez! Okay, we know each other, all right? What's the problem?"

"Dude, we know *everyone* you know and hang out with, because we hang out with them too. And we've never hung out with *her,*" Jean Paul pointed out.

Twin tag team time—Hannah's turn: "So when did you start hanging out with B? And don't say months or years because we'd know."

"Yeah, don't say months!" Jean Paul parroted.

Thankfully the previews were starting, so the lights started to dim. "Can we talk about this later?" I asked.

"You know we're not letting this go, right?" Hannah whispered.

"Yeah, we will get to the bottom of this," Jean Paul added.

"Get to the bottom of what?" I whispered back, all annoyed.

"How you two know each other," Jean Paul said.

"Be *quiet!*" Someone *shushed* us because we were starting to disrupt the previews with our talking.

"Yeah, yeah, we're shushing! We're shushing!" Jean Paul said loudly.

I winced. "Look, let's hit Friendly's after the movie and talk about it there, okay?" I hissed.

Jean Paul let out a breath. "Yeah, fine, we'll hit Friendly's. Now stop hogging the popcorn."

"Here, I've lost my appetite anyway." I just passed him the tub.

Well, that bought me a couple of hours at least.

And just barely. As the credits rolled and the lights went up, the interrogation resumed. We hadn't even left the theater yet.

"Okay, start talking!" Jean Paul said. "Tell us the whole story, and don't leave out *any* details, because we'll know."

I threw up my hands. "I thought we agreed we'd wait and talk at Friendly's?"

Jean Paul's eyes narrowed. "Why are you stalling? Why won't you tell us? We'd tell you." He followed this up with . . .

Wait for it . . . three . . . two . . . one. . .

"I thought we were *best friends!*"

He'd played the best friend's card! I couldn't believe it. He followed that one up with "Best friends don't keep secrets from each other." These trump cards have been played by best friends forever, because they work. *Well played, Jean Paul. Well played.*

"Seriously, dude? You're hitting me with the best friend card?" I pointed at the bathrooms and said, "Look, we *are* best friends, but I really need to hit the head. My back teeth are floating here. Can we talk about this when I get out?"

He waved his hand at me dismissively. "Yeah, yeah fine. Go ahead."

"We'll be waiting out here," Hannah said, a mischievous smirk on her face.

Well, thank you, God! At least I have a few minutes to think. It's not like I'm trying to protect some big corporate secret or anything. It's not the secret formula for Coke. It's just a quick story really. A few days ago, I started hanging out with the smartest, prettiest girl in school, that's all. What's to tell? But I guess that's not all. The real issue is I'm not ready to share her yet. Not with the twins, not with anybody.

She and I are just starting to connect. I know it's only been a couple of days, but somehow this girl is different. I just want to keep our relationship, if that's what we're calling it, private for now.

The stars must have heard my silent prayers and aligned. As I took my long walk back to the lobby, Professor Michaels, the twins' dad, pulled up outside the theater and honked his horn.

I'd forgotten they had been dropped off by their folks that night. I wanted to jump for joy.

"Oh man, no Friendly's tonight. I'm so *sorry*, guys." I couldn't hold back my sarcastic tone. They deserved it.

But Jean Paul was quick on his feet. "Wait, you can drop us off, can't you?"

Another honk and hand wave from their dad.

I held my palms up, as if there was just nothing I could do. "Sorry, guys, it really looks like you have to go." I pointed to their dad in the car. "Oh, it looks like he's starting to get angry." I smiled and waved at the professor. "Good evening, Professor Michaels."

Dejected, the twins walked to their car.

"I'll talk to you guys tomorrow," I said, then laughed, maybe a little too wickedly.

"You're damn right you will!" Jean Paul said.

"Yeah, we'll talk to you tomorrow," Hannah said.

"Sorry again about Friendly's," I hollered as they drove away, followed by a silent prayer of thanks.

"Did I just hear someone mention Friendly's?" someone whispered in my ear.

"*Whoa!!*" I yelled as I leapt. "What are you, part ninja? Don't you know it's not nice to sneak up on people?"

"Yes, I'm a blond ninja, so watch out. And stop being such a wuss," B joked.

Damn, lady, be nice! There's a sensitive male ego somewhere in here.

"So, what were you saying about Friendly's?" she asked.

"Oh, yeah, that. I was here with Jean Paul and Hannah Michaels. You know them from school, right?"

She said that she did.

"Yeah, so we usually go to Friendly's after we see a movie, but Professor Michaels picked them up, so I'm heading home."

Besides, the only reason we were going to Friendly's was to talk about you. And I'm not ready to talk about you. I don't even know what to say about you, to be honest.

"Oh, you're going to head home? Oh, um, okay then. Well, I guess I'll see you tomorrow at two o'clock, as long as it doesn't rain, right?" It sounded like she was disappointed about something. *What is that all about?* Then she said goodbye and joined her friends, who were off to the side, giggling. Then it hit me.

Oh, you idiot! She was practically asking you to take her to Friendly's. Come on, man, stop her and ask her to Friendly's before she leaves.

Of course, before I could strike up the courage to ask her to Friendly's, she was hopping into a church minivan with her friends and off they went.

Moron!

4 - The Pop Over

*P*lease mow the lawn, Ma's note read.

    Jesus, Ma, not today! It finally stopped raining, and the sun is out, for Christ's sake! And besides, B's coming over today! We're going swimming!

I needed this like I needed another hole in the head. Unfortunately, I had two choices: mow the lawn, or suffer the consequences of an angry Latina.

So I cut the lawn. It took me a couple of hours. First, I rolled up all the garden hoses and put them away. You don't want to have to explain how you ran over a ten-dollar hose because you were too lazy to check first.

After all, did I think that we were the Rockefellers or something? That was my mother's go-to card whenever making a financial point. It was either the Rockefellers, or the dreaded, "What do ju think I'm made of—money?" she'd ask in her Spanish accent.

After rolling up the hoses, I removed all of the dog toys from the back, as well as any large stones, bricks, or any other potentially fatal flying projectile. As any landscaper will tell you, these things will ruin your lawnmower blades, or worse.

I remember one year my dad got a big gash on his leg because he didn't check the lawn before mowing. Good thing Ma was a doctor. While she patched him up, I remember a lot of "coños!" and "hijo de la gran putas!"

In our house growing up, my parents spoke both Spanish and English. It was very common for them to incorporate both languages into one sentence. For example, "Pass me the butter, por favor."

Unless they were pissed off. If they were upset, it was all Spanish, all the time. And Ma's favorite word when upset? The word coño!

Ah, the word *coño*. It's one of the filthiest words in Spanish and a favorite used in my house growing up. As I understand it, it was my first word. It must have been a proud moment too. Like many languages, this word has various meanings in different Spanish-speaking regions.

For example, it means something a little different in Spain than in Latin America. It's like using the word *fanny* in England versus in the United States. It's the same word, but with two very different meanings.

It was one of my mother's favorite words, which was funny really. She was an extremely intelligent, diminutive, prim and proper, well-respected surgeon and pillar of the community, but when she was angry, she swore like a Spanish sailor, which made my brothers and me laugh.

Another of her favorite words was *pendejo!* It's the Spanish equivalent of *dumbass*—as in the sentence, "Way to go, pendejo, coño!"

Once I finished mowing the lawn, I tidied up the house a bit, at least the teenage-boy version of tidy. What's a teenage-boy version, you ask? That's when you grab all the dirty laundry in your room and stuff it in your closet. You then replace the empty toilet paper roll in the downstairs bathroom, wipe down the bathroom counter, and spray half a can of Lysol. You put all the dirty dishes into the dishwasher alongside the clean ones and run it. Lastly, you take out the trash.

At one o'clock, there was a knock at my front door. *Shit, she's early!* When I opened it, Jean Paul and Hannah were standing there, towels wrapped around their necks, a backpack over Jean Paul's shoulder, and smiles on their faces. Apparently they'd ridden their bikes over and wanted to go swimming.

Seriously, not today!

"Oh hey, guys, what's up?" I asked as I tried to block them from entering the front door, which worked for all of a nanosecond. They just barged right into the house like they owned the place.

"We thought we'd pop over and go swimming, *dumbass,* what's it look like?" Jean Paul said, giving me a weird look as he passed. Hannah grabbed her bathing suit from the backpack and went into the downstairs bathroom to change.

"I didn't know you guys were coming over," I said.

"What's the big deal, bro? We always crash your house. You didn't have plans, did you?" Jean Paul asked as he went to the refrigerator.

They were family, which meant they could come and go as they pleased. If they were hungry or thirsty, they could simply help themselves. This is a standard we use in my house to this day, with my children and their friends.

The first time you visit, you get the tour. *This is where we keep the glasses, and this is where we keep our snacks. Please feel free to help yourself, and throw out your trash.* The second time you visit and ask for something, you're told, *"You know where it is, right? Help yourself."*

We run our home on the honor system. If we trust you enough to have you *in our home*, then we trust you enough to make yourself *at home*.

5 - The Impromptu Pool Party

Hannah stepped out of the bathroom in her solid blue Speedo bathing suit with a towel wrapped around her waist. "Where's Jean Paul?" she asked.

I nodded in the direction of the kitchen. "He's in the fridge, where else?"

She sat on a sofa in the family room and beckoned me over, like she was my mother or something. She patted the cushion next to her.

My relationship with Hannah was different than my relationship with Jean Paul. Of the two, he was my best friend, but Hannah wasn't a far second. Jean Paul and I joked around, played sports, chased girls, and went comic book shopping together. The latter drove Hannah crazy, as she thought it was beneath us. I told her she didn't understand great reading material.

Hannah was more of a trusted confidant. She and I could talk about anything, and I knew she could keep a secret if I asked her.

"So, what's the story with B?" she asked.

For some reason, she was very protective of me. I guess I felt the same way about her. Whenever she started dating someone, the guy would get "the conversation" from Jean Paul and me. We'd let the suitor know he'd receive a beating from both of us if he mistreated Hannah.

Clearly the twins had planned this, because Jean Paul walked outside without saying a word, dropped his backpack, and jumped into the pool.

"There's no story there, Hann. It's not like she and I are strangers. We're in the same grade at the same school."

"Yeah, I know, but you've never hung out with her before. She's not in any of your classes or anything. You've never even mentioned her to *me*, and you tell me about *every* girl."

Damn it! She's right! I do tell her about every girl. Me and my big mouth! "Yeah, that's true. We've never hung out before . . ." I said, letting the words trail off. I didn't know exactly what to say at his point.

"Before *what*? What aren't you telling me?" she prodded.

"Jeez, Hann, come on, give me a break, would ya? It's not a big deal," I said. "Okay, so here's the story." And I proceeded to tell her most of the story, holding back very little.

"Do you like her?"

"I'm not sure yet. I'm just getting to know her."

"She's really pretty," Hannah said. "She also seems nice whenever I talk to her at school."

Wait a minute. You've talked to her at school? Why haven't you ever introduced me to her before? I thought I was one of your best friends!

"Yeah, I guess she is. Anyway, I sort of invited her over today to go swimming," I said as I started standing. "So if you don't mind grabbing Jean Paul and leaving, I'd really appreciate it."

She laughed at me. "Oh, hell no! We're not going anywhere. We're not missing this. You must be crazy!" She stood up from the couch and yelled for Jean Paul.

What does she mean, I must be crazy? I'm not crazy! "Hannah, *you're* crazy if you think I'm letting you guys stay here. That's not happening."

"What's not happening?" A wet Jean Paul asked from the doorway, a towel wrapped around his waist. "What did I miss? What's going on?"

"She's coming over, and he wants us to leave," Hannah said, flipping her thumb in my direction.

"Dude, *you're* crazy! We were planning on hanging out for a while this afternoon. We're *definitely* not leaving now!" Jean Paul stated.

"Come on, guys. Be reasonable! I'd leave if it were one of you!" I pleaded.

Hannah wasn't buying it. "Ha, no you wouldn't! You'd probably strip down to your underwear and start watching TV."

"Dude, I hate to tell you this, but we're staying," Jean Paul said. "And be happy we don't strip down to *our* underwear and start watching TV!"

Damn It! They were right! I wouldn't leave and the underwear . . . that is something I'd do. "Okay, fine, I'll just call her and tell her not to come. Are you happy now?" I bluffed.

"Seriously, you'd do that? You're being ridiculous." Hannah was sounding sisterly again. "You know we won't embarrass you. We're not animals, for God's sake! Okay, let me rephrase that: *I'm* not an animal." She looked pointedly at her brother then laughed. "We actually know how to behave ourselves. We're usually better than you. When you think about it, we're really doing you a favor and saving you from yourself."

"Hey! What's that supposed to mean?" I asked.

"Oh come on, do you really want to get into this now? When is she coming over?" Hannah asked.

"She's supposed to get here in about twenty minutes . . . why?"

"*Twenty minutes!* Why didn't you say so? That really doesn't give us much time. Okay, Jean Paul, quickly now . . . go to his room and find him something nicer to wear than whatever *this* is!" She wrinkled her nose at my clothes. *Sniff, sniff.* "Dude, you stink! What the hell have you been doing today?"

Before I could answer, she raised her hand. "You know what? I don't care. We need to get you out of those stinky clothes and into something nice, but we don't have a lot of time. Besides, I know you. We don't have time for one of your yearlong showers. You're worse than a woman."

Damn, Hann!

"Go jump in the pool and rinse that stink off! Move it! Go!" she ordered.

"What are you gonna do?" I asked, nervous that she'd take out all the cleaning supplies, and start scrubbing down the house from top to bottom. First, we didn't have time for that, and second, I'd already cleaned the house. It looked fine.

"Don't worry about me. Go rinse yourself off!" she said, switching from sister to drill sergeant. I tossed off my shirt and jumped into the pool. Hannah, with a look of disgust on her face, picked up my smelly T-shirt and took it to the laundry room.

I did my best Mark Spitz impersonation and swam back and forth, trying to clean off. Who is Mark Spitz? He was our 1970's version of Michael Phelps.

Shit, I forgot my towel!

Hannah must have read my mind. As I climbed out of the pool, a towel hit me in the face. "Thanks," I mumbled behind the towel.

"Thank me later. Let's go! You have, like, eight minutes, and everyone knows her reputation for being on time for everything! She's more accurate than a Swiss clock!" she said, her tone pitching higher with each passing minute. "Jean Paul is waiting for you in your room. *Go!*"

You could tell she was starting to enjoy herself . . . *Wait a minute. How does Hann know she's always on time? Have they hung out together before? I thought we kept no secrets from each other.*

I slid through the family room, ran up a flight of stairs, and met Jean Paul in my bedroom. It looked like a tornado had blown through, and its name was Jean Paul Michaels. All of my dresser drawers were open. If it weren't Jean Paul, I'd feel violated, but we'd known each other for years. We'd even seen each other naked in the locker room, so there were no secrets between us.

On my bed were a pair of underwear, a plain polo shirt, and khaki shorts. "Towel off and throw that stuff on, quickly!" he said in his best Hannah voice as he threw my underwear at me.

"Okay, okay. I'm changing, I'm changing! Jeez, you're worse than your sister!"

"Well we *are* twins. We're essentially the same, but *different*. I'm the cooler one!"

I changed quickly. "Tell him to brush his teeth and hair!" Hannah yelled from downstairs.

"You heard her. Go brush your hair and teeth, you slob!" Jean Paul said, laughing hysterically.

"Don't start, dude. Not now, seriously!" I said as I ran to my bathroom.

My hair gets super curly when it gets wet. Women pay good money to perm their hair for curls like mine. *Me?* I hated them! I wish I had straight hair. Someone actually once asked me if I Jheri curled my hair. *I swear, some people are morons.* I brushed my teeth with my index finger and then primped my hair. I didn't have time to blow it dry. *Oh, screw it. Natural it is!*

It was two o'clock on the nose. As I started down the stairs, someone was knocking on the front door. Hannah was waiting for me at the bottom of the stairs, so she just turned around and answered the door, switching into hostess mode. It was B, so Hannah invited her in.

B looked up at me and smiled.

Wow! Did my heart just skip a beat?

She wore white shorts, a blue tank top with some beach design on it, and flip-flops.

Man, does she wear it well or what?

Her Ray-Bans were pushed up in her hair, which she had pulled back into a ponytail.

"Hi, Hannah, I didn't know you'd be here," B said in a curious tone. "Is Jean Paul here with you or is it just you two?" She shot a look between us.

Uncomfortable! That was when I jumped in. "Oh no, no, Hannah and Jean Paul just dropped by *unexpectedly.*" I gave Hannah the stink eye.

That was when we heard a flush from the upstairs bathroom, followed by my partner in crime walking down the stairs. "Hi, Jean Paul," B said.

"Hey B, how's it going?" he replied.

"Not bad. Are you guys going to stick around and go swimming too?"

Before I could interject, Hannah said, "That's the plan. You don't mind, do you?" She raised an eyebrow.

Han-NAH! Knock it the fuck off!!

"No, not at all. The more the merrier, I always say," B replied; and you could tell she actually meant it.

Who is this person? And how well did *she know the Michaels twins? Is there some secret relationship here that I'm not aware of?*

B had a yellow and white striped beach tote slung over her shoulder. I invited her in while Hannah shut the door behind her. I escorted her into the back yard, where she put her stuff down under one of the wooden picnic benches we had on our patio.

"Is anyone thirsty?" Hannah asked.

"Sure. I'll help you," B replied, and off they went, leaving Jean Paul and me alone outside.

"What the fuck is happening here?" I whispered.

"It beats me, bro. I just came over to hang out and swim for the afternoon. You're the one with the date."

"Dude, it's not a date. I just invited her to come over to swim. We're just hanging out. It's *not* a date."

"You could have fooled me."

Moments later, B and Hannah walked outside carrying two glasses of iced tea each. We always kept a full jug in the fridge over the summer. *And great, they found the old McDonald's glasses we have in our cabinets from the '70s!*

B handed me the Hamburglar glass. *Hannah, I swear to God, I'm going to friggin' kill you!* Hannah smiled and handed the Ronald McDonald glass to Jean Paul. *You seriously couldn't find any other glasses? We have plenty!*

"I love these glasses. I didn't think anyone else collected them. I think we have the whole set at our house too," *My* B said. *Wait a minute, did I just think of her as "my" B?*

You know, the glasses weren't so bad after all. "Yeah, we collected them back in the '70s. When we played little league, we'd hit McDonald's for dinner after the game. I think they came with every meal."

B took a sip of her tea, nodding her head and laughing, as if she recalled a similar memory. Hannah stood there, stifling a giggle. *Oh shut up, Hannah!*

We all sat down at the picnic table and chatted for a while. *Man, I could sit here forever. I love the way the sun just glistens off her shoulders.* Out of the corner of my eye, I noticed Hann watching me. Self-consciously I shifted positions, which made her laugh.

Oh, shut up.

Our conversation was broken by the first of many drum solos. *Well, if that's not a cue, I don't know what is.* "Who wants to jump in the pool?"

"Sure. Where can I change?" B asked.

"Oh, you can use the downstairs bathroom." I pointed in that direction.

"Let me show you where it is," Hannah said. As they walked by, Hannah flicked me behind my ear. *Ow! What the frig, Hann!*

Jean Paul and I swam in our regular shorts. One of the advantages of being guys, I supposed. We could wear whatever we wanted to go swimming, and no one cared. Girls, on the other hand, had so many things to consider: *Do I shave, wax, or go au naturel? Do I wear a one-piece or bikini? Is "Aunt Flo" visiting this week? Will this suit make me look fat, skinny, tall, short, slutty, or stupid? How's my ass in this suit? How're my boobs?* And the list goes on.

Hannah joined us at the picnic table outside while B changed. "I think it is going well," she said.

"I think so too," I admitted. "I haven't said anything stupid yet."

"Well, it's still early, so don't get cocky," Hannah said. "And control the staring. It can get creepy."

Out of the corner of my eye, through the glass door, I noticed the light from the downstairs bathroom as B opened the bathroom door. It was like a heavenly choir started singing as an angel stepped out.

We are not worthy! We are not worthy!

B wore a green print bikini. The bottoms were tied on the side, while the top was tied behind her neck and back. Her hair was still in a ponytail, and she was now barefoot. She carried her beach bag with flip-flops sticking out the top. She wore her Ray-Bans and had a heavenly smile on her face as she stepped outside. *She's clearly done this before.*

I was speechless. My jaw dropped, and I couldn't move. Hannah gave me a quick elbow to the ribs and snapped me out of it. *"Stop staring!"* she hissed. Jean Paul had missed her entrance as he was already in the pool and underwater. *Sorry for your loss, bro!*

B walked out to the patio and placed her bag under a picnic table. "Hey, do you have a box?" she asked.

"A box, sure," I replied.

"Great! I brought some tapes!"

"Okay, cool. Let me grab it. I'll be right back."

So what's a box? A box is what we used to call our portable radios, and some came with cassette players. Eventually, boxes were replaced with portable CD players, then iPods, thumb drives, iPhones, and the list goes on.

I went inside and grabbed my old box and returned to the patio, plugging it in. Everyone was already in the pool, playing volleyball with a beach ball. B hopped out of the water and joined me. *Sweet Jesus on a stick! You're killing me! Stop staring!*

She still had her Ray-Bans on, but no longer had her ponytail. Instead, her wet, golden locks flowed down her shoulders and back. *Deep breaths, deep breaths!* She walked past me, went over to her beach bag, and grabbed a cassette. "May I?"

I just nodded my head.

B ejected a mixed tape I had in there, carefully put it on the patio table, and inserted her cassette. I figured we'd hear Madonna, Prince, Michael Jackson, or something like that. Instead, we heard, *"Free, free, set them free! Free, free, set them free! Whoa! Whoa!"*

She was playing Sting's first solo album. His album came out that summer, and his first single was "If You Love Somebody Set Them Free." They played the video all the time on MTV. I loved The Police, but wasn't sure about solo Sting. I wasn't used to the Caribbean-influenced, funky sound he produced.

B turned to me and asked, "Is this okay?"

Let's be honest, she could have played an hour of someone scratching a nail across a blackboard, and I would have given her two thumbs up. "Yeah, it's great! I love Sting!" Okay, so I fudged a little. Sue me.

"You do? So do I! I just love his new stuff, don't you? It's so different from the stuff he plays with The Police, you know?"

Again, nails on a blackboard. "Oh yeah, it's great!" I replied in my most enthusiastic voice.

With that, she put her sunglasses in her beach bag, grabbed my hand, and led me to the pool. "Come on!" she said.

I'll follow you anywhere.

Instead of jumping right in, she went over to the diving board. She hopped up, took a few steps, leapt up on one leg, came down, and delivered a great dive into the pool. It was a thing of grace and beauty. *So she plays tennis, bowls, and is an Olympic-level diver—got it.*

She popped up and asked me, "Hey, are you coming in?"

Goddamn right, I'm coming in! I leapt into the air and cannonballed into the deep end. She had her specialties, and I had mine.

For the rest of the afternoon, the four of us just laughed and hung out. We tossed the pool ball around, splashed each other, played chicken, and even played Marco Polo until Jean Paul cheated.

Hannah was it and was yelling, "Marco!"

B and I were giggling in the deep end, yelling back, "Polo!"

Jean Paul was closest to her in the little end, almost whispering, "Polo."

Hannah sensed she was close to her prey. I was guessing it had something to do with the twin thing. They could finish each other's sentences and knew what the other one was thinking, without saying a word. At dinner, Hannah would pass Jean Paul the salt without him even asking. It was just weird, but you got used to it.

As she leapt at him, he jumped out of the pool, clearly cheating. She missed and became frustrated. Hannah yelled again, "Marco!" B and I giggled again and yelled back, "Polo!" Jean Paul laughed as he ran and dove back into the pool. What a moron! He totally gave himself away. Hannah knew right away what he did. "You cheated! You're it!" she yelled.

"I'm tired of playing," he replied and hopped out of the pool again, grabbing a spot on one of the lounge chairs we had around the pool area. *One* of the lounge chairs, but not *the* lounge chair. He and Hannah were family, so they knew the rules of the house, including: no one uses Aunt Mary's lounge chair. Aunt Mary was our neighbor and second mother.

It all started one afternoon, before my dad passed away. Aunt Mary came over with her own lounge chair and cushion and placed it on our pool deck. It became like Archie Bunker's chair. No one was allowed to sit or lay in it.

Hannah, B, and I swam for a little while longer. The cassette ended, so B hopped out to turn it over. Hannah took that moment to whisper to me,

"You're doing really well. Jean Paul and I will leave soon. I'll make up an excuse, so he doesn't start whining." Then we hopped out of the pool.

"Jean Paul, grab your stuff, we're leaving! We've got to get home and help Mom," Hannah said.

Jean Paul gave her a confused look. "What are you talking about? We helped her yesterday."

Through gritted teeth, Hannah answered, "I said, *grab your stuff*, we've got to get home and *help Mom*."

In all the years I've known the Michaels twins, whenever Hannah gritted her teeth and spoke, you'd better listen. Since Jean Paul was her twin, he'd had longer to learn this lesson, because he got up immediately.

"*Fine*, I'll go grab my stuff!" he responded with attitude. He wrapped his towel around his waist and went inside, as B joined Hannah and me in the pool area.

"You guys need to go?" I asked innocently. Hannah just rolled her eyes.

"Yeah, we promised Mom we'd only hang out here for a little while and then get home to help her with her garden."

"Oh got it, her garden. Well, if you have to go . . ." I replied with a smile. We wrapped our towels around our waists and all went inside. Still in his wet shorts, Jean Paul came downstairs from my room with his towel wrapped around his neck, while Hannah stepped into the downstairs bathroom to change.

"My brother, it was another epic adventure," Jean Paul said.

"You know it!" We high-fived each other.

Hannah stepped out of the bathroom with her regular clothes on, her bathing suit wrapped in her towel. She just shoved everything into Jean Paul's backpack.

"Thanks, kiddo, we had fun," she said to me and then looked at her brother. "Jean Paul, aren't you going to change out of those wet shorts?" She was both his twin *and* his mother at times. Technically she was the older of the two by a few minutes, so I guess she'd earned the position.

"No! These will be dry by the time we get home. Quit bugging me, Hann!"

Hannah turned to B and me, apologizing for her brother. "Sorry, we've tried to train him, but this is the best you can do when you have so little to work with."

"Hey, I'm standing right here!" Jean Paul said.

I didn't see the big deal. He was right. They'd be dry by the time they got home. But I didn't say a thing. She'd had my back all afternoon. B and I walked them out to their bikes and said our goodbyes. They rode off, bickering and laughing. *Ya gotta love the twins!*

B then turned to me and asked, "So what's next on our agenda?"

Um . . . next?

6 - B Meets Belle

*B*link, blink, blink . . .

"Um, I don't know. Are you thirsty?" I asked.

"Sure. Would you mind if I use the restroom first, though?" She called it a *restroom*, not a bathroom—how classy.

"Oh, yeah, go ahead. I'll meet you in the kitchen," I replied as we entered the house. She headed to the *restroom*, and I went to the kitchen. I opened the fridge and began surveying the contents.

Let's see, what we've got in here? We have orange juice, nah! We have milk, pass! There's a jug of water, boring! Lipton Iced Tea? Why do we have such a boring refrigerator? Where are the cool drinks?

As I was surveying the contents, I felt a warm hand rest on my lower back; B was leaning in to have a look for herself.

"So what do we have? Oh good, more iced tea!" she said.

Forget about what I said, Ma! You rock!

She reached around me, grabbed the jug out of the refrigerator, and walked out the back door. I followed a few steps behind her in happy amazement.

As she was pouring more iced tea into our glasses, my brother popped his head out of the back door. "Hey, I'm heading to Rick's. Tell Ma I'll be home for dinner."

"Okay, see ya later. Tell Rick I said hey," I said.

And without skipping a beat, B adds, "Yeah, tell Rick hey from me too!"

Ha! Is she kidding me? Who is this girl anyway? My brother just smiled, shook his head, and left.

"So what do you want to do?" she asked.

Gulp! Hmm, let's see, we have a boy and girl, alone, and one of us looks like you, and you want to know what I want to do? Seriously? You're killing me!

"I don't know. Do you want to swim some more?" I asked.

She said that she did, jogged to the pool, and dove in.

I think I'll just sit here while my boner goes away, thanks.

"Hey, are you coming in?"

"Yeah, I'm, uh, just turning the tape back over."

"Oh, okay," she said, and dove underwater.

Fast thinking, sir! Fast thinking indeed!

I flipped the tape back over to the first side, and then joined B in the pool. We swam for a while. She showed me a few different dives off the diving board, and I just marveled at her. I couldn't help it; she was stunning and didn't even seem to know it. After a while, she got out . . . and walked over to *THE Lounge Chair,* spreading out her towel and stretching out on it.

Oh, fudge . . . but I'm not really thinking "oh, fudge." I'm thinking "oh, f . . ." Well, what's the worst that can happen? I'm too old to get spanked or grounded, right? It's not like I have a lunatic Latina for a mother. Think, man, think!*

"Hey, uh, want to go inside and watch some MTV?" I said quickly.

She leaned up on her elbows. "Are you sure? We're still wet, and I don't want to get you in trouble."

Man, is she nice.

"Yeah, it's no big deal. We do it all the time. As long as we dry off a little first, we'll be fine. Just remember to put your towel down, that's all." And it was true. We did do it all the time.

Like a gymnast, she twirled off the lounge, wrapped her towel around herself, and walked toward the back door. I jumped out of the pool and grabbed my towel off the fence. I tried not to trip and kill myself while wrapping myself up.

How'd he die? He tried walking and wrapping a towel at the same time. Yeah, we lose a lot of horny, teenage boys that way.

Before heading inside, I turned off the box and grabbed our drinks. Now remember, this was the mid-'80s. Cable TV was still in its infancy. There were only about forty-eight channels at that time.

There was no Comedy Central, FX, or any of the other popular channels. There was no Internet either, which meant no Netflix. But we did have HBO and MTV. I turned on our twenty-five inch TV console with stereo surround sound and turned it to MTV.

B found a spot on the couch, while I put our drinks down. That was when I heard my dog whining from the laundry room. *Belle! Shit, is she still in the laundry room?* That was where she spent most of the day.

"Is everything okay?" B asked.

I tossed her the remote. "Yeah, I've just got to check on my dog. I'll be right back."

As I approached the door, I heard Belle whining in her sleep. I inched the door open just a smidge and accidently woke her up. She was lying on her doggie bed, dreaming away. She heard me at the door and opened her sweet, brown eyes. When she saw me, her tail started wagging.

What a face. Who could hate a face like that?

That was our great dog, Belle. She was a chocolate Lab mix. She wore a red collar over her beautiful, short, chocolate coat. She was as sweet as the day was long. She loved everyone and everyone loved her.

Ma got her after my dad passed away from a heart attack, back when I was eleven. Ma's friends told her it would help her sons grieve and deal with the loss of their father. A few days after the funeral, she went to the pound and brought Belle home. She completed our family.

"Hey, baby girl, were you napping?" She simply stretched, then got to her feet.

She walked over and licked my hand as I scratched her right behind her ears. It was her spot. She shook herself awake, a shake that started from her head and worked its way to her curved tail. As she finished her shake, she looked past me. Her tail started wagging, and she barked.

I turned and found B standing in the doorway behind me. "Belle, be nice!" I commanded. She barked one more time. *You won't tell me what to do!* She started panting and walked past me straight to B.

"What a pretty doggie." B bent down and stuck out her hand so Belle could sniff her.

Please don't bite her, please don't bite her! And please don't put your nose in her crotch! Belle, her tail still wagging, walked over, sniffed B's hand, and licked it.

Oh, thank God!

B bent down further, showing me a nice view—*quit staring, moron*—and gave Belle a big old hug and a rub behind the ears.

Yep, that was her spot. You want to make friends with Belle? Give her a good old rubbing behind her ears, and you've made a friend for life.

"Aw, you're a good girl! You're a *good* girl! You want to come watch TV with us?" B cooed.

Belle just stood there wagging her tail, and both of them looked up at me with puppy dog eyes. "Fine, let's go," I acquiesced.

"Yay, let's go Belle," B said as we walked back to the family room. Belle jumped onto the couch and placed herself between B and me, stretching out so B could rub her belly.

Uh, Belle, she's here for me, not you. Sigh! Never mind.

Could you blame Belle? If I were her, I'd do exactly the same thing. As a matter of fact, I wanted to do the same thing.

"So what movie did you see last night?" B asked.

"We saw *The Lost Boys*. It was really good. It was about teenage vampires, and it had a great soundtrack too."

"That sounds good."

"What about you?" I asked. "What did you see?"

"We saw *Dirty Dancing*. 'Nobody puts Baby in a corner!'" she said in her best Patrick Swayze impersonation. "It was a great movie! It was so much fun!" She spent the next few minutes telling me about the movie, without revealing any spoilers.

Whitney Houston's "I Wanna Dance with Somebody" came on MTV.

"Oh my God, I love this song!" B announced and she soon had me up dancing. Belle sat on the couch and barked along while we danced. *Is this really happening? Am I really dancing with B in my family room?* We laughed as we danced. She had the greatest laugh. It was light and airy.

We sat back down after a commercial came on. "That was fun," she commented, as I nodded.

You're fun.

"So, who were all those people you were there with last night?" I asked.

"Oh, those were kids from my youth group at church. I've been going to the same church since, like, kindergarten. I practically grew up in that church. We usually get together every Wednesday night. Sometimes we just hang out at church. Other times, we'll go to the movies like last night, or the beach, or bowling."

She was very animated as she spoke and her eyes lit up. "Each summer we go on a mission trip too. This year we went to a small town in West Virginia and helped clean up a rural church summer camp. The place was a real mess. This was the first year they were going to use it as a summer camp in, like, thirty years."

B went on to explain how much work they put into it this year. She shared how they painted the facilities and put a new roof on the main hall with some local help. They also mowed the lawn, planted new shrubs, and put in a new playground set, which was her primary task.

"What about you? Do you belong to a youth group?" she asked.

"No, I don't belong to a youth group. We're not really a church-going family. I mean, we go at Christmas and Easter, but not like every week, you know?" I shrugged.

"Oh, that's too bad. You don't know what you're missing," she said, but not in judgmental way.

It was that moment that Belle started snoring. Apparently she'd become real comfortable on the couch. We both looked at each other and laughed, which disturbed Belle's slumber. She looked at us, jumped off the couch, and made her way back to the laundry room.

B called after her, "Oh, sorry, girl, you don't have to leave. We didn't mean to laugh at you."

Belle continued to the laundry room, unfazed. It was her safe place, and I guess she'd figured out that B wasn't a threat to one of her toys, so she went back to her doggie pillow. Whenever things got too loud, or if she wanted to take a nap, that was where she went, except at night. Then, she would either sleep on the floor in the family room or patrol the house.

We had carpet throughout most of the house, but tile in the dining room and formal living room. You could hear her nails clicking and clacking as she made her way through the house at night. It was a sound that made you feel safe.

B noticed the time and said she had to get going. Instead of going back into the bathroom to change, she simply threw her shorts and T-shirt over her partially-dry bikini. She then pulled her hair back into a ponytail, slipped her beautiful feet into her flip-flops, and put on her sunglasses.

She checked her reflection in the glass and merely shrugged her shoulders, "Meh."

Meh? Is she kidding me? How about, "Holy shit, you look awesome!"

"This was a lot of fun. Thank you for inviting me over and letting me hang out."

"Oh yeah, you're welcome anytime. I had fun too. Clearly, Belle likes you. She doesn't let just anybody rub her belly. It took Jean Paul, like, five visits before she would let him into the family room, let alone rub her. It was very funny. She would growl at him when she was a puppy," I told her, which made her laugh. "She just tolerates Hannah. She'll let her pet her for a bit and then walks away."

Of course, I didn't tell her about their first meeting. Belle had nailed Hann with the *nose in the crotch*. It was so embarrassing.

"So what's the deal with you guys?" B asked.

"What do you mean? They're my best friends. I thought everyone knew that."

"So there's nothing going on, you know, between you and Hannah?"

"With Hannah? Oh, *God* no. Plus, Jean Paul would probably kill me, so no. There's nothing going on between me and Hannah." I paused. "Why do you ask?"

"Oh, no reason. It's just that when I came over, I thought . . . I mean, *she* was here, and I didn't know *Jean Paul* was here, so at first I thought that maybe I was *interrupting something*, even though you invited me over, and, well, I guess it really doesn't matter if that's the case," she rambled, which made me laugh to myself.

"They're just my best friends. Really, they're more like family. Also, I think she has her eye on some football player or something. She still won't tell me who, but I'll figure it out."

B giggled. "I bet you will. Well, thanks again."

"Sure, let's do it again sometime." *And please wear your green bikini again!*

"That would be nice. I gave you my number, right?"

"Um, no, actually I don't think I have it." *As a matter of fact, I know I don't have it because if I did, it would be my most valuable possession. Sorry, comic book collection!* "Let me grab a piece of paper and pen." I said, as we walked into the kitchen and found a pad and pen in our catch-all drawer.

She wrote her name in cursive and her number underneath, handing me back the pad and pen. "Here you go. I have yours, obviously. Give me a call later, if you want to go do something," she said.

Yes!

"Cool, I'll call you later." I told her.

"Good, I'd like that."

She'd like that, she said. I can't wait to tell Hannah!

With that, she smiled, and I damn near melted right there in my kitchen. She then twirled around and went out to the patio to grab her stuff.

I just love the way she twirls and how her ponytail whips around. Man, she is so graceful.

We walked to her car, and before she got in, she gave me a hug, a real one. We're talking a skin-on-skin, honest-to-goodness hug. And it felt great!

Please don't let this be a dream!

"Thanks again. You have a really nice house, and I love Belle. She's a real sweetie."

Screw the dog, I got a hug! I got a hug!

"Thanks. And, uh, thanks again for coming over." *And for the hug!* "I'll call you later." I looked at the pad of paper, which I had still had in my hand—in a death grip.

Please let this be your real number. Please don't tell me I'm on Candid Camera!

"Sounds great. I'll talk to you later then, but not too late, okay? My parents hate it when the phone rings past nine thirty."

She adjusted her Ray-Bans before getting into her car. She then backed out of my driveway, rolled down her window, waved goodbye and smiled, which went right through my soul.

7 - Friendly's

Ma got home around five thirty, temporarily taking my mind off of B. Ma changed and started making dinner. As she made dinner, we talked about her day at the hospital, while I fed Belle, who was lying down in the kitchen near Ma. While Belle loved her toys, Ma was her favorite. The moment Ma got home, Belle was right by her side until Ma went to bed.

Around seven, I finally worked up the nerve to call B. I went to Ma's bedroom, for privacy. We didn't have phones in all of our bedrooms. Ma didn't believe in it. We had a cordless phone downstairs in the family room, a phone in the drum room, and one in her bedroom.

My older brother had argued with her during his high school years that he *needed* one in his room too, for privacy. But she'd stuck to her guns and said "N-O, no! Ju're not getting a telefono in jur bedroom. If ju need to use the phone, ju can go to my room."

I closed the door behind me and sat on her bed, staring at the phone. After a few seconds, I picked up the handset, heard the dial tone, and put it back down. *Coward!* B's number sat on my mother's dresser, and I just stared at it. I stood, fixed my hair in her mirror, and took another deep breath.

Idiot, this isn't Star Trek! She can't see you! You could be standing here in your underwear, bloodied and on fire, and she would have no idea. Pick up the phone and call her. She's waiting for your call. You told her you'd call, and she said she's looking forward to it, remember? What are you waiting for? Grow a pair, for Christ's sake! Come on!

I picked up the phone and dialed. Unfortunately, my younger brother picked up the phone at the same time and also started dialing. "Dude, get off the phone! I have to make a call!" I yelled.

"No! *You* get off the phone. I have to make a call too!"

This pissed me off, so I opened Ma's bedroom door and yelled downstairs, "Ma, would you tell that *idiot* to get off the phone! I've got to make a call!"

The drum room door opened, and my brother yelled, "Ma, tell *him* to get off the phone! I was on first, and I've got to make a call too!"

Ma was at her wit's end with two teenagers hollering at her from two different ends of the house. "Okay, enough! Stop *jelling* at me! If ju want to talk to me, come to the family room, coño!" Exasperated, I ran downstairs while my brother walked into the family room.

"Ma, I've got an important call to make," I said.

"I do too," my brother said.

She looked at my brother first. "Okay, how long will jur call take?"

"I don't know, a while I guess."

I huffed and rolled my eyes.

She then looked at me and said, "Mira, enough of that, okay? How about ju? How long is jur call going to take?" It was like going before King Solomon.

Okay, important piece of advice. Whenever possible, always go last. It allows you to hear the previous answers, gauge your audience, and come up with a better one. "Not long at all," I replied, raising an eyebrow at my brother.

Ha! Bite me! Check!

"Okay ju have fifteen minutes to make jur call, then jur brother gets the phone."

"Ma, that's not fair!" my brother whined as he narrowed his eyes at me. "Who do you need to call? Is it *the girl* that came over to swim today?"

Damn it, I didn't see that one coming. This kid's good! Well played, my friend, well played. Clearly, you've received exceptional training in the ways of The Force. If I weren't so pissed, I'd be proud.

Ma's radar went into hyperdrive. "What girl?" she asked. "Did ju have a girl over to the house today? Ju know how I feel about that. I don't want any *jodienda* happening when I'm not home!"

"I know, Ma, I know. Yes, Ma, my friend B was over. So were Hannah and Jean Paul, and we all went swimming. You told me they could come over when you're not home." I pointed at my brother. "He knows that."

When she heard it was Hannah and Jean Paul, her radar dropped and her demeanor changed immediately. She loved the twins and trusted them, sometimes more than she trusted me, I suspected.

"Ohhh, that's different," she said, nodding her head. Then she eyeballed my brother. "Ju know they're allowed over to the house. Why'd ju say it like that? Ju know what? I don't want to know. Stop being tan necio, okay?" That meant "stop being foolish." My brother just nodded. Then her eyes were back on me. "Okay, ju have fifteen minutes and not a minute more. Now leave me alone. I want to watch my shows in peace."

"Thanks, Ma," I replied with a kiss on the cheek.

As I left the room, I quickly flipped my brother the finger in victory. *Ha! Checkmate, bitch!!* I returned to my mother's room and was ready to make the call. My adrenalin was pumping from the argument downstairs. When I picked up the phone, my brother was waiting for me. "You have fifteen minutes, asshole!" he hissed. "I'm picking up and dialing the phone in fifteen minutes exactly."

"Hang up the phone! Ma, he's still on the phone!" I yelled. He then hung up immediately.

"Knock it off, pendejos, or no one's jusing the phone tonight!" Yep, she's just like King Solomon, only shorter, scarier, and has a Spanish accent.

Okay, fifteen minutes. That was plenty of time. I picked up her number from my mother's bureau, clicked the phone for a new dial tone, and started dialing.

Busy signal! Seriously, I'm getting a busy signal? I fought so hard to get the phone, and you're busy? Un-friggin-believable! Who doesn't have call waiting?

I hung up and waited five seconds before dialing her number again. *Still busy! Come on!* Twelve seconds. *Busy!* Twenty seconds. *Busy!* Minutes started ticking away. *Ma only gave me fifteen minutes! Come on! Get off the phone! You're killing me!*

I had twelve minutes left. Click, dial, *busy!* It was becoming a routine. I started pacing, running my hand through my hair. I looked over at the alarm clock. Ten minutes. I jumped back on Ma's bed, picked up the entire phone, then picked up the handset and dialed one more time.

Ring! Seriously, you're really ringing? This isn't a ruse? You're not screwing with me, are you? Shit, did I misdial? Ring! Shit, what if I did misdial and I have the wrong number? I better hang up and try it again.

"Hello?" It was B's voice.

I didn't misdial! Who's the man? Who is the man?

"Oh, hey B, what's happenin'?" I said, trying to sound cool—the exact opposite of what I was feeling.

"I'm sorry, who's this?" she said.

Wait a minute, what? She doesn't recognize my voice? We've spent a couple of days together. She came to my house today, and we swam together. We danced and watched MTV together. You played with my dog! What do you mean, who is this?

A pit developed in my stomach. Then I heard her giggle. *Oh, good Lord. Thank you, God!*

"I was wondering when you were going to call," she said. "My sister's been on the phone for a while. I was worried that you'd try calling and when you heard the busy signal, you'd just give up and not call back."

Um, no friggin way! "Oh, was your phone busy? It rang the minute I dialed," I said. *Real smooth there, Romeo, real smooth!*

"Oh good, so what are you doing?"

"Nothing, I was just watching TV. What are you doing?"

"Not much. I just finished doing the dishes a few minutes ago."

"That's cool." *That's cool? Really, dummy, what's cool about doing dishes? Idiot!* "Hey, so did you have, uh, dessert after dinner?" I asked.

"No, we don't usually do dessert too often after dinner. Why do you ask?"

"Oh, I, uh, figured, you know, if you were, you know, up for it, we could, um, you know, go to, uh, Friendly's if you want. I'll treat," I said.

Real smooth there, Ex-Lax!

"That sounds like fun," she said, as I silently breathed a sigh of relief. "But you've been spending a lot of money on me. Can I treat tonight? Unless it would bother you having a girl treat you, that is."

"I wouldn't mind at all. My mother treats me all the time," I replied. *Sweet Jesus, did I really just friggin say that?* "I mean, no, I don't mind at all. Do you want me to pick you up?"

"No, don't be silly. You live right by Friendly's," she said. "I'll swing by and pick you up, okay? Besides, I'm treating, remember?"

"Yeah, okay, cool. I'm ready when you are," I told her.

"Okay, let me clean up, and I'll be over at eight thirty, okay? It's only seven twenty-seven now, so that should be enough time."

Seven twenty-seven! Shit! I've got three minutes before that asshole picks up the phone! "Yep, eight thirty works. I will see you then," I said, and then accidently hung up as she was saying, "Okay, bye." *Shmuck! Well, it's 7:28 p.m. now. I'm good!*

I opened the bedroom door and yelled, "Okay, you can have the phone now!" *Asshole!* This last part went unsaid, of course. I had about an hour to kill, so I went to my room and watched TV. After a half hour, I started the process of choosing the right outfit for the evening.

Should I change my shirt? I should change my shirt. Shit, do these shorts have a stain? Dammit, Belle! Why'd you jump on me with your dirty paws! Now I've got to change my shirt and shorts. I'll wear this polo shirt. It smells clean, doesn't it? I should ask Ma. Wait, are you out of your mind? You'd field a million questions. Yeah, this is clean. All right, which shorts? Should I wear the khakis? No. How about the white ones with blue pinstripes? Nah, I'd look like something out of a Brooks Brothers catalog. How about the red ones? Screw it, I'll wear the khakis. You can't go wrong with khakis. Where the hell are my boat shoes?

"Ma, are my boat shoes down there?"

"How would I know? Come look for jurself, pendejo."

Groan! Thanks for nothing, Ma! Okay, it's eight twenty. I still have enough time to brush my teeth and fix my hair. Hopefully I'll find my boat shoes before she gets here. Now, where are my house keys, watch, and wallet?

"Hey, Ma, are my house keys, watch, and wallet on the counter?"

"Sí!"

"Thanks, Ma." I splashed on a little cologne, and then I raced to the bathroom to brush my teeth and hair. As I headed downstairs full of confidence, I realized that B would be coming to the front door.

Gasp! I'll have to ask her in and introduce her to Ma. And she's wearing her comfortable T-shirt, sweatpants, and fuzzy chancletas. Ma, you're killing me. I don't have enough time to clean you up.

I raced into the family room and grabbed my watch, wallet, and keys. I noticed my boat shoes were five feet away from Ma, in her line of sight actually. *Thanks for looking, Ma!* I kissed her on her cheek and headed toward the door.

"I'll see you later," I said as I threw on my shoes.

"Are ju going over to Jean Paul and Hannah's?"

"Um, no, I'm heading to Friendly's to meet up with some . . . friends."

"Did someone say Friendly's?" My brother had just walked out of the drum room. *What timing!*

"I'm not getting you anything from Friendly's, so don't bother asking," I told him.

"Why not? I'd get something for you."

"I don't have enough money."

Ma waved her hands in the air. "Just go get me my purse, and I'll give ju money. What do ju want?" she asked my brother. *Ma, you're killing me!*

"I want a Reese's Pieces sundae," he said as he handed Ma her purse.

"Okay, go write down what ju want from Friendly's for jur brother, and he'll get it for ju." She handed me a twenty-dollar bill. "Y quiero mi cambio."

"Yeah, yeah, you'll get your change. He doesn't need to write it down. I'll see you later," I said. My brother returned to his drum room, while my mother changed the TV to Channel 11 for the start of the Yankees game. She loved her béisbol.

I waited for B in my driveway and she arrived at eight twenty-eight. Yep, she was punctual. *What did Hannah say, something about setting a clock?* I walked over to the passenger side as she reached over to unlock the door.

"Hey," I said, getting into her car.

"Hi. I hope you weren't waiting long."

"Nope, I just stepped outside."

"You didn't have to wait for me outside. I would have come to the front door." She laughed.

No friggin way! Not with Ma in her comfort mode. "It's no big deal. Like I said, I just stepped out."

"Okay, cool. You ready to go?" she asked as we backed out of my driveway. *Should I have hugged her when I got in? Is that our thing? Are we huggers?* She wore her hair up using a black ribbon, and she smelled great. She wore a Levi's jeans jacket over a white shirt, green shorts, and matching green sneakers. *She really knows how to put herself together.* She wore no makeup except for a light shade of pink lipstick.

Man, why haven't I noticed you before?

Even though she had a cassette sticking out of her radio, we listened to WBAB, our local rock station. I loved BAB, as we called it, so I was fine.

"Thanks again for today," she said as we drove to Friendly's.

"Yeah, sure, no problem; I'm glad you came over," I said. "I know Belle enjoyed your visit."

She smiled.

What a great smile.

We pulled into the parking lot and found a spot near the takeout window. As we walked toward the front door, she grabbed my arm and huddled in close. *Holy shit, is this really happening?* When we got to the front door, I held it open for her. There was another door inside, so I ran and held that one open too.

"You don't have to hold the doors open for me. I'm capable of getting the door myself," she said, but I could tell it pleased her.

"It's the way I was raised. If my mother found out I didn't hold the door for a lady, she'd kill me."

"She raised you well."

The hostess greeted us and told us it would be about a ten-minute wait, so we took a seat in the lobby.

"So what are you in the mood for?" I asked her.

"I don't know. What about you? What'd you have for dinner?"

I shrugged. "Nothing special. Just barbecue steaks, baked potatoes, and broccoli."

"Wow. Do you eat like that all the time?"

"What do you mean? Eat like what?" I was baffled by her question.

"Have barbecue steaks, potatoes, and broccoli on a weeknight?"

What's so weird about that? I shrugged again. "I guess so. I don't know. We eat normal."

"Well, if that's normal, then I want to move in. Do you think your mom would mind?" she joked.

I know I won't mind! Bye-bye, baby bro! "Oh sure, she'd be okay with it. She's always wanted a pretty, blond daughter."

B giggled. "Great, let's go grab my stuff and I'll move in tonight," she said. Then she did something unexpected.

She nuzzled her face into my neck and *smelled* me. "I thought that was you. You smell nice. What are you wearing?" she asked.

"Oh, uh, thanks, it's called Fahrenheit. I got if for Christmas last year."

"Well, it smells nice," she said and scooted closer to me.

There go those butterflies in my stomach.

Moments later, the hostess directed us to a booth, and we slid in opposite each other.

Shit, did I just kick her? "Sorry, did I just kick you?"

"Like this, you mean?" She gave me a light kick then laughed.

"No, and it was more like that," I replied, returning the light kick.

The server approached just then and, in a tired monotone voice, asked us what we'd like to order. We stopped giggling and looked up at her. This was when B decided to kick me again, which caused us to start laughing again.

I coughed into my fist. "Sorry about that. My friend's a bit of a spaz," I said, which caused B to kick me again, harder. *Ow!*

She batted her eyelashes at me, then grinned at the server. "He's right. I *am* a bit of a spaz."

"Uh huh, so would you like something to drink?" the waitress asked impatiently.

"Oh, um, okay. B, what would you like?"

"I don't know. Am I in the mood for a milkshake or a Fribble? Then again, I may want a sundae. Can I have water while I decide?" she asked, which caused our waitress to roll her eyes.

Clearly, someone's in a bad mood. "I'll have the same, please," I said.

"So, two waters?" the waitress asked.

"Yes, for now," I said and gave her my best grin. She snapped her pad closed and walked away, clearly annoyed. "I'm guessing she's *not* a fan," I said, lightening the mood.

"Yeah, I noticed that too."

"I wonder what her problem is," I said.

"Maybe she's just having a rough night. It happens," B said empathetically. No judgment, just forgiveness. *Who are you?*

Our server returned with two straws and glasses of ice water. "So have you decided what you're having this evening?"

We hadn't gotten that far yet, and I winced inwardly thinking about how that might go over with our grumpy waitress.

B flipped open her menu. "What are you thinking of having?"

Since she's paying, I better go with a regular sundae. Plus, I don't want to make a pig out of myself.

"I don't know. I'll probably just get a regular sundae. What about you?"

"I think I'll be a little more adventurous," she said, then looked up at the waitress. "Can I have a Jim Dandy, please?"

Damn! Did she just order a Jim Dandy? Is she crazy? That sundae is huge! It comes with five scoops of ice cream, chocolate syrup, marshmallow topping, strawberry topping, hot fudge, nuts, two bananas, whipped cream, sprinkles, and a cherry on top. Maybe she's thinking we're going to share. That's sweet.

You could tell by the expression on the face of our waitress, she was surprised as well. B couldn't weigh more than a hundred fifteen pounds, and she'd just ordered the largest sundae on the menu. "So will you need two spoons?" the waitress asked.

"No just one spoon," B replied.

"Are you *sure,* sweetie? That's an awful big sundae."

"Yes, I'm sure."

The server raised her eyebrows. "Okay, honey, it's your body. What kind of ice cream would you like in it?"

"Um, I'll have two scoops of mint chocolate chip, one scoop of butter pecan, one scoop of butter crunch, and a scoop of black raspberry, in that order, please," B ordered with a smile.

Okay, she's not playing around here, folks. Clearly, she's done this before. Instead of following suit, I ordered a regular sundae with scoops of mint chocolate chip. Again, she was paying after all.

After the baffled waitress walked away, B said, "Are you sure you didn't want a Jim Dandy too? My older brother and guys from my youth group usually order them. I figured you'd get one too. You didn't hold back because I'm paying, did you?"

"No, not at all. I mean, I do order them sometimes, but tonight I just wanted a regular sundae. Besides, I think her head would explode if I changed my order," I said, showing my hand a little.

B laughed. "I think you're right, but next time order a Jim Dandy if you want one."

Next time. Yes! "Okay, next time I'll get one." I replied.

B picked up her straw, poked it on the table, and then blew the paper wrapper into my face.

Nice! Two can play at this game. Swing and a miss! My wrapper blew past her and landed on the table behind her, where a family was having dinner. *Oops!*

The father turned around, looking annoyed.

"I'm so sorry about that. I was actually aiming for her," I confessed, which made B giggle.

"Uh huh, please don't do it again," the man said.

"It won't happen again," I promised, and he just turned around.

"I can't take you anywhere," B joked. "You're nothing but trouble. First, you bother our waitress, and then our neighbors. I'm having second thoughts about moving in." She waggled her eyebrows and kicked me softly under the table.

Moments later, our desserts arrived. The monstrous Jim Dandy sat in front of B and the regular sundae sat in front of me, along with a pair of sundae spoons and extra napkins. *I guess Ma called ahead.* I can be a bit messy.

"You're really gonna eat all that, huh?" I joked.

"Are you kidding me? I'll be finished before you."

"There's no way you'll finish before me."

"You don't think so, huh? Care to bet on that?"

Like my father used to say, never enter a bet unless you know the outcome. I agreed to the wager; the loser would pay the bill.

She said, "You know, I'm starting to feel a little guilty with you paying for everything." Then she winked.

"I just hope you brought your wallet, because there's no way I'm losing," I replied.

"Do you need to go to the bathroom or anything? I don't want to hear any excuses when I win." There was a gleam in her eye.

I think it's time to take little Miss B down a peg. Good luck, sister! Ain't no way you're beating me!

"Nope, I'm good to go. What about you?" I asked.

"Nope, I'm ready to go." She then removed her jacket, giving me a full frontal view of her white shirt.

Gulp! Stop staring. Look at something else. You're here to eat ice cream. Stop staring. Focus, idiot, focus!

She looked at me and giggled, knowing the exact effect she was having on me. *Well played, blondie, well played.* What can I say? She was gorgeous. She picked up her spoon, and I picked up mine. We gave each other our best Clint Eastwood glare.

"Ready?" I asked.

"Yup, are you?" she asked as she popped a cherry in her mouth, stem and all.

Ewww! That's disgusting!

A moment later, she stuck her tongue out. The cherry was gone, and the stem was tied into a knot. She just sat there and raised an eyebrow.

Holy crap! What the . . . ?

"Um, youth group?" I inquired.

"Yep," she replied as she placed the stem on the table and started in on her sundae.

Before I knew it, she'd made her way past the whipped cream and sprinkles, and devoured a couple of scoops. That was when I knew I was in trouble. Her sundae became a multicolored mess. Strawberries were smashed to the side; smeared chocolate syrup and small pieces of bananas were mixed with her ice cream. But she worked her way to the bottom like a champ. I was captivated.

I was still navigating my way around my cherry, whipped cream, and first scoop as she downed a piece of banana and a half scoop of ice cream. She simply wiped her mouth with her napkin and took a sip of water. "How're you doing over there?" she asked.

I just scrunched my nose at her and kept eating. Then she really surprised me. She burped!

It wasn't an earth-shattering, guttural burp, but it was a burp nonetheless. *Whoa! That was awesome!* I sat back and gave her a golf clap.

"Very nice. Youth group again?" I asked.

"Nope, older brother," she replied.

"Excellent! Your parents must be proud," I teased.

"Yes, very. Um, I'm almost done here; are you ready to give up?"

"I *never* give up!" I boasted.

"Okay, just remember, I gave you the option."

"Whatever, Burps, just finish your ice cream," I said.

She then picked up her spoon and devoured the remainder of her sundae. It was like she had unhinged her jaw and swallowed the whole thing. *Holy crap!!*

I tried to copy her, which was my near fatal mistake. *Brain Freeze!!* I winced as she almost spat out her ice cream from laughter.

She slid my water to me. "Here, drink some water. It'll help."

Of course, she was right. She picked up her sundae dish and slurped on the remnants as I drank my water.

"You won," I conceded. "I've only seen my younger brother devour a sundae like that," I said.

"I told you I'd win. I know how to eat ice cream."

"Well, a bet's a bet."

She waved a hand at me. "You don't have to pay. I was just kidding. Really, I'll pay. I really don't mind."

"And I don't mind either." *I was planning on it anyway.*

"Can I at least leave the tip?"

"Sure, leave the tip. And the next time we go out, you can pay, cool?"

"When do you think that will be?" she asked with a glimmer in her blue eyes.

Don't stare into her eyes, don't stare into her eyes. Crap, you're staring into her eyes!

"Um, I don't know. What are you doing tomorrow?"

"I have nothing big planned. My neighbor is away and asked me to take in her mail and water her plants. Aside from that, I've got nothing planned. What are you thinking?"

"Well, Macy's is having a sale tomorrow, so I was going to go back-to-school shopping. Want to join me? We can hang out in the mall afterward."

"I'll go as long as I'm allowed to buy lunch. Besides, I have to do some back-to-school shopping too. I'll help you pick stuff out, and you can help me, okay?"

She's so cute. Like I need help picking out clothes.

"That sounds like a plan," I agreed.

B shared her shopping list for the coming school year. I was always curious about what the smarties bought that normal students didn't. She rattled off a new day planner, assorted notebooks, new Trapper Keeper, colored pens, pencils, and index cards for school and her SATs in October. I just sat there trying not to stare, but how could I help myself?

She had the most amazing blue eyes and the cutest tiny freckles on her pretty nose, not to mention a great smile. The waitress came back and left the check, which I grabbed before B could. "You can pay for that up front," our waitress said with a slight smile. *A smile this time! We've made progress.*

"It's been a long night, huh?" B asked her.

"Honey, you've said a mouthful. You kids have a good night." She gave one more little smile and walked away.

That was B—she cared. Other people had that continual resting bitch face. B's "resting bitch face" was a smile. *Who is this girl?*

She left a five-dollar tip under her water glass and then grabbed her things. She stood and put her jacket back on in a very fluid motion, which made me laugh for some reason.

"What's so funny?" she asked.

"It's nothing." I couldn't wipe the smirk from my face.

"It has to be something."

"I just like the way you put your jacket on, that's all."

"You're so weird."

"You don't know the half of it."

We were at the register when I realized I'd forgotten something. *Shit! My brother's sundae!* "Oh, hey listen," I told the cashier, "I need to put in a to-go order too." She seemed annoyed by this. *I'm just making friends everywhere tonight.* "I promised my brother that I'd bring him home a sundae," I explained to B.

I ordered my brother's sundae, and handed the woman Ma's twenty-dollar bill to pay the entire tab.

Ma, thanks for treating for dessert tonight!

8 - The Drive Home

I got the sundae, and we made our way to the parking lot. As we walked to B's car, she wrapped her arm around mine and snuggled in close. *Does it get any better than this?* As we drove away, she looked over at me and said, "I really had a good time tonight. I enjoy spending time with you."

"Thanks, B. I like spending time with you too." I turned to her, and in the reflection of the oncoming headlights, I saw her smile.

During the drive back to my house, we laughed about the evening, from the straw incident to our *friendly* waitress.

When we pulled into my driveway, B turned off the radio and parked the car. We sat there for a moment, looking at each other, grinning. *Gulp! Should I kiss her? Does she want me to kiss her? What do I do here?*

She saved me from myself with conversation. "So, tomorrow we're hitting the mall, right?" she asked.

"Yep, that's the plan, Stan."

"Do I look like a Stan to you?"

"Does Stan-ella work better?"

She just laughed and playfully smacked me. "*Jerk.* So what time do you want to go tomorrow?"

"Well, the mall opens at nine, so do you want to go at maybe ten thirty? We can shop, eat lunch, and then come back here to go swimming again," I said.

"That sounds like fun. Do you want to drive, or do you want me to drive?" she asked.

Well, this is a first. I get to drive? Sweet! "I'll drive."

"Okay, that sounds good. So do you know where I live?"

Heaven. "Uh, no, I actually don't. Where do you live?"

She gave me her address and directions to her house. It was a fairly direct route, and I knew the area pretty well, so even I wouldn't get lost. She lived about fifteen minutes away, just past the school, near the golf course.

"That sounds pretty easy." I said.

"Yeah, it shouldn't be too tough, even for you." She laughed at her own joke while I just grinned. *Man, I love that laugh.*

"Nice. *Now* who's being a jerk?"

"Oh, stop being so sensitive." Before I could jab back, she leaned over and kissed me on the cheek. "There, does *that* make you feel better?"

Holy shit! I've never felt better in my entire life! "Uh huh!" was all I could get out. She'd actually left me tongue-tied, and I'm never tongue-tied!

"Good, then I'll see you tomorrow at ten thirty at my house," she said.

Well, I can take a hint. It's time for me to go. "I'll be there at ten thirty on the dot." I opened the passenger door to get out.

"You better be," she said. "Don't make me send out a search party to look for you."

I smiled and nodded as I shut the door. I was almost to the front door when she rolled her window down and hollered, "Hey, aren't you forgetting something?" She was holding my Friendly's bag out the window. *Sigh!*

"Thanks. My brother would have a hissy fit if I forgot it." I went to the window and took the sack, then hesitated. *Should I lean in for a kiss?*

"See you tomorrow," she said as she put her car in reverse.

Nope, I guess not.

I waved as she drove away and then stood in my driveway for a few minutes.

I should have kissed her. Next time I'll kiss her, right? I mean I should, right? Argh! I'll figure it out!

"Ma, I'm home," I yelled as I walked into a relatively quiet house. "I have his ice cream. Where is he?" I asked, gesturing toward the drum room.

"He's spending la noche at Rick's. Ju have my change?" she asked, holding out her hand. I gave her the change, which she placed in her purse.

"What do you mean he's sleeping at Rick's?" I asked, all annoyed. "He had such a hissy fit before. What am I supposed to do with this?" I held up the bag.

"Put it inside la nevera."

I just grumbled to myself and put his sundae into the freezer.

I then joined Ma in the family room to watch the Yankees, and must have had a funny look on my face as I sat down. "Que te pasa hijo de mi vida?" Ma asked.

"Nothing's the matter, why?"

"No razón. ¿Con quien fuiste a Friendly's?" She was probing my brain for information. I could feel it. I wasn't her first teenage rodeo. She'd already perfected her skills on my older brother.

"Just a friend from school."

"¿Fuiste con Jean Paul y la Hannah?"

"No, Ma, not Jean Paul and Hannah."

"So, ¿con quien fuiste?" she asked again. And like a typical teen, I went from zero to sixty in seconds.

"*Ma*, what's with the third degree?"

"What third degree?" She pulled her chin back, acting offended. "I just asked ju an esimple question, ¿y por qué me estas gritando?" Then she gave me *the look,* so I took a deep breath.

"I'm not yelling at you, Ma. Look, I went to Friendly's with my friend B. There, are you happy now?" I said it with the attitude that every snot-nosed teenager shot at his or her parents on occasion. "I'm going to my room." I got up to make my exit.

As I hit the stairs, I overhead Ma mutter, "Coño, must be some girl."

Damn, Ma knew me too well.

9 - The Mall

I got up early the next morning—well, early for me in the summer anyway—8:30 a.m. Thankfully, I didn't have a note waiting for me when I got downstairs. It was overcast, so I took Belle for a quick walk and hoped the bad weather would hold off. Belle did her business, and we returned to the house. I put some food in her bowl and gave her fresh water.

Next I skimmed leaves out of the pool and turned the cushions over on the lounge chairs, except for *THE Lounge Chair.* I didn't bother touching that one, other than to wipe it down. By nine thirty, I had jumped in the shower and worked my way through my daily routine, which is the same routine I use to this day. After my shower, I moisturize my face, neck, and arms. Today, I use Aveeno brand skin lotion, because I like the way it feels. In the '80s, I used whatever free samples Ma brought home from the hospital. It was usually Lubriderm.

After moisturizing, I shave what little facial hair decided to make an appearance. To this day, I still can't really grow a mustache. After shaving, I Q-tip my ears, brush my teeth, and put deodorant on. And that, ladies and gentlemen, was and is my morning routine. Hey, it keeps me looking young regardless of the gray hairs in my goatee.

After I finished, I went to my bedroom and got dressed. I wanted to make sure I looked good, but noticed I was running late, so I tossed on blue shorts and a blue and white striped polo shirt. I threw on socks and sneakers then ran to the bathroom to blow-dry my hair.

Hopefully I don't look too much like a douche. I tossed on some cologne, went downstairs, grabbed my watch, keys, and wallet, checked on Belle, and then left the house. I hopped into my car and noticed I was low on gas. *I'll pick up B and then fill up at Hess on the way to the mall.*

I hit every red light possible. *Damn, I only have eight minutes to get to B's, and I'm still about twelve minutes away! I'm going to be late!* I turned up a side street and sped my way through various neighborhoods at fifty-five mph instead of the posted thirty.

The speeding, of course, is not something I would recommend today, especially to my own children. *So, kids, if you're reading this, don't speed. It's not worth it. It's better to get to your destination safe and sound and a few minutes late than to crash your car or worse. Oh, and just say no to drugs! Thank you, Nancy Reagan.*

I landed in her driveway at ten thirty on the dot. *Who's the man? I'm the man!* I took a deep breath and checked my look in the mirror before getting out of the car. *Meh!* And before I forget, here's some quick advice for all you gentlemen out there.

When picking up your lady, never pull into her driveway and honk your horn for her. It's not cool nor is it funny. It makes you look like a jerk and proves to her parent(s) that she chose the wrong guy . . . again!

Show some class and get your ass out of the car. Walk up to the door and introduce yourself to her parent(s). Smile and say things like, "What a lovely home you have," even if it's a pigsty. Another one is, "I can see where your daughter gets her great taste, or fashion sense, or sense of humor . . ." It's called being polite. Her parents will appreciate it, trust me.

She lived in a split-level, two-story house, which had a landing that separated both levels. I rang the doorbell and waited patiently. Moments later, her mother answered the door. "Hello, can I help you?"

Her mom was an older version of B. They were about the same height, with shoulder-length blond hair and blue eyes. She was just a little heavier than B, by maybe five pounds; then again, one was a teenager and the other was a mother in her early- to mid-fifties, I would guess.

"Good morning, ma'am, I'm here to pick up B. We're planning on going to the mall together."

She looked down her nose at me, arched her blond eyebrow, and hollered over her shoulder, "B, there's a boy here for you."

"I'm coming."

"She'll be right here," her mom said while giving me another once-over. I just smiled. She, of course, did not. Nor did she invite me in. She just squinted her eyes slightly and walked away. About ten seconds later, B appeared at the door. "Hey, I'll be right out. Just wait for me in your car, okay?"

"Oh, uh, sure. Okay, so I'll go start my car and wait for you."

B came out shortly after that and made her way toward my car. She had her purse over her shoulder and her tote in her hand. I hopped out of the car and met her halfway, taking her beach tote. "Thank you," she said.

I put her tote into my trunk and then went to the passenger side, holding the door open for her. I felt someone staring at me, and that was when I noticed her mother looking at us through their picture window overlooking the front yard, near the split-level landing. I smiled and received no response, so I closed the passenger door and went around to the driver's side and hopped in.

I noticed immediately that something was off with B. Don't get me wrong, she looked amazing. She wore a yellow headband, which offset her gorgeous, blond hair. She wore a pretty blue, white, and yellow print summer dress that came down to her knees, and white flats. No, it wasn't her clothes that were amiss; it was her attitude.

"Hey, are you okay?" I asked as she stared into the sky, out the passenger window.

"Can we just get out of here please?" she quietly replied without turning.

"Sure, I just need to grab gas, cool?"

"That's fine, as long as we get out of here," she replied as she cleared her throat.

Obviously I've missed something. As we pulled away, I noticed her glaring at her house.

When she noticed me watching her, she stopped glaring and immediately transformed back into the person I knew. "So, how are you?" She smiled, pretending nothing was wrong.

Okay, I'll play along.

"I'm great. I took *your friend* Belle for a walk and then took care of the pool this morning."

"How is my friend Belle? I can't wait to give her a big hug later."

Yep, she's back to normal.

After stopping for gas, we made our way to the mall, chatting and singing along with the radio.

"So, where to first?" I asked, after parking. I figured we could knock her stuff out, and then move on to my stuff.

"Well, what's on your list?"

"Not much. I just want to hit Macy's. What about you?"

"I really don't need anything, to be honest. I usually go clothes shopping with my mother." She said this with an eye roll.

Ha! So it's not just me!

"How about we just walk around," she suggested.

"Sounds like a plan, Stan-ella. Ha!"

"Laugh it up, fuzzball," she replied with an arched eyebrow.

I put a hand over my heart in mock horror. "Wait a minute, did you just *Star Wars* me?"

"Oh yeah, I just *Star Wars*'d you. Surprised?"

Who is this girl? She's quoting Star Wars *and doing it right!*

"A little bit," I replied.

"Hmm, so if I called you a *half-witted, scruffy-looking, Nerf-herder*, would you feel insulted?"

"Wow! No, but I do prefer scoundrel to Nerf-herder."

"Duly noted," she laughed.

So she quotes Star Wars, *can take a joke, and looks like, well,* that. *Awesome! Just . . . awesome!* "Okay, *Princess*, let's go shopping," I said.

"You've got it, scoundrel," she replied and took my arm as we went in.

"So, you're a *Star Wars* fan, huh?" I asked.

"Not really."

"Okay, now I'm confused. You just quoted *Star Wars* to me."

"Lighten up, scoundrel. I have an older brother and sister. We used to watch it all the time. I guess it's in my blood now, just like *Star Trek*." She shrugged. "Sometimes when I finish my homework early, I stay up late and watch it after the *Honeymooners* on Channel 11."

I think I'm in love. She quotes Star Wars *and watches* Star Trek. *If she starts quoting* The Odd Couple, *I will marry her!*

"Spock's my favorite." She then did the Vulcan hand salute.

"I love Spock too." I returned the salute. *Live long and prosper! This girl is awesome!*

We walked past a few stores and came upon Spencer's Gifts. Let's see, how do I describe this store?

It's the kind of store where you didn't want anyone you knew seeing you enter or exit the place, especially with a Spencer's bag in your hand.

Throughout the years, they've transformed, but it has always had an adult theme.

Back in the '80s, they sold a lot of pot paraphernalia, from pipes to two-headed bongs. They also had the best black-light posters. Their T-shirts were very funny too. You couldn't wear them at my school, but they were funny nonetheless. One of my favorites was one with a nun flipping you off.

"Do you want to go in?" she asked, raising an eyebrow.

"Sure," I said, all casual and cool.

She took my arm and we entered. The front half of the store was full of dark lights, bongs, and assorted smoking paraphernalia. "You guys need any help?" the dirtbag behind the counter asked.

I waved him off. "No thanks."

B giggled as we passed a mannequin wearing a T-shirt with a glow-in-the-dark smoking pot leaf on the front with a saying, *Let's Get High.*

It was like the bar scene from *Star Wars.*

We stopped and checked out their assortment of posters. They had everything from *Jaws* to the Beatles to an assortment of Rolling Stones posters.

"I love Mick, don't you?" she squealed.

"He's okay, but I'm more of a Beatles fan." You know how there are Mac people versus PC people? That's how some people are with the Stones and the Beatles. Can you guess which type B was?

"Well, maybe you just haven't heard all their good stuff. I mean, the Beatles are *okay*, but they're no Rolling Stones," she argued.

I didn't want to waste precious time debating this point, so I just said, "Maybe you're right. I'll have to listen to them again sometime."

"Well . . . what are you doing tonight?" she asked.

"Nothing planned, why?"

"Do you want to come over tonight and listen to some music?"

"Sure, as long as it's okay with your parents."

"Why wouldn't it be okay with my parents?" Her brow furrowed as she looked at me. *Oh shit. Way to go, putz!*

"Uh, I don't know. I, uh, usually have to ask my mother first, that's all."

"Of course I'll let my parents know, silly. And it'll be fine, trust me, I'm a lifeguard," she joked.

Okay, sister, I'll take your word for it. I just don't think your mom liked me. I guess I'll find out tonight. "Great," I replied as she smiled, which became intense due to the black lights. For some reason, white teeth really pop under black lights and not just teeth. T-shirts, sneakers, really anything white.

In the distance, I could see the sex toys and adult games, so I nonchalantly turned us around to exit the store. Those toys are funny, especially to toss to your friends, but not when you're with a girl you're trying to impress.

We stopped by Claire's next, and B purchased an assortment of headbands and accessories. From there, we entered a women's clothing store. "Do you mind?" she asked.

"No, not at all." And I didn't. I was the rare breed of male who liked the mall—still do to this day. I like walking around, window shopping, or I'll sit and people watch. Styles have changed, but people haven't.

We walked over to the young ladies' section and looked at various dresses. B would pull one out, put it up against herself, shake her head, and put it back.

"Can I help you find something today?" the salesperson asked.

"Do you have this blue dress in a size . . ." B gave her dress size, but frankly I didn't pay attention. I was busy trying to act cool while standing in the middle of this clothing store. While I truly didn't mind, I was still out of my element.

"Hmm, let me see. We just got a shipment in. Let me check my inventory sheet. I'll be right back," the lady replied. We walked around the store while she checked her inventory. B found a pair of slacks, a pink top, and a yellow print top—all very stylish and pretty, just like B.

The clerk finally came back with B's dress.

"It looks like one did come in today. Do you want to go try all these things on?"

B looked at me and asked, "Do you mind?"

"What kind of scoundrel would I be if I minded?" I smiled.

B laughed, while the clerk gave me a funny look. "Uh, okay, the dressing room's this way."

B went in, and I stood outside the dressing room, like a fish out of water. I tried not to look at anything or anyone specifically. Like I said, I was out of my element. I was a teenage boy in a women's clothing store and didn't want to look or act like some kind of pervert.

"Hey, what do you think?" B asked as she modeled the blue dress.

Wow! Is there anything she can't wear? "Wow, you look great."

"You really think so? It doesn't make me look fat?"

She's kidding me, right? Does she even have an ounce of fat on her? "Oh God, no. You look *great*!" I told her with a bit of enthusiasm.

"Thanks, Nerf-herder." She giggled and returned to the dressing room. She proceeded to model all the clothes, asking me each time if they made her look bad.

I didn't grow up with sisters, so I didn't understand that teenage girls really have to fight to keep a healthy self-image. They're constantly bombarded with images of *the perfect girl*. The perfect girl is thin, not fat. She wears this style and not that one. She wears this shade of makeup and this perfume. I'm amazed they can get out of the house every day.

B purchased the blue dress, the slacks, and the yellow top.

After we left that store, we window-shopped for a while, then I heard someone call my name. It was my neighbor Rick with a bag from the local record store, Sam Goody, in his hand. I introduced him to B.

"So what's going on?" Rick asked.

"Not much," I said. "Just clothes shopping. Macy's is having a sale, so I'm picking up some polo shirts."

I'd known Rick my whole life. He was like family, so he knew all of my quirks, including my preference for polos. "Dude, *more* polo shirts?" He did the big-eyes thing, like I was completely over the edge.

Dude, not in front of this girl! "First, you can't have too many polo shirts. Second, you get most of my hand-me-downs, so what do you care?"

"True," Rick agreed, then grinned.

"So what'd you buy?" I pointed at his Sam Goody bag. He handed me U2's recent release, *Joshua Tree.*

I nodded appreciatively at his choice. "U2, good call. I love *The Unforgettable Fire.* I hear this one's excellent."

"That's what I heard too. Anyway, I've got to get home. My mom doesn't know I'm here," he said.

"I never saw you, dude," I replied.

"Yeah, neither did I, dude," B chimed in, which made Rick laugh. "And it was nice meeting you," she added as we all waved goodbye. She turned to me. "Are you hungry?"

Did she really just ask a seventeen-year-old guy if he was hungry? "Yeah, I could definitely eat. Want to hit Sbarro?"

"Yep, and remember I'm paying, okay?"

I raised my hands. "Not a problem, Princess."

She giggled, grabbed my arm, and we headed to Sbarro, where we ordered a couple of slices and Cokes, then grabbed a booth.

As we sat, I quickly grabbed my straw, poked it on the table, and blew the straw paper into her hair! "*Shot, score!*" I mock-yelled.

"Hey, I wasn't ready." Not to be outdone, she did the same maneuver with her straw and nailed me square in the chest.

"I still got you first."

"Easy, kid, don't get cocky."

"Remember I'm a scoundrel, Princess."

We then hunkered down for our meal, enjoying the food and each other's company. Even though I made the offer to pay, she reminded me it was her turn and she'd have it no other way. Afterward, we headed for Macy's and the polo shirts.

10 - Macy's and Swimming

M acy's, the epicenter for men's fashion. It was like walking into a store in New York City. The employees dressed nicer. The counters were cleaner. *Can I offer you a cologne sample? Would you like a facial today?* They carried the latest in men's fashion, not that I could afford most of it. Back then, though, there was no place like it.

The men's department was on the second floor, so we hit the escalators, rode up to men's fashion paradise and the polo shirts were calling my name like the sirens they were. I led the way.

Back in the '80s, Ralph Lauren owned the polo shirt market. There were other brands, but Ralph Lauren's were the best. Guys would wear their collars popped up, or down; the tails tucked in or casually untucked over a pair of shorts. Ralph Lauren had the best Oxford dress shirts and sweaters too.

The polos were on sale today, and I was happy to see there were a variety of colors available in my size. I unfolded them, held them up, and asked B what she thought.

"They're okay."

Okay? That's it? "Don't you like them?" I asked,

"It's not that. I'd just like to see you in something else." She bit her lip and started looking around the displays.

Uh-oh, she wants to change my style. "Really, like what?" I cautiously asked.

"Well, how about this?" She picked up a blue cable-knit V-neck sweater vest.

A clerk approached us before I could respond. "Can I help you?"

"No, I think I've got this," B replied confidently. She then grabbed a white T-shirt and a yellow T-shirt. "What do you think?" she asked, putting the T-shirts up against the sweaters.

I had to admit; it wasn't half bad. "Hmm, it actually looks nice."

"This vest is versatile too. You can wear it with a T-shirt, a polo shirt, or with one of your Oxfords." *How'd she know I wore Oxfords? Has she noticed me at school?* "And they're actually cheaper than the polo shirts." She then looked over at the clerk, who nodded in agreement.

"Cool, let's start making a pile," I said. And we did. In the end, I left with four sweaters, a couple of T-shirts, and a blue-and-white-striped polo shirt.

"Are you happy with what you picked out?" she asked as we left the store.

"You mean what *we* picked out?" I corrected, but with a grin. She grinned too, clearly pleased with herself.

We decided to end the shopping day and head to my house for a swim. It was overcast outside but still good swimming weather. We sang along to the radio and laughed as we drove to my house. She put her hand on top of mine and held my hand. *She's holding my hand! She's holding my hand! This is awesome!*

The house was already vibrating from the music pumping out of my brother's drum room. *Jesus, dude, seriously? Can't you give it a friggin' rest for one friggin' day?* I just smiled as I unlocked the front door, letting B in first.

"Make yourself at home," I said over the music. "I'll be right back."

I opened the vibrating door of the drum room and hit a wall of sound. "Dude, can you turn this down?" I yelled as I flicked the lights. I had to do that sometimes to get his attention.

He was sitting behind his drum kit, pounding away as Rush blasted out of his speakers. "Huh?" he replied. *Exactly, pendejo!*

"I said, "Can you turn this down a little? I have a friend over." He didn't move, at least not fast enough for me, so I lowered the volume on the stereo myself.

"Oh yeah, sure, go ahead. I thought I was home alone."

"Thanks. Oh, I saw Rick at the mall. He got the new U2 tape."

"That's cool. Oh, and thanks for the sundae. I had it for breakfast."

Reese's Pieces sundae, the breakfast of champions! "Sure."

When I walked into the family room, I found the Bs playing together. Belle had her old tennis ball in her mouth. She dropped it in front of B, who picked it up and threw it across the room. Belle went after it with excitement and dropped it once again in front of B. "What a good girl you are, Belle." B hugged her and rubbed her back.

"Well, you've clearly made a lifelong friend," I said.

"I think so." B giggled as Belle rolled over, begging for a belly rub. B obliged.

You lucky dog! "At least we can hear ourselves think now," I said.

"I didn't mind. He's really good."

"Yeah, he really is. He's been playing since he was real young, so I guess I'm just used to it. Some days though, I'd like to blow those things up."

"Oh, you're mean," she said, still rubbing Belle's belly. "Isn't he a mean old man, Belle?"

Did Belle just nod?

We decided to get to swimming. B went into the bathroom with her tote while I headed upstairs to change, Macy's bag in hand.

I laid my new clothes on the bed and gave them a once-over. *She's got good taste. I'm gonna look good this year.* I threw on a T-shirt and my bathing suit, grabbed my box, and headed to the family room to wait for B.

She joined me moments later, wearing a flower print T-shirt, an ocean-blue bikini, flip-flops, black Ray-Bans on top of her head holding back her hair, and a smile. *Another great entrance.*

We went into the kitchen to see what was available for drinks. As I leaned over to look in the fridge, she put her hand on the middle of my back and rubbed it lightly. I didn't think she realized she was doing it—she was very nonchalant about it as she peered over my shoulder into the fridge. I, on the other hand, entered *the holy shit this is really great* zone. "Iced tea good?" I said, trying not to sound like a voice-changing Peter Brady.

She nodded and I poured us some tea and handed her glass to her.

"Did you bring any tapes in that tote of yours?" I asked. "If not, we can listen to a mixed tape or the radio."

"Why don't you play a mixed tape? I'd love to hear what songs you like," she said.

That made me feel good. "Sure. I've got something in the box already."

I rewound the tape, pressed play, and out came "Sussudio" by Phil Collins. B gave me a nod of approval, and we walked into the pool area. *Thank God I passed that test!*

We threw our stuff on two lounge chairs, then I dipped my toe in the water.

"How's the water today?" she asked.

"It's perfect. Come on over and check it out," I said.

She removed her Ray-Bans and T-shirt, revealing her amazing bikini. *Good Lord! Gulp!*

She then made a mistake. She trusted me. She walked next to me and stuck her toes in the water. *And you call yourself a lifeguard. What a rookie!* I immediately pushed her into the pool. *Score!*

"Hey! That wasn't fair! I wasn't ready!"

I dove in next to her. "I can't believe you fell for that!" I laughed as she splashed me. She then dunked me, and that was pretty much how it went that afternoon—splashing, swimming, laughing, talking, and discovering more about each other.

The skies grew more overcast until eventually raindrops intruded on the day. We grabbed our clothes and took off for the house.

"I need to call my mom about you coming over tonight. Can I use your phone?" she asked as we dried off in the family room.

I handed her the cordless phone, and she walked into the kitchen. I stayed in the family room, allowing her some privacy.

Still, I could see her from the couch and noticed her tense body language. It didn't seem like a happy conversation. I saw her nodding, then shaking her head, and then nodding again. I could make out the words "okay" and "thank you" just before she hung up.

"Is everything okay?" I asked when she walked back to the family room and laid the phone down. Then she plopped down on the couch with a sigh.

"Everything's fine. She wanted to know what time I *planned* on coming home, like I was five years old or something. I don't understand why she always gives me a hard time. I'm nothing like my older sister." Another sigh. "I get good grades, I go to church, I'm a youth leader in my youth group, and she's always on my case, giving me a hard time."

I nodded and just listened as she vented.

"You don't want to hear any of this," she finally said, looking a little embarrassed.

"I don't mind. Really I don't."

"That's because you're sweet. Hey, what are you doing for dinner tonight?"

"Probably eating at home, why?" I asked.

"Would you like to have dinner at my house tonight?"

"Are you sure it's okay? I mean, I don't want to get you in trouble." After the conversation she had with her mom, I was not so sure this was a great idea. But she waved it off.

"Don't worry about it, it'll be fine. Remember, you can trust me, I'm a lifeguard." She winked. I still wasn't so sure, but I just laughed at her joke and let it go.

"Do you like fish?" she asked.

I hate fish! "Sure, I love fish, why?"

"Good, we're having lutefisk with boiled potatoes and peas. My mom is making it special for my brother and sister tonight, because they're going back to college this weekend." She looked at me and tilted her head. "Have you ever had lutefisk?"

I never even heard of—what'd she call it? Luckfist, I think? "No, is it good?"

"We think so, but to be honest, it's not everyone's cup of tea," she said as she adjusted her towel.

You're really not doing a great job here selling me on this meal, sister. "I'm sure I'll like it, but are you sure your folks will be okay with me crashing the party?"

"They won't mind. The more the merrier. And if you don't like the lutefisk, you can smother it in mustard. That's what my sister does. She hates lutefisk."

My eyebrow went up on that one. *So let me get this straight. You're serving some fish dish that your sister hates, even though the meal is supposed to be partially in her honor. It's also a food I've never heard of, that'll require me to smother it in mustard. And after dinner, we're going to listen to the Stones. Oh, and let's not forget, I don't think your mom likes me. Yep, this'll be a great evening.*

"Sounds great, what time should we get you home?" I asked.

"Four thirty will work," she said.

We still had plenty of time to kill. B adjusted her towel and tossed on her T-shirt while I flipped the TV to HBO. We settled back into the couch and began watching *Gremlins*. It was playing for the umpteenth time.

"I love this movie," she said as she nuzzled up against me. "Remember, never feed them . . ." she started.

". . . after midnight!" we say together.

"*Jinx*, Ha! You owe me a beer!" she yelled.

"Damn! Fine, I owe you a beer." I put my arm around her, which felt right. It was the second time I'd caught her natural scent. *Is this what angels smell like?* This was also the second time I got to see how beautiful her skin was. Her flawless skin was golden brown, with some freckles and beauty spots. I was hardly watching the movie at all, and sure enough, she caught me staring.

She looked up at me with her beautiful blue eyes and smiled. *Oh, eat my chair! Gulp!* I quickly returned to the movie, which made her giggle. *Real smooth, champ!* She continued to watch me, which caused me to return her gaze and smile. We sat there staring into each other's eyes, smiling.

God, you are so pretty!

If this were any other girl, I'd have kissed her, but there was something different about B. She was flawless and delicate at the same time. All I could do was sit there and stare into her eyes.

Wait, is she leaning in? Are we going to . . .?

11 - My Room

That was the moment that my brother decided to exit his drum room, walk through the family room, and make his way into the kitchen for something to drink. *Dude, your timing sucks! Sigh!* B and I jumped away from each other.

"Hey," he said.

"Hey," I replied. This was brother-speak.

"What're you guys watching?" he asked with his head inside the fridge.

With that, the moment was completely gone. *Sigh!*

"We're watching *Gremlins*," I muttered.

"Oh God, it's always on."

"It was either that or General Hospital," I said. *Oh my God, will you please just go away?*

"What's Ma making for dinner?"

"No idea, besides I'm having dinner at B's house tonight."

"That's cool." He then went back into his drum room. Moments later, we heard another song start, followed by his drums.

Yep, the moment was gone. *It's dead, Jim!* We sat there watching the movie until the credits started rolling around four or so when she rose from the couch. *But I was so comfortable!* "I have to get home soon," she said as she started gathering her things.

I quickly stood. "Okay, I'll go grab my shoes and be right back."

"Am I allowed to see your room?"

Warning, Will Robinson! There are no girls allowed upstairs!

"Uh sure, I guess so," I said, trying to sound like it was no big deal.

"Lead the way." She smiled.

Please don't get busted! Please don't get busted!

I led her upstairs to my bedroom, shutting my brother's door as we passed. *Did I forget to mention my room is across from the warden's room, a/k/a Ma's bedroom? Thankfully she had me clean my room earlier this week.*

Was I nervous about getting caught? Nah! I was *terrified!*

This was the first time I had a girl up in my room. Aside from my brother, who was busy playing his drums, we were relatively alone. *Oh crap, oh crap! Am I really doing this?*

"So this is my room." I gestured her through the door. My bedroom was your basic teenage boy's room. I had a full-size bed with your basic blue and white sheets and comforter set. I had a stereo, a TV, a desk and chair, and a dresser. There were a few posters hanging on the walls. She immediately walked over to my bed and bounced on it, laughing.

What are you doing? Are you out of your mind? My brother will hear you and rat me out! She then pressed her face to my pillow. *Dude! What are you doing?* She then sat up laughing, clearly enjoying herself.

"You have a really nice room, and this bed is really comfy." She bounced on it some more. "I didn't know you played little league," she said, pointing at the trophies on my dresser. She hopped off my bed and inspected the trophies. *Oh thank God!*

"Wow, you played on a lot of championship teams. That must have been fun."

"Yeah, it was fun. I didn't feel like playing on the traveling team this summer," I told her as she returned a trophy to the top of my dresser.

"That's too bad." She gazed up at me with her stunning, blue eyes. *Whoa!*

"Yep, so this is my room," I said while trying to escort her out. *We've been up here* way *too long. Either Ma will come home early or little drummer boy will catch us and rat me out. Either way, it's time to go.*

But she had other things in mind. She grabbed my hand and pulled me away from the door, closer to her. *Hamana, hamana, hamana!* She gazed deeply into my eyes and smiled. "I really like spending time with you," she whispered.

"Thanks, I feel the same way about you." I smiled back and tried not to gulp. We just stood there, *in my bedroom*, staring into each other's eyes. *Kiss her, you idiot!! No, don't* kiss her, *you moron! You need to get her out of your room! If you don't, you may never leave. They'll find you both years from now, withered away, locked in an embrace.*

Unfortunately, I blinked first. *Damnit!*

"I better take you home," I said. *Pussy!*

She smiled and nodded in agreement. She looked at my room one last time as I threw on my shoes before heading down stairs.

Thank you, Jesus!

12 - Dinner with Her Family

After dropping her at home, I hit the deli near my house to pick up dessert. Ma drilled it into us to always bring something with you when invited over to eat. On the ride home, B mentioned that her father liked Entenmann's danish rings and the deli always had the best selection. They had two kinds of danish rings, so I picked up both.

If I'm going to suck up, I might as well do it right.

Once I got home, I called the twins. They'd spent the day helping their parents prepare their classrooms for the upcoming school year. I explained that I was heading to B's for dinner, which concerned Hannah.

"Do you know what you're going to wear?" she asked.

"Yeah, we hit the mall today, and she helped me pick out a few sweater vests and T-shirts. I also picked up a new polo shirt."

"Well, for tonight, wear one of the outfits she picked out for you today," she instructed.

"First of all, they're not outfits," I protested. "Second of all, *we* picked them out, not her."

"Uh-huh, if that's what you want to believe, fine," She giggled, then paused. That was her segue to a more serious question. "Have you met her parents before?"

"Sort of, why?" I asked.

"What do you mean 'sort of'? How do you 'sort of' meet someone?"

I gave her the quick rundown about meeting B's mom.

"Hmm, you're going to have to work on her. She's notoriously unpleasant to people of, um, *color*, if you know what I mean," she said.

Hannah shared how B's mom apparently was overheard using derogatory language to describe some students. She also supposedly dressed down a few teachers as well, which I imagine embarrassed the hell out of B.

Anyway, I told her not to worry about it and assured her I'd be on my guard and best behavior.

"Well, good, I know you'll do fine."

I hung up the phone, went to feed Belle, and then started getting ready for the evening. I picked out an "outfit"—*shut up, Hannah*—and was almost done dressing when I heard Ma come through the front door. I threw on my shoes and headed down the stairs.

"Hey, Ma," I said as I kissed her cheek.

"Hola, where are ju off to?"

"I'm having dinner at a friend's house," I replied as I tried to squeeze past her. As I mentioned before, this wasn't Ma's first rodeo; she gave me the once-over.

"La casa de quién?" she asked.

"It's just a friend from school." I had a hand on the doorknob and had just cracked the door open, when Ma stuck her foot out and jammed the door closed. In other words: *not so fast, señor, I'm not finished with my interrogation.*

"Do I know jur friend?" She clearly knew something was up, so I figured I might as well spill the beans.

"Uh, I think so. We go to school together. Listen, Ma, I've got to go. I already fed Belle." I tried again for my escape.

"Are ju taking anything?"

Sigh! "Yes, Ma, I'm taking a couple of Entenmann's with me." I held up the bag from the deli.

She gave me another once-over and nodded. "Okay, dame un beso," she said, so I gave her a quick kiss and ran out of there.

The rain had stopped, and I pulled up to B's house in good time. There were a couple of extra cars in her driveway, all packed to the gills with clothes, books, and furniture, so I parked in the street. Before getting out of the car, I checked my look in the mirror one last time. *You look good, son!* I grabbed the desserts and walked to the front door.

I took a deep breath, said a quick prayer to whoever listened, and knocked on the door. A few seconds later, a six-foot tall, thin-framed guy with messy, dirty-blond hair and blue eyes answered the door. "Hey, you must be B's friend. I'm her brother, Nils," he said, inviting me in with a smile and handshake.

B came bouncing down the stairs just then. "Hey, you made it! And right on time," she said as she hugged and kissed me on the cheek. Her brother went downstairs on the split-level while I followed B upstairs to the kitchen.

"Oh, I brought Entenmann's. I couldn't decide which danish ring to buy, so I bought two."

"You silly, you didn't have to bring two, but thank you," she said graciously as I handed her the bag. As we entered the kitchen, her mom was busy putting the final touches to the meal.

"Mamma, you remember my friend," she said in a formal voice. "And look, he brought Pappa's favorite, Entenmann's." She held up the grocery bag.

I extended my hand to her mother. "Nice to see you again, ma'am. Thank you for inviting me over for dinner." Her hands were full of who-knew-what, so we didn't shake hands, but at least I got a smile.

"Yes, it's nice to see you again. B, please put those over there," her mom said, pointing to an empty spot on the kitchen counter. B did as she was asked. "And help me start getting this on the dinner table." B picked up some dishes. "And please let Pappa know that dinner is almost ready."

"Yes, Mamma."

Yep, she definitely keeps her on a short leash. I wonder why?

Maybe it was a cultural thing, or maybe it due to an incident with B, not that I could imagine her causing an incident. Who knows? It's one of those mysteries I never solved.

B motioned toward the stairs with her head. "Why don't you go make yourself at home downstairs? That's where our family and dining rooms are. I'll join you in a few minutes."

"Okay," I said as she left the kitchen. I turned toward her mom. "Can I help you with anything, ma'am?"

"Oh, that's very nice of you. But no, thank you. B and her sister will help me. Go downstairs, like B suggested, okay?"

"Okay, ma'am." *Well, I tried.* I went downstairs and found her brother watching TV. *Shit, what's his name again? Neal, Nigel, Noel, no wait, Nils! Yes, it's Nils!*

"Hi. *Nils*, right? What are you watching?" I asked.

"Hey, I'm just flipping the channels until dinner is ready," he said, then added, "We typically don't watch a lot of TV."

"Yeah, us either," I lied as I took in the family room. They had rows and rows of bookshelves, full of books.

No wonder she's so smart.

"Grab a seat," he said.

He seems friendly enough. Just as I sat down, a man in his mid- to late fifties walked down the stairs, followed by a cocker spaniel. B's dad, I guessed. He was about six two with a slim build, balding, like Murray from *The Mary Tyler Moore Show*, but with blond hair instead of gray. He wore a light cardigan and had on a pair of horn-rimmed glasses.

"Oh, hello. You must be the young man joining us for dinner," he said as he approached.

The moment he hit the bottom step, I was already standing. "Yes sir. It's a pleasure to meet you," I said, extending my hand. "You have a lovely home. Thank you for having me over for dinner."

He took my hand in his large *paw* and shook it with a firm grip. *Easy, crusher!*

"Oh, well, yes, thank you very much. Please, please, sit, sit," he said. "My wife's just finishing up. Please sit, sit." He sat in an armchair as I sat back on the couch. The dog immediately came over to me to check me out.

Oh good, nose in the crotch. What is it with dogs? They go right for your crotch!

"Gabriel, stop that!" the dad shouted at the dog, then looked at me apologetically. "I'm so sorry. He does that." Nils snickered, and his dad wagged a finger at him. "Oh, knock it off, college boy."

"It's all right," I said, chuckling. "He probably just smells my dog, Belle."

"Yes, that's probably it. Say, what kind of dog do you have?"

"She's a chocolate Lab. A great dog. My mom got her a few years ago, after my dad passed away."

I could see the familiar look of sympathy in his eyes. "Oh, I'm sorry to hear about your loss. Those Labs are good dogs. They're very loyal, just like this one," he said, patting Gabriel on the head. We chatted for a few minutes, and then the ladies came down the stairs, holding platters of food in their hands.

Nils, B's dad, and I stood and headed toward the dining room and got situated around the table. B and I sat next to each other, and she introduced me to her sister Ellie, who sat across from us.

"I think I know your older brother," Ellie said, then added with a sarcastic tone. "I hope you like fish."

"Oh, stop it now. You know you like lutefisk," her father chided.

B jumped in. "Oh, Pappa, he brought over Entenmann's for dessert."

Her dad's eyes lit up. "Is it the one with the walnuts or pecans?"

"I brought both, sir."

"That was very nice of you, but I already made dessert," B's mother said.

Did someone just turn on the air-conditioning? Why is it suddenly so cold in this room?

Ellie and Nils just looked down at their plates, while B squirmed slightly in her chair.

"Yes, well, he did bring them over, after all, Mamma," B's father diplomatically said. "Maybe we can make room for at least one after dinner?"

"We'll see," the mom replied.

The father turned to me. "Do you like lutefisk?" All of a sudden, all eyes were on me.

"I've, uh, never had it before, sir."

"Do you like fish?"

"Uh, yes, I eat fish." *Notice I didn't say I liked fish, just that I ate fish.*

"Oh, well, good, then you'll love Mamma's lutefisk. It's the best on Long Island," He smiled proudly, while his wife served him.

Out of the corner of my eye, I noticed Ellie crinkle her nose with a look of disgust on her face. *This is a heck of a goodbye dinner for you, huh?*

Soon, everyone passed around trays of food. B poured ice water into our glasses. She then placed a piece of what I assumed was the famous lutefisk, along with boiled white potatoes, onions, and peas on my plate. I followed everyone's lead and placed some Gulden's mustard on my plate as well. We held hands, said a quick prayer, and started eating. B was my Sherpa for the meal.

Cut off a piece of fish and put on mustard . . . got it. Add a piece of potato and onion, pop it in your mouth and chew. Okay, here we go . . . Holy shit! This is awful! How do you people eat this shit? No wonder her father is so thin.

"Mm, this is delicious, ma'am. It's really good," I lied as I swallowed my first awful mouthful.

"See, I told you that you'd like it," the father said. "See, Ellie, it's just you."

Ellie rolled her eyes.

"I'm glad you like it," B's mom said.

"Do you really like it?" B whispered.

"Oh yeah, it's really good. My mom never serves anything like this. You'll have to give me the recipe," I said as I choked down another terrible mouthful.

Yeah, give me the recipe, so I can take it out back and set fire to it! I may have to mainline the Gulden's!

"So tell me, young man, what sort of food do you usually eat at your house?" B's father asked.

It was like watching a tennis match. Suddenly all heads turned from him to me.

"We eat, uh, regular food," I said. "You know, chicken and rice, steaks, potatoes, pork chops . . . oh, and of course, fish."

"Oh, good, a growing boy needs good food, right, college boy?" He gestured at Nils and chuckled.

"You know it, Pappa," Nils replied.

"You mentioned earlier that your father passed away. What does your mother do?" B's father asked. *Volley back to me.*

"Your father passed away?" her mom interjected, "I'm so very sorry."

"Thank you, ma'am. Yes, a few years ago. He had a heart attack at work. My mom's been raising us alone ever since." B placed a sympathetic hand over mine and squeezed.

"We're all doing well, though," I added. "My older brother recently graduated Magna Cum Laude from Dartmouth and now works in Boston. It's just my younger brother and me at home, at least until I graduate in June."

"Are you planning on going to Dartmouth too?" B's father asked. *Volley.*

"I've applied to a few schools, but I hope to go to Penn like my mother."

He nodded in understanding.

"I have backups too," I said.

"It's always good to have backups, right, young lady?" her father said, looking at B now.

"Yes, *Pappa.* NYU, Brown, Harvard, and Yale *are* my backups," she said as he chuckled.

Those are your backup schools? Jesus, how smart is *this girl?*

The father turned back to me. "So your mother went to Penn? That's an excellent school. What did she study?"

"Medicine. She's a surgeon, the head of pediatric surgery at St. Agnes." All of a sudden, everyone sort of perked up.

"Your mother is a physician?" B's father asked with surprise in his voice.

"Yes, she's a surgeon," I replied with pride.

"Well, very good! Yes, indeed, *very good*! See that, Ellie? His *mother* is a surgeon," he said to his eldest daughter.

She rolled her eyes. "I heard, Pappa." Then she turned to me and said, "You must be very proud."

"Um, I am." *I'm clearly missing something.*

"Well, these two attend NYU. That's where Mamma and I met," B's father said. "B will probably attend as well, isn't that right, daughter?"

B sighed. "We'll see, Pappa, we'll see."

Thankfully, the conversation shifted to the upcoming road trip for Nils and Ellie. What route would they take back? What classes were they taking in the fall? Things like that.

As dinner wrapped up, B's mom stood. "Would anyone like more?"

"I didn't want this piece," Ellie mumbled to herself.

Her mom ignored her and looked down the table at me. "Would you like another piece?"

"No thank you, ma'am," I replied, as disappointment appeared in her eyes.

And there goes my sympathy card.

"Very well then," she said. "Girls, help me clear the table."

It was like watching a professional production. They were the von Trapps of clearing a table. B stacked and scraped all the plates. Ellie grabbed the platters and utensils, while their mom grabbed everything else. This would only take one trip to the kitchen, where I heard water running and the fridge opening and closing. All that was missing was Julie Andrews.

"Nils, please feed Gabriel and take out the trash," B's father said. Nils nodded and headed upstairs. After he left, the father turned his attention back to me. "So, my boy . . ." He picked up a pipe but didn't light it. "You attend that prep school with B, is that right?"

The way he said it—*that prep school*—was peculiar.

"Yes sir, since the seventh grade."

"So you like that school then?"

"Um, yes sir, I do."

"Do you think you receive a better education there than, say, at the local public school?"

I shrugged, feeling a little uneasy. "My mom seems to think so."

"Yes, yes, I'm sure, but what about you? What do *you* think? Certainly, someone who's attended since the seventh grade has an opinion, no?"

Okay, what's going on here? A few minutes ago, we were buddies. I brought your favorite dessert, both of them, in fact. We laughed together at dinner. Now you're grilling me. What gives?

"I agree with my mom, sir," I replied.

"Yes, I see." He started to say something else, but was interrupted by B walking in with some sort of vanilla sponge cake with white icing. Ellie was right behind her with six coffee cups, six teaspoons, and sugar all balanced on a tray. Nils was next, presumably done taking out the trash and feeding the dog. Their mom came last, carrying a pot of coffee, cream, sugar, and a white doily, upon which the coffeepot would be placed.

"Oh, Pappa, put that *pipe* away," B's mom said as she sat. He nodded and placed it on a side table. Ellie placed all the cups and spoons in front of everyone, while B returned to the kitchen for plates, utensils, a spatula, and an Entenmann's dessert on a plate. She smiled at me as she placed it down near her father, whose eyes lit up again. "Yes, this *is* the good one. Nice job, my boy!"

I guess we're buddies again.

B returned to her seat and jokingly squeezed my leg, which made me jump. Ellie looked at me, "You okay?"

"Yeah, I'm fine."

"Is that dog bothering you again?" the father asked.

"No sir, I, uh, slipped."

You slipped? Moron!

"Oh, well be careful," he said as his eyes went back to the dessert.

B giggled. "Nice," I whispered, which made her turn and stick her tongue out and giggle some more. Nils caught it all but didn't say a thing. He just shook his head and poured himself some coffee.

"So what are you guys doing tonight?" Ellie asked as we ate our dessert.

"We're going to listen to a few Stones records. *He* thinks the Beatles are better than the Stones." B said.

"You *do*? Maybe you haven't heard enough Rolling Stones yet," Ellie said.

This argument sounds familiar.

"I didn't say I didn't *like* them, I just prefer the Beatles," I replied, defending my position, "but I am open-minded."

Then Nils chimed in. "The Rolling Stones . . . please. They're okay, but they're no Neil Young."

"Oh, don't start with your Neil Young rant again," Ellie said.

"Neil Young with Crazy Horse is the best period. The Stones never put out anything better than *Everybody Knows This Is Nowhere,* and you know it. Plus, the Stones would be nowhere without the Beatles. John and Paul wrote their first songs." He challenged his sister, "Name one album better than that one."

"Let's see. How about *Let It Bleed, Sticky Fingers, Exile on Main Street, Some Girls, and Tattoo You?* How's that for a list? What's that, *five albums* to your *one*? What else have *you* got?"

"Yeah, what else have you got?" B chimed in, taking her sister's side.

But it was B's father who responded. "Okay, enough of that down there. Besides, neither of them can hold a candle to Bob Dylan."

His children just groaned as he chuckled.

13 - The Stones

D inner was thankfully over, and we had gotten the okay from B's dad to listen to music in her room as long as we kept the door open. As we walked toward her room, Ellie stepped out of the bathroom, wearing makeup and perfume. She was clearly ready to head out for the evening.

How do I describe Ellie? She was a couple of years older than B. You could tell they were related. Like everyone else in the family, she had blond hair and blue eyes, but her hair was a shade darker and a bit shorter. She and B had a similar build, and Ellie was certainly pretty, but she carried herself differently than B.

She also looked more mature than B. I guess two years does make a difference. Where B had a confidence about herself, she also had humility. Ellie, on the other hand, was missing that last quality, at least that night. That night she was full of confidence, and piss and vinegar.

"Give me your keys; I'm heading into Port Jeff tonight and need to use your car," Ellie demanded as she extended her hand.

At first B told her no. They argued back and forth in front of me for a bit, but Ellie eventually got her way, once she'd agreed to gas up the car. With that, B took my hand and escorted me to her room, where she closed the door, leaving it open just a crack.

"He said to leave it open, but not how much," she said with a giggle.

Maybe she's more of a rebel than I thought, not that I'm going to complain. This is a heck of a lot better than playing verbal ping pong at the dinner table.

B kept her record collection in red and blue milk crates. She pulled out an assortment of albums as I checked out her room. It was definitely a girl's room. She had a full-size bed like mine, but with a white, frilly comforter that had yellow flowers on it and matching pillowcases. There was a desk and a dresser with a mirror. There were posters on her walls; Mick Jagger hung on the back of her door, while the Stones tongue was hung sideways on her wall.

On her dresser was perfume and an assortment of jewelry, hair clips, and other personal items. Her record player and speakers sat between her dresser and window.

Once she had finished picking out the albums, she kicked off her shoes, and invited me to do the same. "Okay, I picked out a few albums. I love all of them, and after tonight, I think you will too," she said. "As a matter of fact, I think you'll love the Stones more than the Beatles after tonight." She was full of confidence.

No pressure.

"Like I said, I'm open. And while I can't make any promises, I trust you; you're a lifeguard," I joked.

She laughed and placed the first album onto the player. She then sat on the floor, against her bed. I slid next to her as Keith Richards's riffs kicked off "Gimme Shelter" followed by Mick Jagger's vocals.

B's head started to bob along to the music.

"You look real pretty tonight," I said, which embarrassed her.

"Thanks, so do you," she said, then corrected herself, "I mean, you don't look pretty, you look nice too." She giggled and shook her head.

Nice, she gets tongue-tied too.

She then took my hand, caressing it with her thumb, and we sat there holding hands while listening to my *new* favorite band of all time, The Rolling Stones. For the record, I'm still a Beatles guy, but that night, I was a Stones guy. Suddenly, the door creaked open a bit, and we immediately let go of each other's hand.

We turned and saw her mother shake her head and walk away. We looked at each other and laughed before B scooted over and changed the album. *Wow, what a nice ass! Hey, I'm a seventeen-year old boy, what do you expect?* She scooted back and took my hand again as the music started.

I couldn't tell you which albums we listened to the rest of the evening. I just remember sitting in her room, holding her hand as Mick serenaded us. I couldn't have asked for a better Friday night. It was heaven.

She turned and gazed into my eyes, "So, what do you think?"

"What do you mean?" I whispered.

"What do *you mean*, what do *I mean*? The Stones, what do you think?"

My problem wasn't that I didn't hear or understand her question. The problem was that I was getting lost in her amazing blue eyes.

I finally managed to say, "Oh, the Stones, yeah they're great!"

"I told you," she replied triumphantly. I just took it all in. *Sigh!* There was a knock on her bedroom door, and we stopped holding hands again.

"It's getting late, and Pappa and I are turning in. I think you need to say goodnight to your friend," B's mom said.

"Okay, Mamma. I'll turn off the music, and we'll go downstairs, okay?" B replied as we both stood up.

"Okay, but not too much longer. We have a busy day tomorrow."

"Yes, Mamma, not too much longer."

"Thank you for dinner, ma'am. I enjoyed it," I said, just as she looked at my feet and saw that my shoes were off, which made her frown.

"Oh, yes, you're welcome. Thank you for, um, coming. You were very, uh, polite." She turned to go, then doubled back. "And thank you for bringing dessert. My husband enjoyed it."

"Thank you, ma'am, you're welcome," I replied as she walked away.

I slid my sneakers back on while B turned off her stereo and returned all of her albums to her milk crates. She then gave me a big hug in the middle of her bedroom as we stood.

Holy shit, is she crazy? Her parents will kill me!

"Thanks for coming over tonight and putting up with my family. I hope it wasn't too much for you," she whispered as she stepped back with a smile.

"Are you kidding me? Thanks for having me over. Besides, you should see my family. We're a loud bunch of Latinos, especially when my older brother's in town."

"That sounds like fun actually."

She took my hand and walked me to the front door. "So what are you doing tomorrow?" she asked.

"I'll probably have to mow the lawn," I replied. "What about you? It sounds like you're going to be real busy tomorrow."

"Yeah, we're going to drive to the city tomorrow and be gone all day, helping my brother and sister move into their shared apartment. Then afterward, we'll probably go out for dinner somewhere in the city. Sometimes we go to Chinatown or Little Italy, depending on everyone's mood. We'll get back late and then get up early the next morning for church. I'll be exhausted by the time Sunday afternoon rolls around. How about you? What are you doing on Sunday?"

"I don't know, why?" I asked.

"Do you want to go to West Meadow Beach?" It was a local beach.

"Yeah, that sounds perfect."

"Great. It'll be after church, though, if that's okay."

"Sounds good to me. Call me when you get home from church, and I'll pick you up." I said.

"Great, then I'll see you Sunday."

"B, it's getting late," her mother said from downstairs.

"Yes, Mamma." She rolled her eyes. "You'd better go," she whispered. Then she smiled and stared into my eyes with her perfect blues.

"Okay, goodnight," I whispered back, trapped in her stare. She leaned in and gently kissed my cheek then whispered goodnight in my ear. I damn near melted on the spot.

I floated to my car, and we waved at each other as I pulled away.

What a night!

14 - Hanging with the Twins

The following day was uneventful. While B was in the city, I was busy doing chores around the house. I mowed and edged the lawn and then vacuumed the pool. After a quick swim, I checked in with Jean Paul, who suggested a round of tennis.

As we played, I did my best Howard Cosell sportscaster impersonation.

"Ladies and gentlemen, that was the most pathetic serve I've ever witnessed," I commented as Jean Paul served. Of course, to shut my mouth, his next serve was an ace, but that didn't stop my bantering.

We played for a few hours, and eventually stopped keeping score. As we were enjoying our freedom, Hannah rode up and joined us. As always, her timing was uncanny.

"Hey," I said.

"Hey. So who won?" she asked.

"I did!" we both replied.

"Uh-huh. So you stopped keeping score again?"

"Yeah, pretty much," I said.

"What do you want, Hann?" Jean Paul sniped.

"Nothing, why are you always such a snot?"

"I'm not being a snot. I'm just getting tired of you showing up to tell me I have to come home and do something. I can't wait to graduate and get out of this town," Jean Paul lamented.

"Dude, you can't have senioritis already, do you?" I asked. "School hasn't even started yet. I'm actually looking forward to this year." I smiled.

Mistake! I just showed my hand, and now the sharks smell blood in the water! The best way to keep a secret is to not share the secret.

"Oh really? Do tell," Jean Paul said.

"Yeah, what's with the smile?" Hannah asked. "At the end of last year, you couldn't wait to graduate. Now you're looking forward to this year? That seems odd, doesn't it, Jean Paul?"

Shit, I'm trapped!

"It sure does, Hann. I wonder what's new in our boy's life," he said, turning to me with a wicked grin. "Spill it!"

"So I take it that last night went well?" Hannah asked.

"Oh yeah, I forgot about last night," Jean Paul said. "So did you *get any*?"

"Jean Paul! Don't be crude!" Hannah said. "So how'd it go? We want details."

"Yeah, we want details," Jean Paul agreed, raising his eyebrows and making kissing sounds.

"You're such a pig." Hannah said as he laughed. I spent the next fifteen minutes debriefing them. I walked them through the entire evening, including the hug and kiss.

"She kissed your cheek? What is this, 1950? Dude, you're lame," Jean Paul said.

"Shut up, Jean Paul, I think it's sweet," his sister defended. "I can't believe we're related," she added in disgust.

Jean Paul just laughed and threw a tennis ball at his sister. She then flipped him off.

"So do you guys want to come over?" I asked, attempting to defuse the situation.

They agreed it was a good idea—we'd go swimming and have dinner at my house.

But first . . . the always-sensible Hannah: "We should check with our parents first, though."

"What's to check? They love me!" I said.

"Uh-huh. They love your mother. The jury's still out on you," she said, laughing.

"I don't care what you say. They *love* me!"

We went to their house and got the okay from their mom, and about thirty minutes later, we rode up my driveway on our bikes.

"Hey, Ma, we're here," I yelled as Jean Paul and I walked to the back yard. Hannah went to the bathroom to change.

"Hola, mijo. Hola, Jean Paul. Where is la Hannah?" Ma asked. She was out on the patio, cleaning off the barbecue grill.

"Oh, she's changing," I replied, Moments later, Hannah joined us outside, holding three towels from the laundry room.

She hugged Ma hello and offered to help her clean the grill. "Oh no, mija, it's okay. Go enjoy jurself con los pendejos."

We spent the rest of the afternoon swimming. My younger brother and Rick joined us a little while later. Jean Paul and Hannah knew Rick, so no introductions were needed. We were one big extended family.

My mother made a bunch of hamburgers and hot dogs, along with a large garden salad. It was a nice summer day to eat outside. We all worked together and set the table. We all ate like royalty, enjoying the food and each other's company.

As we ate, I got lost in a daydream about B and our time at her house the night before.

"Penny for your thoughts," Hannah whispered.

"Oh, I was just thinking about last night," I replied. "I really like her, Hann. I know it's only been a few days, but there's something, I don't know, different about her."

"I'm happy for you," she replied with a mix of happiness and what sounded like disappointment, for some reason, in her voice. "Just be careful, okay?"

"I will. Thanks, sis."

We finished dinner and put the leftovers in the fridge. "Por favor someone feed Belle," Ma said.

"Not it!" My brother and I shouted.

Hannah then shoved me and said, "Go feed your dog!"

"Ha!" my brother said.

Hannah looked at him. "What are you laughing at? You're walking her when she's finished, smartass."

"Ha!" I shot back.

Everyone always obeyed the *Great* Hannah Michaels. We all loved and feared her, so I fed Belle, and my brother walked her when she finished eating.

"Quieren Friendly's; it's my treat," Ma announced.

I'm sorry, but did you just offer to treat five perpetually hungry teenagers to Friendly's? Were you expecting a no?

She handed me forty dollars.

"Thanks, Ma. Do you want anything?"

"Sí, bring me a small chocolate Fribble por favor."

"Sure, Ma. Can we take your car?" I asked as I grabbed her keys.

"Sí," she replied.

"Shotgun!" my brother and Jean Paul shouted as we piled out the front door. As they argued, Hannah slipped by them and took the front seat like a champ.

"Hey!" they both whined.

I cranked the radio and drove us to Friendly's. We went to the takeout line and screwed around while waiting. Hannah ordered everyone to start making their selections. "And don't forget your mother's Fribble."

"Jeez, Hann, I remembered," I replied.

Thank God she said something. I totally forgot.

We were grabbing our desserts, including Ma's Fribble, when I heard my brother say, "Hey, isn't that your friend B?"

Sure enough, B was walking out of *our* Friendly's with a couple of people I knew from school, Mary and Kyle Fergusen.

B must have heard her name, because she turned around. When she saw me, she smiled and came right over.

"Hey, guys," she said. "You're getting Friendly's tonight too, huh?"

"Yeah, Ma's treat," I replied quietly, looking past her at the Fergusens. "I guess you made it back from the city early, huh?"

What the hell is she doing here at our *Friendly's with Mary and Kyle Fergusen, of all people? Mary walks around school like her shit doesn't stink. And her older brother, Kyle, is just as much of a dickhead. I guess she doesn't have a no-asshole policy.*

"Uh, yeah, that's a funny story, actually. We didn't make it into the city today," she said. "Remember how my sister went out last night? Well, she got wasted, stayed out partying all night with her friends, and didn't get home until eight this morning. My parents found her passed out on the couch, and they were pissed! They threatened to pull her out of NYU and send her to Suffolk Community College." She laughed. Me, not so much.

For some reason, the more we stood there, the more my mood soured. I felt possessive, jealous, and angry all at the same time.

That's teenagers, folks! They go from zero to sixty for no logical reason! Thank you, hormones!

"So they're going tomorrow instead, while I stay home and go to church," she continued. "So what'd you do all day?"

So let me get this straight. You were home all day and didn't call me?
Instead, you chose to hang out with the Fergusens and bring them to our
Friendly's?

Again, illogical, irrational, and zero to sixty, folks!

"Just, uh, yard work and stuff," I briskly replied.

"Are you okay?" she asked as I glared.

"Yeah, I'm fine, why?" I replied curtly.

"I'm sorry I didn't call you today. Mary called me and asked if I wanted
to hang out. You don't mind, do you?" she probed.

Hannah noticed my glaring and lightly elbowed me, bringing me back to
my senses. "Huh? No, no, not at all. Um, we're still on for tomorrow, right?"

"West Meadow, yes, unless you don't want to go." There was hesitation
in her voice.

"What? No!" I said, almost shouting. "I mean, no, no, I still want to go."

"Good, I'm glad," she said, then turned to Jean Paul and Hannah. "Hey,
do you guys want to join us too?"

"What time are you guys going?" Jean Paul asked.

"After lunch, which I guess I'll now fend for myself," B replied.

"Hey, bitch, are you coming?" Mary Fergusen yelled.

Go screw yourself, Mary! She's talking to me right now! You can wait!

B hollered over her shoulder, "Yeah, I'm coming," then said to us,
"Listen, I've got to go. You guys are welcome to join us. I guess I'll see you
tomorrow," she said as she walked away, a bit downcast.

"Why don't you ask her to lunch tomorrow?" Hannah whispered.

Brilliant!

"B!" I yelled as I ran across the parking lot to her.

"Yeah, did you forget something?"

"What? No. I, uh, wanted to know if we could have lunch tomorrow."

She took a deep breath, smiled and caressed my cheek, which
immediately had a calming effect on me. It was like she knew how to
immediately defuse me with her caress.

"That would be nice," she whispered. "I'll call you when I get home from
church, okay?" She held me captive with her eyes.

Where'd everyone else go? How'd she do that?

"Cool, call me and I'll pick you up, okay?" I replied as I came out of my
state of euphoria.

"Okay, I will. I better go before they leave without me," she said
motioning toward her friends.

Screw them! I'll drive you home. Like the Boss said, "The night's busting open, and these two lanes will take us anywhere."

"Okay. I'll see you tomorrow." I waved goodbye and just as I was heading back, I heard Mary say, "Is that *him*? Yeah, I think I know him *now.*"

Seriously? You've sat next to me in Spanish for three years. Hell, you've cheated off me for three years. What do you mean you think *you know me? God, what a bitch.*

"So, West Meadow tomorrow, huh?" Hannah asked when I walked back.

"Did I forget to mention it?" I innocently replied.

"Yeah, you left that part out, but that's okay. Right, Jean Paul?"

"Yeah, we understand," he replied as we headed toward the Caddy.

"Shotgun!" my brother and Jean Paul yelled.

Hannah ignored them again and hopped into the front seat.

"Hey!" they both whined again.

We spent the rest of the evening enjoying our Friendly's, while watching *Weird Science* for the umpteenth time. Afterward, we loaded the twins' bikes into Ma's trunk, and I drove them home.

"Do you guys really want to go to the beach tomorrow?" I asked as we unloaded their bikes.

"Yeah, we want to go," Jean Paul said. "Don't worry, bro, we won't cramp your style."

Hannah cut in. "Listen, we don't have to come, but be careful tomorrow, okay? You chucked her attitude tonight for no reason. You don't own her. She's allowed to have a life."

Am I that transparent?

"No, you're right. I tried to catch myself, but it just got away from me," I said. "She caught me off guard, that's all. I can't explain it. It's just that I thought she'd be in the city all day with her family, and then I see her at *our* Friendly's, with the Fergusens, of all people, and . . . I don't know."

"I understand, but she may not," Hannah said.

"I know. Thanks for suggesting lunch. I would have totally blown that one too."

"What time are you picking us up?" Jean Paul asked.

"What do you mean? You're riding your ass to the beach."

"Dude, we're not riding our bikes to the beach. Who do you think we are, my folks? Just call us when you finish having *lunch*," he said while moving his eyebrows.

You're lucky you're my best friend . . .

15 - The Diner

I got up earlier than my "summer usual" the next morning, so I made myself a *healthy* three-egg omelet with ham, cheese, and salami, two slices of white toast, and a large orange juice.

After breakfast, I took care of Belle, then grabbed a shower and got ready for my lunch date with B. Just after eleven, B called.

"Good morning, sunshine. I hope I didn't wake you, did I?"

"Nope, I've been up a while. I usually get up early on Sundays," I lied. "Did you just get back from church, or are you heading out?"

"I just got home. Are you ready for lunch?" she asked.

"Sure. What time do you want me to pick you up?"

"Can you be here at noon?"

"Absolutely, I'll see you at noon," I replied, then we said our goodbyes.

Ma came down to the kitchen as I was tossing my towel into my beach bag.

"You look nice. Adonde vas?" she asked as she poured coffee. She slept in Sunday mornings.

"I'm going out to lunch and then heading to the beach. Which reminds me, can I borrow twenty dollars?" I asked. I handed her purse to her.

Important safety tip: if you want something from Ma, always ask before her first coffee or right before she's going to bed; she is at her most vulnerable and usually says yes.

"Just take it. I don't feel like digging through mi cartera," she said, and I took a twenty. "Thanks, Ma," I replied as I put it into my wallet. *Oh look, there's her change from last night. Oops!*

"Con quien vas a comer?"

"Oh, uh, it's just my friend B."

"Ju're spending a lot of time con her."

"We've only hung out a few times," I replied defensively. *Again, zero to sixty, especially with parents!* "Jean Paul and Hannah will be there too," I added, trying to confuse her. But I wasn't dealing with an amateur.

She saw right through my *bullshit*. She squinted her eyes and gave me the mom look, but fortunately let me off the hook. Again, she hadn't had her coffee yet.

"I've got to go. I'll see you later," I kissed her cheek.

As I hit the front door, I heard her yell, "Hey did ju give me back mi cambio from Friendly's?"

Time to make my escape!

"Okay, Ma. Thanks! I love you too! Bye!" I yelled as I closed the front door behind me.

"Hey! Get back here, ju hijo de la . . ."

Yeah, I'll pay for it later, but extra cash is extra cash.

I made it to B's in good time. I was still a bit nervous because of the previous night. *Should I have brought flowers? Nah, that's stupid, right? Yeah, that's dumb. She sounded okay on the phone. Yeah, we're cool. Okay, breath check . . . yep, good to go. Go get her, champ.*

Moments later, I was knocking on B's door. "Hey, you're early. Give me one minute, okay? I just have to get off the phone with Mary," she said. "Come in and wait for me in the kitchen. I'll be done soon."

See? She's fine.

"Take your time."

Let's see, Better Homes and Gardens, Time Magazine, *or* National Geographic*? Pass, pass, and pass.*

"Well, he just got here. I've got to go. Yeah, I'll talk to him about it, but if he doesn't want to go, neither will I," I overheard B saying. "I don't care. Listen, I've got to go. I'll call you later. Bye." Then she yelled to me, "I'll be right there, okay?"

"No problem."

Moments later, she walked in carrying her beach bag and purse, looking amazing as usual. She wore a knee-length summer dress with pastel patterns.

She had a black headband on and white sandals. Her only makeup was a very light shade of pink lipstick.

"I'm sorry I've kept you waiting. I think it's so rude. I think Mary makes me late on purpose half the time. She always tells me I'm too uptight and need to lighten up," she rambled and seemed jumpy as I took her beach bag.

Oh yeah, we're fine. *She's not nervous at all. You're a dumbass. You should have brought flowers.*

"Hi," I whispered as I took her hand, which seemed to calm her down.

"Hi."

Man, she even smells great! She smells like rose petals.

"Sorry I'm late," she whispered.

"It's okay," I replied. *I'd wait for you forever!* "You ready for lunch?"

"God yes, I'm starving. Where do you want to go?"

"How about that restaurant up in Setauket, near the church at the top of the hill?"

"I know that place. That sounds great. They've got a really good lunch menu. Do you go there a lot, or do you just stick close to home?"

"I've eaten there a few times," I replied. "Plus, it's close to Hannah and Jean Paul's. Remember, you invited them to the beach last night?"

"Do you think they'd want to join us for lunch?"

"Probably not. They usually eat lunch with their parents on Sunday."

"Let's call them and find out," she suggested.

Groan! "Okay."

She handed me the phone.

"Hello, this is Professor Michaels."

"Hi, Professor Michaels, may I speak with Jean Paul or Hannah, please?" I asked.

"Good afternoon, fine sir, I'll get Jean Paul for you," he said in a jovial manner. He shouted for Jean Paul, then said, "And how is your mother doing? She's such a wonderful—"

"I've got it, Dad," Jean Paul said, probably from the phone in his kitchen.

"Very good. Have a good day, gentlemen," Professor Michaels said, and then hung up.

"Yo, dude, how's it hanging?" I asked.

"A little to the left, thanks for asking. What up?" Jean Paul asked.

"B wants to know if you guys want to join us for lunch," I explained, my eyes on B. "Oh, you can't? Man, that's too bad." I shook my head as I made a sad face for B's benefit. "Okay, we'll pick you up after lunch. Bye."

As I quickly hung up, I could hear him saying, "Hey, we can go, don't you dare hang . . ."

Click, oops!

"Yeah, they can't come. I told him we'd pick them up after lunch."

B squinted and gave me the once-over. "So, if I call him back, he'll say the same thing?" she asked while reaching for the phone.

"Hey, hey, you don't need to do that," I quickly said.

"I'm sure they won't mind . . . unless there's a reason I shouldn't call, like say, you don't want them to join us?" Her eyes narrowed.

Busted! Damn it! Sigh! "Yeah, uh, it's um, that," I admitted, embarrassed.

"Well, why didn't you just say so?" She caressed my cheek. "Next time, just be honest, okay?"

"Yes ma'am," I sighed.

"Good. Let's eat. I'm starving," she said as she lightly patted my cheek and then took my hand as we left her house.

We made it to the restaurant in no time.

"How many?" the hostess/waitress asked as we walked in.

"Two, please."

The smiling waitress seated us in a cozy booth and took our drink orders.

"She's much nicer than the waitress *you* bothered the other night."

"Oh? The one *I* bothered, huh?" she replied with a laugh.

After the waitress brought us our drinks, we still weren't ready to order. She encouraged us to take our time and left us to it.

"I guess we should— Hey!" B had nailed me again with the straw wrapper. She laughed and moved her eyebrows up and down.

"Like I was *saying*, I guess we should look at the menus, since *you're* the one who's starving," I said as she continued giggling. *She really does look pretty today.* "You look real pretty today."

This made her blush a bit. "Thanks. You look nice today too." She glanced down at the menu. "So what looks good? I mean, on the menu, uh, um, you know, for lunch," she rambled.

"I think it all looks good to me," I replied flirtatiously, which earned me a light kick.

"You *know* what I meant," she whispered, smiling, her eyes still on the menu.

"*Ow!* Oh, lunch, right. I don't know. I was thinking maybe a burger or something. What about you?"

"A burger sounds good, and theirs come with curly fries too," she replied.

"Burgers and curly fries sound like a plan." I waved to our waitress, who came over and took the order.

About five minutes later, she brought us ketchup and mustard. "Your burgers will be out in just a few minutes."

We spent the better part of an hour in the café, eating, laughing, and talking. I loved the sound of her voice. It just lit up the room. She told me the whole Ellie story and how her parents had completely come off the rails, blaming Ellie for being a bad influence on B.

"My mother treats me like I'm three years old or something. I'm graduating high school this year, for goodness sake."

I could relate. "Parents, right? What are you gonna do? My mom does the same thing with me."

She just laughed in agreement and excused herself.

"Did you two lovebirds leave room for dessert?" the waitress asked me.

Lovebirds, huh? Nice. I'm stuffed. I could barely finish my burger and fries.

"I think we're good," I said, taking the check. I paid the bill as B returned to the table. "Keep the change," I told the waitress, just as B sat down.

"They have a pay phone in the back. Should we call the twins before going over?"

"Nah, let's just head over there," I replied as we headed toward the door.

"Have a nice day, you two," the waitress said as we left. "He's a keeper, honey."

"I think so too," B said as she took my hand and grinned.

She thinks so too! She thinks so too! Yes!

I just smiled—okay, beamed really—as we drove over to pick up the twins.

16 - West Meadow Beach

As we pulled into the driveway of the Michaels family, I honked my horn, announcing our arrival. *Okay, remember what I said earlier about honking the horn in someone's driveway? That doesn't apply to your best friends.*

B and I hopped out of the car and held hands as we walked to the front door. Hannah met us and noticed us holding hands, but didn't say anything. She just smiled and gestured subtly, letting me know she noticed. I smiled back.

"You guys ready?" I asked.

"Yeah, just about, but beware, *it's* in a mood," Hannah informed us with a roll of her eyes.

Moments later, *it* joined us, glaring at me for hanging up on him earlier. I just gave him my *get over it dude* look. He just nodded, got over it, and led the way to the car.

"Holding hands, huh? Nice!" he whispered as we loaded everything into my trunk. Grinning, he grabbed shotgun before I could say anything.

Dude!

I looked up at B and she grabbed my arm, "It's okay," she said, so I let it go.

Hannah and B hopped into the back seat, and we hit the beach.

West Meadow Beach was a small beach located in Setauket, on the North Shore of Long Island. On clear days, you could see Connecticut across the Long Island Sound. It satisfied the needs of the locals from Stony Brook to

Setauket, especially young families and the elderly, who didn't want to go to the Hamptons, Jones Beach, or Smith Point.

After parking under a tree, we grabbed our gear and hit the public restrooms to change.

"Dude, why'd you hang up on me?" Jean Paul barked as the men's room door shut behind us.

Here we go. Let the whining begin!

"Why do you think?" I entered a stall and started changing.

"You afraid I'll embarrass you or something?" he asked.

"You could say that."

"Dude, you're much worse than I am. You're the biggest pig on the planet," he laughed.

"This *is* true." I laughed too and exited the stall.

"So have you kissed her yet?"

A fair question from your best friend, but one I wasn't ready to answer.

"Come on, dude. Show some class."

"So that's a *no* then. Got it."

"It's more like a *nunya*, as in *none-ya-damn-bidness!*"

"Yep, that's definitely a *no*," he laughed.

"Oh shut up."

We met the girls outside moments later. Hannah wore the same blue bikini I'd seen a million times. B, on the other hand, wore this amazing coral bikini. It showed off her sun-kissed skin and blond locks.

Both she and Hannah wore sunglasses. B smiled, and I damn near melted on the spot. Who needed the sun? I had B. Even her gravity pulled me in. Icarus be damned, I'm flying toward the sun.

Jean Paul led the way to the beach—he was actually strutting. *It's his world, folks. We're just visitors.* He picked a spot for us to unload our stuff, then he grabbed his soccer ball and headed toward the water.

"Come on, dude. The water's calling," he beckoned, then he tossed his ball into the water and dove into an oncoming wave.

I turned to B, who was applying suntan lotion on her arms and legs.

That's some lucky lotion.

"Do you mind? If I don't play with him, he pouts," I explained.

"It's true," Hannah confirmed. "If they don't play together at least once a day, they *both* turn into big babies."

"Big babies, huh?" B laughed. "Go have fun."

"Hey, dumbass, wait for me!" I yelled as I jogged toward Jean Paul, who was already talking to two girls in the water.

There's one thing you need to know about Jean Paul. He's a perpetual flirt. He's six feet, one inch tall and lean with a muscular soccer body, which girls love. I'd always been his wingman, so I'd get the cast-offs, which worked just fine with me, since pretty girls seemed to travel in packs.

Of course, I didn't need his cast-offs today, so I didn't mind crashing his party. After all, what are best friends for? Once I hit the water, I jumped him and totally ruined his groove. The girls just shook their heads and got out of the water because I'd accidentally splashed them. *Sorry, ladies!*

"Dude!" Jean Paul growled at me.

I just laughed.

Soon B and Hannah joined us in the water, splashing us. And that was the beginning of an afternoon toying around in the water, throwing the Frisbee, kicking the soccer ball around—just your average teens at the beach.

Hannah and B eventually returned to their towels while Jean Paul and I continued to play, until he noticed a new pair of honeys and *accidentally* kicked his soccer ball near them.

That was my cue, and I joined the girls. Hannah was lying face down working on her tan, and B was on her back.

She leaned up on her elbows. "So are you children done playing?"

"Yeah, he found something else to distract him," I replied, motioning toward Jean Paul showing off for his new friends. "He'll be a while."

She laughed at that, then asked, "Want to take a walk?"

I'd walk through hot coals in gasoline-soaked sweatpants if you asked me to.

"Sure."

B turned to Hannah. "Do you mind?"

Hannah just waved her hand as I helped B stand, who then hugged me for my troubles.

Do I hear angels singing?

She took my hand, and we started our walk along the beach. It was a perfect summer afternoon. The sun was shining, and there was hardly a cloud in the sky. B and I were alone in our own little world.

"It's a beautiful day out," B said. Her tone was pensive, almost sad.

"Is something wrong?"

"I'm that transparent, huh?"

"I wouldn't say transparent. I'd just say you look like you want to talk about something, that's all," I replied with caution.

"Well, it's about last night at Friendly's."

Sigh! I thought we were past this. I guess not.

"Look, I don't want to upset you, especially here at the beach. But I *do* want to talk about last night."

That put me on the defensive. "O-*kay*, so what do you want to talk about?"

"See, you're getting upset already. You know what? Never mind. Forget about it." She tried walking away.

Dude, you're being a dick! Stop her and fix this!

I grabbed her hand. "B, wait a minute. I'm sorry. Seriously, you can talk to me about anything."

"Are you *sure*?"

"Yes, I'm sure. Trust me, I was a camp counselor." I replied, trying to defuse the situation.

She just rolled her eyes, shook her head, and smiled at my joke, "Good, because Hannah said I should just talk to you about it."

Great, so Hannah knows. Terrific! How about a heads-up next time, Hann?

"Well, you seemed upset last night at Friendly's. You made me feel like I hurt your feelings or something." She paused, then said, "Even though I explained what happened, I still felt guilty for some reason."

Crap. Way to go, moron.

"I didn't mean to hurt your feelings. I knew we would be seeing each other today, plus I haven't seen Mary in, like, a week. So when she called, I thought I'd hang out with her and catch up on things, know what I mean?"

You're an idiot, dude. This girl cares about you. Don't be a jerk!

"B, I'm sorry," I sighed. "To be honest, when I saw you last night at our Friendly's with somebody else, it bothered me for some reason. I can't explain it. I guess I thought you lied to me about going to the city."

"But I *explained* what happened with my sister. Don't you trust me? Do you really think I'd lie to you and hurt you *on purpose*?" There was hurt in her voice and it killed me.

"Oh God no, I don't think that at all. Listen, I'm a jerk. I'm really sorry about last night and how I made you feel." I released her hand and started walking away in shame.

"Hey, where are you going?" she asked as she grabbed my wrist to stop me.

"I just thought . . ." I started, but she placed her hand on my cheek and smiled.

"You thought what? That I hated you or something? You're so silly. I don't hate you. If I hated you, I wouldn't be here with you. I don't think you're a jerk, okay?"

"Are you sure?" I replied, downcast.

"Yes, I'm sure. You just didn't know the whole story, that's all. I just wanted to clear the air and not have anything weird between us, okay?"

I allowed myself to smile. "Yeah, okay."

"Good. Are we okay?" She was smiling now too, which made her eyes sparkle, reflecting the sunlight.

Man, how does she make them sparkle like that?

"Yeah, we're definitely okay. We're more than okay," I replied, giving her a hug.

"*Our* Friendly's, huh? I like it."

"So do I."

We frolicked for a while in the water and eventually made our way back to our towels, where I proceeded to shake my wet hair all over Hannah.

"*Hey! Stop it, you jerk!* What's *wrong* with you?!" she yelled as I cackled. "You're a big child. Where's your idiot friend?"

"He's still over there showing off," I said, pointing. Jean Paul was acting like a seal at Sea World, balancing a ball on his head.

Should I throw him a fish?

Hannah laughed. "You two were made for each other."

"Well, he *is* my brother from another mother."

"*Uh-huh,* so what does that make me?"

I shrugged my shoulders and then threw myself on top of her. "My sister from another mister!" I said, laughing as she screamed.

"Get off, you animal! You're worse than my idiot brother."

"Thank you! I'll take that as a compliment!"

B watched from her towel, smirking the whole time at our "sibling love." When Jean Paul heard the ruckus, he left his fans and joined us.

"So'd you get their digits?" I asked as I hopped off Hannah.

"What do you think?" He smiled, while holding up their phone numbers.

"You're a *dog,* dude. I don't know how you do it."

"Hey, when you've got it, you've got it. Am I right, B?"

She snickered. "Whatever you say, Jean Paul."

Shortly thereafter, we packed up and headed home, dropping the twins at their house first. As we drove to B's house, I asked her, "So what are your plans for dinner?"

"Dinner with the parents, I'm sure. They should be home soon. What about you?"

"Same. How about after dinner?" I hoped I wasn't coming off as too pushy, but honestly, I just loved spending time with her.

"Nothing, why?" she asked.

I pulled into her driveway. "Do you want to walk around Port Jeff tonight?"

"Aren't you tired of me yet?"

"Not yet, but I'm getting there," I teased.

"*Hey!*" She laughed and smacked me in the chest.

I held my hands up to ward off the next attack. "*Ow!* I mean, no, not at all."

"That's better. Port Jeff sounds nice. Let me just check with my parents first. Plus, I want to shower the beach off of me."

I'll shower the beach off of you.

"I'll call you after dinner," she said then leaned over and gave me a warm kiss on the cheek. "I had fun today. Thanks for making it so special," she whispered.

Oh, sweet Lord!

We grabbed her things, and I walked her to her front door. As we stood there, she gave me another hug, right there in the open.

"Thanks again," she said. "Talk to you later." She stared deeply into my eyes as she said this and everything inside me just melted.

"Yeah, okay," I squeaked out, lost in her gaze. Then she smiled as she opened the door. Yep, she knew the impact she was having on me.

She stood in the open doorway, watching me get into my car and back out of the driveway. We waved at each other, and then . . . then . . . she kissed her hand and held it up to me.

She blew me a kiss! She just blew me a kiss!

17 - It's About Time

Mmhmm . . . I loved the smell of Ma's *arroz con pollo*! It smelled great, and tasted even better. She made it "old school"— Carolina white rice mixed with saffron, sliced Spanish green olives, and Goya spices. Then she'd add the chicken, allowing it to simmer until the chicken melted off the bone.

She always made enough for leftovers, unless we had company. If we had company, the only thing left over were the satisfied people around the table, loosening their pants and patting their bellies.

"Is anyone joining us for dinner tonight?" I asked as I kissed her on the cheek.

"No sé, ¿por qué?"

"No reason. I just hate sharing," I replied, which made her smile. "Also, I was planning on going out tonight after dinner."

"Ju're going out again? ¿Adonde vas y con quien?"

"Uh, to Port Jeff with my friend B," I replied, which made her stop stirring the food pot and start stirring mine.

Here we go.

"Didn't ju just spend all day with her today? Why don't ju stay in tonight? We need to start planning for back-to-school shopping."

Crap, she's bringing her A game!

"Ma, we have plenty of time for back-to-school shopping. Going out tonight's not going to make a difference."

She gave me the once-over, which took just ten seconds or so, but felt like an eternity.

She sighed dramatically, "Well, go shower. Ju can't go out looking like that."

Yes! "Thanks, Ma!" I kissed her cheek and ran upstairs to clean up as she smiled and shook her head. Again, it wasn't her first rodeo.

After dinner I sat on the couch, which was next to the phone, pretending to watch TV. Seven o'clock came and went as I sat there, staring at the numbers on the clock that hung on the wall above the television.

7:10 p.m. . . .

7:13 . . .

7:15 . . .

Shit, was I supposed to call her? Is my idiot brother on the line? I told everyone I was expecting a call, but that's never stopped him before.

I checked the phone. No one was on the line.

Shit, should I just call? What if she really doesn't want to go? What if she was just lying and didn't enjoy the day? What if her parents won't allow her to go? Fuck!

I was clearly getting myself wound up.

Zero to sixty, folks. Zero to sixty!

7:18 . . .

7:19 . . .

I began to pace back and forth from the family room to the kitchen, which drove Ma crazy. "Por Dios hijo de mi vida!" she yelled, so I stomped out of the family room and started up the stairs to my bedroom, to get out of her hair and to pout in private.

Of course, halfway up the stairs, the phone rang.

Shit! I'm halfway up the stairs! Do I run to the family room or to Ma's room? I don't want Ma answering the phone, especially if it's B.

"I've got it!" I yelled and ran up to Ma's room.

Second ring. Third ring. I literally dove across Ma's bed and grabbed the phone.

"Hello?" I answered, slightly out of breath.

"Hi, it's B. Are you *okay*?"

She called! Yes!

"Huh? Oh yeah, I'm fine. I was, um, just playing with Belle," I lied, regaining my composure, while reaching out with my left foot to shut the bedroom door.

"Aw, that's sweet. Give her a hug from me. So, my parents said it was okay to go out tonight, as long as I don't stay out too late."

"Cool! My mom said the same thing. It's almost seven thirty now. When do you want me to pick you up?"

"How soon can you get here?"

Scotty, beam me to B's!

We agreed I would pick her at seven forty-five. I grabbed my stuff, gave Ma a kiss on the cheek, and ran to my car, tossing one of my high school sweatshirts into the back seat, just in case it was cold by the water.

I made it there in eight minutes, making every green light!

Don't try that at home, folks, remember, I'm a professional.

When I pulled into her driveway, I noticed her interior front door was open. I heard Gabriel barking at the sound of my knock, then through the screen I saw B bounding down the steps.

Who needs a nightlight with a smile like that?

"Are you ready to go?" she asked.

"I was born ready," I replied in my best Southern accent.

We headed up Route 25A to Port Jeff—a short ten minutes. Once there, I parked in a lot near the corner of 25A and Main Street.

"Do you think I'll need this sweater?" B asked. She was wearing a pair of black-patterned culottes, a white top, and a beige cardigan sweater.

"Well, I brought a sweatshirt just in case."

She took my sweatshirt and smelled it. "This smells like you," she replied as she left her sweater in the car and took my sweatshirt.

We walked hand in hand around "downtown," as some locals used to call it.

Downtown Port Jefferson is located right along the Long Island Sound, with various sailboats and motorboats docked in boat slips. It's known for its ferry that takes passengers across to Connecticut daily. The forty-five-minute ferry ride always beat taking the two-hour ride on the Long Island Expressway through the city to get to Upstate New York or New England.

At night, cars cruised Main Street while people strolled along the sidewalk, hitting the various shops along both sides of the strip. They sold your standard tourist memorabilia that all said *Port Jeff* or *Port Jefferson*. There were also shops that carried charm bracelets, puka shell anklets, necklaces, and a variety of things. We checked out every store.

Seventy-five bucks for a glass figurine! Are they crazy?

"See anything you like?" B asked.

I looked right at her and smiled, "Yep."

That earned me an elbow to the ribs.

"I meant here in the store," she giggled.

"Oh, in the store. Got it. Not really. You?" I was fishing to see what she might like.

"Not really. The things here are pretty expensive, don't you think?" she whispered as I nodded.

"Want some ice cream?"

"Sure," she said.

We held hands and walked to a local ice cream parlor with twenty flavors of homemade ice cream. B and I both sampled the mint chocolate chip ice cream.

Confession time. I'm a mint chocolate chip snob. Growing up, Baskin-Robbins was the best, followed closely by Carvel. Friendly's came in third, followed by the various brands you bought at the supermarket. This one blew them all away!

It was the perfect blend of mint and chocolate.

"*Oh my God,*" B purred.

"Not bad," I said, nodding to myself. Then I noticed that B was looking at me like I had three heads.

"Did you just say *not bad?*" she asked, her expression incredulous. "This is the best mint chocolate chip ice cream I've ever had."

The clerk behind the counter smiled at her with pride.

Easy, Bucko. The blonde's with me!

"That's what I said. *Not bad.* It's really good." To the clerk, I said, "We'll take two scoops each." Looking at B, I added, "Unless you want to try another flavor?"

"Two scoops sound perfect. Can I have mine in a sugar cone, please?"

"I'll have the same, please."

The clerk handed us our cones. B's scoops were clearly bigger than mine, but I didn't care. We left the store and became lost in our time together. We made it to the end of the block, where the shops gave way to residential apartments, so we carefully crossed the street and made our way back down the other side.

I finished my cone first, wiped my face with a little napkin, and tossed my garbage into a trash can.

Swish! Three points!

"Finished already?"

"I don't mess around, sister. I figured the way you killed that Jim Dandy the other night, you'd be finished already."

"I'm choosing to *enjoy* this ice cream, thank you very much."

"Ah, *that's* what you're doing," I joked as I wiped ice cream from her cheek with my thumb.

"You're on a roll tonight. Remind me again . . . why did I come out with you tonight?"

"Because I'm magnetic, and you just couldn't stay away from me," I said full of bravado and moxie.

She raised her eyebrows at me. "Wow, someone is *very* full of himself tonight."

"Let's just say, I'm fun to be around when I'm in good company."

"Mmhmm, nice save. Come on, mister." She grabbed me around the waist, so I put my arm around her shoulder.

We continued window shopping as she finished her ice cream. Once she finished, she gave me her trash, which I tossed in a garbage can ten feet away.

"It's in the hole!" I said, faking a crowd cheering, which earned me a high-five.

Yep, she gets me.

We walked into another store with basically the same type of trinkets as previous stores, give or take. I checked the prices on a few things while B browsed the assorted figurines.

They're actually reasonably priced.

"Find anything good?" B asked.

"I think so." I held out a rope anklet for her to see.

"It's pretty."

"Would you like one?" I asked.

"What? *No.* You've already spent too much money on me."

Yeah, but not all of my money. Thanks, Ma.

"Let me worry about that. Which one do you like?"

"I don't know. Which one do *you* like?"

I stepped back and gave her the once-over. She raised her arms and posed for me, giggling as she tossed her hair back.

Whoa! Please do that again!

Her ankles were bare, so I handed her an ankle bracelet. "What do you think?" I asked as she looked at the price.

"It's pretty, but seriously, don't you think you've spent enough money on me for one day?"

"I want to get it for you. Is that okay?"

She finally acquiesced and smiled.

As I paid, B came up with her own rope bracelet. This one was thicker and made for a wrist.

"I'll take this, please," she said to the lady at the register. Then she looked at me and stuck out her tongue. I just stepped away so she could finish her transaction.

"You didn't have to do that," I said as we stepped outside.

"Do what?"

"Get me a bracelet."

"What makes you think it's for you, *mister?*" Her face had a look of innocence and whimsy.

"Uh, well, uh . . ."

"*Uh, well, uh* . . . what? The cat got your tongue?"

"Uh, well, uh, then uh, what makes you think *this* is for you then?" I countered. It was weak, I know, but it was all the game I had.

She stepped to the side, hands on her hips, feigning shock. "Oh, so is that how it's going to be? You're going to hold my gift hostage now?"

"I don't know, maybe I will, at least until I find out who that's for." I pointed at the bag in her hand.

"Well, I guess you'll just have to wait and see, *mister*," she said, tying my sweatshirt around her shoulders and leaving me standing there with my mouth open.

Don't let her get away! Catch her!

I quickly caught up, hugged her from behind, and started tickling her, which caused us to slip into a fit of laughter. People stared as they walked by, but we didn't care.

Keep walking . . . nothing to see here, people.

We stood there in the lights of the various shops, staring deeply into each other's eyes.

I could get lost in those blue eyes of yours. Man, you give me butterflies.

She reached out her arms, and we hugged right there in the midst of passersby without a care in the world.

After our hug, we held hands and walked to the end of the block. We carefully crossed the street and took a stroll along the docks. It was a pretty evening, with hardly a cloud in the sky. The moonlight was shining beautifully on the water.

I guided her to sit on one of the many benches along the docks, placing my arm around her shoulder, I held her close as we enjoyed the view.

"So, I got you something," I said nonchalantly.

"You *did*? What'd you get me?" she asked in faux surprise.

"I got you this," I said, dangling the ankle bracelet from my index finger.

"Thank you," she whispered. "I really do love it. Can you put it on me?" She straightened her right leg out in front of her.

Don't need to ask me twice!!

"Sure."

I got down on one knee and carefully removed her right shoe. She giggled as I playfully tickled her foot, causing her to wiggle her cute toes. I adjusted the bracelet, slipped it past her toes, and laid it perfectly against her ankle, adjusting it so it wouldn't slip off.

"Is this okay? It's not too tight, is it?" I asked.

"It's perfect," she whispered, admiring her gift as I joined her back on the bench.

A cool breeze blew past us, forcing B to huddle closer. The water gently rocked the docks, while the moonlight reflected off the waves as they lightly crashed on the shore.

B lifted her head and looked up at me, smiling warmly. I met her gaze with my baby browns and smiled back as I felt my heart pounding in my chest.

Is it getting warm out here, or is it just me? There go those butterflies again.

As we both leaned in slowly, she held me captive in her crystal-blue eyes. *My God, I could drown in your eyes.*

We shut our eyes and tilted our heads slightly to the right. And there, sitting on the docks of Port Jefferson, overlooking the moonlit water as the waves caressed the docks, B and I shared our first kiss.

And it was perfect.

"Well it's about time." she whispered.

18 - The Blow-Off

Our first kiss was eternal. It was gentle and sweet. There were no tongues fighting for dominance. It was a pair of soft, innocent lips coming together for the first time. I tasted her lips and didn't want to stop.

They were naturally sweet and a bit salty from the breeze coming off the water. They also had a hint of chocolate and mint from the ice cream as well.

She gently caressed my face while I held her in my arms. When we parted, we both smiled and stared into each other's eyes.

"I was wondering when you were going to kiss me," she whispered.

I was speechless.

"You've had plenty of opportunities too," she continued. "But I'm glad we waited."

I felt her soft breath on my neck and the warmth of her body as she snuggled closer.

I had plenty of opportunities? It's official. I'm a moron!

"I've wanted to kiss you since the first time I saw you at the market," I said. "But I didn't want to rush you. I'm not that type of guy, you know?" I pulled back to look at her. "Now, had I *known* what I was waiting for, I wouldn't have waited," I teased, which made her laugh.

"God, B, you have the most beautiful eyes I've ever seen," I caught myself whispering, which made her blush.

"Thank you."

"You're welcome."

And we kissed again, which was better than our first.

This was an open-mouthed French kiss. As the tips of our tongues gently caressed each other, I gently stroked her hair. I felt my heart pounding in my ears, chest, stomach, and groin. I couldn't believe this was happening!

I'm the luckiest person on the planet.

More kissing, some talking, more kissing . . . the minutes flew by in a heartbeat.

"It's getting late," she said through a sigh.

I looked at my watch. It was almost eleven, and I felt like we'd just arrived.

"I better get you home."

I felt like I was floating on air as we walked back to my car. Before getting into the car, she gently kissed me, which simply took my breath away. I held her hand as Port Jeff slowly shrank into my rearview mirror along 25A.

Thanks for the great memories, Port Jeff!

"I had a great time tonight," she said softly as I walked her to her door.

"Me too."

"Thank you for my pretty gift."

"You're welcome. You're more than worth it." We kissed.

"I better get inside, before my parents come outside."

"Okay," I said, getting lost in her beautiful blues.

She giggled. "Don't start that again. I really have to go."

"I know." I smiled as she gave me one last kiss.

"There, that will have to hold you, mister," she said as she opened her front door. "I'll call you after I get home from work, okay? It's my last week."

I nodded. "Sure, I don't have plans tomorrow."

"Okay," she said from behind her screen door.

"I'll talk to you tomorrow," I said, and then heard Gabriel bark in the distance.

"Okay, good night." She smiled.

She was simply stunning. "Good night," I said.

I finally broke myself away and headed back to my car with a huge grin on my face.

All of a sudden, I heard a screen door slam behind me as someone ran toward me. I turned quickly as B jumped into my arms.

She pressed in close, and we kissed on her front lawn, under the moonlight. This was our big finale. Our last kiss of the evening and it was spectacular.

As I drove home that night, I sang along to Prince's "Let's Go Crazy."

You said it, brother!

~ ~ ~

Belle greeted me at the front door, barking, licking, and wagging her tail. "Settle down, Belle," I whispered.

Even Ma's list of chores that she left on my pillow didn't spoil my mood. My heart and mind raced with the memories of the evening.

I can't believe we finally kissed. It was awesome! Her lips were mint! They were so soft, and her tongue was amazing. And we fit so perfectly together, like a pair of Legos. And she looked so hot tonight. And what a great laugh.

And she's funny too. Who knew? Why'd it take me this long to say something to her? I've certainly noticed her at school. She's the prettiest, smartest girl in our grade. I guess I thought she was too unattainable.

Man, I can't wait for this year to start. I can't wait to go to Homecoming with her in October. I bet she'll look amazing. Oh, and I can't forget about the winter formal in February and the prom in the spring.

I can't wait to see everyone's faces when they see us together. Here's this gorgeous genius of a girl going out with average-looking me. This year is going to be epic!

I woke up the next morning in a great mood. I grabbed breakfast, then hit Ma's list running. She had me trimming the bushes along the back yard, which took me a few hours. I built up a hard sweat and eventually my brother helped me finish after a five-minute argument and a five-dollar bribe.

Jean Paul called to check in at three thirty. "What's going on, bro?" he asked.

"Not much. Ma had me trim the bushes today. She'll probably have me trim the trees tomorrow, in case you're up to helping?"

"Yeah, isn't it supposed to snow tomorrow?" he joked. "Also, I think I'm going to Europe."

"Oh yeah, I forgot all about that dreaded summer snowstorm and your trip to Europe tomorrow, Rome, isn't it? Man, I must be getting old," I said. "So I'll see you tomorrow morning at ten?"

"Are we swimming afterward?"

"Does a bear shit in the woods?"

"What about lunch?"

"Yes, I'll make lunch. Anything else?"

"Hey, don't rush me. I'm thinking, I'm thinking."

"So that's a no. Got it. I'll see you at ten."

"Yep, see you at ten. What are you doing the rest of this afternoon? Are you up for some tennis?"

How do I get out of this? B's getting off work soon, and I really want to see her.

"Would you be angry if I said no?" I asked.

"What, do you have other plans or something?"

"Not really, but—"

"So let's play. Come on, dude. It's a beautiful day outside and I've got to get out of this house."

"I'm, um, sort of waiting for B's call," I admitted.

"Did you make plans?" he asked.

"Well, not really, but—"

"Well then, come play tennis. You can see her later, dude. Come on. Don't tell me you're pussy-whipped already."

"Come on, dude. That's not fair. And no, I'm not pussy-whipped," I said.

"Great, then grab your racquet, find your *balls*, and meet me on the courts in a half hour."

Buzz, buzz! Call waiting . . . great!

"Hold on, dude. Call waiting," I said and hit the flash button on the phone. *Click.*

"Hello?" I answered.

"It's still me, dude," Jean Paul said.

Shit!

"Shit, hold on . . ."

Click.

"Hello?" I answered again.

"Hey, mister, how're you?"

Yes!

"I'm doing great. What're you up to?" I asked.

"Well, I just got home from work, so I thought I'd call *my man*."

I'm her man!

"So what'd you do today?" she asked.

"Not much. Ma had me trim the bushes. It took me a few hours, but my brother helped me finish, after I gave him five bucks. So now I'm just hanging by the pool, chillaxing. How about you? How was work? Did you save anyone today, or did you just hang out on your lifeguard stand wearing your cool black sunglasses and twirling your whistle?" I teased.

Buzz, buzz. Shit, Jean Paul.

"Hey, can you hold on a sec? I have Jean Paul on the other line."

"Oh, I'm sorry, I didn't mean to interrupt. Finish your call with him and call me back."

Yeah, I don't think so.

"It's okay. I'll be right back."

"Okay, I'll wait."

Click.

"Yo, dude!"

"It's still me, *dude*," B teased, laughing.

Shit, I did it again! Sigh!

"Sorry about that, don't hang up. I'll be right back. I promise."

Moron! Let's try this again.

Click.

"Hello?"

"Dude, I thought you forgot about me," Jean Paul said. "So was it your blond hottie? Are you allowed to come out and play?"

"First of all, I don't need to ask permission. Second, I haven't asked yet and shut up! Listen, I'll call you back, cool?"

"No, dude, it's not *cool*. You have all year to hang out with her," he whined. "We only have a week left to play tennis. Grow a pair and meet me at the courts."

He's got a point. We really only have a week left to screw around before school starts up again, and then we're back to the old grind.

"All right, let me see what I can do. I'll call you back in a few minutes, okay?"

"Don't leave me hanging!" he said.

"Yeah, yeah, I'll call you back."

Click.

"Hey, are you still there?" I asked.

"Yep, I told you I'd wait. So was he mad that you had to go?"

"No, he was all right."

"Well, that's good. So you're home *swimming*, huh? That sounds like *fun*," her tone was flirtatious.

Sorry, bro, tennis is off the table!

"Why, yes I am. And the water is *sooo* nice. It's a shame I'm here all alone," I flirted back.

"Did I forget to mention I picked up a new bikini today at work? Yeah, it was on sale, and it'd be a shame if I couldn't wear it today. If you'd *like* some company, I *could* come over, but only if you wanted," she purred.

Boing! Apparently I wasn't the only one that heard her. Down, boy!

"I don't know. Would you *like* to come over? You *did* spend the whole morning at a pool already. Plus, I doubt I'll need a lifeguard."

"Well, if you keep *that up*, you *will* need a lifeguard."

"That sounds like a threat," I said.

She countered with, "It's more like a promise."

"Well, since I'm not a fan of getting beat up by girls, I better have you come over, just to be on the safe side."

"Of course, just to be on the safe side. Let me grab a few things, and I'll be right over, okay?"

"Awesome, I'll see you soon."

"Okay, see you soon."

"Okay, bye."

"Okay, um . . . *bye.*"

And neither of us hung up.

Let the games begin. In this corner, we have a sarcastic, horny, Hispanic, teenage male. And in that corner, we have a gorgeous, intelligent, blonde of Swedish descent, teenage female. Ding, ding, and begin the battle!

"Are we really going to do this?" she giggled.

"Do what?" I innocently replied.

"*Okay*, I guess we're going to do this. Now you do realize the longer we waste on the phone, the less time we'll have to spend together. And I did mention I bought a new *bikini* today, right? So really, it's your call."

Dammit, Jim, I'm just a country doctor!

"Okay, bye!" I quickly hung up.

She's good! Crap, I've got to call Jean Paul!

I dialed and Hannah picked up. "Hi, Hann. Is he around?"

"Nope, he's waiting for you at the courts. He told me to tell you, and I quote, "*Don't blow me off for the blond hottie*," end quote."

Crap!

"So things are getting serious between you two, huh?"

How do I fix this? I'm not blowing off B and her new bikini.

"Yeah, I guess so. We hung out in Port Jeff last night," I said.

Think, man, think!

"Remember to take things slow. We don't want you getting your heart broken this close to school."

"What's that supposed to mean? I *am* taking it slow. I'm not going to get my heart broken. I really like her, Hann."

"Listen, calm down. I know you really like her," she said. "Trust me, everybody at the beach yesterday could tell. I just don't want you to get hurt, that's all. I'm just telling you as a friend to take things slow."

"Fair enough. So, um . . . *Hann?*"

"What do you want?" she quickly replied, recognizing my tone.

"Not much, really."

"Good, because I'm not going down to the tennis courts and telling him you're not coming."

How'd she know? Am I that transparent?

I laughed. "How'd you know?"

"Because I know you, that's how," she said. "What do you want me to tell him?"

That's my Hannah! My lifesaver!

"Um, can you tell him that I'm really sorry and will make it up to him tomorrow, when he comes over to help me trim some trees?"

"Wait a minute. Let me get this straight. You're blowing off your best friend, presumably for your *new* female friend, *and* you're still expecting him to come over tomorrow to help *you trim some trees?*"

Sigh!

"Um . . . *yes?* How mad do you think he'll be?" I asked.

"You know the prince; he's going to be *pissed!* I wouldn't hold your breath waiting for him tomorrow. I certainly wouldn't want him around sharp objects. You know how he gets. He'll be worse than a woman scorned." She laughed.

For years, Jean Paul referred to this as *the Blow-Off Incident!* As in, "Remember that time you blew me off . . .?"

"Looks like I'm paying my brother another five bucks tomorrow," I said.

"Screw him! How about giving me five bucks for my troubles?"

"Will you accept a hug instead?" I sheepishly asked.

"Uh-huh, I thought so," she scoffed.

"You're the best! Thanks, Hann!"

"Yeah, yeah, you owe me . . . *again!* And by the way, your tab is getting awfully long. When are you going to start paying up?"

"Hey, you're taking Spanish 2 this year, right? We both know you'll need my help again. When you get your A, we'll call it even."

"Yeah, okay. Let me go disappoint your brother from another mother. I can't guarantee he won't come over and beat you silly."

"I know, I know. Tell him (a) I'm sorry, (b) to get over it, and (c) I'll see him tomorrow," I said. "And Hann, seriously, thanks."

"Yeah, yeah, what are friends for?" She sighed.

She's the best, but enough about Hannah.
B's coming over and has a new bikini!
Yes!

19 - Let's Go Swimming

I quickly changed out of my ratty gym shorts and into a bathing suit. I also grabbed a clean towel, one without all my dirt and sweat on it. About fifteen minutes later, an angel pulled into my driveway.

"Is it okay that I parked behind your car?" she asked. "I don't want your mom getting mad with me."

That's B, always thinking of others.

"Yeah, you're fine right there," I assured her as she ran to me and pressed her heavenly body against mine, followed by a sweet kiss.

"Hi," I said, grinning.

She laughed, looking coy. "Hi. Sorry, I needed to get that out of my system."

"Better?"

"Much," she replied, followed by another quick kiss.

"Good. So are you ready to go swimming?"

"You ready to get wet?" she asked.

I'm already wet.

"Yup, but I do feel a little bad for you," I teased. "You're going to get dunked *so many times*. Good thing you're a lifeguard."

"You don't say. Just remember, I'm a trained professional. So don't be surprised if you're the one getting dunked a lot."

We walked inside to the sound of drums when she added, "Plus, if you get in trouble, I can give you mouth to mouth." She smiled as she moved her eyebrows up and down, then excused herself to change while I grabbed my box and set things up outside.

Two minutes later, she stepped outside wearing her sunglasses and wrapped in a towel. As she shook her hair out and removed her towel, time itself seemed to slow down. There she stood, wearing this white bikini, and it took my breath away.

Her top and bottom were both pure white with white tassels. Her blond hair and golden skin just popped against the white contrast of her bikini. She simply looked amazing.

Holy fuck balls!

"Whoa." I whispered, and she blushed slightly.

"So, do you *like* it?"

"Yeah, you could say that."

"Good, I'm glad. I see you grabbed your box. I actually brought some more tapes with me."

She fumbled through her bag and handed me Peter Gabriel's *So, The Eagles: Their Greatest Hits (1971–1975),* Sting again, and a double cassette from the Stones, *Hot Rocks 1964–1971.*

Nice.

"So what do you think?

"Wow, these are all really good albums."

"You sound surprised."

"Well, you're a girl. Who knows what you people listen to?" I teased and received a playful shove. "So what do you want to hear first?" I asked.

"Do you *really* need to ask?"

"The Stones. Got it." I popped a cassette into the box, pressed play, and heard the sound of organs playing the intro to "Time Is on My Side."

This'll work.

I took her hand and walked her to the pool area.

"Happy?" I asked as we neared the pool. What I meant was, *are you happy I put your Rolling Stones on?*

She took it differently.

"I'm *very* happy now. I'm here with you, and we're about to go swimming. I couldn't be any happier." She dipped her toe into the pool, but I didn't push her in . . . yet.

"So are you just going to stand there staring all day, or are we going swimming?" she purred.

I bum-rushed her, grabbed her around the waist, and pulled her into the pool, entwining our bodies as we fell in. We both came up laughing and splashing each other.

She dunked me immediately, and I hit the bottom of the pool, which I used to push off and come up behind her. Unfortunately for B, I had home-field advantage and knew every nook and cranny of that rectangular, crystal clear pool.

I grew up in it and could swim it blindfolded. I splashed her from behind, and then dropped like a stone, coming up at the shallow end, while she tried to track my movements.

Good luck, sister. I'm like a fish in this pool.

I popped up, splashed her, and then dropped back down. To her credit, B was a trained lifeguard and also knew how to swim really well. Plus, she was extremely intelligent, so it didn't take her long to get her bearings. Once she had them, she had no problem tracking my movements.

She grabbed hold of my legs and wrapped me up in the shallow end.

Damn! She is friggin strong.

I popped up, and she splashed me while laughing. "You didn't think I'd let you get away from me for that long, *did you*?"

She then dunked me again, but I easily swam up behind her and wrapped my arms around her waist, holding her closely. She turned around and put her arms around my neck, both of us laughing. We stood there, dripping wet, and stared into each other's eyes for a long moment.

Man, you're beautiful.

Staring transitioned to kissing. The sun was shining, the birds were singing, and we were in paradise. Our mouths slowly opened, allowing our tongues to softly explore one another. She tasted great.

Pool water? What pool water?

We released each other, and I brushed hair out of her face. This was when she cupped some water into her hands and splashed me, the water shooting up my nose. She escaped into the deep end.

"You'll pay for that."

"I've heard that one before! You'll have to catch me first." She then dove underwater, slicing it like a knife. And I knew right where she was going—under the diving board.

Amateur! At least try to come up under the slide. Make this challenging at least.

Ha! Gotcha!

Or not.

Damn!

She slipped right out of my hands and jumped out of the pool. "Ha, missed me," she taunted and then dove off the diving board, right past me.

"Damn!" I dove after her, but she had a solid lead on me.

Clearly, she was a powerful swimmer. She stood in the shallow end before I got halfway there, so I decided to tread water and watch her plan her next move.

Using the ladder in the shallow end, she slowly climbed out of the pool, looking over her shoulder to keep an eye on me. Water dripped down the back of her gorgeous body.

Wow, do that again, please?

She ran past me and dove back into the water, coming up catty-corner to the diving board, laughing.

"You might as well give up now. You'll never catch me."

"I'm just letting you build your confidence. You'll be in my arms before you know it."

"Oh, promises, promises." She lifted herself out of the pool again and was back on the diving board. She removed a wedgie and got her *girls* back in order before diving past me.

While she dove, I pushed off the bottom and met her in the shallow end. She screamed as I surprised her. She wasn't the only strong swimmer in this pool.

She was caught and knew it. She laughed and splashed as I stalked forward, my eyes peeking slightly above the water. I then dove to the bottom and grabbed her ankles, pulling her under.

We came up laughing and playfully splashing. We were inches apart at this point. We giggled like a pair of teens in *like* with each other. Soon the splashing stopped as did the giggling. That was when I felt butterflies in my stomach again.

There was a look of anticipation on her face as she used her powerfully athletic legs to pull me closer. She wrapped her arms around my neck as we began kissing again.

I caressed her from the back of her head to her perfect bottom. My hands gently glided over her bottom, while our lips and tongues explored each other.

Her soft moans drove me crazy. I wanted to rip off her bikini and have her right there in the pool. Of course, it was the middle of the afternoon . . . and there was that *other* thing.

I was a virgin!

Holy shit, I can't believe we're doing this! I actually have my hands on her ass! Please don't let this be a dream!

When we stopped and regained our composure, I damn near poked her in the stomach with my boner.

I just made out with this blond vision in my pool! And got to caress her perfect ass! We're talking about a pair of athletically toned golden legs that come up to here . . . and create The Perfect Ass!

She took a few steps back and turned around to adjust herself before stepping up the ladder and out of the pool, which I took pleasure in watching again. I dipped under water and, um, *adjusted* myself too.

Crap, I may never lose this boner! Come on, buddy, down you go. That's it, go on. There you go.

Boner-free, I joined B, who was sipping on her iced tea and changing the music. As I approached, I heard Peter Gabriel sing, "*Red rain is coming down; re-e-d rain.*"

"This okay?" she asked. "I figure I've tortured you enough with *my* Rolling Stones."

"Yeah, I like Peter Gabriel." Then I added, "Also, it wasn't torture. I told you the other night that I liked *your* Stones."

And the afternoon went on much the same, filled with swimming, kissing, and just hanging out on the lounge chairs, holding hands. Around four thirty, my neighbor, Aunt Mary, appeared with suntan lotion and *People Magazine* in hand, taking possession of *her* lounge chair.

Did she just snicker?

After making the appropriate introductions and receiving a modicum of teasing from Aunt Mary, B and I decided the swimming portion of our day was over.

"Hey, you want to get out of here?" I asked.

"Sure, what do you want to do?" she asked.

You!

"I don't know. Do you want to hit the mall?" I asked.

When in doubt, go to the mall

"Sure, that sounds like fun."

We gathered our things, said our goodbyes to Aunt Mary, and headed inside to change. As B was entering the bathroom, I placed my hands around her waist and spun her around. I then kissed her softly.

"Too bad your brother's home," she purred.

Boing! Every damn time!

That was when Belle decided to join us. B bent down and played with her as Belle rolled over, wagging her tail and licking B's arm. B just looked up at me and smiled.

Oh my God, those eyes! Thanks for the cock block, Belle!

"Okay, I'll be down in a minute," I said, and headed to my room. I dried off, changed into a T-shirt, shorts, and sneakers. I quickly hit the bathroom to check my look in the mirror. After some minor primping, I went downstairs and into the kitchen.

I cleaned up while I waited, putting the iced tea glasses in the sink. Moments later, B joined me, looking as amazing as ever, her hair up in a ponytail and wearing the same outfit she wore over earlier.

I know I gush a lot, but what can I say . . . I'm in, um, like.

20 - Ma, I Hit the Mall

I left Ma a note, and we took B's car to the mall. The place was swamped, and it took us a while to find parking.

"I didn't think we'd ever find a spot. I wish they had valet parking, like they do at hotels and restaurants. You pull up, hand someone your keys, and just walk inside," B commented.

Come on, girl. Get real. Valet parking at the mall? That's the stupidest idea I've ever heard. What's next, valet parking at the hospital?

Clearly, one of us was a visionary while the other one was me.

"Yeah, that *would be* nice. I just don't see it happening anytime soon."

Cough—less than twenty-five years, genius—cough!

"Holy smokes, Batman, this place is a madhouse. What do you think? Yay or nay?" I asked as we stepped inside the main entrance.

"Well, we've come this far. Let's give it a shot. What's the worst that can happen?"

What are they doing—giving the shit away?

"Want some ice cream, my treat?" B asked.

"That sounds good to me. Is your machete ready?"

"I was born ready; lead the way, McDuff," she laughed, while pretending to hold a machete. We navigated our way to Baskin-Robbins for a couple of mint chocolate chip cones, which fell short of last night's delicious scoops.

"Are you thinking what I'm thinking?" I asked.

"Toto, we're not in Port Jeff anymore," she joked, taking another lick.

"Well, at least I'm in good company." I smiled as she placed her arm around my waist and hugged me.

"B! Is that you?" shouted a familiar voice.

Oh look, it's everyone's favorite stuck-up friend, Mary Friggin Fergusen!

"Hey, Mary!" B said, and the two did air kisses. "What are you doing here?

"I thought you finished your back-to-school shopping last week in the Hamptons?" B nodded at Mary's multiple shopping bags.

"Bitch, I'm never done shopping, especially when I have my daddy's Amex," she replied, showing off her father's platinum card. "Am I interrupting anything?"

B popped her on the arm. "Oh stop it. No, you're not interrupting anything."

She's not?

"We just finished swimming at his house and decided to come to the mall for some ice cream."

"I thought Friendly's was your special place," Mary jibed.

Man, I hate this bitch! How can B stand her?

"Oh, Mary, stop teasing. Besides, everyplace we go is our special place, right?"

"Damn right," I replied with a kiss on her cheek and a smile.

"Oh brother, gag me," Mary said.

Biiiiiitch!

Then she asked, "So, what are you doing tonight?"

B looked at me. "I don't know, what *are* we doing tonight?"

"Want to see a movie?" I asked.

B nodded and said that she did. Then Mary reared her ugly head again.

"A movie tonight does sound like fun. What are we going to see?" she asked.

Sigh!

"I don't know. I thought we'd just go to the triplex and see what's playing at around seven," I replied, trying hard to hide the annoyance from my voice.

"Great, it'll give me enough time to finish shopping."

Finish shopping?

Then Mary added, "And I'll call my brother and see if he and his *new* girlfriend want to join us."

At the mention of Mary's brother, I felt B tense up.

"Do you really think that's such a good idea?" B asked.

"Oh, come on. You're not still mad at him, are you? Besides, you've clearly gotten over him," Mary said, pointing at me. "What's the big deal?"

Wait a minute. Hold on a second. Is she telling me that B dated her douche bag of a brother? Eww! That guy's a bigger tool than this bitch! No, that can't be right.

B shrugged. "Whatever, fine."

"Great, I'll meet you up there around seven," Mary said and air-kissed B again.

We watched her walk away, then took a couple more licks of our ice cream cones before tossing our cones into the nearby garbage can in tandem.

Nope, we're definitely not in Port Jeff anymore.

21 - Time to Swallow My Pride

"Do you want to invite Hannah and Jean Paul to join us?" B asked.

"That sounds like a good idea, but I don't think they'll come. Jean Paul is kind of pissed off at me."

"Why?"

I then explained how I blew him off today.

She smacked me. "Why didn't you tell me you had plans this afternoon, silly? I would have understood. Come on. Let's go find a pay phone so you can make this right and apologize to him." She then paused for a moment.

"Listen, I clearly love spending time with you, but the last thing I want to do is come between you and your best friend. So from now on, if you have plans, just let me know. I'll understand. I mean, I'll *probably* miss you, but I'll totally understand."

"Hey, what do you mean—*probably*?" I asked as she giggled. We searched for a pay phone, which ironically was inside the movie theater in the mall.

"Hello, Michaels residence," Hannah said.

God, it's all in your hands now.

"Hey, Hann, how's it going? I don't suppose *he's* around, is he?" I meekly asked, and she laughed.

"You're funny. Oh yeah, *he's* here. Are you sure you really want me to get him? He's *really* pissed off at you."

Sigh!

"I figured. Well, I told B about it and she *ordered me* to apologize immediately."

"I'm really starting to like this girl of yours."

"Shut up and get your brother."

"Okay, but it's your funeral."

A few seconds later, I could hear Jean Paul's raised voice in the background. "Are you friggin kidding me? He blows me off for some chick, and now he wants to talk to me? No! Hang up on him! I don't care if he's calling to apologize. Tell him to go fuck himself! Sorry, Mom."

Another few seconds ticked away, then, "Fine, just hand me the phone. I'll talk to him, but he's not gonna be happy." I heard the shuffling of the phone; he was on the line. "Yeah what?"

Here we go.

"Hey, buddy, listen . . . I'm *really* sorry for what happened today. I promise it won't happen again."

"Dude, you totally blew me off today! You made me feel like a total dick!" He kind of hiss-whispered the last part. "And for what—some chick you barely know? Not cool, bro! Not cool at all!"

"I know, I know, you're right, I'm sorry."

But, dude, if you saw what she was wearing this afternoon, you'd have totally done the same thing to me!

"It was a dick move, and I'm sorry. Let me make it up to you."

"I'm listening."

"How about I treat you and Hannah to the movies tonight?"

I heard the wheels in his head spinning.

Okay, folks, let the negotiations begin! I know my best friend. He clearly has me over a barrel and will make me pay for it!

"Popcorn and soda too, and not just for me, I mean for both of us."

Got him! He's in!

I nodded to B and gave her a thumbs-up. She smiled and nodded back.

"Yes, popcorn and soda included for both of you."

"For both of us, no arguments!"

"Yeah, yeah, I heard you."

"Oh, and Twizzlers too, but those are for me. Hannah can get her own," he whispered.

That's my boy, always thinking of others!

"Okay, Twizzlers too, but it also includes you helping me tomorrow," I countered.

"Yeah, yeah, fine. You take care of tonight, and I'll help you out tomorrow."

"Meet us at the triplex around six forty-five, okay?"

"Yeah, okay, cool. We'll see you tonight. Smell ya later!" Then he hung up.

"It took some negotiating, as you probably overheard, but they'll meet us at six forty-five." I took B's hand in mine.

"That's good. Did you tell him who's joining us? I didn't hear you mention Mary's name."

Shit! I knew I forgot something!

"Um, I sort of forgot to mention that last part. Please don't make me call him back," I pleaded, which made her roll her eyes.

"Come on, Mr. Kissinger. Let's go to Herman's."

We spent time inside Herman's Sporting Goods playing with various sporting equipment, before being asked nicely to leave. Someone knocked over a display . . . okay, it was me. We then spent the remainder of our time holding hands, laughing, and walking around the mall.

As we were leaving the mall, B remembered she never let her parents know about our impromptu plans. "Oh my gosh, I can't believe I forgot to tell my parents. Do you mind? Do you want to call your mother too?"

"Nah, I left her a note. She knows I'm staying out late," I lied.

"Oh, okay. Well, I'm still going to call my parents." So we returned to the pay phones and called her parents for her version of negotiations.

"Hi, Mamma, it's me. Well, that's why I'm calling. We're at the mall and ran into Mary. She invited us to go to the movies tonight. It'll be an early show, so I shouldn't be home too late."

Excuse me, who invited you?

"Besides, I have to work tomorrow. Yes, he'll probably be there too, with his new girlfriend," she said edgily. "Of course he's coming with me. No, everything will be fine. No, I don't want any trouble either. Yes, Mamma, I understand. No, I won't be home too late. Okay, Mamma, I'll see you later. Okay . . . bye-bye."

Man, she really does keep her on a tight leash.

22 - What's the Story with Kyle?

Every time Kyle's name comes up, she gets all tense. And why would there be any trouble? I may not be a genius like her, but there's clearly something going on here. Now I'm glad Jean Paul's coming tonight.

"So is everything cool?" I asked.

"Of course. Why do you ask?" she responded with a smile.

"Well, it's just that . . . how do I say this?" I started.

"Just say it. You can say anything to me, you know that," she replied while caressing my cheek and gazing into my eyes.

"Yeah, I know," I said softly. "It's just that, whenever Kyle Fergusen's name is brought up, you get all, I don't know . . . tense."

She frowned, dropped her hand, and began shifting back and forth on her feet.

"Listen, I don't want to talk about it, if that's okay." Her tone was sharp, and then she turned to walk away, but I grabbed her hand and stopped her.

"Hey, hold on, B, what is it? You know you can tell me anything too. Did you guys go out or something? Did things end, um, badly?" I asked reluctantly.

She guffawed, "Yeah, you could say that. We went out at the beginning of the year for a few months. I guess he was my first real boyfriend. People warned me about him, including Mary, but I ignored them. I was young and I thought I was in love. I thought everyone else was jealous. He was always sweet and generous with me, not the *jerk* everyone said."

I nodded, though I didn't know why, and just waited. After a pause, she continued.

"Then one night I walked in on him with another girl. It turns out that he'd been cheating on me from the beginning. He actually blamed *me* for *him* cheating on me. He was mad because I wouldn't *give it up*." She pursed her lips after she said this, then added, "Can you believe that? What a jerk."

I didn't know what to say. I didn't know whether to nod or shake my head in response, so I just listened.

"He was like 'guys have needs.' If I wasn't going to give it up, then he'd get it elsewhere, he told me. I dumped him on the spot, after trashing his room. He's been trying to get me back ever since. He's even tried stopping by my house late at night, at the beginning of the summer, which really upset my parents."

Finally, I thought of something to say. "No shit?! What an *asshole!*"

"I know, right? My parents threatened to call the police on him a few times. It got real ugly. Fortunately, I had my ten-day youth trip around the same time, so things stopped. To be honest with you, I'm surprised my parents are even letting me go out with you, even though you're nothing like Kyle." Then she reached out and pushed a curl off my forehead.

"There's something different about you. You definitely impressed them the other night. They both commented on how polite you were and how nice you seemed. My dad said you 'seem like a boy with ambition,'" she said, which made me smile.

"Anyway, I guess he's dating someone else now, so the heck with him. It's probably that skank he cheated with."

Man, what a loser!

"Wow, B, I'm so sorry. You know I'd never do anything like that, right? That's not how I was raised. I was raised to respect women. Especially women I care about, and I care about you, B. You know that, right?"

"I know that. And I care about you too. I still can't believe we've only really known each other for a little over a week. I mean we sort of knew each other, but we didn't hang out or anything."

"That's pretty funny; I was thinking the exact same thing earlier this week. I guess great minds *do* think alike," I joked.

She countered with, "Well, I wouldn't say *two* great minds, but I get your point." Then she poked me in the ribs.

"Laugh it up, fuzzball."

"Hey, that's my joke!" She giggled and gave me another poke.

I rubbed my ribs. "You know you're going to leave a mark soon."

"Oh, I'll leave a mark all right!"

"Don't write a check your mouth can't cash, as my father used to say."

"Who said I couldn't cash *that* check?" Then she leaned in and softly kissed my neck.

There go those butterflies again!

"Okay, okay, I believe you."

She laughed and went for my neck again, this time blowing a raspberry. I responded by tickling her, and after the giggle-fest was over, we left the mall and drove over to Giuseppe's for a couple of slices and Cokes.

23 - Dirty Dancing

According to the marquee on the corner, the three movies playing were *Dirty Dancing, No Way Out,* and *The Big Easy.* After finishing our slices, we walked over to the movie theater to see what times the movies started.

So we've got two cool movies and Dirty Dancing. *I'd like to see* No Way Out. *I heard there's a really hot scene in the back of a limo, but I guess we can see that another night.*

"So, what would you like to see?" I asked.

"I wouldn't mind seeing *Dirty Dancing* again. I think you'd like the movie."

Certainly not my first choice, but I'd sit there and watch paint dry as long as you're with me.

"That sounds good. Let's wait and see who actually shows up. The movie starts at seven thirty, so we still have plenty of time."

"Yo!" I heard a very familiar voice yell from across the parking lot.

I turned and saw Hannah and Jean Paul walking toward us, smiling.

"Yo!" I yelled back. Jean Paul and I did our bro handshake while the girls greeted each other.

"So are we going to see *No Way Out* with my man Kevin Costner?" Jean Paul asked enthusiastically.

Someone is about to get disappointed. Sorry, bro.

"We're actually thinking about seeing *Dirty Dancing.*" I tried not to choke on the words, and as soon as I said them, Jean Paul's face dropped.

"B said it was a really good movie. She said we'd all like the movie."

Please don't be a dick, I pleaded with my eyes as he mulled it over.

"All right, fine, but next time we see Costner," he said.

"Agreed, but next time I'm not paying," I mumbled as I bought our four tickets.

"Check it out," Jean Paul said, twirling a set of keys.

"Wow, they actually let you take the car out again, huh? Nice!" I said.

He grinned. "They trust me every now and then."

I was handing out the tickets when I heard, "Yo, B!" from across the parking lot.

B tensed immediately as she grabbed my hand, almost out of fear. Kyle walked toward us, smoking a cigarette and holding the hand of some skanky-looking girl in a T-shirt and ripped jean shorts.

"Is Mary here yet, or is she still trying to max out Dad's Amex?" he asked.

"No, she's not here yet," B replied sheepishly. I hadn't seen her like this before and I didn't like it. This wasn't the B I knew and, um, liked a lot.

"So what are we seeing tonight?" Kyle asked, giving Hannah, Jean Paul, and me a head nod.

Jean Paul and Hannah turned and shot me a look that said, *What the fuck, who invited them?* I just ignored them.

"She's late to everything," Kyle said while blowing smoke in my face.

Dick! Do that again, and you'll be eating that fucking cigarette!

"But you know that better than anyone," he said to B, jokingly poking her in the stomach.

I felt my nostrils flare as I tensed up.

"Please stop that," B replied sharply, smacking his hand away from her stomach.

"Okay, jeez, I'm sorry. I didn't realize you were still angry with me. I won't do it again."

You've got that right, asshole! If you fucking touch her again, I'll break your arm off and shove the stump down your fucking throat!

"So what are we seeing?" he asked B.

"We're seeing *Dirty Dancing*," I replied, which earned me the *I wasn't talking to you* look as he sized me up.

Then he said, "Oh, hey, everyone, this is Beth. Beth, this is B and, uh, *this guy* and the Michaels twins."

Another puff of smoke hit my face, and I looked at B as I coughed, and my eyes narrowed.

You really dated this douche, huh?

"Nice to meet you," the skank replied and gave B a dead-fish handshake.

"It's nice to meet you. You might as well get your tickets. We'll wait here for Mary. Hopefully she'll show up soon," B said, her eyes narrowed. She was definitely annoyed.

"Yeah, okay, do you want me to get your ticket too?" Kyle asked.

I held up our tickets and smiled. "I took care of it, thanks."

He shrugged his shoulders, took another puff of his cancer stick. "Just thought I'd ask. No offense, amigo."

Asshole!

B pulled me in tight. "Thank you for doing this tonight. I owe you big," she whispered.

"First, you don't need to thank me. Second, I'd do anything for you. And third, I don't keep score, okay?"

She nuzzled and kissed my chest. "Okay."

"Bro, that guy's a *douche!* Do you want me to take him out back and *adjust his attitude?*" Jean Paul whispered.

"I appreciate the offer, but if anyone's going to adjust his attitude, it'll be me. And it wouldn't take me very long."

My buddy laughed and slapped me on the back in agreement. Hannah and B ignored us as they searched for Mary, who finally showed up.

"I'm not *too* late, am I?" she asked as she walked up.

She could tell B was annoyed. "Oh, don't be angry. You know how I am. Oh, hey, Kyle! Did you get my ticket?"

"I didn't know if you'd actually show up, so no," her brother replied.

"Fine, I'll get it myself. What are we seeing tonight anyway?" she asked as she got in line. "And please don't tell me *Dirty Dancing*."

"Yes, we're seeing *Dirty Dancing*," B snapped.

"Fine, jeez, don't bite my head off."

Can I?

"Okay, is everyone ready?" Mary the Cruise Director asked. We all just ignored her and entered the theater.

"I'll get our seats, while you get Jean Paul and Hannah their snacks," B said to me.

"Okay, do you want anything?"

"No, I'll just share yours." She smiled and kissed my cheek as she walked away.

Kyle and Skanky got in line behind us at the concession stand.

"What'll it be?" the clerk asked.

"Well, go ahead, you two. A promise is a promise." I said to the twins, so they ordered a medium popcorn and Coke each.

"For only fifty cents more, you can upgrade to a large," the clerk informed us.

"Fine, I'll have three large popcorns and Cokes, with very little ice, and a pack of Twizzlers please. Can't forget the Twizzlers, right, bro?" I said.

"Damn skippy," he replied.

"Will there be anything else?" the clerk asked.

"Hey amigo, are you treating everyone, or just your two friends here?" Kyle chimed in.

If I say no, I'll look like a dick. If I say yes, I'll look like a chump.

Before I could answer, "I'm only kidding with you, amigo. Lighten up."

"That'll be all," I told the clerk behind gritted teeth.

B had secured seats in the middle of the theater, but there wasn't room for Kyle and his skank, so they sat right behind us, which was fine until he started kicking my seat when B and I started cuddling.

I swear to God, I'm going to friggin kill someone!

Halfway through the movie, I'd had enough, "Dude! Do you mind? Stop kicking my seat!"

He just smirked at me, "Oh, amigo, sorry. I didn't realize I was doing that. Yeah, I'll stop. No problem."

Didn't realize, huh? Well, you won't realize me punching my fist through your skull after the movie either.

Thankfully, the rest of the movie was incident-free. B and I snuggled together, sharing our popcorn and soda, and kissing periodically. I felt Kyle's eyes burning a hole in the back of my head.

Sorry for your loss, bud!

"So what'd you think? Did you like it?" B asked as the lights came up.

"Yeah, it was actually really good," Mary replied.

"Um, I think she was asking me," I said as Mary mouthed, *Oh, I'm sorry.*

"I liked it a lot. I loved the music," I said. "I think Patrick Swayze is on the soundtrack too. What'd you guys think?" I asked the twins.

"Hey, we're going to head outside for a smoke. We'll meet you guys out front," Kyle informed us as he left the theater with his skank.

We ignored him, "I really liked it too. Patrick Swayze is hot! He's got such a nice butt!" Hannah said, cupping her hands as B and Mary giggled in agreement.

"Hey, hey, settle down, you three," I said as they ignored me and continued laughing.

"It was good. But Swayze's no Costner," Jean Paul chimed in, which earned him boos from the ladies as well as some flying popcorn.

"Hey, watch the threads," he said, backing away. I pointed at him and laughed.

"What are you laughing at?" he asked, then threw some popcorn at me.

Once we hit the lobby, the girls excused themselves and went to the restroom, while Jean Paul and I followed suit, hitting the men's room.

"She's really cool, bro. I'm happy for you," Jean Paul said as we ponied up to the urinals.

"Thanks, bro. I appreciate it."

While we waited outside the restrooms for the girls to join us, Jean Paul and I were discussing our plans for the following day's yard work at my house. He'd come over around ten to get started on what would surely be a job that would last several hours.

Neither one of us was really looking forward to it, but a man's gotta do what a man's gotta do. When the girls showed up, we all stepped outside, and I asked B if she was working tomorrow.

"Yeah, but I get off at two."

Then Kyle interrupted, "Hey, thanks for the movie, B. Good call. We both enjoyed it." He turned to me and added, "Sorry again for kicking your seat there, amigo. We're cool, right?" He beat his chest like a moron, and I just pursed my lips and nodded.

"Hey, listen, I can take B home if you want," he informed me.

Jeez, this guy's a piece of work. I really may *have to really take him around back and beat the shit out of him.*

B put her arm around my waist. "No, thanks, Kyle. I drove tonight," she said.

"Oh, you drove, huh? What, you've got no wheels, amigo?" Before I could respond, he went on, "That's cool. Just thought I'd offer. No big deal. I guess I'll see you next weekend at our Labor Day party, right, B?"

Again, I could feel B tense up.

"I don't know, maybe," she replied as her face went flush.

"What do you mean *maybe*?" Mary asked, offended. "You always come to our Labor Day party. It's our tradition. You're not going to break our tradition, are you?"

B gave a quick glance in my direction, then sighed and said, "We'll probably come." She pulled me in closer as if I were some sort of shield.

"Oh yeah, of course you're all invited too," Mary waved her hand, gesturing at all of us. "B will give you the details and you don't need to bring anything either. My dad supplies *everything,* unless there's something special you prefer to drink with your lobster."

Braggart.

"To be frank, I'm not a big fan of lobster," I said. "Actually, I'm more of a filet mignon guy." Mary deflated a little, while B giggled.

"Well, maybe you can bring some guacamole or tacos if you want," Kyle interjected.

I wasn't going to be baited. Ignoring him, I said, "Yeah, well, we've got to run. Nice to see you guys again." I turned to Jean Paul and we did our handshake. "See you tomorrow, bro."

I invited Hannah to come over too, if she wanted to swim and hang out. We all parted ways, and B and I headed to her car. When we got there, Kyle and his skank pulled up in his car, blocking B's car.

"Hey, B, got a minute?" he yelled.

"No, Kyle, I don't. Please move your car."

"Come on, you can spare *one* minute, can't you? You'll be okay without her for one minute, won't you, amigo?"

B and I exchanged looks. She said in a weary voice, "Come and get me please if I'm there more than a minute."

"I will," I promised and gave her a soft kiss.

B walked around to Kyle's window. I couldn't make out what they were saying, but I could tell from B's hand gestures and headshakes that she was annoyed. Moments later, she came back to her car and fell into my arms, shaking in anger as Kyle drove off.

"He's such a jerk. Can you believe he actually called me over there to ask me to dinner this week? His girlfriend was right there, and *you're* standing right *here*! He's such an *asshole*!"

It was the first time I'd heard her curse, but she was right. He was an asshole.

"I'll talk to him," I said.

"You mean you'll take him out back and *adjust his attitude*?" She shook her head. "No, I can handle him. But if he doesn't get the message soon, then you have my permission to *talk* to him." She giggled as I held her.

24 - B, Meet Ma

"Do you want to come inside?" I asked as we pulled into my driveway. "Sure, as long as I don't stay out too late. I have to work in the morning and I need my beauty sleep." She playfully batted her eyelashes.

"B, if there's one thing you don't need, it's beauty sleep. You're perfect just the way you are," I replied, which made her blush.

"Okay, Shakespeare, let's get inside."

As we walked to the front door, I felt a cold shiver run down my spine and glanced around, but I didn't see anything out of the ordinary.

"Are you okay?"

I glanced around one more time. "Yeah, um, I'm fine."

It's like someone's watching us or something. Weird. Nahhh, it's probably nothing.

I placed my arm around her waist and escorted her inside.

"Hey, I'm home," I announced as we walked in.

Belle barked and immediately greeted us at the door. B bent down and rubbed her belly when Belle rolled over.

Clearly someone's developed a habit.

"Who's a good girl? Who's a pretty girl?" B cooed as Belle wagged her tail.

"All right, Belle, that's enough. Go on, scoot," I said.

"Oh, your pappa's a big meanie," B said, giving the belly one more rub before Belle stood up, shook, and walked back to the family room.

"Yeah, yeah, that's me, a big meanie. She'll get over it." I said, taking B's hand. "Come on, I'll introduce you to Ma."

She held me back suddenly, "Wait a minute, how do I look? Do I look okay?"

Checking her reflection in our dusty hallway mirror, she tried fixing her hair, removing the ponytail, brushing it left, then right, then to the back, and finally shaking her head in frustration and putting it back into a ponytail. I just giggled.

"Shut up, it's not funny," she whispered while smacking my arm. "This is a big deal. I don't want to look bad when I meet your mother for the first time."

"B, seriously, you look fine," I assured her. "You look better than fine; you look amazing."

She giggled and smacked me again. "Okay, let's go meet your *Ma*."

We held hands and walked into the family room to find Ma knitting and watching the Yankees play.

"Mijo, por que tan tarde?" she asked looking at her wristwatch.

"That was probably my fault," B answered, which caused Ma to look up in surprise.

"Oh, hello, who are ju?" she asked B, while shooting me a look.

"Ma, this is the friend I've been telling you about. This is B."

Then, to my utter shock, B said to Ma, "Es un placer conocerte, Doctora."

Holy shit, she speaks Spanish? Since when does she speak Spanish?

"Usted habla español? Y sin acento," Ma replied approvingly, nodding her head and smiling at me.

"Sí, Doctora, gracias."

"Mira, ju can drop that doctora stuff. ¿Okay? Siéntate aquí." Ma pointed to a spot on the couch next to her. B followed instructions and sat down next to her, looking up at me with a smile. I gave her a smile and thumbs-up.

"Mijo tráeme un iced tea por favor," Ma said. "Would ju like something to drink?" she asked B.

"Some iced tea would be nice."

I grinned. "Two iced teas, coming right up."

From the fridge, I heard B giggling with my mother.

All right what the hell is going on over there? What's she telling B? It better not be embarrassing! Ma, you're killing me! This was clearly a mistake!

I poured three glasses and delivered two of them to the ladies, while keeping one for myself.

"Oh my gosh, I love your mother! She is so funny!" B told me as I sat down.

My mother smiled with pride. "Mira, it's getting late, and these bums aren't going to win tonight, coño! Oh, excuse me, I meant to say darn it," Ma corrected herself. "I'm going to bed. B, what are ju doing Wednesday night?"

Ma, what are you doing?

"I don't have any plans."

"Well ju do now. Would you like to join us for dinner? I'll barbecue some steaks on the grill. Do ju eat steak?"

"Sí, señora, yo como carne," B replied in a perfect Spanish accent, which made Ma smile.

"Good. Come over for dinner Wednesday night then."

"Thank you, I'd love to."

"Bueno, te veo el miércoles," Ma said and excused herself, but not before making a point of kissing me on the cheek and getting one back.

Sigh! Ma! You're killing me!

"Good night, B," Ma said as she left the family room and went up to her bedroom.

"Buenas noches, señora," B replied, which put a smile on both their faces.

I grabbed the TV remote and flipped the channel to MTV.

"I didn't know you spoke Spanish."

"I bet there're a lot of things about me that you don't know," she replied with a whimsical smile.

"Oh yeah, like what?"

"Well, that I speak Spanish, for one."

"So how does a girl, with clearly no Latin blood in her, speak such perfect Spanish?"

"Remember the youth mission trips I mentioned?"

I nodded.

"That's where I learned to speak Spanish. Some summers we went to Honduras and Panama. That's where I learned Spanish. I also made many friends too. We still write each other. We always correspond in Spanish, which forces me to think in Spanish, if that makes sense."

Who is this girl and how is it I've only truly discovered her this past week?

"Yeah, I know exactly what you mean. My brain is wired the same way. I'll speak to my mother in Spanish but think in English and vice versa. B, I had no idea you did all this," I said, genuinely in awe of her.

"See, I'm not your average seventeen-year-old."

"Well that's true, but I think they've found a cure for it in the Amazon recently," I teased.

"Hey, you jerk!" she said and jumped me.

I started tickling her ribs, which made her laugh and squeal. She tried jumping off of me, but I held on to her.

"Okay, okay, stop, stop, you win, you win, let me catch my breath."

I stopped so she could compose herself, but then she dogpiled me again, and we laughed and wrestled on the couch, eventually stopping with B straddling me. She shook out her ponytail, allowing her blond locks to fall into my face, and smiled.

As I gently brushed them aside, she stared deeply into my eyes and she bent forward to kiss me with her full lips.

We lay there a while, kissing and caressing one another. She groaned with pleasure as our tongues did some exploring. Soon, she began to slowly grind herself into me, eliciting a moan as she felt my immediate response.

From there, we went from zero to sixty. As I began caressing her perfect bottom, Belle started growling. It was guttural at first, but quickly transformed into full-blown jumping and barking at the sliding glass door overlooking the back yard.

What now?

B hopped off me, and I turned on our patio lights, "What's the matter, girl?" I asked as I looked out into the back yard and saw nothing. Belle, on the other hand, continued to jump, bark, and scratch at the back door.

"Belle, knock it off! There's nothing out there. Go lie down!" I chastised her. She whimpered and put her tail between her legs as she skulked away toward the laundry room.

Stupid dog! Well, that *killed the mood! Thanks, Belle!*

"Sorry about that. I've no idea what's gotten into her. She probably saw a squirrel or something."

"It's okay. Things were starting to get a little intense."

"I know. I'm sorry about that. I didn't mean for that to happen."

"Oh no, you don't need to apologize, no. I'm just as guilty, trust me." Then she added in a whisper, "Besides, you're a *really* good kisser."

"Thanks, you're a really good kisser too." I inched closer, and we locked eyes once more.

Is that the universe I see in there?

I leaned in and we began to slowly kiss. She began to moan again but then abruptly pulled away.

"*Ohhh* . . . I'm sorry, but I've got to go. It's getting late. Plus, I don't want your mother thinking I'm *that* kind of girl."

I nodded in agreement as I ran a hand through my hair.

"So what're you doing tomorrow?" I asked.

"Well, while we were saying our goodbyes, Mary invited me to join her for a manicure. She has a standing weekly Tuesday afternoon appointment at a local salon. I really want to talk to her about her brother. I hope you don't mind."

"I don't mind at all. You already know what I'm doing tomorrow."

"You should have fun though. Jean Paul and Hannah seem really cool."

"They are. You're going to like getting to know them better."

"I can't wait." She smiled her pearly whites. "Okay, walk me to my car, mister."

As she buckled up, she rolled down her window and gestured to me with her index finger, to come closer.

"Yes?" I asked.

"I want to leave you with a little *something* to remember me, since I probably won't see you tomorrow," she purred.

BOING! I think I just poked a hole in her car!

I inched closer and she pulled me in for a passionate kiss, sticking her tongue practically down my throat.

"I think that'll do the trick," she said as she released me a minute later.

"I miss you already," I replied in a daze, which made her laugh.

"Good, then my work here is done." With that, she backed out, kissing her hand as she did so, and waving as she drove away.

What a great friggin night! I'm really falling hard and fast for this girl. She's not like anyone I've ever met. Who knew she spoke Spanish? And that make-out session, woof! And that last kiss. Wow! Just wow! I can't wait to see her again.

25 - While the Cat's Away

The following day went off without a hitch, even though I didn't get to see B. Jean Paul came over around ten with breakfast in hand, two bagels and two chocolate milks, which surprised me. I guess it was his way of letting me know there were no hard feelings. We spent the morning trimming trees and were done by half past noon.

Hannah showed up and helped us finish bagging branches. She was like that, always willing to lend a hand. It was one of her many awesome qualities. B seemed that way too. Maybe it was a common theme for the girls in my life.

We spent the rest of the day, swimming, eating, and enjoying each other's company. Aunt Mary even came over, making sure to hug and kiss *her favorite twins*, as she called them. Again, they were family.

Ma gave Hannah and Jean Paul each twenty bucks for helping, which they refused at first, until realizing Ma wouldn't take no for an answer. Ma ordered pizza for dinner and invited the twins to stay. We spent part of the evening watching TV and the other part with the twins busting my balls about B.

Yep, all was normal in the world.

Before leaving, Ma invited the twins to join us for dinner the following day as well.

"B is coming, and I'm making steaks," she said.

Their eyes lit up when they heard who was coming over and what Ma planned on serving. I guess they didn't get their fill of busting my shoes, so they immediately agreed.

Ma, you're killing me! Wasn't one day of getting my balls busted enough?

The following morning, Ma took the day off so that she could take my younger brother and me out for our annual torture session—back-to-school shopping. Of course, as a parent today, I don't know who's in more pain, the kids or the parent. Our whining must have been torture for Ma. Anyway, we spent the morning going from Sears, to JC Penney's, and finally ending up at Marshalls.

"Son las mismas cosas," Ma said.

"No, Ma, they're not the same things. A Sears polo shirt isn't the same as a Ralph Lauren polo shirt," I argued.

She merely shrugged and walked away. Even though she was a surgeon, she was still a single parent with one salary. Unlike many of her male counterparts, Ma was not swimming in cash. Not even close.

We were lucky she bought us anything, but we never fully appreciated it back then. We were self-centered, self-absorbed teenagers, not unlike today's variety. We were home by noon, with multiple bags of clothes. Ma still had errands to run so she left us with some instructions.

"Can ju please start the fire by four thirty?" Ma asked before leaving.

"Sure, Ma. I'll take care of it," I replied.

"Gracias, and give Belle agua and empty the dishwasher por favor."

Sarcastically, I replied, "Okay, Ma, anything else?"

Ma immediately nipped my attitude in the bud, "Cuidado con the attitude, y no, there's nothing else."

B called at just after one that afternoon.

"Hey you!" she said cheerily.

"Hey," I grumbled, still in a bad mood from shopping.

"I just got home a few minutes ago and can't wait to see you. Can I come over?" she asked, which immediately improved my mood. I couldn't believe how much I missed seeing her, even though it was just one day.

"Hell yeah, you can come over!"

"Yay, I'll be over in twelve minutes, okay?"

"Excellent! I can't wait. You understand that it's okay if you make it here in fifteen minutes though, right? We don't want you getting into an accident."

"Ha, ha, very funny. Fine, I'll see you in fifteen minutes, better?"

"No, not better! Get over here already! I miss you!" I laughed.

"*Grrrr,* you know I'm going to make you pay for this."

"It's totally worth it."

"I'll remember you said that when I hit you with a dead leg!" she threatened.

"Listen, you're wasting time. Hang up and get over here already."

"I'll see you in a few minutes."

Twelve minutes later, I greeted her in my driveway in a T-shirt and shorts. *How does she do that? To the minute!*

She wore a pair of khaki shorts and a floral print T-shirt. She dropped her purse on the driveway, squealed, and leapt into my arms. It was like we hadn't seen each other in months, instead of a whole day.

We stood on my driveway, kissing for the whole world to see, eventually releasing one another and catching our breath.

"Hi," she whispered with a giggle.

"Hi. I missed you," I whispered.

"I missed you too." She brushed my hair back. "Well, now that we have that out of our systems, don't I owe you a dead leg?"

I feigned ignorance while blocking my legs from her knees. "Uh, I don't know what you're talking about. What's this dead leg thing you're referring to?"

"Uh-huh, just help me with my stuff," she replied, flicking me behind the ear.

As she opened the trunk, a familiar scent hit me, "Mm, are those homemade brownies I smell?" I asked, reaching for a container full of them. She smacked my hand.

"Ah, don't touch. These are for dessert. I had to fight Pappa off yesterday. You can't have any until you've finished dinner *and* helped clean up. Remember, I have a brother too. I know how you men are, wanting us to wait on you hand and foot. I may be forced to do that at my house, but I won't be doing it here, got it, slick?"

"Yes, ma'am, I got it." I salivated as I sniffed the brownie aroma. "They better be worth the wait," I mumbled.

"Is there anything about me that isn't worth the wait?" she whispered and licked my ear.

Whoa! Boing!

I stood there stunned.

"That's what I thought." She winked, grabbed her things and proceeded to walk into the house.

Belle was waiting for us—okay, B—at the front door. As we stepped inside, we were immediately hit by a wall of sound and pounding drums, coming from my brother's drum room. As soon as B stepped in, Belle rolled over. Unfortunately for Belle, B's hands were full.

"Belle, get out of the way," I yelled.

"Oh, be nice. Hi, Miss Belle. Pay no attention to Mr. Grumpy Pants," B said as she walked into the kitchen.

B made room in the fridge for her brownies and then went to the family room, getting on the floor to play with Belle, who groaned happily.

"You've clearly made a friend for life there," I said as B rubbed Belle's tummy while smiling up at me.

"Okay, Miss Belle, I love playing with you, but I going to play with your daddy now."

Belle just rolled over and groaned, as if she understood every word.

"Aww, you'll be okay, Miss Belle." B scratched her behind her ear. "Why don't you go lie down in your special place?"

Belle licked her cheek and then dutifully headed toward the laundry room. *Amazing! Not even Ma can do that, and she's Belle's favorite.*

B stood and didn't realize how close I was when she spun around, accidently bumping into me.

"Oh! I didn't realize you were standing so close," she said taking a step back.

"Not so fast." I snagged her around the waist. "I recall you mentioning something about playing with Belle's daddy?" I purred.

"I did indeed. Where *is* that brother of yours?" she said, tapping her finger on her chin. Then she laughed, "Oh burn!"

"Damn! You're *brutal!*"

"You need to be quicker when you're around me, mister." She jabbed my stomach playfully. "That's not hot air up here," she said pointing to her head. "I'm no dumb blonde."

"*Hmm* . . . dumb blonde, huh? I'd say we have a new nickname, but you probably wouldn't understand it. Oh burn!"

"Oh really? Well, you better be nice to me, mister, or I won't be nice to you. And trust me, you'll like it when I'm *nice*." She licked my earlobe again and slowly sauntered away.

BOING! I think I'm getting lightheaded!

She rendered me speechless.

"No response? I guess you didn't bring your A game today?" she commented over her shoulder.

I caught her around the waist, hugging her from behind. We crash-landed onto the couch, which led to us wrestling a bit before kissing, while my brother's drumbeat provided us a personal soundtrack in the background.

Then for the first time . . . I cupped her breast over her shirt. It wasn't even intentional—it just kind of happened—but she groaned in approval as she straddled me.

There we were, a pair of love-struck, horny teenagers. As we kissed, B bent forward and began nibbling my earlobe. She slowly worked her way down my neck as goosebumps formed all over my body. I groaned in delight as she nibbled, licked, and kissed my neck, using her soft, silky tongue as a guide. I was in heaven.

B groaned as I continued massaging her left breast, kicking up her intensity on my neck. I felt her nipple poking through her shirt and I went from massaging her breast to playing with her nipple. She moaned and slowly returned to my mouth for more tonsil hockey. The more I played with her nipple, the more she moaned.

She soon began pressing her pelvis into mine, and I met her with every thrust.

That was when the drum room door opened. We hadn't noticed that the drumming had stopped.

In a panic, B leapt off of me as my brother walked in, knowing exactly what he'd interrupted. He was no dummy. He just smiled and gave me a thumbs-up behind B's back while walking into the kitchen.

"Sorry, I didn't mean to barge in. I just needed some OJ," he said from the kitchen.

"No need to apologize," B replied.

"Yeah, we were, um, just watching TV," I said, while turning on the TV.

He shook his head, embarrassed by my lame excuse.

Shut up and play along!

"I'll be right back. I'm going to change into my bathing suit." B grabbed her bag off the floor and went to the downstairs bathroom.

After we heard her close the bathroom door, my brother said, "Dude, I'm so sorry. I had no idea she was here and that you guys were . . . you know. She's hot, dude."

"Not a problem. It's my fault. I should have told you. Dude, I have no idea what I stepped in, but damn, this girl's the total package."

"I'm just going to take the orange juice with me, so I don't keep coming out. Just remember, Ma will be home around four, and she mentioned something about Jean Paul and Hannah coming over. And you never know when they'll show up, so be careful."

"Yeah, good point," I replied. And that was how all the brothers in my family were—always looking out for one another.

He went back to his drum room while I waited with anticipation for B, wondering what bikini she would be wearing today.

Please be the white one again! Unless she has a better one!

I heard the bathroom door open and seconds later, B stepped into the family room wearing her T-shirt over a two-tone blue, one-piece swimsuit and flip-flops.

What the—? Where's the bikini?

Apparently I didn't hide the look of disappointment well. "What's with the look?"

"What? I don't have a look. What are you talking about?"

She put her hands on her hips and arched her eyebrow. "Well, I'm waiting."

"It's nothing. I just thought you'd be wearing, you know, another uh . . . bikini, that's all," I sheepishly replied. "I mean you *still* look great, it's just that I'm used to seeing you in a bikini."

"*That's* what's *bothering* you? You're upset because I'm not wearing a *bikini*?" She was incredulous. "You do realize your mother's coming home this afternoon, and I'm trying to make a good impression? Can you imagine what she'd think of me if she walked in and I was wearing my white bikini? She'd toss me out by my hair, and I wouldn't blame her. That would be *very* disrespectful. So, yeah, I chose not to wear my teeny-weeny, white bikini, out of respect for your mother."

She's right. She did the right thing. Still, would it have killed her?

"No, no, you're right. I didn't think about that. I'm sorry, you're right. Forgive me?"

"I don't know," she replied slowly. "What's in it for *me*?"

"Well, what do you want?"

"Oh, *you know* what I *want*," she said with a devilish grin.

Oh my God, yes!

"*Really*, you mean right now, here, *on the couch*?!" I asked, getting all excited.

"*What? No! Not that!* You're a pig! Your brother is home, for goodness sake. What's the matter with you? I was talking about the *dead leg*."

Shit! I thought she forgot about that!

"Oh, *that* again; I thought you forgot about that." I smiled, taking a step toward her.

She wagged a finger at me. "Who said anything about forgetting? I didn't say I forgot. I never forget. I owe you one dead leg, and you *will* pay the piper sooner or later. If I were you, I'd just man up and get it over with. I have no problems doing it in front of your mother," she warned, and I believed her.

I quickly changed the subject. "Oh yeah, that reminds me . . . Ma invited the twins over for dinner tonight too."

"Oh good, maybe I can get Jean Paul to help me." She grinned and stroked her chin like an evil villain, plotting some dastardly scheme.

"Hey, there's no need to get anyone else involved, especially not him. He'd wind up giving me one on my *other* leg. By the time you're both finished, I wouldn't be able to walk right for a solid week."

"Oh now you're just making it sound better," she said with an evil laugh.

I threw my hands in the air. "Okay, okay, fine, you win!"

"Ha! Okay, so where do you want this?"

"How about one of your legs?" I suggested.

"That was quick. Good for you. But no, that's not what I meant. I meant on *you*?"

"Wherever, I don't care. Lady's choice. I can't believe I'm agreeing to do this," I grumbled.

"Remember, the pain won't last, as long as you relax," she coached.

"Yeah, yeah, I know, I know. I have an older brother too. I know what's about to happen. Let's just get this over with," I said, trying to sound relaxed and confident.

I shut my eyes as she stalked me.

I'm an idiot!

"Are you *ready*?"

"Yeah, yeah I'm ready, I'm ready." I tensed in anticipation.

"Are you *sure* you're ready?" she whispered in my ear.

Whoa, I wasn't expecting her to be so close.

"Yeah, I'm ready. Come on, let's get it over with."

Shit, this is going to hurt! Come on, just relax!

I felt her circle me like a lioness circling her prey, trying to decide which leg would become her victim. I briefly opened one eye and watched her as she smiled wickedly and made her decision. It would be my left leg.

She snickered as she came in for the kill.

Okay, here we go! Shit, this is gonna hurt!

Smack!

I yelped immediately as she slapped my ass and started laughing at me.

Oh, holy crap!

My tension immediately ebbed as I felt myself go limp.

She was just screwing with me. I'm a mope, Alice! A mope!

She just stood there, pointing her finger and laughing at me. "I can't believe you actually thought I would hurt you," she laughed. "Seriously, what kind of person do you *take me for*?"

Let's see . . . evil, cruel, wicked . . . I could go on.

"You should have seen your face, all serious and tense. 'Come on, let's get it over with,'" she mimicked. "Mister, you are one funny man. I can't wait to tell Hannah and Jean Paul later!" She then pushed me backward onto the couch and straddled my chest, while pressing her knees onto my arms, holding me down. She then bent forward and tickled my face with her hair.

"So when are they showing up?" she asked as I pretended to struggle.

"I don't know," I answered through clenched teeth.

"You're not getting mad at me now, are you?" She raised her eyebrows then shook her hair in my face some more. "Here, let me give you something to make you feel better," she cooed and started kissing me.

Yep, I definitely feel much better.

She slowly slid off me and rolled me on top of her, wrapping her legs around my lower torso. I immediately took my T-shirt off and tossed it on the floor. As we kissed, she began to rhythmically move her crotch in slow circles, and she pushed herself into me.

I responded immediately, popping a boner. I couldn't help it. Our *nether regions* were saying *hello*. She then started slowly rocking against my boner.

What the fuck is happening? I'm about to lose my mind! If she keeps this up, I swear to God, I'll . . .

She let out soft moans, while working her magic on my lower back with her freshly manicured hands. I spread her legs further, so that I could faux-penetrate her, and she met my every thrust with one of her own.

Dry humping, nibbling, exploring . . . then she placed her lips against mine and began sucking the tip my tongue. I was in heaven, and based on her moans and lustful groans, so was she.

I caressed both of her breasts this time and her nipples responded immediately as they poked through her T-shirt and bathing suit. She arched her back, allowing me better access. I pushed her T-shirt up and began kissing and sucking her breasts through her bathing suit as she closed her eyes and moaned.

The more I caressed, fondled, and sucked, the more she pressed herself into me. I'd never experienced passion like this before. Sure, I'd kissed girls before, felt a boob or two, but never like this. Never with someone I'd truly, um, liked so much.

I was both excited and nervous at the same time. I was a virgin and had no idea what I was doing. Okay, maybe I had some ideas, but not a lot. I didn't want to do anything wrong.

How far are we going to take this?

Unfortunately, I received an immediate answer, as someone began pounding on the front door.

Boom, boom, boom!

Oh C'mon!

26 - They're Here!

We were both startled back to reality. She immediately slid from underneath me as the pounding continued. As we stood, B glanced over at me and then stopped still, her eyes widening.

"What?" I asked.

"I'm so sorry," she giggled and blushed. "I think I gave you a few hickeys," she said while rubbing my neck with her thumb, as if she were trying to erase them.

That's not all you gave me, sister. I need to get rid of this boner before I get to the front door!

"Don't worry about it. I'm sure no one will notice." I adjusted myself as nonchalantly as I could, which sort of worked. I opened the front door and found Hannah standing there, arms crossed, tapping her toe.

"Sorry about that. We couldn't hear you over the pounding," I said, pointing to the drum room. "Where's Jean Paul?"

Before she answered, Belle began barking as Jean Paul entered through the back door.

"Hey, I came around back, just in case you guys were in the pool and couldn't hear us pounding at the front door," he said as he entered and began petting Belle.

"Sorry, bro. Yeah, we couldn't hear you." I gestured toward the drum room.

That was when Hannah inspected my neck and noticed my hickeys. "Mmm hmm," she murmured.

Busted! Oh shut up!

She didn't say a word though. She only raised an eyebrow, then headed to the bathroom to change. Relieved, I turned off the TV, leaving B with Belle while I joined Jean Paul upstairs in my room so he could change.

As we entered my bedroom, Jean Paul jumped on my back the way best friends do. I shoved him off of me and shook my head.

"So, we didn't interrupt anything, did we?" He smirked.

"Let's just say, 'yeah,' and leave it at that." I turned around and grinned.

"*Dude,* you look like a freaking leper!" He pointed at my hickeys and laughed.

"Dude, shut the fuck up. They'll hear you!"

"Let me check those out!"

"Dude, get the hell away from me!"

"Oh come on! Don't be such a baby. I'd show you mine."

"*No!* The last thing I need is you checking out a couple of little hickeys. Grow up."

"Dude, who said there were only a couple and that they were little? Check them out." He pointed at my reflection in my dusty bedroom mirror.

I wiped it off, took off my shirt and began inspecting B's artistry.

Whoa! He's right!

"Damn! How do I hide these from Ma?"

"Does your mom have any makeup in her room?"

"Probably, why do you ask?"

"Why do you think? Let's put some makeup over it. That's what I do whenever I get hickeys. It works like a charm. I never get busted," he boasted.

"Oh, you mean like the ones you got from Jenny last month? And the other ones from that junior girl's counselor . . . Barb, was it?"

"You knew about those?"

"Dude, everyone knew. Do you have any idea how many people I threatened to beat if they laughed at you or said anything? Hey, what are bros for?" I replied, ignoring the fact that he lied about always showing me his hickeys.

He just laughed as I reviewed my love bites. She'd left a pattern from my neck to my chest.

"Yep, I'm screwed!" I sighed.

As we changed into our swim trunks, I noticed an embarrassing white residue in my underwear.

Ugh! I guess I'll be doing my own laundry this week.

We walked across the hall to Ma's room and found her makeup case. We applied foundation over my hickeys and did our best to blend them into my skin. This was the first time I'd worn makeup and, oddly enough, wouldn't be the last. I caught the acting bug in my early twenties, but that's another story for another time.

"Can you still see them?" I asked as he hid his smile. *I hate him!* "Thanks for the support."

I threw my shirt back on in defeat, and we went back downstairs.

"We wondered what was taking you guys so long up there," Hannah said as she grabbed my face and turned my head.

"Oh my God, you two are pathetic." She sighed.

I'm still not sure whom she was referring to: me and her brother, or me and B.

"Sit down and take your shirt off," she commanded.

"Hey, your brother's right there," I said, which earned me a smack.

"Let's see what we can do here. You realize you can't go swimming once I'm done here, right? There's no such thing as waterproof foundation. You're going to have to hang out while we swim, okay?" And then she went to work.

B joined us, giggling out of embarrassment, and mouthed, "I'm so sorry!"

How can I be angry with her? I think I'm falling in love with this girl, and we've only been together a week. Besides, these are her love bites! I will wear them proudly.

I just smiled back and said it was okay. Five minutes later, which felt like an eternity, they stepped back and inspected her work. There were nods of approval and praise for Hannah on a job well done.

I hated the thought of missing out on swimming with my friends, but . . . *if you can't do the time, then don't do the crime!*

"Come on, there's a pool out there waiting for you guys. I'll set up my box. Does anyone need a towel or anything?"

Everyone had brought their own, so I snagged one for myself and we headed for the pool, Belle included. Just before we stepped outside, though, B held me back.

Hannah, Jean Paul, and even Belle, turned around to see what was happening and watched as B turned to talk to me. They decided to leave us alone and went to the pool area.

"What's the matter? Is everything okay?" I asked with concern.

"It's nothing," she said, shaking her head. "Well, it's just that . . ." She shook her head again, then leaned in and embraced me.

Is she trembling?

"Hey, hey, what's the matter? Hey, if it's about these hickeys, it's not a big deal. I consider them my personal battle scars! If I could, I'd turn them into permanent tattoos. Really, I would."

She pulled away, with her eyes turned down. "You're always trying to make me laugh." She then lifted her eyes and met my gaze while holding back tears.

I caressed her cheek. "What's the matter, B?"

"I don't deserve you."

I put my hand under her chin so she couldn't look away. "You're kidding me, right? *You* don't deserve *me?* B, *I'm* the lucky one here. You could have your choice of any guy in the whole universe and you're here with me? I still don't know what I did to deserve you, but I'd do it again in a heartbeat. I'm the luckiest guy in the entire universe," I confessed, which made her smile.

"See, this is why I *care* about you. You're like no one I've ever known. Do you have any idea how special you are?" She paused. "I-I lo—just wanted to apologize for giving you those. I'm a little embarrassed, I guess. I feel so stupid. I hope your mother doesn't notice them and lose respect for me, or worse, hate me."

"First, that's not possible. No one in their right mind could ever hate you. Secondly, I'll handle Ma, okay? Look, let's go enjoy the afternoon." I kissed her forehead.

She tilted her head back and kissed me softly on the lips.

"Better?" I asked.

"Yes, much."

"Good, ready to have fun?"

She nodded.

While I searched for a good mixed tape to play, she joined the twins in the pool. Moments later, we heard the initial bass, drums, and talkbox that Richie Sambora used on Bon Jovi's "Livin' on a Prayer."

On my way to the pool, I noticed a cigarette butt on the patio near the sliding glass door. *Shit, is Ma smoking again? Sigh! I thought she quit for good this time.*

I rolled my eyes, then picked it up and flicked it into the grass.

Instead of jumping into the pool, I grabbed a lounge chair and lay there shirtless, dog by my side, with makeup on my body, as I absorbed the last bit of summer sunshine, while my beloved best friends and my girl splashed around in the pool, enjoying the afternoon.

They took turns checking on me. Hannah stopped by first. "How're you doing, champ?"

"Hey, Hann. I'm doing okay. Hell, I'm doing better than okay." I grinned.

"Oh . . . do tell."

"I think I'm falling for her, Hann. I know it sounds silly, but I really like her," I whispered. "And I think she's falling for me too. She told me she's never met anyone like me before and that she really cares about me. For the first time ever, I'm really looking forward to school."

"Wow, I didn't realize things were getting so real so fast. Just be careful, okay? I won't beat a dead horse, but just take it slow. You may not know this, but the last guy she dated—"

"You mean Kyle Fergusen? Yeah, I know."

"Oh. Well good, I didn't know if she told you. Did she tell you why they broke up?"

"Yeah, she told me," I grumbled.

"Good, because rumor has it, he kept pressuring her to have sex," she said. "The way I hear it, he still holds a torch for her and won't leave her alone. So watch your back."

"Yeah, yeah."

"I'm just saying. So if you take it slow, you *will* have a great year, Mr. Hickey!" she teased and squeezed my hand affectionately.

"Yeah, yeah," I said again. "Thanks, Hann."

B came next. I had my eyes closed when I felt water dripping on my face, followed by giggles. I opened one eye, and saw B standing over me, dripping her wet hair onto my face.

"Nice," I said as she continued to giggle.

"Aww, I'm sorry." She wiped my face. "Is that better?"

"Almost," I replied and grabbed her wet body and started tickling her. She wiggled around like a fish, screaming and laughing.

"Okay, stop, you win, you win!" she screamed, so I stopped, victorious. "Oh, you're so mean," she said as she settled into my lap, putting her arms around my neck

"That's right, and don't forget it. They don't call me the Grinch for nothing."

"I think we finally have a nickname that fits."

"Oh really, you really think so? And how about now . . . still?" I asked as I restarted the tickles. She squirmed and screamed with delight.

"Okay, okay, you're not the Grinch . . . okay, you win, you *win*!" she squealed.

"So what am I then?" I asked, not letting up.

"You're . . . you're . . . ha, ha, ha . . . you're *awesome*! You're awesome!"

I let up. "That's right, I'm awesome. Hey, I forgot to ask you about yesterday with Mary. How did it go?"

"It went okay. I talked to her about it and asked her to talk to her brother. She said she would, but you never know with Mary. She has great intentions sometimes, but isn't very dependable," she explained.

"So what do you want to do?"

"Let's just leave it alone for now and see if she'll talk to him. If she doesn't, then I will. If that doesn't work, then you can talk to him," she said. "But just talk."

"Yeah, yeah. Let's hope Mary takes care of it, because if she doesn't, I will."

"Okay, Mister Awesome, enough about them. I'm going to lie down for a few minutes. Give me a kiss so I can relax in peace," she said, followed by a sweet kiss.

Minutes later, Jean Paul came over.

"Yo! You just going to sit there all day?" he teased.

"That's the plan, unless you can think of a better idea."

"How about you put your big-boy panties on and join us in the pool?" he challenged. "Dude, nobody cares about a couple of hickeys. I'll just tell your mom I gave them to you by accident, while we were screwing around in the pool."

You know what . . . that's actually not a bad idea.

"You'll take the heat?"

"Well, not all of the heat. I'll say you started it and I finished it."

"What are you guys talking about?" Hannah yelled from the pool, while B leaned up on her elbow to listen, so I explained our new plan.

"You think it'll work?" Hannah asked.

"Of course it'll work! I thought it up!" Jean Paul bragged.

"That's why I'm asking," Hannah replied, bursting his bubble.

"Hey!!" he replied and jumped into the pool after her. B followed, trying to defend Hannah. I just shrugged and threw caution to the wind, diving in after B.

Who else is going to protect my brother from another mother?

27 - Dinnertime

*G*entlemen, it's time to rev your engines. Game on!
It was guys versus girls. It didn't matter that the girl I was falling for was on the opposite side. This was a battle, and our side wouldn't lose—especially with my home-field advantage. Forget about tennis and bowling. we're talking about my own pool, where I was the master.

Let the games begin, ladies.

Jean Paul and I put our heads together for a brief strategy session as the girls watched from the deep end. We chose our individual opponents, devised our winning plan, and now were prepared to put it into action. It was go time! Even the girls knew they were in trouble the moment we went into action.

I dove toward them from the shallow end, while Jean Paul hopped out of the pool to cut off their retreat. We took everything into account. Everything except the number one safety rule for every pool owner. It was like a neon sign flashing in my head the moment it happened.

No running around the pool.

Jean Paul took three steps then immediately took a spill on the concrete as he was running toward the diving board to cut the ladies off. We all gasped as he fell.

Shit!

We all immediately jumped out of the pool to go to his aid. There was a huge skin burn along his thigh. He writhed in pain as we did our best to fix him up. Between B's first-aid training from lifeguarding and mine from camp, we were able to take care of him.

We bandaged his leg, gave him some Tylenol for the pain, and spent the rest of the afternoon playing board games and watching TV. Swimming was officially off the table.

Ma showed up as *General Hospital* was ending. Can you guess who wanted to watch it? Yep, Jean Paul. It was his favorite soap and something he secretly taped daily. Looks like the secret's out now—oops.

The moment Ma saw Jean Paul, she asked what happened and immediately switched from mom mode to doctor mode. She had him sit back on the couch and examined his wound. While she took care of him, Hannah, B, and I grabbed the groceries from Ma's car. She bought enough to feed an army. We put everything away, except for the steaks, which B placed on a plate. After Ma finished examining Jean Paul, she went upstairs to change and asked me to join her in her room.

Crap, what did I do now?

"I'll be right back. I'll meet you guys outside in a minute," I told my friends.

I felt like a dead man walking as I followed Ma to her room, shutting the door behind me.

"What did I do?"

"Nada, mijo, nada. I just wanted to tell ju that ju did a good job with Jean Paul, that's all."

A weight immediately lifted from my shoulders.

Oh, thank God!

"Thanks, Ma. If there's nothing else, I'm going to head back down."

As I turned to leave, she said, "Oh, by the way . . ."

"Yeah?"

"Nice love bites on jur neck," she said through her giggles as she entered her bathroom, closing the door behind her.

My cheeks were immediately ablaze.

Sigh! I hate my life.

I just shook my head, went back downstairs, and met everyone outside, where I was bombarded with a million questions at once.

"So what did she want?" Jean Paul asked.

"Did you get in trouble?" Hannah asked.

"Is everything okay? Do we need to leave?" B asked.

I just held up my hands. "Whoa. Everything's fine. No one's in trouble. She wanted to tell me we all did a really good job tending to the injury, that's all." Of course, I kept the hickey comment to myself.

Ma came down and put a bunch of sirloins on the grill. B and Hann joined her at the barbecue, while Jean Paul and I sat at one of the picnic tables. At one point, B turned and pointed at me, laughing.

Ma, I swear to God, I will kill you!

"So did your mom say anything *else* while you were up there?" Jean Paul whispered.

I made sure the coast was clear before responding. "Oh yeah, she totally busted my balls about the hickeys . . . in her own special way. I was escaping, and she shot one across my bow," I said, mimicking a gunshot, and Jean Paul started cracking up. "Don't you dare say anything to B. It'll embarrass her."

Of course, this didn't stop him from teasing me during dinner. At one point, he wiped my neck, saying that it looked like I got barbecue sauce on it or something.

"Oh my bad, that's not sauce," he joked as everyone laughed.

Aside from Mister Laughs, dinner was a complete success, including B's homemade double-chocolate brownies. We devoured them. B insisted that Ma relax, which she appreciated, so she sat and watched *Wheel of Fortune* as we cleaned up.

"So what do you guys want to do?" I asked after we finished.

"Would you hate me if I said I wanted to head home?" Hannah asked.

"No, not at all. We can load your bikes into Ma's car and drive you guys home."

"Are you sure? I've had such a great day, and dinner was excellent. I can't tell you the last time we ate like this." She patted her stomach, and the others nodded in agreement.

As we loaded up the bikes, B and I made plans to hang out some more, after dropping the twins at their house.

"Do you need to ask your parents first?"

"If I do, they'll tell me it's late and to come inside, so let's just drop my car off and head out, okay?"

B, a rebel without a cause. I like it.

So we agreed to drop off her car at her house, then go hang out somewhere in Ma's Caddy.

After the obligatory goodbyes and thank-yous for dinner, we hopped into Ma's Caddy, Jean Paul riding shotgun, of course, with Hannah in the back.

We followed B to her house and dropped her car off, before heading to the twin's house.

Once there, Hannah and I took the bikes out of the trunk and walked them up the driveway, since Jean Paul was still nursing his leg.

I said to him, "Hey, if your parents freak out about your leg, have them call my mom, okay?"

"Will do." he said, then added, "Hey, don't do anything I wouldn't do tonight." He waggled his eyebrows.

"Well, *that* doesn't leave much." I whispered.

28 - Love and the Sand Fleas

In the Michaels' driveway, we debating what to do next. She had her T-shirt and shorts over her swimsuit, and I was still in mine, which gave me an idea: West Meadow Beach. She enthusiastically agreed, and off we went.

The beach closed after sunset, but back in the '80s, West Meadow didn't have a gate, so I drove right in and parked in a secluded spot. All we had to worry about were nosy locals, the local authorities, who never patrolled the beach anyway, or people out for late-night frolicking and swimming, like us.

We grabbed her beach bag, found a spot on the sand, and stripped down to our swimsuits. We were alone, holding hands as we walked to the water.

"I've never done this before, have you?" she asked.

To be frank, I hadn't. It's something my older brother used to do, but I'd never had the opportunity until now. "Nope. Neither have I."

B spun into my arms and placed her arms around my neck as we stepped into the water, and shared a tender kiss. It was a perfect summer evening. The moon and stars reflected off the water as it splashed onto the beach. We stood there kissing and gazing deeply into each other's eyes.

"Do you want to go into the water or head back to the towel?" I nervously asked.

She smiled, took my hand, and walked us into the water. I don't know who splashed first, but we were soon playfully splashing each other, back and forth. I dove under and came up right next to her. She wrapped her arms around my neck, and I wrapped mine around her waist. I pulled her close and we began kissing, or at least tried to kiss. Regardless of what you see in the movies, it's not very easy.

We tried wading and kissing, me floating on my back, her wrapping her legs around my torso, side-by-side swimming . . . nothing worked. We just laughed and gave up, then walked back to our spot on the sand. We only had the one towel, so we shared it, semi-drying ourselves off.

I now had her natural scent all over me and loved it. I then placed the towel back on the sand, so we could lie on it. We lay there, focused only on each other, and whispered sweet nothings, as the saying goes. Her eyes seemed to sparkle in the reflection of the stars and moon. I gently pushed her hair from her face, while she caressed my chest and side. We huddled closer together and kissed.

She placed one leg over mine, interweaving our bodies, and I was in heaven.

That was when the real fun started.

I gently smacked my leg.

She followed this up by gently smacking her arm.

Smack . . . smack . . . smack.

We were kissing, while swatting at our own bodies at the same time.

What the—

It didn't take long to realize what was happening.

Sand Fleas! Son of a bitch! The movies lied. This isn't romantic at all. This sucks!

"Uh, B, I think it's time to go," I said, still swatting at my limbs.

"Yeah, I think so too!" she replied as we both stood and shook off the towel.

We gathered our things, went back to Ma's car, and placed it all in the trunk, just in case the sand fleas decided to hitch a ride.

"Well, *that* was an adventure," I joked as I shut the door.

"Yeah, *that's* what I'd call it," she laughed.

"I'm sorry. If I knew we'd be dealing with sand fleas, I'd have come up with a different plan."

She smiled and softly stroked my cheek. "Don't be silly, it's okay. Neither of us had any idea. It certainly isn't something that a little Benadryl cream can't fix." She scooted closer.

That was the great thing about Ma's Caddy: no bucket seats.

"Man, how is it that you're still beautiful even with bug bites? They clearly have great taste," I teased as I pulled her close and kissed her.

She parted her lips and slowly slipped the tip of her tongue into my mouth. I gently caressed her wet hair as she sucked on the tip of my tongue, something that drove me crazy. I moaned with pleasure, which elicited a smile out of her.

We soon got comfortable in the front seat. She pushed me back and lay on top of me. She then sat up and threw her wet T-shirt into the back seat. I followed her lead and did the same. She bent back down and sucked on my lower lip, working her way slowly from my lip to my earlobe. Her lips were so full and soft. As she lay on me, I caressed her back, from her tanned shoulders down to her perfect backside, cupping, stroking, cupping, stroking.

She responded with a moan and continued attacking my earlobe and neck. Soon she began rocking her pelvis into me, grinding deeply so she could feel my now very swollen member in her most sacred area.

I was losing my mind. I caressed her breasts and protruding nipples, tweaking them softly. We were both completely lost in the moment. The more I played with her nipples, the deeper she pressed herself into me.

I soon felt a familiar pressure building within me.

Oh crap, not now! Please don't do it!

I was about to explode, so I sat up quickly.

"What's the matter?" she asked, slightly out of breath.

"Nothing, nothing, I, uh, thought we'd slow it down for a minute." I brushed her hair from her face.

"Oh, okay, but wow. That was awesome! Where'd you learn how to do that?" she asked.

Do what? What did I do?

"Uh, watching a lot of movies?" I replied, followed by a wince.

Did you just really say that? You couldn't have said, "It just comes naturally to me?" You're an idiot!

"Oh? Well, you learned really well." She giggled and gave me a weird look as she began inching closer again.

Smooth move, Ex-Lax! Okay, round two! Try not to explode into your pants, okay, Chief?

Moments later, we're at it again. This time with me on top of her, kissing, fondling, groping. I then looked into her blue eyes and wrapped my fingers around the strap of her bathing suit top. She smiled and nodded slightly, inviting me to go further.

Holy crap, I'm finally going to meet her glorious breasts, in person. She's actually arching her back, inviting me to enjoy myself!

Thank you, God!

That was when we heard . . .

Tap, tap, tap!

Followed by a flashlight shining into the car window.

Noooooo! Are you friggin kidding me? Can't you give me twenty minutes? Seriously, God, do you really hate me that much?

We immediately sat up—sixty to zero this time—and grabbed and threw on our T-shirts from the back seat.

I then rolled down the window. "Evening, officer, can I help you?"

"Did you kids know it's after hours here at the beach?"

"Oh, is it? I hadn't noticed." I replied, imploring for mercy with my eyes.

"You're not allowed to be here after the beach closes. I'll let you off with a warning this time, but if I catch you here again, I'll be forced to give you a ticket. You need to vacate the premises immediately."

I gave him the "yes sir, thank you sir" routine, trying my best not to look completely disappointed. But I was.

Damn, so close!

After the officer left, I turned to B, dejected, and said, "I'm so sorry. Had I known we'd be dealing with sand fleas *and* the cops, I wouldn't have come here."

But she placed her hand on my cheek and laughed, "Oh, sweetie, it's okay. Don't feel bad. Look at it as an *interesting adventure* we can tell people one day."

She then smiled that sensational smile. "Think about it, we came to the beach after hours, swam at night, made out on the beach, were attacked by sand fleas, and then were asked to leave by the police! That, *my friend*, is an interesting adventure!"

I had to admit . . . she had a point.

She continued, "How many of our friends could lay claim to any part of that story? We're true adventurers, ready to take on the world!" She raised her fist in victory, laughing.

Goddamn it, she's right! Hell, not even my older brother could tell this story, and he's done it all. Look at me, setting a new standard! I love this girl— WHOA, what was that? Did I really just think that? Do I really love this girl?

I looked at her as she laughed. Really looked at her for a moment.

Last Exit to Montauk 191

Holy crap, I think I just might. Does she feel the same way? It's way too soon, right? It's all the excitement of the evening. Yeah, that's what it is. I just really like her, that's all.

Man, she sure does look great though. And oh, can she kiss! I can't believe I almost got to see her topless! Goddamn cop! You couldn't have given me another twenty minutes? What an asshole!

Then I realized B was asking me a question. "Huh?" I said.

"Don't you agree?" B asked, then playfully shoved my shoulder. "Hello, Earth calling! Are you still with me?"

"What? Yep, yep, I'm here. Yes, you're totally right! You're definitely right!" I grabbed her hand and said, "B, I love the way you turn the negatives into positives," I said.

As we left the beach, we snuggled up and listened to Bryan Adams singing about his younger years, when he was young and wild and free.

29 - Breakfast and a Funeral

"Are you working tomorrow?" I asked as we pulled into B's driveway. "No, I'm not on the schedule tomorrow, why? What do you feel like doing?"

You! It'll be the same answer every single time, folks.

"Do you want to go to Smith Point? I'll drive," I suggested. "We can stop at a deli on the way out and pick stuff up too. I have an Igloo in my garage that we used for baseball. I can ask the twins to join us, and you can call some friends too. We'll make a day of it. What do you think?"

"I think that's a great idea. I'll have to ask my parents, but I don't see them objecting, especially if we have a bunch of people going. I'll call you in the morning at eight o'clock and let you know. If they say yes, it will give us plenty of time to invite others to join us. And if they say no, we'll go out for breakfast or something, spend the day together regardless. Does that sound okay?"

Darlin', you can call me at three o'clock in the morning, and I wouldn't complain!

"Yeah, that sounds like a great idea," I said, leaning in and getting a quick kiss.

I walked her to her door, and she began to give me a passionate kiss goodnight, which I stopped. "We wouldn't want your parents to come out here and kill me."

She giggled and said, "Yeah, you're right. Well, thanks again for such a wonderful day, mister!" Then she whispered in my ear, "I had the best night ever."

Commence melting . . .

"I'll call you tomorrow morning, so no staying up late watching *Star Trek.*" She gave me the Vulcan hand salute.

"Yeah, yeah, no *Star Trek* tonight. It's probably a rerun anyway," I said.

"Aren't they all reruns?" she asked.

"Yeah, good point. You know what I meant. I'll talk to you tomorrow morning." I returned the Vulcan hand salute and smiled at her as she stood behind her screened door.

I started walking to my car when I turned around. "B?"

"Yeah?"

"I just wanted to tell you, um, I really did have a good day today."

She knew exactly what I was telling her, without saying the words. "Me too," she whispered with the same intent.

I smiled and floated back to the Caddy and drove home.

"Hey, Ma," I said as I dropped her keys into her purse and kissed her on the cheek. "We're all thinking of going to Smith Point tomorrow; is that okay?"

"Con quien vas?"

"Me, B, Jean Paul, Hannah and some of B's friends. I won't get home too late."

She smiled as she sat there watching her "bums" play the Royals. "Sí, that's fine. Ju really like this girl, huh?"

I felt awkward, not really wanting to tell her how I was feeling—still trying to understand it myself—so, like a typical teenager, I tried avoiding her question with one of my own. "What do you mean?"

"What do ju mean—*what do I mean?* I may speak with an accent, but ju definitely understood the question, pendejo!"

Sigh.

"I don't know, Ma. I mean, I guess so."

"Well, good. I like her. She's very pretty and extremely polite and respectful, not like some of the girls jur older brother used to bring home at jur age. Some of those girls were estúpida."

I agreed and we laughed.

"Oh, and thank you for not saying anything about the, you know . . ." I said, pointing to my hickeys.

"What do ju think, soy bruta o algo niño? Did ju really think I would say something?" She waved her hand at me dismissively. "Mijo, this is not my first time dealing con los hickeys. One verano, I thought tu hermano caught the plague. Plus, I was young once too, ju know."

"Oh my God, Ma, okay, please stop!"

"What? I was a teenager once too, ju know. Anyway, I just want ju to know that jur mother is not estúpida. I wasn't going to embarrass that nice girl . . . it was her, sí?"

Sigh!

"Yes, Ma, it was her. So he really came home one summer . . ."

"Hijo, ju know I love the three of ju, pero that hermano tuyo almost put me in an early grave one summer with todas las chicas he dated." She laughed and shook her head. "The good news is he prepared me for ju y tu hermanito."

The next morning, B called at eight on the dot.

"How did you sleep?" she asked.

"Great, I dreamt about you all night." Which was pretty much fact.

"Oh *really,* and what did you dream about?" she whispered.

God, I love her voice!

"Oh, not much; just your beautiful smile and perfect lips, that's all."

"That's so sweet," she cooed. "Okay, so I talked to my parents. They weren't too happy that I dropped the car off last night and left without saying anything, but I talked them off the ledge."

"What'd you tell them?"

"I told them the truth, sort of. I explained what happened to Jean Paul and how we had to pack their bikes in your mom's car and drive them home. Since we were driving near my house, we decided to drop my car off and head to the Michaels house and hang out for a while."

So you basically just lied to your parents. I just hope it doesn't come back and bite you on that perfect ass.

"And they believed you?" I asked.

"Oh yeah, I'm the *good* daughter, remember?" She giggled.

"Uh-huh."

"Anyway, I asked about Smith Point, explaining a group of us would be going, and they said fine. What'd your mom say?"

"She gave me the green light too. Why don't you call a few of your friends, and I'll call the twins? I can pick you up in about an hour. Is that enough time? I asked.

"It should be, but with some people you never know. Regardless, be here at nine, and if the others aren't ready yet, we can finish coordinating from here, okay?" she suggested.

"Perfect. I'll see you at nine," I said as I blew her a kiss into the phone, which she reciprocated, before we hung up.

I dialed the twins, talked to Hannah, and made plans to pick them up at around nine thirty. Then I rinsed out the cooler, pulled together a beach bag of stuff, then stopped at the deli for ice and sodas. I figured we'd pick up lunch at the beach. I also grabbed a couple of bagels and coffees for me and B.

When I got to B's door, holding the bag and the two coffees, she giggled and pointed at the food.

Confused, I asked, "What's up?"

She replied by holding up a paper bag and two coffees from a local deli. "I went to the deli and did the same thing."

Great minds really do think alike.

We walked up to her kitchen, and she told me that she'd called a few friends, including Mary, who all agreed to go. Once in the kitchen, she turned and growled at me, making one of the cutest scowling faces I'd ever seen.

"Didn't you forget something?" she asked.

I was lost on this one, "Uh, no?"

She then puckered her pretty lips.

I laughed. "Oh yeah, I did. Sorry about that, Chief," I replied with my best Maxwell Smart impersonation.

After kissing her, I asked, "There, better?" She then planted three quick smooches on my kisser.

"Yes, that's much better. Don't let it happen again." She giggled and headed to the cabinet for some paper plates.

"We're picking the twins up at nine thirty, so it looks like we'll have a little time to eat."

We dug into our sausage, egg and cheese breakfast sandwiches, and decided to save the bagels and extra coffees for the twins.

"So, where're your folks? I asked.

"Pappa's at work and Mamma is out running errands . . . *why?*"

I thought I heard suspicion in her tone, so I quickly said, "Oh, no, no. I don't mean for that reason. I was just making conversation. So, what does your dad do for a living?"

She went on to tell me that he worked for the local lighting company, LILCO, as an engineer, while her mother was a stay-at-home mom.

"So, can I ask you a question?" Her tone was cautious.

Instinctively, I knew where this was going, based on the topic of conversation.

She wants to know about Pop.

I swallowed my bite and said, "You want to know about my dad, right?"

She nodded, "Unless it's too painful." Then she reached across the table and squeezed my hand.

"It's okay, B. I can talk about it. It happened when I was eleven. My older brother was fifteen, and my younger brother was about seven. It seems like forever ago, you know? My younger brother and I were home alone. Ma was pulling into the driveway from picking up my older brother from something, I can't remember what." I paused, thinking.

"I remember looking out the dining room window in the front of the house, as a police car pulled up behind Ma in the driveway. Two officers stepped out and walked up to Ma. As they began talking to her, Aunt Mary crossed the street and held Ma as she received the bad news. I still had no idea what Aunt Mary was doing out there, at that very moment when the officers arrived. Maybe it was a God thing, who knows? Anyway, Ma immediately collapsed into Aunt Mary's arms as my older brother began pointing and screaming at the officers."

"Oh my God," B whispered, putting her hand to her mouth.

I nodded and continued. "My younger brother and I ran out front, and then my brother yelled for us to stay inside, so I grabbed my younger brother and hightailed it back inside to the family room, sitting there wondering what the heck was going on.

"The officers came inside, one with his arm around my older brother, patting his shoulder. They introduced themselves and then the one asked my older brother for permission to speak with us. He could only nod. He was still in shock.

"I remember one had a brown mustache while the other was clean shaven with salt-and-pepper hair. It's strange; I always remember that for some reason. Anyway, the one with the mustache knelt down and explained that our father had passed away at his office. He said, 'Your father was busy working at his desk, when he suddenly died.' It hit me like a ton of bricks. I just stood there and cried."

As I got deeper into the story, B's eyes were filling with tears, so I reached across the table and caressed her face.

"My older brother wrapped his arms around us, and we just stood there hugging and crying," I said, pausing to suck in some air.

I guess it still affects me.

B wiped a tear from her eyes and then pulled her seat next to mine. She kissed my cheek and held both my hands, realizing the impact this retelling was having on me.

In a quieter tone, I continued, "Eventually Ma came in and asked if we understood what happened. From there, my memory's a little fuzzy. I think Ma and Aunt Mary's husband, Uncle Stu, went to the morgue to identify the body, leaving my older brother in charge for the first time. Days later, we held the funeral and all sorts of people spoke, some from his office and some from various clubs he belonged to. I remember going up to his open casket and feeling his head. It was ice cold and didn't feel real. It felt like, I don't know, rubber or plastic. That's really weird, right?"

I didn't wait for her to respond. I just kept on talking. "I remember kissing his forehead and saying a prayer for him, because that's what everyone else was doing. I remember sitting there watching random people touch his chest and finding it offensive, but I never said anything. What I wanted to say was, *Stop touching him, get off my father!* Instead I just sat there and cried.

"It was the longest day of my life. Teachers from school paid their respects as well. It was the first time I met Hannah and Jean Paul's folks actually. The twins stayed home. We buried him out east at Calverton Cemetery since he was a veteran. It was the first time I'd ridden in a limousine. They gave him a 21-gun salute, gave Ma a folded American flag, and then laid him to rest," I whispered as a tear broke loose and rolled down my cheek.

"I am so sorry for your loss. I had no idea," B said as she held and rocked me. "Just let it out. I'm right here."

Just then, her mom came home and found us in the kitchen. "Oh my God, is everything okay?"

B just nodded and whispered to her mom that she'd explain it later. Her mother placed her bags on the kitchen counter, then scuttled out of the kitchen, as B handed me a tissue. I wiped my eyes and nose then blew out a sigh.

"I'm sorry I broke down. I thought I was over it. I guess I'm not." My lips quivered and I bit at them to hold them still. B stayed close, comforting me. Her actions said it all. She truly cared about me. She was an awesome human being, and I was truly falling in love with her.

"Can I get you anything?" B asked.

"No, I'm okay, really. It's just . . . more emotional than I anticipated, I guess. Please go tell your mom I'm okay. You can tell her that Gabriel bit me in the balls, if you want."

She laughed and kissed me on the forehead. "Oh my gosh, you're one sick puppy."

30 - Katie and Iris

B soon returned with her mother in tow. Out of respect, I stood when she entered the room.

She held my hands as she spoke, which I found strangely warm and comforting.

"I am so very sorry for your loss. I, too, lost my father at a young age. It's never easy, but you will eventually learn to live with it."

She then did something I never expected. She *hugged* me. She actually *hugged* me. I was speechless, and by the look of shock on B's face, she was too.

"Uh, thank you, ma'am," was all I could think to say.

She released me, swiping her hands down her skirt—a nervous habit maybe—and said, "Yes, well, B, you said something about going to the beach with your friends. You know how important it is to be on time."

So that's where she gets it from.

"Now off you go then. Have a lovely day," her mom said as she scooted us along. We thanked her, grabbed the food and B's beach bag, and left.

"I'm sorry about Mamma. She's *never* done that before. She's not a hugger, if you know what I mean," B explained.

"I actually thought it was very sweet," I replied as we backed out of the driveway, which made her smile.

We sat at a light, and B snuggled up against me, gently rubbing my chest as I placed my arm around her.

How'd I get this lucky?

We stayed like that all the way to the Michaels house, where we found Jean Paul waiting for us in their driveway, ready to go.

He'd changed his bandages, but otherwise looked fine. "Yo, skillet, what's up?" he greeted.

"Yo, we come bearing gifts." I held up their bagels and coffee.

"Dude, I'm starving! You're awesome!"

Hannah joined us and grabbed her coffee and bagel. "Mm, thank you."

"So what's the plan? We really don't have a lot of room in my car. Who else is coming and who else is driving?" I asked B.

"Well, Mary's coming, as well as my friends Katie and Iris from my youth group. They said they'd drive. Do you think we could squeeze Mary into our car?"

Sure, I think we have room in the trunk.

"Sure, we could probably squeeze her in, right, guys?" I forced a smile at the twins. Hannah and Jean Paul forced a smile back as they nodded.

I mouthed a thanks to them.

After loading the trunk, Jean Paul grabbed shotgun, "Uh-uh," I said through the driver's side window.

"What do you *mean*, uh-uh?" he asked, all insulted.

"B's riding shotgun."

"But I *always* ride shotgun. I'm your wingman and you're my wingman. It's how we always do it." He shook his head like I'd lost my mind.

B intervened. "It's okay, really. I'll sit in the back with Mary and Hannah. Jean Paul, you're his wingman and he's yours. Take the front seat, please. I insist."

Jean Paul snorted at me. "See? She's fine with it. C'mon, let's get going."

I shot him a dirty look and growled as he ignored me.

B then pulled me aside, "Look, we're are going to spend all day together at the beach. I even packed your favorite white bikini, the one with the tassels, so play nice, okay?"

I do love that white bikini! Damnit, how did she know it's my favorite? The Force is strong in this one!

"Okay, I'll play nice. I'm still allowed to make fun of him though, right?" I threw a thumb in Jean Paul's direction.

"Oh, that's to be expected. I'd never deprive you of that," she said, kissing me softly before sliding into the back seat with Hannah. "There'll be more of that later, if you're good."

"Oh, I'll be good," I assured her. "Okay, Sulu, where are we heading?"

B gave me directions to the Fergusen house in Old Field, an exclusive community in Setauket, New York.

I pulled up to a mini-mansion. Apparently, Mr. Fergusen was some mega-wealthy investment banker on Wall Street. Supposedly, when he wasn't working, he and his current wife went to their condo in the Bahamas.

I started to understand why Mary spent the shit out of his money. She was waiting for us in their long circular driveway with two large beach bags packed to the gills.

Jean Paul made a face. "Jesus Christ, *two* friggin bags? We're just going for the day— Ow!" I jabbed him in the ribs, "What the hell, dude?"

"Hey, bitches!" Mary greeted as we stepped out of my car.

"That's an awful lot of stuff, don't you think?" B replied after their air kiss.

"Bitch, please . . . you know I need all my stuff when I go to the beach. We never know who we'll run into, and I always need to look my best." She then gave my old crap-mobile the once-over. "So we're going in *this* car, huh?"

Be nice, be nice, be . . . nice!

"Yep, we sure are," I said, using the most pleasant tone I could muster. "You ready to go?"

"Yeah, I guess," she replied and then turned to B, "Do you want me to drive my car?"

Oh, please drive your car and never come back, pretty please.

"Oh, stop it. Let's put your things in the trunk and get going," B said.

Mary stomped her foot like a three-year-old. "Fine," she pouted, leaving me to load her bags in the trunk.

No, let me get those for you, Princess Grace-less. Jesus, what the hell did she pack . . .

My car dipped a little as I put her things in my trunk. Hannah was squeezed in between B and Mary.

Looks like my Hannah tab just took another hit. I wonder how much I owe her now. I may have to buy her a car soon.

I climbed in and gave Hannah the *I'm sorry* look in the review mirror, and she just nodded.

"So where are we heading next?" I asked, and B gave me directions to our next stop, the S section part of Stony Brook. It's named that because every street started with the letter S, like Sycamore. That was where I met B's friends, Iris Robertson and Katie Larsen, for the first time.

"Oh, *they're* coming too?" Mary whined. "They're never any fun. You know they're not going to let me drink."

"Oh stop it," B said. "You can do whatever you want, just don't get caught, okay? And if you do, please don't cause a scene."

"Yeah, yeah, fine, I won't cause a scene or get anyone in trouble." She responded like a toddler in need of a spanking.

"I need to hear you say you promise," B said.

"What? Okay, I promise already. I'm not an infant."

Says you.

About ten minutes later, I pulled into Iris's driveway to find both girls waiting for us. B and I hopped out of the car, and she ran over squealing and hugging her girlfriends. They spoke rapidly, saying how excited they were. B then introduced me as her *boyfriend.*

Yes! It's official! I'm her boyfriend!!

"Who's *that*?" Iris asked, referring to my wingman sitting shotgun.

Oh no, here we go. Like his ego isn't already out of whack.

"Oh that's B's friend Mary. I thought you knew each other." I joked as both their faces turned sour.

"Yeah, we know who *she* is. No, I'm talking about the guy in the front seat? Who's *that*?" Iris asked again, and B giggled the way teenage girls do.

"Oh, him," I said. "He's my *gay* friend, Jean P— *Ow!*" B had delivered a nice elbow jab to my ribs.

With her hands on her hips, she said to Iris, "Ignore him, he's not *gay!* He's straight and also *his* best friend. His name is Jean Paul. The other girl is his twin sister Hannah. They're really nice. You'll like them."

"Jean Paul . . . are they French?" Katie asked in a faux French accent.

"No, he's just a jackass— *Ow!*" Another shot to the ribs.

Shit, I think that one left a mark.

"I mean, no, they're American. Their parents teach at our school. They're biblical names: Jean Paul translates to John and Paul, from the New Testament, and Hannah is from the Old Testament," I explained as they nodded. They were youth group kids, so they understood the references.

"So are you guys all packed up?" B asked.

"Yep, we're all set," Iris replied, patting her car's trunk. She drove a metallic blue Toyota Celica.

"Cool. Hey, would you guys mind taking Jean Paul with you? We're kind of cramped in my car. You'd really be doing me a huge favor," I said as both girls smiled and nodded.

"Great, thanks." I motioned at Jean Paul, and he got out and limped over.

"Oh, what happened?" they asked in unison when they saw him shuffle over.

"What, this? Oh, this is nothing. It's just a scratch."

Unbelievable! And the Oscar goes to . . .

"Jean Paul, this is Iris and Katie. Katie and Iris, this is Jean Paul Michaels," B said. Jean Paul just smiled his hundred-watt smile, which made them giggle.

Oh, brother.

"Hey, bro," I said, "I was wondering if you would help a brother out?"

"Sure, what do you need?" he asked.

"Since the Batmobile is a bit cramped, would you mind grabbing a ride with Iris and Katie? If we separate, we'll just meet up with you guys at the restrooms, cool?"

The girls continued to nod and smile as Jean Paul looked at me, then the girls, then back at me. This time he was smiling as well. "Sure, I'd love to go with Iris and, uh . . ."

"Katie," I said, helping him out.

"Right, Katie. Yeah, I'd love to ride with them to the beach, as long as they don't mind."

"No, we don't mind at all," Iris said as they each took one of his arms and helped him to their car. He just looked over his shoulder—the cat who ate the canary.

You owe me!

"Oh, it's okay, ladies. I'll be . . . *ow* . . . fine, really," I overheard him say.

Sweet Lord, we're never going to hear the end of this. Who cares, I've got B!

And she called me her boyfriend!

31 - Smith Point

"Did that really just happen?" Hannah asked as B rode shotgun.

"Do *you* really need to ask?" I replied and laughed along with B and Hannah. Mary, not wanting to be left out of the joke, joined in late.

I started the car, turned the radio to *WBAB,* and off to the beach we went.

"Do we really have to listen to this garbage the whole way there?" Mary asked as Paul Simon sung about stepping outside to smoke himself a J.

I felt B take my hand and squeeze it as I took a deep breath, "No, Mary, what would you like to listen to?"

"Here, put this on," she said, handing me a tape. Moments later, we heard a hard guitar riff as Kirk Hammett ripped into Metallica's iconic "Master of Puppets."

Back then, I wasn't as open to different styles of music as I am now. I let three or four riffs go by before ejecting the cassette.

Okay, before you call me a pussy, or say, "Dude, that is one of the greatest songs ever recorded" . . . I know, I know. I like the song today, okay? But when I was seventeen, I didn't. People grow and change; get over it! Okay, back to the story . . .

"Yeah, I don't think so. I don't exactly know what the hell *that* was, but I'm not playing *that* crap in my car," I said, handing Mary her tape back.

"Are you kidding me? That's freaking *Metallica*! They're *awesome*! I can't believe you'd rather listen to this drivel instead of real music like Metallica." She was getting a little heated up about it, "I'll bet you don't even listen to Megadeth or Iron Maiden."

"I'm sorry, Mega what?"

Mary scoffed in disgust. "B, I can't believe you're *dating* this guy! Come on, dude. 'Peace Sells'? 'I Ain't Superstitious'? Nothing?"

I just shook my head no.

"You have to know 'Flight of Icarus' or 'The Trooper,' right?"

I shook my head again.

"I mean, you *are* a guy, aren't you? I can't believe you've never heard these songs before. I know you're on the football team. What do you guys play in the locker room before each game, Barry Manilow? Geez, no wonder our team sucks!"

Deep breath, deep breath! Don't let this bitch get under your skin. Just ignore her! Just focus on B calling you her boyfriend . . . la-la-la, I can't hear you.

That was when Hannah came to my rescue. "Hey, listen, just because he doesn't listen to your heavy-metal barf music doesn't mean he doesn't like music. Plus, he's kind enough to drive your ass to the beach, and that's how you treat him? I don't know what world *you* live in, but it's clearly not the same as mine! Now apologize to him, and then sit back and shut the fuck up!"

D-a-a-amn! Double-barreled blast to the chest! I'm going to have to clean up some mess in the back seat! Hannah, you're fucking awesome!

Mary sat back and pouted as I turned the radio to an alternative rock station, *WLIR,* which made everyone happy, as The Smiths sang "Bigmouth Strikes Again."

Tell me about it, dude.

Ten minutes later, we hit the Long Island Expressway, a.k.a. the LIE, and headed to Exit 68. I held B's hand as Iris blew past me in her Celica. "She better slow down. The cops are out in full force this week," I said.

"She never worries. Her brother is a Suffolk County cop, and he gave her his 'get out of a ticket' card. She always gets off with a warning. I've seen it firsthand, and it's very funny. She's all, 'Officer, my brother's a cop too, see?' And she shows them this card her brother gave her."

"So it's not all prayer circles and mission trips with your youth group, huh?" I teased.

"No, we have fun!" she replied defensively.

Mary did that scoffing thing again. "Yeah right, you don't know the *meaning* of fun."

I bet her meaning of fun involves illegal substances and prison. Just say no, Mary.

B ignored her as I caught up to the Celica. Jean Paul sat in the back seat, smiling from ear to ear.

Jean Paul. You dog!

A few miles west of Exit 68 sat a road sign: Montauk - 65 Miles.

"I love Montauk," B said, then turned to me. "Don't you just love it out there?"

"I've actually never been out there," I replied, and she looked at me like I had three heads.

"Did you just say you've never been to Montauk Point? How long have you lived on Long Island?" B asked.

"My whole life."

"You've been here your whole life and you've *never* been to Montauk? Wow, that's amazing! How is that even possible?" I shrugged my shoulders as she turned to Hannah. "Have you ever been out to Montauk Point?"

"Seriously? Of course. You've taken my parents' classes. They're all, 'We live here and we'll explore every part of Long Island,'" she said, mimicking her father's voice. "We've been all over Long Island, from Orient Point to the Hamptons. My favorite are the vineyards on the North Fork, especially Pindar Vineyards. They even have a store in downtown Port Jeff," she said before flicking me in the back of the head, "Yeah, I don't know what you see in this one. He lives such a sheltered life," she teased.

"I think it's his butt," B said with a giggle as she cupped her hands.

"Yeah, it is cute," Hannah chuckled as I noticed Mary leaning forward to get a peek, and nod in agreement.

"Um, you realize that I'm sitting right here," I said. "And I'm not some piece of veal. I've traveled," I replied as I exited the LIE.

"*Really*, where exactly have you been?" Mary asked. "This ought to be good."

Hannah just snickered because she knew what was coming.

Now to be frank, for a seventeen-year-old, I was well-traveled. Ma spoke at physician conferences all over the world and often took us with her, especially after my dad passed away.

"Well, let's see," I said, tapping my chin. "Last summer we went to Maui for a couple of weeks. At the beginning of this summer, we went to Acapulco. A few years back, we were in Paris, and then London . . . oh, and then there was Rio for a week.

"Rio was one hell of a week for a fourteen-year-old, let me tell you. Can you say nude beaches?" I whispered that last part. "*Annnd*, we've been to the

Grand Canyon, Orlando, Los Angeles . . . oh, and skiing, or in my case, falling, in Vermont. Ma let Jean Paul join us for that trip. And I've been to other places too."

B just sat back and stared at me with her mouth open. Hannah, of course, knew my backstory and the *real* reason we traveled so much. Ma didn't like spending the holidays at home since Pop died, so we usually took winter and summer trips.

"Wow, you really are well-traveled. You've been to more places than me," Mary commented, and she actually sounded impressed. "That's pretty cool. So you went to Brazil? What was *that* like?"

We spent the rest of the ride laughing about our travels, or lack thereof. At the beach, I found a parking spot near Iris. We unloaded everything from my car, including Mary's cement-filled bags.

"So how was the ride?" I asked Jean Paul as he limped over.

He just smiled. "Dude, it was mint. I owe you big time!"

"It was *that* good, huh?"

"Oh yeah. I've got a double date with them Saturday night. Katie has a boyfriend. Iris, you know, the prettier one," *naturally,* "isn't seeing anyone, so we're going out Saturday night."

"Nice job, bro!" We high-fived, then followed behind the girls, who were scoping out the best spot to settle in.

Mary pointed out a good spot, halfway between the concession stand and the ocean. As we all set up, she pulled a red igloo jug from one of her bags and took a swig. "Ah, that's good. Anyone else want some? I made it fresh this morning."

We all shook our heads.

"No? Anyone, no? Really, none of you are going to try some?" she asked, incredulous, trying to pass it around.

Sigh!

I grabbed the jug and took a quick sip.

Sweet Jesus, what the hell is this? Bitch, you better not have poisoned me!

"There you go! What do you think? It's really good, right?" Mary asked.

I gave her a thumbs-up, though my face was twisted up. "Yeah, it's really good." Then Jean Paul reached for it, but I stopped him with a headshake.

"All right, Jean Paul and I will finish setting up if you guys want to go change. Just toss me your towels."

Mistake! Never tell a bunch of teenage girls to throw you their towels.

They looked at each other, giggled, and pelted me with their towels at the same time.

"Whoa!" I yelled as I fell backward into the sand, to their laughter.

Et tu, Hannah, et tu?

"Ha, ha, very funny; now toss me the cooler," I said. "Wait! Never mind. I'll get it myself." The girls were still laughing. "Yeah, yeah, ha, ha, go get changed."

They did—but not before B kissed me. Jean Paul and I spent the next few minutes setting up the spot.

"So dude, how's it going between you and B? She seems to really like you, Lord knows why."

"Really good, dude. She introduced me earlier as her *boyfriend*," I said.

"Nice, dude! It's about goddamn time you had a girlfriend. I'm getting tired of carrying your ass all the time."

"Excuse me, you *carrying* me? Please, everyone knows you're the larger burden. I have to carry you *and* your ego!" I countered. "Do you have any idea what kind of a burden that is?"

"That's only because I'm . . . *whoa*, dude!" he said, gesturing behind me.

"Whoa what?" I asked as I turned around.

Whoa!

Time seemed to slow down as the girls walked toward us. It was like watching a suntan lotion commercial, as every head turned as they walked by. The sun seemed to glisten off their heavenly bodies, as the wind tossed their hair. Even Hannah looked hot in her navy-blue bikini, and so did the pale-skinned Mary in her black bikini.

B was stunning. She had a leather strap tying her blond hair back and looked sexy as hell in her white bikini. She walked so gracefully, laughing with her girlfriends, seemingly clueless to the effect they were all having on the rest of the beach attendees.

32 - Beach-Blanket Guidos

"Hey, guys, sorry we took so long. There was a line to get into the bathroom," B said as they sat down and grabbed the suntan lotion. Jean Paul already had his suit on, so he stood and slowly peeled off his T-shirt, making sure all the girls were watching. Hannah and I just looked at each other, rolled our eyes, and shook our heads.

He received the obligatory oohs and aahs from Katie and Iris, while B giggled—she knew what I thinking by the look on my face. Mary just settled back, and started applying baby oil to her pale skin.

Jesus, she's nuts. Enjoy your sun poisoning!

"All right, I'm going to go to the bathroom and change. I'll be right back," I announced.

"I'll come with you," B said, taking hold of my hand.

"I hope you didn't mind me introducing you as my boyfriend to Iris and Katie earlier," she said as we reached the restrooms.

"Are you kidding me? I didn't mind at all! Does this mean I can call you my girlfriend now?" I teased.

"Oh, I think it's okay. I actually like the way that sounds." She grinned.

"Well, all right, I'll be right out, *girlfriend*," I said, kissing her before going in to change.

It didn't take long. I changed quickly, relieved myself, and as I was washing my hands, I overheard, "No thank you, I'm here with someone. No, really, thanks anyway. Yes, I'm sure. My boyfriend will be out in a . . . oh, here he is."

So, here are the pros and cons of coming to a large public beach, like Smith Point, on Long Island. The pros are you will always find a cross-section of people. The cons—this cross-section usually includes *Guidos*.

What's a Guido? A Guido is a guy of, let's call it, Mediterranean descent or a wannabe. He'll usually have a cheesy mustache, slicked-back, jet-black hair, and wearing a gold chain around his neck with a gold horn dangling over his hairy chest.

He'll be in Speedos, have faux muscles, and a permanent five-o'clock shadow. He will smell of Drakkar Noir cologne and act like Andrew Dice Clay—toothpicks and Marlboro Lights optional.

And that was what I found surrounding my new girlfriend. Three Guidos trying to pick her up.

Great, just what I need! Sigh!

"This is your boyfriend, *really*?" the alpha Guido said, pointing at me and then snickering to his buddies.

"Is there a problem?" I asked.

"Ay oh, ain't any problems here. We were just making *nice* with your, ah, you know, *friend* here," Alpha said as his friends grunted in agreement.

"Yeah, thanks, we have enough friends . . . 'scuse us." I placed my arm around B and tried leaving.

"Whoa, what's the rush?" Alpha asked as he and his clones blocked our exit.

And speaking of friends . . . "Hey, is there a problem?" Jean Paul asked as he came up behind the Guidos.

They turned and saw an impressively sculptured and pissed-off Jean Paul, ready to throw down.

Boys, let me introduce you to Mongo. Mongo don't like Guidos. He eats them for lunch.

When they realized they were about to lose some teeth, Alpha said, "Ay, look, we don't want problems. We were just, you know, kidding around. Have a nice day. Come on, boys. Let's get out of here."

Alpha led his Guido clones away, probably already on the hunt for their next prey, God help her.

"Thanks, bro, but I had it," I said.

"I know you did, bro, but I wasn't going to let you have *all* the fun." We did our handshake, and he walked into the bathroom, shouting, "I'll see you back at the towels."

"Well that was fun, huh?" I joked as B and I walked back.

"Yeah, *that's* what we'll call it." She seemed a little shaken.

I stopped and turned her to face me. "You know I'd never let anyone hurt you, right? Especially not a pack of Guidos. You're too important to me."

Her frown turned into a sweet smile . . . then a sly one. "Really? How important?" she purred as she placed her arms around my neck, pulling me in for a kiss.

People stared at us as they walked by, but we didn't care. We just giggled like the pair of teenagers we were, then headed back to our spot on the beach.

As we approached, Katie, Hannah, and Iris giggled and made kissy faces at B.

"Oh shut up!" she said, laughing.

Mary was already tuned out as she listened to her Walkman. I was glad to see Hannah made fast friends with Katie and Iris. I had been mildly concerned that she'd feel like a fifth wheel or something. I'd forgotten she was the friendliest person on the planet and could make friends with anyone—except for Mary, of course.

Only Saint B could befriend that one, which simply didn't make sense to my teenage self. Later in life, as I came across other damaged teens, I figured it out. I guess B looked beyond the façade and damage, and saw the potential of the person buried underneath the rude, obnoxious, self-centered exterior.

With age comes wisdom. I guess B matured faster than most. Faster than me, at least.

"Do you want me to put lotion on your back?" I asked B.

"Would you mind?"

"No, not at all. That's why I asked." Then I leaned close to her ear and added, "I'll take any excuse to touch you."

She giggled, handed me the lotion, and flipped over.

Sweet Lord, what a view! I can't believe all that *belongs to* my *girlfriend.*

"When you're finished, I'll get yours," B said.

"Cool."

First, I warmed the lotion in my hands and then applied it, starting at her shoulders, neck and upper back. I slowly worked my way south, to the top of her butt crack.

"*Ahem!*"

"Sorry, I'm just making sure you're covered." I grinned like a kid sneaking a piece of candy before dinner.

"Uh-huh, just watch the hands in public, mister."

I giggled to myself like Muttley, the cartoon dog.

"Yeah, okay, I think we're finished back there."

"Oh man!" I whined as she flipped back around.

"Okay, now let me get you." She motioned for me to turn as she shook the lotion with her other hand.

I did, and she squirted the cold lotion directly onto my warm back, laughing, as did Iris, who was watching us. It caused me to yelp.

"Oh, I'm sorry. My bad."

She giggled as she applied the lotion, goosing my butt when she finished.

"Really, you want to play that game, huh? Because I'll play too; it's one of my favorite games." I laughed wickedly as we stood, readying for battle.

She held up her hands. "No, no, it was an accident. Don't do anything you're going to regret, *mister*." She kicked sand at me and then took off toward the water.

I then chased her down toward the water, playfully reaching for her butt as she ran. Eventually, I had her cornered between the ocean and the beach. She might try to fake right and go left, but it would be to no avail. We both knew I had caught my prey.

Luckily for her, Jean Paul, Katie, Iris, and Hannah were making their way to the water as well. So, due to the witnesses, I settled down.

"We'll settle this later," I joked.

"Promises, promises," she said, slowly backing into the water and then splashing me.

"Oh, you're dead."

She immediately dove into the water, with me hot on her tail.

We all swam for a while. Periodically, I'd pull B in close and give her a salty kiss. Due to our previous beach adventure, though, we chose not to go any further. The last thing either one of us wanted was to drown while attempting to make out in the ocean, especially in front of our friends.

Of course, this didn't stop me from goosing her occasionally. *What can I say? I gotta be me.*

"Want to go back and grab a soda or something?" I asked B.

"Sure, what'd you pack?"

"Cokes and Sprites."

"That sounds good."

"Hey, we're heading back," I announced to our friends who were still frolicking in the water, and received a thumbs-up from Jean Paul.

"So what'll you have?" I asked as I opened my cooler.

"I'll take a Coke please."

As I grabbed us both Cokes, I glanced over at Mary, who was lying there, seemingly ignoring everyone and quietly listening to her Walkman.

"Is she always like this?" I whispered, gesturing to Mary.

"Sometimes, yeah. One moment, she's really happy, and the next, she's almost suicidal. You just never know which Mary you're going to get. I worry about her."

"I *can* hear you, you know," Mary said.

"Sorry, Mary, but I do, and you know it," B said defensively.

"Yeah, yeah, don't worry about me, B. I'm fine. I just have my moments, that's all, and then they're gone." She turned her face in my direction. "Hey, slick, do you have any ice you can spare? My drink's starting to get warm."

"Yeah, take as much as you'd like," I replied.

Not that you wouldn't anyway.

"Thanks. You know, you're cooler than I thought you'd be." She started digging around for ice.

"Um, thanks."

"So, what plans do you lovebirds have today?"

B and I just shrugged.

"Oh Jesus, you guys are pathetic. If I were you two, I'd find a nice quiet spot and get naked. You're both hot, plus you're only young once. Why waste it?" She took a long swig of her witch's brew, before settling back down on her towel.

Of course I'd love to go off someplace and get naked with B, but let's be honest here, it just wasn't' gonna happen. First, we're not in Rio. Second, B's not that type of girl, right?

We turned to each other, speechless. I tried speaking, but couldn't find the right words to say. They came out as incoherent sounds. She too had a hard time putting a sentence together, but she managed to say, "I am *so sorry* about that. I mean, it's not that, um, you know, I um, you know, we uh, just . . . um . . ."

I just held my hand up.

"B, it's okay, relax. I know. We're not there yet."

She let out a deep breath, smiled, and seemed to relax a bit. Then she pushed me back onto my towel, giggling and kissing me at the same time.

"Oh God, get a room!" Mary said, which earned her the middle finger from B.

Mary just shook her head and laughed.

Maybe Mary's cooler than I thought.

33 - Hannah and the Concession Stand

The crazies eventually came out of the water, ravenous for lunch. I took B's lunch order, a cheeseburger and fries, and headed over to the concession stand. As I walked away, Jean Paul asked if I'd grab him one too, as he stretched out on his towel.

I simply flipped him a bird and kept walking, as Hannah caught up to me. "I'll get the prince his food," she said, laughing.

"Yeah, he's a real prince all right," I said. "Hey, did you hear that B introduced me as her boyfriend?"

"Good for you. That's really nice," she said sincerely. "She's actually turned out to be a really nice girl. She wasn't who I thought she was, you know? I thought she was more like Mary. I'm glad to see I was wrong about her."

"Thanks, Hann. It means a lot, having the Hannah Michaels stamp of approval." I replied as we grabbed a spot in line.

"But enough about me. What's happening in your world?" I asked.

"Not much. To be honest, I'm a little nervous and excited about our senior year," she said as we slowly inched forward.

"Really? How come? You crushed the SATs and you have a great GPA. Plus, all of your extracurricular activities are there. What's the problem?"

"I don't know. I mean, I know I'm doing well in school and stuff. It's just that—" Before she could finish, we made it to the front of the line, where a not-so-pleasant cashier rang up our orders.

As we headed out, carrying our food on red trays, Jean Paul, Iris and Katie were making their way in.

"Hey, get in that line over there," I told them, gesturing to the line we just left. "You'll love the cashier. We'll wait for you guys outside."

"Cool, bro. Thanks," Jean Paul said, stealing a fry before getting in line.

Hannah cackled with glee, "Oh, that was so mean. I love it!"

"Yeah, well, it's good for him. It'll add some character. Anyway, you were saying inside that you're doing well in school and stuff but . . ." I did a rolling gesture with my arm, for her to continue her story.

She let out a deep sigh, "Look it's nothing, forget I even brought it up."

"Yeah I don't think so, McFly. You're not getting off that easy. You wouldn't let me get off that easy, that's for sure."

"Okay, fine. You're worse than a dog with a bone."

"Damn right I am. So go on, Hann. I mean seriously, all kidding aside, it's me. You know you can tell me anything," I said and took her hand.

I call this "the B move," but please don't cry on me. Jean Paul will kill me if I make you cry. Speaking of which, how're they doing in there?

I craned my neck to see if they'd made it to the counter yet.

Oh snap, he's almost there.

"I know, but this is more girlfriend to girlfriend stuff, that's all. Sometimes I wish I had more girlfriends locally than across the country," she said, then let loose a big sigh.

I understood.

It was the advantage and disadvantage of going to a boarding school. You literally made friends from across the planet. To this day, thanks to Facebook, I'm still in touch with people from my high school who now live in Europe, South America, and Asia, not to mention various states across the US.

"I get it, and I'm sorry, Hann. I guess I always thought of you as one of the guys, which clearly you're not," I said, pointing to her bikini. "By the way, if you don't mind me saying, *damn*! I'm so used to seeing you in shorts or a one-piece that I forgot you can look all *POW!*" I said with flourish, which made her blush.

"Oh stop, I do not." A pause, then, "Do I really?"

I laughed. "Uh, yeah, dummy! You're hot! And I say that in a brotherly way, not that a brother should think of his sister as hot. I mean that would be gross and wrong and, um . . ."

"Oh my God, please stop. I understand what you're trying to say, and thank you. It means a lot coming from you. Oh look, here they come! I can't wait to hear about their cashier experience." She waved at them, then said to me, "Oh, he looks pissed! This ought to be good!"

And with that, we ended our conversation. It would be years later that I eventually found out what was bothering her, but more on that later.

Jean Paul strolled over, carrying a tray full of food, with Kate and Iris giggling on either side of him.

"Man, that lady was a bitch! Was she actually *nice* to you two?" he asked, disbelief in his voice.

"Oh yeah, bro, she was awesome. She loved us," I replied with a smile.

"It must have been *you*. What'd you say to her?" Hannah asked her brother, tilting her head and cocking an eyebrow.

"Nothing. We just walked up there, and the girls gave her their order—" He stopped suddenly and gave us the once-over.

I broke first and threw my head back in laughter. "Ha!"

"Jean Paul, you're such a fool!" Hannah laughed.

"Dude, this is how you do me? Damn!" he said, but there was a partial smile on his face. "That's all right. Just remember, payback's a bitch."

I just wiggled my fingers in that "ooh, scary" way. "Sorry, bro, it had to be done. It was a moral imperative," I said, quoting Val Kilmer in *Real Genius*.

Hey, what are best friends for?

34 - An Uninvited Guest

A s we all walked back, I noticed that B and Mary weren't alone.
Sigh, seriously? Who invited Kyle Fergusen and his skank from the other night? I guess his conversation with his sister didn't work.

"Hey, look, it's Amigo and his buddies. How's it going, *Amigo?*" Kyle Fergusen asked.

I just faked a smile, nodded, and then glanced at B, who seemed equally apologetic and mortified.

"How's it going, Kyle?" I replied flatly. There he stood, wearing a pair of cutoff jeans and ratty T-shirt, toasting me with one of my Cokes, and with a lit cigarette sticking out of his stupid face.

As I sat down, B whispered, "I'm so sorry. I had no idea *he* was coming."

"Don't worry about it," I assured her as I handed her a cheeseburger. "But if this jerk disrespects you in any way, I'll take *care* of it."

"Take care of it how?" she asked with concern in her voice.

"I'll just politely pull him aside, and *'splain* to him that it's in his best interest to change his ways. If that doesn't work, then I'll adjust his attitude." I popped some fries into my mouth.

"Mmhmm, well *you* need to understand that I'm not a fan of violence, even if it is over me, so don't go all Rambo on him, okay? I *won't* like it," she hissed.

I just pursed my lips and nodded as Kyle stepped closer, "Hey, what are you guys all hush-hush about over here? Hey, what're you eating, B? Mind if I take a couple of fries?" he asked while grabbing some fries.

I started getting up, but B placed her hand on my lap, pushing me down. *Grrrr!!*

"Oh, you know . . . boyfriend/girlfriend stuff," B said smiling.

"Boyfriend/girlfriend stuff, huh? Well, I didn't know you and *Amigo* here were that serious," he said as he slapped me on the shoulder. "Congratulations, *A-migo*, you've got yourself a real catch there; and I ought to know, since I caught her first."

Laughing at his own joke, he stole some more fries, then took another puff from his cancer stick before walking back to his skank.

Oh look, the skank helped herself to one of my Sprites. No, no, help yourself. Want a bite of my burger or some of my fries?

"B, I swear to God, if that asshole calls me *amigo* one more time . . ."

"Just *ignore* him. He's trying to get under your skin. Plus, he knows how I feel about violence. I'm guessing that he thinks if you get into a fight in front of me, I'll break up with you. Let's just ignore him, okay?" she pleaded with her sweet voice of reason and a gentle hand squeeze, which immediately calmed me down. It was like someone released a pressure valve.

"Okay, but only for you. Now if he happens to fall down a flight of stairs, gets swept away by some rogue wave, or gets hit by a bus in the parking lot, it's not my fault."

She giggled. "Okay, if something like that happens, I won't blame you."

"Right, we'll just call it a *happy* coincidence," I replied with an evil laugh.

"You're incorrigible." She leaned in, kissing me on the lips, and I could feel Kyle's glare.

I merely turned and toasted him with my Coke.

Same to you, asshole! Same to you.

As we ate our lunch, B and I would periodically kiss. She tasted like suntan lotion, sea salt, and ketchup. We must have kissed once too often for Kyle's liking.

"Come on, let's go swimming," he told his skank, yanking at her arm.

"Ow, Kyle, that hurt! No, I don't feel like swimming," she whined.

"Fine, I don't care, do what you want. I'm going swimming." He flicked his cigarette into the sand, took off his shirt and ran into the ocean in his cut-off shorts.

Aw, did your little feelings get hurt when you saw us kissing? I'm so sorry. Tell you what, why don't you go fuck yourself and drown!

"I wonder what got into him," I said, smirking.

"Who knows? Maybe it's his time of the month or something," Mary said, and we all laughed at Kyle's expense.

After we all finished our lunch, Jean Paul and I grabbed the garbage and took it back to the trash cans near the concession stand.

"Dude, so what's the deal with Kyle Fergusen?" Jean Paul spat out. "He's such a douche! Who *invited* him here anyway? Isn't he too old to be hanging out with us?"

I blew out some air, trying to stay calm, "Who knows? All I know is, I told B that if the bullshit continues, I would *'splain* to him the errors of his ways." I punched my right fist into my left palm. "She's not a fan of violence, so I'm not allowed to touch him, unless I really, *really* have to."

"Does this mean *I* can't *'splain* things to him?" Jean Paul asked.

"Dude, everyone knows we share a brain, so, yeah, this applies to you too," I replied.

"So what's the plan for the rest of the day?"

"At this point, we don't know," I replied, mimicking Jim Belushi from the movie, *About Last Night*. "Seriously though, I've got to take a leak, so I'm going to the head. After that, who knows? Maybe B and I will take a stroll along the beach. What about you?"

"Actually a stroll along the beach with Iris sounds like a good idea. And don't worry. We won't let you cramp our style. We'll let you go first."

"Oh, *us* cramp *your* style, huh?" I gave him a friendly shove as we walked into the restroom.

We were washing our hands after taking care of business, and who strolled in? Kyle. We both saw him in the reflection in the mirrors. When he saw us, he froze. He clearly wasn't expecting to see us there. Jean Paul and I simply gave him the head-nod greeting from the mirrors.

"Oh, uh, hey guys," he said cautiously while walking to a urinal. He kept looking over his shoulder as he took care of his business. Maybe he was expecting us to beat his ass or something, but I'd promised B, and I was a man of my word.

Of course, I never promised I wouldn't fuck with him a little. So, before leaving, I slammed the hand-dryer button and began to slowly dry my hands. This caused him to flinch and pee himself a little, which put a grin on my face.

Next time, Amigo!

35 - A Stroll Along the Beach

When Jean Paul and I made it back to our spot, I reached down for B's hand, "Want to go for a walk?" I asked.

"You know it, mister." She smiled as I helped her up, receiving a hug for my troubles.

"We're going to go for a walk. We'll be back in a little while," B announced as Katie giggled and made kissy faces. B stuck out her tongue. Everyone joined in on the teasing as we walked away hand in hand.

As we walked, I slipped my arm around her shoulder and she wrapped her arm around my waist, caressing my back as we walked. We simply walked along the beach, enjoying the sights and sounds—people bodysurfing, kids building sandcastles, teens tossing footballs, and fathers chasing toddlers. You couldn't ask for a better day.

B looked like the type of girl the Beach Boys sang about back in the '60s—white bikini, golden skin, and flowing blond hair tied back with that leather band. The tassels on her bikini swayed back and forth as we walked along, lost in our own little world.

We found a somewhat deserted spot along the beach and sat down in the sand, watching the ocean waves caress the sand as they hit the beach. As we baked in the summer sun, we turned and smiled, taking each other in. She pushed her sunglasses into her hair, while leaning in closer.

I followed suit, meeting her halfway, and we kissed. We slowly leaned back onto the warm sand, and B snuggled into the crook of my arm. I gently caressed her back, while she reciprocated, rubbing my chest.

She leaned over and pressed her chest against mine, allowing me access to her lower back and perfectly shaped bottom.

I made slight circles, softly massaging my way down her back. As I did this, she placed the tip of her tongue in my mouth, allowing me to taste the sweetness from her soda and the saltiness of the ocean.

"Oh my God, this is amazing," she purred.

Boing! Houston, we have lift-off!

Her words immediately elicited that *certain response.* In a moment, we'd be able to use me as a sundial.

Normally that would've embarrassed the hell out of me, but we were relatively alone, and frankly, I simply didn't care. It was a natural response to the girl in my arms, purring in my ears, and softly breathing on my neck, with her soft and salty lips on mine and the tip of her silky tongue exploring my mouth.

Eventually, seagulls snapped us out of it as they landed nearby and started squawking. We looked up, saw a flock of seagulls—*the actual birds, not the band*—and giggled.

"I guess we have an audience," I said as we sat up and stared out at the ocean. We sat there, lost in a love trance.

Our trance was eventually broken by a familiar voice. "Dude, get a room!"

We looked up to see Jean Paul and Iris approaching us. "Hey, don't let us interrupt. By the way, our *uninvited guests* left the beach."

"What happened?" I asked.

"Who knows?" Iris said with a shrug. "All I know is, when he got back from swimming, they started arguing. He wanted to leave, and she wanted to stay."

Jean Paul added, "The next thing you know, he's forcing her up, and they left. We could hear her whining all the way to the parking lot."

Iris nodded. "It was pretty pathetic. B, I love you like a sister, but I still don't know what you saw in that guy," she said, which made me smile and feel good. "This is more of the type of guy you should be with," she added, pointing at me.

She then took Jean Paul's hand and pulled him down the beach. Jean Paul looked over his shoulder at us and flashed his hundred-watt smile.

B and I giggled.

It's your world, bro. We're just living in it.

36 - Time to Go Home, Princess

B and I stayed there for a while, doing what teenage lovebirds do, before eventually making our way back to our spot. Hannah, Mary, and Katie were lying there, enjoying the sunshine and the ocean breeze. Mary was still drinking her concoction, which concerned me.

Please don't puke in my car.

B noticed the look of concern on my face, so she went to check on Mary.

"Hey, how're you doing?" she asked as she removed one of Mary's headphones from her ear.

"Huh? What? I'm fine," she drunkenly slurred, which made B scowl, so she bent down and picked up Mary's concoction.

"I think you've had enough of whatever this is," she said while pouring the contents into the sand.

"Hey, why'd you do *that*? I wasn't done!" she slurred.

"Because you've clearly had enough. Now stop acting like a baby and have a Coke instead," she replied, while reaching over to the cooler and grabbing a Coke. She opened the can and forced it into Mary's hand. "Here, drink this."

"Fine." Mary took a swig of soda. "Happy now?"

"Very."

Mary went back to listening to her music.

"What do you want to do?" I whispered.

"I don't know."

"We can head out if you want. It is getting late."

"You wouldn't mind?"

"No, I wouldn't mind."

As we were talking, Jean Paul and Iris came back from their walk. I let him know we were leaving soon, which was fine with him.

I then addressed the group. "Hey, guys, it's getting late. Do you mind if we head out?"

No one objected, so we all policed the area, packed up our things, and made our way back to the parking lot. As we headed back to the cars, Jean Paul told me about his stroll. Apparently, he and Iris had a lot in common—they both ran track-and-field in the spring. He also discovered the she was a good kisser. I was happy for him.

That was when he reminded me about his upcoming double date on Saturday, so he wouldn't be joining us at the Fergusen party.

"No worries, bro. I don't plan on staying long," I replied as we walked up to my car and popped the trunk.

"Hey, Mary isn't, um, *feeling* too well, if you catch my drift," Hannah whispered as she walked over and mimicked someone puking.

Oh fuck. Now I've got to deal with that sick bitch in my car for the next forty-five minutes.

"Thanks for the warning. She'll get the window seat on the way home, and I'm dropping her ass home first, if you guys don't mind," I said.

"Hey, as long as she doesn't throw up on me, I don't care. I still have shotgun, though, right?" Jean Paul asked.

He was nothing if not persistent. "Yeah, that's fine. Let's just get everything into the trunk."

Just as we'd finished with most of the packing, B came to the back of the car and said to the twins. "Katie and Iris offered to drive you guys home if you want."

They declined, with Hannah adding, "You may need our help getting her inside."

Jean Paul seemed to blanch at the thought, and I felt the same way. We said our goodbyes to Katie and Iris and then poured Mary into the back of my car.

I put the A/C on as soon as I started the car, which caused Mary to cough. We all froze and stared at her.

Is this bitch going to puke?

Hannah brought an extra can of Coke with her, just in case Mary needed it to settle her stomach.

Thankfully, she didn't puke. She just settled onto B's shoulder. Not wanting her to puke on B, I reached back and gently pushed her against the open rear window. I looked at B and shrugged, then buckled up and left Smith Point, for what turned out to be a very long time.

During the drive to Mary's, she threatened to spew a few times. Each time, I would pull over and B would open the car door, but nothing happened. They were all false alarms.

"I'm not going to puke, you fucking amateurs," she would slur and then pass out again.

Once we finally arrived at her house, Jean Paul and I grabbed her things from my trunk, while Hannah and B took her into her house. They only had to stop once for her to throw up in the shrubs by her front door.

"Our Mexican can take of that tomorrow! Ha!" she drunkenly exclaimed, presumably referring to her gardener.

B grimaced as we followed them inside. She pointed Jean Paul and me to the kitchen, "Why don't you go put her stuff in the kitchen while we put her to bed," she said.

I noticed immediately, that the inside of the house was as large as I imagined. The moment you walked in, you stepped into a large foyer with a gaudy chandelier hanging from a high, vaulted ceiling.

The foyer led to many rooms as well as a winding staircase leading to the upstairs portion of the mini-mansion. There was a hallway, which led to a large, modern kitchen. It had a center island with a sink and butcher block— where we dropped Mary's things—and all the latest in stainless steel appliances.

There were two rooms leading off the opposite sides of the kitchen, as well as a patio door that led to a large wooden deck overlooking an even larger back yard full of large trees.

As we waited, we heard footsteps approaching us, which turned out to belong to Kyle, coming to fetch himself something to drink from his fridge. The moment he entered the kitchen and saw Jean Paul and me standing there, he froze and turned a minor shade of pale.

"What are you guys doing here?" he asked suspiciously, positioning himself behind the center island.

We've come to kick the living shit out of you, Kyle, what do you think?

"We're here dropping off your sister. Hannah and B had to put her to bed, if you know what I mean," I replied.

"Yeah, she was in, um, no condition to, you know, do it herself," Jean Paul said, mimicking someone puking, which made Kyle chuckle.

"She left a gift in the bushes just outside the front door," I informed him.

"Nice. I'll let the Mexican know," he said nonchalantly. "That's my sister. She just can't seem to hold her liquor."

Realizing we weren't there for him, he went to his fridge and took out a Budweiser, never taking his eyes off of us.

"Hey, dude, where's your bathroom?" Jean Paul asked.

"Oh, uh, it's right down the hall there, on the right. The light is on the left, inside the door."

"Cool, I'll be right back. I've gotta go see a man about a horse."

And just like that, Kyle and I were alone for the first time.

Kyle's stance changed a bit after Jean Paul stepped away. He became more confident, which made me laugh internally.

Dude, you may have home-field advantage, but I'll still fucking crush you! So be a smart boy and don't start anything, especially while no one's here to stop me. Be a good boy and walk away.

"So, you and B are going out, huh?" he asked as he took a sip of his beer.

"Yeah. What of it?" I wasn't going to let this douche push me around, even in his house. It just wasn't going to happen.

"Whoa, settle down, dude. I was just asking. There's no reason to get all, you know," he said, pointing at me with his beer. "How long do you think it'll last? She has expensive tastes, you know. She likes high-end things." I just stared at him as he blathered on. "She's like a fine thoroughbred that needs constant pampering, if you know what I'm saying?"

I took a deep breath and gave him my best Clint Eastwood squint. "Yeah, I think this conversation's over," I said as Hannah and B entered the kitchen.

"What conversation?" B asked.

"It's not important. How's Mary?" I asked, trying to change the subject, but I could tell B was taking the temperature of the room and was not buying it.

"She's going to be fine. She got a little sick again in her bathroom, but it's mostly air at this point. We stripped her down, and put her into a pair of PJs. Hannah put a cold compress on her forehead, and I put a garbage can next to her bed, just in case."

"What a friggin lightweight," Kyle said as Jean Paul joined us in the kitchen. "Well, I believe you know your way out," he added, doing the Vanna wave at the door.

"Yeah, we know the way, thanks," I said and grabbed B's hand, putting myself between her and Kyle. Hannah and Jean Paul walked out behind us, with Jean Paul bringing up the rear. Kyle must not have wanted to get too close to Jean Paul, because he didn't follow.

Instead, he called out from the kitchen doorway, "Oh, hey, don't forget about the party on Saturday night. It should be another blowout. Unfortunately, B, you won't get to play hostess again this year, I guess."

"Oh, we'll be here," I replied. "But I wouldn't worry about B. She'll be plenty busy with me to worry about playing hostess. Besides, the way she tells it, I'm more fun. 'Night." *Asshole!*

Jean Paul snickered as he shut the door behind him.

Was that a glass bottle I heard shatter against the front door? Hey, buddy, you mess with the bull, you'll get the horns!

37 - Hercules and the Two Virgins

Once we arrived at the twins' house, B and I helped them unload their things. We hung out there for a little while, finishing off a Domino's pizza that their mom had ordered for dinner. We also finished off the rest of the sodas from my cooler, so it was a win-win.

We sat at their dining room table, laughing about the day. After we finished eating, Jean Paul and I did our normal bro handshake, while Hannah and B hugged. "Thanks for helping me with Mary," B said to her.

"Sure. I wasn't going to let you deal with that on your own."

I gave Hannah a quick hug while B hugged Jean Paul, who gave me a big smile and thumbs-up behind her back.

I just rolled my eyes.

"You're a douche," I whispered to him.

"Why is he a douche? What'd I miss?" B asked.

"Nothing. He knows."

Jean Paul grinned. "Are you up for some tennis tomorrow?"

I shrugged, looked at B. She said, "Don't look at me; it's my last day of work, so if you want to go play tennis, then go play."

"Does ten o'clock work?" I asked Jean Paul.

"Sure, as long as you don't blow me off again."

"Yeah, yeah. I'll see you at ten, smart-ass."

With that, B and I left their house, hopped in my car and headed out.

"So why was Jean Paul a douche?" she asked.

So I explained to her what he did, and she just giggled, "I *thought* he was doing something behind my back. That's okay, I'll get him back."

Bro, you're in trouble! This chick is evil. She doesn't mess around!

"So, miss, where to?" I asked as we pulled up a stop light.

"Well, it's not too late. What do you feel like doing?"

You! (Yeah, that one never gets old.)

"I don't know. I'm open. Do you want to hit West Meadow again?" I asked.

She made a face, "No, I think one night of fleas and police are enough. I think I have a better idea. Do you trust me?"

"Of course, you're a lifeguard," I replied, which made her chuckle, before giving me directions to our next destination.

Ten minutes later, we were parking in a nice secluded spot alongside the Stony Brook Harbor, across from the locally famous Hercules Pavilion that houses the figurehead and anchor from the USS *Ohio*, the first ship launched from the Brooklyn Navy Yard in 1820.

She was right; this was a better idea. We didn't have to worry about the beach closing, late night strollers or parking restrictions. Best of all, neither of us had to be home anytime soon.

"Good call. Youth group again?"

"Nope, older sister."

"Ah."

I suggested a walk, since it was a perfect evening for a walk.

She had other things in mind.

With a raised eyebrow and a *cat that caught the canary* glint in her eyes, she said, "I think we've walked enough for today, don't you?" She unbuckled her seatbelt and slid closer.

Gulp! She's going to eat me alive!

"Can't argue with that," I stammered out.

Under the light of a lamppost, she softly caressed my cheek. At that moment, she was the most precious thing in the world to me. Our eyes locked. I gazed into her exquisite blue eyes and couldn't believe she was here with me.

I leaned in, tilting my head as I continued staring into her eyes, lost in her beauty. "God, you're so beautiful!" I caught myself whispering, and she smiled, leaning in too.

We shared the most innocent of kisses. Our kiss lasted for an eternity. Soon eternity transformed from sweet and soft kisses to something more sensual. We became lost in our passion.

She slowly slipped the tip of her tongue into my mouth, which I happily accepted, both of us moaning with pleasure. I could still taste the ocean on her lips as we kissed. I could still feel the sunshine radiating off her sun-kissed skin, as she slowly arched her back.

She climbed across the gearshift and straddled me, as I awkwardly reached down and pushed the seat as far back as it would go, providing us with more room.

Her eyes bored into my soul as she removed her T-shirt and tossed it into the passenger seat, and I followed her example.

Then I cupped her bikini-covered left breast and began massaging it gently as we continued kissing. I felt her nipple respond immediately, as it poked against my thumb. She left my lips and began to nibble my neck with her pouty lips. As she sucked away, I moaned with pleasure, my hand never leaving her breast.

Her tongue worked its way up and down my neck, which drove me crazy. *She* drove me crazy. I pulled her off my neck and kissed her deeply, and she responded by pressing herself into me.

Then she did something that blew my mind. She leaned back slightly, untied the back of her bikini top, and removed it, fully exposing her breasts to me for the first time.

Oh Sweet Jesus! Yes!

They were better than I imagined. Smiling, she leaned back and allowed me to marvel at her naked breasts. Their perfection blew me away. They were just the right size, not too big and not too small. They were full on top, firm and round. Her nipples were pink and hard, beckoning me to consume them.

I had to feel those breasts. Had to taste them. I had to have them. I reached up and felt them for the first time, causing me to stand at attention.

She then pressed herself against my swollen companion.

Good soldier!

We were both nervous and excited. I removed my hands from her breasts, held her and caressed her face, doing my best to convey that she was safe with me. I would never take advantage of her. I wasn't wired that way.

She smiled, removed my hand from her face and placed it on her left breast and whispered, "I trust you," and then began to slowly and rhythmically grind into me.

I soon matched her thrusts with my own as I leaned in and gently sucked on her left nipple. I tasted the salt of the ocean as I placed her pink nipple into my mouth.

We slowly rocked back and forth as our breathing patterns increased. I changed breasts, lightly flicking the tip of my tongue from one erect nipple to the other.

The more I flicked, sucked, and caressed her breasts, the deeper she would grind into me. There was nothing else in the world at that moment, but our passion.

I reached down and grabbed her butt with both hands, trying to control her thrusts as she rode me harder and faster. The harder she rode, the more I squeezed her butt and sucked her nipple.

I soon felt a familiar pressure building. It started in my toes and worked its way up to my stomach. B leaned in and grabbed the back of the seat, bearing down even harder and longer.

She leaned her head back, and I held her as she continued to grind into my swollen member. Her naked breasts bounced as she closed her eyes and bit her bottom lip, rotating her hips into mine. I tried my best to lean back and meet her thrusts.

The pressure traveled from my stomach to my groin, as B and I now worked in tandem, grinding and moaning. The deeper B went, the more she bit her lip. The more she bit her lip, the more the pressure in my groin grew. I could no longer hold it in. I lost control. I grabbed her ass and brought her down onto my exploding member.

It was like someone opened a bottle of champagne in my bathing suit. The cork popped, and the contents spilled out into my lining. B rode me to her completion and then collapsed on top of me.

We held each other as we caught our breath. We were a sweaty mess. And it was . . .

"*Amazing!*" she whispered.

38 - Brotherly Advice

As I held her, I noticed freckles on her chest for the first time, which made me smile. I found them cute.

"What are you smiling at, mister?"

"Nothing. Just your freckles. I've never noticed them before. I like them."

"You're so weird," she giggled, as she leaned forward, placing her head on my shoulder.

"B," I whispered.

"Yeah?"

"I, uh . . ." I stammered.

She sat up and held my gaze. "What is it? You know you can tell me anything." I suddenly felt safe and secure.

It was strange. I'd never felt like that before in my entire life, so safe and secure. There was something so intimate and loving about the expression in her eyes. It was so comforting that I felt like I could expose my very soul to her.

"I've never done this," I said as I cast my eyes downward, a bit embarrassed. "I'm still a, uh . . . virgin."

She placed her hands on either side of my face, lifting it up, so I could meet her eyes once more.

"Please never feel embarrassed about that, not with me, okay? I've never done this before either. I'm a virgin too," she said, and her eyes sparkled brighter than her smile.

At that moment, I couldn't have loved her more. I felt safe and at peace, as she exposed herself to me too—in more ways than one.

There was so much I wanted to say, so much I wanted to tell her, but I didn't want to break this moment of intimacy. But the longer we embraced each other, the harder it was to stay silent.

"B?" I whispered.

"Yeah?"

"I love you."

As the words fell from my lips, I felt the pit of fear and trepidation form in my stomach. She simply held me tighter, breathed in, and released me.

"I love you too."

Thank you, God!

I held her closely, as those words echoed in my ears. A moment later, B explained how she'd been wanting to tell me this for a few days now, but was afraid it would scare me away. She told me she'd never felt this way before about anyone.

As she shared this information with me, tears of joy filled my eyes, which caused her to tear up as well. We sat there half naked, holding each other in a sacred embrace. I told her this was the greatest news I'd ever heard.

She loves me! She truly loves me!

It was getting late, so we dressed quickly and I drove her home. I'd love to say that we expressed our undying love for one another as I drove her home, but we didn't. Instead, we drove to B's house while listening to Steve Winwood sing "Higher Love".

As the song played, I had one hand on the steering wheel and the other holding my girl. I felt more content than I'd ever before in my life. After a long goodbye in her driveway, followed by another at her front door, I headed home in a blissful fog, replaying the events of the evening in my head.

As I pulled into my driveway, I felt the need to talk to someone about how I was feeling. But I couldn't talk to Ma, or my kid brother. I certainly couldn't talk to Jean Paul about it—he would make it about him and ruin it somehow—and I didn't feel like talking with Hannah either.

"Hey, Ma, I'm home," I said, taking in the delicious aroma from Ma's kitchen. I was starving. I guess I'd worked up an appetite.

I wonder if B's as hungry as I am right now?

"Hola, mijo. How was jur day?"

I gave her a peck on the cheek as I made my way to the kitchen.

"We had a great day. The beach was awesome."

"That's good. I made pork chops tonight and saved ju a plate in la nevera."

But as hungry as I was, I was more anxious to talk to someone about my evening—and my older brother was just the right person to talk to. I thanked her, told her I'd be down in a few, and grabbed the cordless, heading to my room.

As I sat on my bed, staring at the phone, I began to gather my thoughts. *What do I say to him? How do I even start this conversation? Screw it, just call him.*

So I blew out a breath of air and dialed his number in Boston. When he finally picked up, I could hear the TV on in the background.

"Hello?" he said.

"Yo! What's happening?"

"Hey, what's going on, little bro? Is everything okay? You're calling kind of late," he said, sounding concerned.

"Yeah, yeah, no, everything is fine. Great, actually," I paused for a moment, not sure where to go from there. "Uh, we haven't talked in a while, that's all."

But he wasn't buying it. "Uh-huh," he said, and I heard the TV volume go down. "What's going on?" he asked in that older-brother tone.

"I'm that transparent, even from Boston, huh?"

"Yes, very. So what's going on? Spill it."

I had to lighten this up. "Okay, okay, but first let me get this out—Boston sucks and the Red Sox swallow!"

He blew out a long, exaggerated sigh. Then he chuckled. "Are you done? Are you ready to talk for real, or did you just call me to bust my balls?"

"Hey, I gotta be me, bro. Anyway, yeah, no, um, I guess I did call for another reason. So I, uh, um, I um," I started.

"Uh-huhhh, you what?"

"I have a girlfriend," I blurted out.

He congratulated me and then asked me a how we met. I told him everything about B, and I mean *everything*—how we met, what happened at Hercules, our confessions of love for each other, everything. It felt great getting it all off my chest.

"Phew, okay, that's a lot to take in," my brother said. "It sounds like you guys are getting pretty serious and, I gotta say, moving pretty fast, little bro."

Knowing my brother, this was his preamble to his pearls of wisdom, and that was exactly why I'd called. I needed his opinion, so I waited as he gathered his thoughts.

"Okay, remember I say this because I care, so please try not to get too angry," he started.

"Okay, I understand."

"Well, bro, in my opinion, you need to slow things down. I understand it's probably not what you want to hear. Listen, I've been there. I know all about new love and the excitement you feel, especially when things are moving fast. The thing is, that tends to lead to things even more intimate than you've ever experienced, I'm assuming. Do you know what I mean?"

"Um . . ."

He cut it in. "Look, you know what I'm talking about, and unless you're both ready, and I mean truly ready to cross that line, you should slow things down. It's serious stuff, bro."

"Yeah, I hear ya," I said, just to say something. Because I didn't know what else to say.

"Remember, it wasn't *that* long ago that I was seventeen, so I know what I'm talking about. You're probably still discovering each other, which is exciting, awesome, and even a little scary, to be honest," he said.

"It's even a bit scary at my age, so take your time. The discovery is the best part. The actual act of sex really only lasts a few minutes at best, especially when you're first starting out. So take it slow. Don't rush it. Get to know what she likes; get to know what you like too."

What I like?

"I—"

"Let me ask you something, what's her favorite flower?" he asked.

"Um . . . I don't know," I replied, feeling stupid.

"What about her favorite food?"

"I think . . . pizza?"

"Okay, that's *your* favorite, but are you sure it's *hers*? What about her favorite color? When is her birthday? What does she want to be when she grows up? Where does she want to go to college? I could go on, but I think you get my drift."

My head was spinning as I realized how little I knew about B. She was still a mystery to me.

My brother kept ramming it home. "These are the basics, bro. You should know all this stuff before you rush in and start getting intimate with someone, know what I mean?" he asked.

"Yeah, I do. God, I feel so stupid. I can't believe I don't even know when her birthday is," I said as I slapped my forehead with the palm of my hand.

"So what do I do? We've already kind of started down that path, you know what I mean? How do I suddenly put on the brakes without it causing a problem?" I asked.

"Well now, that's a tough one, little bro. It's something you're going to have to figure out yourself. You know this girl better than I do, so follow your gut. Look, I'm not saying you need to stop getting *closer*. Again, it's all a part of the discovery process. All I'm saying is, don't miss the big picture either. Really get to know her, and allow her to really know you as well. Trust me, you'll have a stronger relationship, in the long run."

I was nodding into the phone, mentally taking notes, "Okay, got it. So we don't have to stop getting, um, intimate, but we should slow things down a bit and get to know each other better. Yeah, I guess we can do that. Besides, we have all year to look forward to."

"That's right, you do. Now here's my last bit of advice."

More? Jesus, what's left?

His tone got serious, "Listen, if you don't take any other piece of advice, please take this one."

"Yeah okay, what is it?"

"Okay, listen to me. I don't care if you do this tomorrow or over the weekend, but it's something you want to do sooner rather than later, and I'm being very serious now. I want you to buy yourself a box of condoms."

Gasp!

"You can keep them in your underwear drawer, like I used to, but whenever you go out with this girl, even if it's to go to Friendly's, put them in your glove compartment, just in case. But never leave them there," he cautioned.

"The sun can bake them, dry them out, and make them useless. Just put them back in your underwear drawer when you get home. Of course, if you *do* use them, remember to throw them away. And lastly, do *not* leave one in your wallet like an amateur."

Then he hit me with a comment that hit closest to home—something I hadn't considered.

"Bro, you're way too young to become a father, and I'm *way* too young to become an uncle."

Shit, this is *getting serious, but he's right.*

"I understand. I'll take care of it tomorrow," I promised.

"Good. So what else is going on? How's my boy Jean Paul doing?"

We spent the rest of the call talking about Jean Paul and listening to my brother's latest adventures in Boston.

As we wrapped up our call, I said, "Thanks for all the advice, bro. I really appreciate it."

"You bet. You can call me anytime, you know that. Let me know how things are going. Oh, and tell Ma I'll call her Sunday," he said before hanging up.

I sat there on my bed for a moment, staring at the phone and thinking about everything he'd said. As I did this, my eyes drifted to my shorts and I peeked inside.

Sweet Jesus, I think I've got a science experiment happening in my pants. Shower time!

39 - Keeping a Promise

I woke up early the next morning feeling both great and confused. The previous day felt like a whirlwind. So many things happened, from the beach to Hercules, to my conversation with my older brother—there was so much information to process. I did sleep like a champ though, and based on the residue in my underwear, I had dreamt about B.

I grabbed a quick shower and breakfast, and then headed out to the courts, making sure I showed up early, to make a point. I try to keep my promises, most of the time. I beat Jean Paul by ten minutes, which surprised him.

It would be our last game of the summer, and of the year, as it turned out, and I had all of my best insults waiting to go. It's how we rolled, we were best friends. But he gave as good as he got.

I did my Cosell impersonation: "Ladies and Gentlemen, this is the poorest display of sportsmanship I've ever seen. He must be a soccer player," I teased. "And look at the way he's dressed. It's like his parents hate him or something."

"Sir, it's called a tennis racquet, not a baseball bat. You have to get the ball over the net, not over the fence," he teased back.

We spent the better part of three hours playing tennis, until his mom showed up at the court to take him back-to-school shopping.

After tennis, I hit a deli, grabbed lunch, and then hit the road. I had no clear destination in mind; I was just driving. One minute I was heading eastbound on 25A and the next I was heading southbound on Nicolls Road.

As I drove, I thought of B, since the car still smelled of her. I smiled as I listened to the radio while her essence filled my senses.

Before I knew it, I'd driven past Suffolk Community College, the LIE, and Montauk Highway. I soon found myself passing a Welcome to Patchogue sign, a solid forty minutes away from my house.

As I drove around Main Street, I notice a Genovese Drug Store, so I turned into the lot and parked my car. As I mentioned earlier, I attended a boarding school, with boarders and day students. As I parked, I remembered that a few students from my school lived in Patchogue, which made me sweat a little.

Jesus, please don't let there be anyone I know in there.

For some reason, the store had an ominous feel to it. Like something evil was waiting for me to enter or something. I took a deep breath, left my car, and entered the store, making a beeline to the candy aisle in the middle of the store.

Shit, where do they keep these things? Do I ask someone? Man, I didn't really think this one through. Screw it, I should just leave and forget about it.

"Can I help you find something?" asked a male employee wearing a blue vest and assistant manager's badge.

A guy, oh thank God!

"Yeah, um, I need to buy, uh, condoms," I mumbled.

He leaned in a little. "Sorry, I didn't catch that."

Come on, dude. You're killing me!

I stepped closer and mumbled a little louder, "Condoms?"

He nodded. "Your first time buying them?"

I was slightly embarrassed. "How can you tell?"

"Just a hunch. Follow me."

I followed him to the pharmacy counter, my eyes darting furtively left and right, praying that no one would come near us, or worse, recognize me. I could hear it now: *Oh, look who's here buying condoms! Who's the lucky girl?*

Keeping his voice low, he leaned in and asked, "Do you know what you want?"

"Not really," I whispered.

"In that case, I recommend your basic Trojans."

"That sounds good to me."

The clerk took a box of twelve from behind the counter and placed them in a white prescription bag. After paying for them, I practically ran out of the store.

Mission accomplished!

My heart raced as I felt the thrill of victory on my drive home.

Now, where the hell am I going to hide these so Ma won't find them? Should I put them in my underwear drawer like he suggested? Nah, she'll find them.

After hiding them in an old pair of sneakers in the back of my closet, I grabbed a quick shower and removed the stink of tennis off my body. As I dressed, curiosity got the better of me. I'd never actually seen a condom before, let alone held one in my hands.

I wonder what they look and feel like?

I locked my bedroom door, looked out my bedroom window just in case a Russian satellite was spying on me, and grabbed the package from my old Chucks.

I removed them from the paper bag and just marveled at the box on my bed. I looked for directions, but couldn't really find any. I opened the box, took one out and ripped open the package, getting smelly lubricant on my fingers. I wrinkled my nose at the scent.

Eww, that's kinda gross.

I held the silicone tip and unrolled it. It looked like an empty beige balloon and smelled even worse. It was slick to the touch, which made me wonder, *oh God, do these things ever slip off?*

After examining my new purchase, I hid the box back in my closet, wrapped the open condom in toilet paper, and flushed it down the toilet. Now, it's not something I recommend doing today, since it can clog the toilet, but back then I wasn't going to risk it.

There's no way Ma's gonna bust me. Got to get rid of the evidence.

40 - Youth Lock-In

A bout twenty minutes later, B called. She told me all about her last day at work and how they threw her a party. They gave her a nice card signed by club members and staff. They also gave her a really nice end of the summer bonus too, which she said she'd use for back-to-school shopping, and ice cream, if I was nice.

"So apparently I'm not the only one who loves you, huh?" I teased.

"Well, maybe not the only one, but certainly my favorite one."

Nice!

When I brought up plans for the evening, our conversation took an unexpected turn. She actually had plans for the evening already. She explained it was her annual end of the summer youth lock-in, and as a youth leader, she was not only expected to attend, but had responsibilities as well. She had to set things up, make sure everyone was following the rules, etc.

"Oh, okay. Well, that, um, sounds like fun. What time do you have to head over?" I asked, trying to mask my disappointment.

She told me she had to be there in about an hour, but . . .

"Would you like to come? It's open to everyone, not just our youth group. Katie's bringing her boyfriend, and he's not a member of our youth group. I'd love it if you could make it."

She'd mentioned her youth group a few times to me, so I knew it was important to her. I told her I'd have to ask Ma, but sure, I'd love to go, so she gave me all the details: what time I needed to get there, what to pack, and what to bring. It all seemed easy enough.

We spent the remainder of our call flirting and telling each other "I love you"—you know, the normal stuff for a blossoming relationship. After hanging up, I packed an overnight duffle bag, including my pillow, my toiletries, and even some VHS movies, as she'd suggested. I even packed my school Bible. I figured when in Rome . . . and tossed it all into my car.

When Ma got home, we did the back and forth approval dance, but she eventually acquiesced and allowed me to go. On my way over, I stopped by Carvel, since B told me people brought stuff. Hey, who doesn't love Carvel, right? Since I didn't know how many people would be there, Carvel Flying Saucers were off the table. So, I went with a Fudgie the Whale ice cream cake.

He's better than Cookie Puss!

"Would you like anything written on it?" the clerk asked.

I guess I should write something on it, but what?

"Um, yeah, can you write Psalm 23, please?"

It was the only scripture I knew off the top of my head. It was either that or John 3:16, but everyone knows to save that one for football games.

"I'm sorry . . . Palm 23?" she asked.

Jeez, she's worse than I am.

"No, *Psalm*. You know what? Hand me your pen, and I'll write it out for you."

Ten minutes later, I walked out of Carvel with a Fudgie the Whale cake with Psalm 23 written across it.

Thank God Jean Paul's not here.

From there, I went directly to B's church and found some girl waiting for me in the parking lot.

"Hi, are you B's boyfriend?" she asked as I stepped out of my car.

"Yeah, I am."

"Oh good, I'm Nancy. B asked me to wait for you. She told me to watch for your car."

She explained that B was busy inside with preparations. She went on to brag what a great youth leader B was, which didn't surprise me. Was there anything she wasn't good at?

As we walked in, I saw B right away, across the room at a table, setting things up.

"Oh, there she is. B, look who I found wandering outside," Nancy gestured at me.

B smiled and waved me over.

"Hey, mister, you made it!" she said as she hugged me. "Let's see what you brought."

"Here you go. I stopped by Carvel. I figured you can't go wrong with Carvel."

She slid the cake out of the bag, and the moment she saw Fudgie the Whale with Psalm 23 written across it, she started giggling.

"Oh my gosh, this is perfect!" she said, hugging me once again.

Then she pulled back and looked at me and said, "Hi."

Her eyes sparkled as bright as her smile.

How do you do that?

"Hi." I smiled back. "Is this okay?" I asked, gesturing to our public display of affection.

She giggled and nodded, "Yes, it's okay, but thank you for asking. This is another reason why I love you." She kissed me softly on the cheek.

She explained to me that she still had things to do, so she pointed me toward the kitchen and told me to find a spot in the walk-in freezer for Fudgie.

"When you finish with that, you can drop your stuff over there. You'll find my pillow over there somewhere. It's the one with the yellow sunflowers on the pillowcase," she said. "We can sort everything else out later."

I did as she asked and put the cake in the walk-in freezer. I goosed B as I passed her on my way to drop off my duffel bag. It startled her, and made me laugh. I couldn't help myself. I found B's pillow, just like she described it, and placed my stuff next to it.

Okay, now what do I do? She's busy getting things ready, and I don't know another soul. I guess it's time to extend my hand and meet some new people.

I walked around and started checking out the joint. There were kids everywhere, and I greeted them as I walked around. Everyone seemed friendly enough, which was nice. I ended up in a combination TV room/lounge. There were kids playing ping pong, video games, reading, and even strumming on guitars.

I walked over and introduced myself to the two guys playing video games. They asked me the usual questions: *Who are you here with? Where do you go to school?* And so on.

They teased me a bit about going to a private school—calling me a "rich kid." That was when a girl sitting off in the corner reading chimed in.

"Pay no attention to those troglodytes. They think everyone with their own car is a rich kid." She was sitting on a beanbag in the corner, book in her hand. She added, "My name's Violet. Everyone calls me Vi."

"Not everyone," the boys teased.

"Oh, bite me!"

"Okay, you two, be nice to Vi, or *I'll* stop being nice to you," B threatened as she entered the room.

"Yes, ma'am, we'll be nice." They giggled before returning to their video game.

"Just ignore those two, Vi," B said as she walked over.

"I always do," Vi replied, pretending to go back to her book, but still keeping an eye on us.

"So have you introduced yourself to everyone yet?" B asked.

Vi answered for me. "He was just getting to it."

"Well, good. Let's go meet people," B said as she grabbed my hand.

"Lead on, McDuff," I said.

We walked around, and B introduced me to a bunch of people as her boyfriend, which put a smile on my face. I still wasn't used to being called someone's *boyfriend*. We eventually bumped into someone I knew from elementary school, Jack Sanger.

"Hey, Jack, long time no see, man! How've you been?"

We shook hands and he dragged me away from B, over to a set of couches so we could do some catching up. B smiled as we walked away—I guess she felt I was in good hands.

Jack and I talked for a while. He introduced me to a few people, telling them, "He was one of the funniest guys in school. He used to joke around all the time, but never got in trouble."

Ha, if he only knew.

B eventually joined us and we held hands as Jack continued regaling about the good old days. Everyone laughed as he shared the stories. But my favorite part was sharing it with B.

God, her gorgeous blue eyes sure do twinkle when she laughs.

Everyone's favorite story was, "Do you remember that time your dog peed on me?"

For a moment everyone paused, then burst out in howling laughter. Belle was a pup at the time, but it was still embarrassing as hell.

"What can I say, she liked you so much that she wanted to mark her territory—on your right foot," I joked.

Soon, others joined in with their own embarrassing stories, including B. Apparently, when she was in third grade, she was so nervous before a chorus concert that she literally peed herself.

"I was dying from embarrassment. I was in the bathroom, and I remember throwing my red leggings and underwear into the garbage. I cleaned myself up as best I could, and went out there with nothing on underneath," she told us.

"Oh my gosh, I wanted to die! Thankfully, my dress came down to my knees, so no one knew. My mother took me home right after the concert, and to this day, she has never asked me about those leggings and underwear."

As we sat there laughing, B's youth pastor and his wife interrupted the share-fest with the announcement that pizza had arrived. It was like a fire alarm had gone off. Teens from all over came rushing into the makeshift dining area and practically hurled themselves at the boxes of Domino's Pizza. Ever the strategist, B suggested I grab our drinks while she grabbed our slices.

"You know what I like," she said as I nodded and giggled. Suddenly realizing how I'd taken her comment, her eyes widened, then narrowed, and she mouthed, "I'll kill you" with a mock mean face, which made me chuckle.

As I returned with our drinks, B's youth pastor, Rev. Mike Thompson, and his wife, Emily, made their way over to introduce themselves.

"Mike and Emily, this is my boyfriend. I invited him to join us tonight. I told him he'd be safe tonight, since we only sacrifice freshmen," B teased.

Mike slapped me on the back. "Well, we're glad to have you. We hope you enjoy yourself tonight. Come back anytime," he said as a paper plate flew past his head.

"Excuse me, apparently I need to go beat a child! Hey, that almost hit me, Brian! You realize this means war!" he yelled as he took off toward a pack of scattering boys.

Emily smiled and shook her head as she watched her husband run off.

"You'll have to excuse him. He's as big a child as those boys. Well, it's a pleasure to meet you. We do hope you enjoy yourself tonight, and again, you're welcome back anytime. Our unwritten motto is 'the more the merrier,'" Emily then excused herself as more youth began to show up.

B and I returned to the couch and ate our dinner. Soon, others joined us, and they began reminiscing about various youth trips and events they had participated in over the years. They were a really busy group, which surprised me, for some reason.

This was my first exposure to a youth group, so I didn't really know what to expect. Part of me expected a cult-like setting or something. I was thinking Jonestown or something, for some reason. But it wasn't like that at all. It was just a group of kids my age hanging out. It was really nice and very comfortable.

After eating, B offered to give me a tour of the facility. We started in the main sanctuary. It was a nice, old-school sanctuary, with deep-red carpeting, stained glass windows, and wooden padded pews for the congregation.

"I was baptized right up there," B said, pointing to the baptismal font. The sanctuary had a solemn and holy feel to it. The moonlight coming in through the stained glass windows gave it an almost bluish hue. It was a quiet and peaceful setting. We grabbed a seat in one of the middle pews and quietly held each other, as we took in the whole place.

"Can you see yourself getting married here too?" I whispered.

"You're not proposing already, are you, mister?" she asked with a sly smile. "You're moving kind of fast there, don't you think?"

"*What*?" I replied louder than I anticipated.

She just laughed, shook her head, and gave me an elbow before standing, "Let's go, mister, before you have a heart attack or say something you'll regret."

"Well, um, it's just that, uh . . ." I stammered as she placed her index finger on my lips.

"Shhh . . ." She stopped me in my tracks and wrapped her arms around my neck. "Just kiss me, silly."

This was the first of three times I would ever kiss a woman in church. The second would be when I proposed to my wife, and the third was at my wedding. All three were equally unforgettable and special.

I'd never felt this type of peace in my life. It was even more intimate than the previous evening in my car. There we were, wrapped in God's presence, kissing.

When our lips separated, we simply stared into each other's eyes, fully aware of how truly special this moment was. "God, I love you, mister," she whispered.

"I love you too," I replied as I held her in my arms. I never wanted to let her go. At that moment, her love penetrated me and filled the entire sanctuary. It was in that moment that I knew I'd love her forever.

"It's time to go," she said, and I nodded in agreement. As we left the sanctuary, I looked up at the altar one last time and smiled.

One day, B. One day . . . I'll marry you up there.

41 - The Scavenger Hunt

We toured the rest of the property, including the church cemetery and the senior pastor's home. Twenty minutes later, Katie greeted us with a knowing smile and a raised eyebrow as we returned to the youth center, "So where've you guys been?"

Busted!

"I was just giving him a tour," B replied while subtly giving Katie the middle finger as she scratched her nose, making Katie giggle.

Katie had only just arrived with her boyfriend Chad. And after doing the prerequisite introductions, they went off to find some grub before the next event started. B and I grabbed more soda and walked into the makeshift TV room/lounge, where people were playing cards, watching TV, playing board games, and some were playing instruments.

We walked over to the musicians. "Hey, guys. What do you have planned for tonight?" B asked.

"Oh you know, the usual," one of them said.

"So we're talking Sabbath, Ozzy and Dio?" I joked.

"This guy's all right!" another one said.

"Hey, I only bring the best to our lock-ins," B said.

"Can you imagine if we played that here? Mike would shit himself." This guy was playing an electric guitar, and he punctuated his comment with an Eddie Van Halen riff. Then he looked up at B and asked, "You're still planning on joining us tonight, right?"

"*Maybe*, we'll see how I'm feeling," she said slyly.

Eddie turned to me, "That means *yes*, in case you didn't already know. Anyway, we have a few good ones for you tonight that I think are in your range," he said.

Wait, she has a range? Since when does she sing? Why don't I know this? She's not in our school choir. I'm in our choir, and I would've noticed.

"Good, I look forward to it. We'll leave you alone, so you can practice," B said, and we walked away, leaving them to it. B then excused herself. She had to help set up the desserts, leaving me to fend for myself once again.

That was when I noticed Vi quietly sitting across the room reading a book among all the activity and noise.

"So what are you reading?" I asked as I sat down on the floor across from her.

"C. S. Lewis's *The Screwtape Letters*." She showed me the book cover.

"Is it any good?"

"You're really interested in hearing about some book versus watching TV or playing video games?" she asked incredulously.

"Yeah, I guess, why?"

She shrugged and fiddled with the book. "I don't know. No one ever asks me what I'm reading, except for B. I guess I can see why you two are together."

"Uh, thanks, I guess. So what's it about?"

She then sat up and proceeded to tell me about the book. She told me it was the third time she'd read it, and it was one of her favorite books, next to the *Lord of The Rings* trilogy. In those few moments, she transformed from an introverted, book-reading, nerdy type to an artist describing a masterpiece.

"But you should really read it for yourself. I'm really not giving it the justice it deserves," she concluded.

"Really? Hell, if the book is as half as good as you've just described it, I think I'd finish it in a day, and I'm a slow reader."

"Really, you'd actually read this book after I just described it to you?" she asked, looking at me with an expression of surprise.

"Yeah, of course. You really made it sound good!" I said with a smile.

"Thanks," she replied with a smile of her own.

(It's no wonder she became a bestselling author as an adult. Vi published her first novel during her junior year of college, which became an immediate bestseller on the New York Times Best Sellers list. Oprah even chose one of her novels as one of her book-of-the-month selections.)

B popped back in the room, announcing that dessert was available, which caused another near-stampede of hungry teenagers.

We loaded up on dessert, or rather, B loaded up on dessert. I took a few brownies and a cookie. As we sat down, I marveled at the amount of dessert on her plate.

"What? I have a fast metabolism," she said defensively.

"What? I didn't say anything," I replied.

She mimicked me, *"What? I didn't say anything . . .* I know what you were thinking, mister."

I then leaned closer, "Really? What am I thinking now?" I snickered.

"Ha! Keep dreaming. That's not on the dessert menu tonight, you bad boy," she said, before leaning over and adding, "But then again, you never know."

Boing! Damn it! She did it to me again and at church! I'm definitely going to hell!

After dessert, Pastor Mike gathered everyone and announced it was time for the annual scavenger hunt. Whoops and hollers rippled through the crowd.

The room was split up into four teams. The team leaders were Katie, B, Emily, and Pastor Mike. Each team had an hour to gather as many items as possible from the list of items. The team with the most items won. He gave us five minutes to clean up and return so the captains could start picking their teams. As we cleaned up, Iris showed up, which made B and Katie squeal with happiness as they hugged her.

Girls . . .

Emily told Iris that she'd saved her some dinner and dessert if she was interested before the game began.

Iris gave her a hug and said, "Thanks, Em. I'm starving, but I think I'll eat after the hunt. There's no way I'm missing out on winning the third time in a row," she said full of confidence and bravado.

Jeez, you and Jean Paul are perfect for each other.

"That's my girl!" Emily said, giving her a double high-five.

Emily then called for order and announced the captains would start picking teams. Katie went first and, to no one's surprise, picked Chad. B's choice, on the other hand, surprised everyone.

"Iris," she said defiantly, which was met with a lot of *whoa* sounds.

"Wait a minute, you're picking Iris, *my* Iris?" Emily asked, incredulous.

"Yep, that's right. I'm breaking up the team," B said.

Mike chose next, followed by Emily, who chose me, eliciting some gasps from the attendees, including B.

"Sorry, babe, but she did say she wanted to win," I teased as I high-fived Emily and got in line behind her.

"Oh, I like this guy, B. He's a keeper," Emily said.

B just shook her head, then winked at me, pointed and mouthed, "It's on."

"Whoa! It looks like people are out for blood here tonight," Pastor Mike said with a grin. "Remember, people, this is just a game, so play nice."

B then stuck her tongue out at me, which earned some laughter.

Oh, it's on!

They finished picking teams and Mike started the countdown. The room shook with kinetic teenage energy and excitement.

Finally, Mike broke the tension, announcing, "Oh the heck with it, go! See you all at midnight! And remember, have fun and be careful!"

Our team huddled around Emily, who began handing out assignments.

"Okay, since B stole our squirrel this year, we're going to need a new one. Who's a really good climber?" she asked.

Vi stuck her hand up, which surprised everyone, including Emily.

"Really, Vi? Okay, you're my new squirrel." Emily announced, then looked at the rest of us, "She's going to need some help out there, so who's going to partner with our new squirrel?"

Before anyone could answer, Vi grabbed my arm and said, "He will. He's all I need."

"Are you sure Vi? There's a lot of ground to cover out there," Emily replied.

"I'm sure," Vi replied confidently.

Emily just shrugged and said okay. She then proceeded to hand out our buddy assignments, a flashlight, and a final reminder regarding the property boundaries.

"We'll meet back here at midnight. Now go make me proud, and remember, be careful and have fun!" Emily instructed as we left.

Our first task: *retrieve a plastic beach ball stuck in a tree.*

Vi and I walked the property for a few minutes, when she finally pointed upward, "Is *that* it up there?"

I shined the flashlight up and sure enough, there it was, a plastic beach ball stuck high up in the trees. Of course, once I flashed a light on it, others started coming our way.

I said, "*Shit*, I mean *shoot*. Quick, give me your leg, and I'll toss you up there, cool?"

She was cool with it, so I cupped my hands together, and tossed her up to the first branch.

Damn! She is just like a squirrel.

She climbed that tree like a champ. Iris stepped up next to me and marveled as Vi expertly navigated the limbs of the tree. I guess everyone was accustomed to Vi the book nerd, not Vi the squirrel.

Moments later, she tossed the ball down to me, which I deflated as she expertly descended the tree. I gave her a high-five when she got down, as did a few others. She took it all in stride. She really was an introvert, I realized, and open praises made her uncomfortable.

The teams split up again, and the next item on our list was: *retrieve Frisbee from roof.*

"How good are you at holding ladders?" Vi asked.

"Fine, I guess, why?" I replied.

She gave a wicked smile, "You'll see."

Soon we were off running through some dense woods on the property and came out in front of an old tool shed behind the youth center.

"Awesome, no one else is here," she said.

I grabbed an orange workman's ladder from the shed and carried it to the front of the youth center. I set it next to the ledge and held it as Squirrel scurried up the ladder. Moments later, she tossed down a green Frisbee and then expertly slid down the ladder, like a professional firefighter.

"I saw it in a movie once," she joked as I tucked the Frisbee into the back of my shorts.

Two down, two to go.

The next item on the list was a blue kite stuck in a tree.

We tore off toward the trees again, only to discover Iris climbing down a tree with the kite in her hand.

Make that three down and one to go.

The final item was a red balloon stuck in a tree.

We only had fifteen minutes left on the clock, and we both knew we'd need every second on that clock if we wanted to retrieve the item and make it back in time.

"I know exactly where this is," Vi whispered to me. "Follow me."

With that, we took off, past the front of the youth center and ran straight into the woods near the front of the property.

"I remember this happening at the beginning of the summer," she explained as we ran through the woods, avoiding branches and stumps along the way. We exited the trees and found ourselves in front of a narrow brook with running water. "Look, we have two choices," she said. "We can jump across this brook, which I've done a million times, or we can cross the bridge down there." She pointed at a wooden bridge thirty yards in the wrong direction.

Hell, if she can do it, so can I.

"Let's jump," I replied.

"Okay, ready?" she asked.

"Born ready."

She then took off like a bullet, as we heard Iris and her teammates exiting the woods behind us.

Damn, she's faster than she looks.

We all just watched her as she gracefully leapt into the air like a gazelle, landing safely on the other side of the brook.

Wow, who is this girl?

We all just stood there with our mouths open. This obviously wasn't the Violet they thought they knew. And it wasn't, because tonight, she was the Squirrel.

"What are you waiting for?" Vi yelled, breaking me from my trance.

I ran like hell then leapt across the brook, gracefully wiping out on the other side of the brook.

Vi came running up to me, "Shit, you okay?"

I stood up, embarrassed, and brushed myself off. "Yeah, I'm fine, I'm fine. Let's go, let's go," I replied as the other team prepared to attempt a flight across the brook.

Three out of the four made it across successfully. The third person slipped and fell, stopping short of the water.

Vi and I ran and found our prey, a slightly deflated red balloon stuck up in an old gnarly tree. Just like before, I cupped my hands and tossed her up to the first branch. As she got herself situated, Iris and her team pulled up next to me.

Like me, one of her teammates cupped his hands and tossed Iris up in the tree. She landed on a branch opposite Vi. The race was on. The Original Squirrel versus Squirrel, The Next-Generation.

They both deftly climbed the gnarly old tree like a pair of . . . well, squirrels. Unlike the beach ball, the balloon was higher and tougher to reach.

Tree limbs shook as they climbed higher, causing leaves and branches to rain down.

"Are you guys okay down there?" Vi yelled as she continued her climb, pulling ahead of Iris.

"Yeah, we're all fine," I hollered back, surveying everyone, who all nodded their heads. "Just be careful and get the balloon. Don't worry about us."

The string tied to the balloon was almost within Vi's grasp. All she had to do was stretch for it, but as she did this, we heard the threatening sounds of limbs breaking.

"Hey, Vi, be careful up there!" I yelled.

"I've almost got it," she screeched, excited as her fingertips almost touched the balloon string. She was determined to get that stupid balloon. Who knew why? Maybe she was trying to prove something to this group of kids who saw her as a bookworm. Maybe she was trying to prove something to herself.

To this day, I have no idea what motivated her, but there was no way I was going to watch this girl fall to her death over a stupid balloon.

"Be careful, Violet," Iris said as she stopped a few limbs below Vi and merely watched as Vi continued to stretch for the balloon.

"I've got to go higher," Vi yelled down to us.

"Hey, it's too dangerous. Wait a minute, I've got an idea. Do you trust me?" I yelled.

"Yeah, I guess so, why?"

"Just hold on a sec, and get ready to grab the balloon okay? And you'll want to lean back a little," I yelled as everyone looked at me.

"Okay, but hurry up, or I'll just climb higher and get it."

Clearly I was dealing with a crazy person here.

I searched the ground and found exactly what I was looking for, a skipping stone. Finally, my misspent youth chucking rocks with my kid brother would come in handy.

"All right, Squirrel, lean back, while I do my job," I yelled as I eyeballed the balloon.

Everyone around me then stepped back to give me room. With the flick of my wrist, I threw the stone at the balloon.

POP!

Yes!

The balloon popped and fell right into Vi's outstretched hand.

"I got it!" Vi yelled and bounced on the tree limb full of excitement. That was when we heard the familiar sound.

Cra-a-a-ck!

The limb Vi was on gave way, and she fell like a stone.

She shot straight down, right past Iris and landed squarely in my arms. We tumbled to the ground as she landed. Talk about being in the right place at the right time.

We both quickly sat up; she was still holding the balloon, and I was still holding her. She immediately collapsed into my chest and cried.

Holy fuck! (Sorry, Lord.)

I held her for a minute before gently releasing her. Iris and the others came to us and checked on Vi as she stood. Fortunately, she was okay, just shaken up a bit. Iris pointed out that we only had a few minutes left, so both teams triumphantly returned to the youth center together.

We dropped our things off with our team captains and patiently waited for the results. Emily immediately noticed how well we did, and I gave Vi her due credit.

"Really, Violet, is that true?" Emily asked.

"Yeah, I guess so," she timidly replied.

"Wow, *that's* awesome, Violet! I'm so proud of you," Emily replied as she gave her an enthusiastic hug.

The team captains then gathered together and tallied all the points.

"Okay, we have our final tallies," Katie announced. "In fourth place this year, Team Mike . . . *again!*" He smirked and waved in defeat. "Okay, in third place by a very small margin, my team!" she said, gracefully accepting her own defeat.

"Surprisingly, this year, it wasn't even close. It was almost a blowout actually. So without further ado, second place goes to . . . drum roll, please?"

Everyone started playing drums on their laps.

"Second place goes to Team B! And for the third year in a row, Team Emily takes first place!" she exclaimed as Emily pumped her fist and high-fived her teammates.

As everyone started dispersing, Emily held everyone back, saying, "Wait a minute, everyone, wait a minute. We haven't announced our MVP this year." She looked at her team, grinning.

"So this year by a unanimous decision, our Class of 1988 MVP is . . . my team's *new* Squirrel, Violet! Vi, get up!"

Everyone clapped enthusiastically, though most had their mouths open in disbelief.

I guess sometimes you just need to step outside your comfort zone to break out of your shell. And that night, Violet didn't just break out of her shell, she shattered it!

42 - Youth Band

"**B**, thanks for inviting me tonight. Man, I'm really having a great time," I enthusiastically told B as Emily dismissed everyone. "I had no idea this is what youth group was all about."

"I'm so glad you're having fun," she replied with a big smile and hug.

"Great job tonight, you guys," Emily said as she walked around hugging her team.

"Thanks, Emily," I replied.

"Listen, you're welcome to join us anytime, and not just for our lock-ins, okay? I mean that. You're a wonderful addition to our group. Anyone who can crack *that* girl out of her shell and have her openly participate is a winner in my book," she whispered while gesturing at Vi.

"We've tried for years to get her to join in, but nothing seemed to work, until tonight. So whatever you did, keep doing it." She hugged me again and walked away, leaving me feeling pretty damn good.

"Hey, do you guys have a second?" we heard a familiar voice ask.

"Hey, Squirrel, congrats on the MVP! You earned it," I said.

She then came straight at me and she hugged me—hard. Boy, there sure was a lot of hugging going on, and I was happy to be one of the recipients.

"Thanks for everything tonight," she whispered as she hugged me.

"Sure thing, anything for a friend," I replied, my voice cracking a little as I was getting a bit choked up in the moment.

"No one's ever believed in me like you did tonight. And then I fell and . . . you caught me and . . ."

"Oh, Vi."

"That's *Squirrel* to you." She wiped tears from her eyes.

"You've got it. Squirrel it is."

Before walking away, Vi turned to B and said, "He's a special one, B. Don't you lose him."

"Trust me, he's not getting away from me that easy," B replied as Vi walked away. "Wow, it looks like someone's made a new friend."

"It looks that way. So what's next?" I asked, as we walked toward our pillows and overnight things.

"Well, the outdoor activities are pretty much over, except for roasting marshmallows out back later, if you want. From here on out, it's all indoor stuff."

"*Really*? You *don't* say?" I said with a sly smile.

She laughed, stomped her foot and playfully shoved me, "No! Not that. Just go put on something comfortable, and meet me over there," she said, pointing to the TV lounge.

As she headed off to change, she goosed me as I bent over to grab my clothes.

"Hey!" I yelped as she turned and stuck her tongue out. Then she casually sashayed toward the restrooms.

After changing into a pair of gray sweatpants and a T-shirt in the men's room, I met B in the lounge. That night she wore a Rolling Stones T-shirt, one from *Tattoo You*, a pair of gray sweatpants similar to mine, and white tube socks pulled up over her sweats. She also braided her hair into a ponytail.

I may be a little biased, but this relaxed, evening version of B was just as beautiful as the daytime version. It made me wonder what the dressed-up version would look like for a formal event, like say, homecoming or our wedding.

Too soon?

"Hey, were you the one who took the ladder from the shed?" she asked as she walked in.

"Uh, yeah, I was. That was okay, wasn't it? I'm not in trouble, am I?"

"What? Oh no, you're not in trouble, although I am upset that my team didn't think of it," she grinned. "Anyway, no, you're not in trouble, but you do need to put it back."

"Oh yeah, sure, that's not a problem. I'll go do it now," I said as I slipped on my sneakers. "I'll be right back."

"You don't have to do it alone. I'll come with you, silly," she said as she slipped her hand into mine. As we left, she called out to Katie, "Hey, we'll be right back. We're going to return the ladder to the shed. Can you have the boys start setting up?"

Katie gave a thumbs-up, and out the door we went with a flashlight to show us the way to the shed.

I propped the ladder back where I found it, and as I closed the shed door, B jumped me from behind and tackled me to the ground.

"Ha! I got you!"

"You're getting good at your sneak attacks, Kato. Have you considered going pro?" I said between laughs.

"I'll keep that in mind. All kidding aside, I'm so glad you came tonight and that you're having a good time."

"Correction, I'm having a *great* time. I've never experienced anything like this before. I'm really surprised," I said as we stood and headed back to the youth center.

"Why are you surprised?" she asked.

"I don't know. To be honest, I didn't know what to expect. All I know is that this wasn't it, and I mean that in a good way."

"Excellent," she replied, before pushing me against the outer wall of the youth center. She trapped me between her arms and stared at me, causing her blue eyes to shimmer like a pair of diamonds in the moonlight.

She then slowly leaned into me, and kissed me. We just stayed there, lost in our own little world, kissing, with God and the universe as our witnesses.

God, she felt so good.

As we kissed, we heard Iris yelling for us. B then did something so sweet and intimate as we finished kissing. She gently brushed her thumb across my bottom lip and smiled.

God, I love this girl.

"We're coming!" B yelled over her shoulder, before taking my hand.

As we walked in, Iris let us know that everything was all set.

"Great, I'm going to powder my nose. Can you start telling people to head in and find a place to sit?" she asked Iris, who knew what she was talking about. "Okay, mister, follow Iris and find a seat. And thanks for, um, returning the ladder," she said with a wink.

"My pleasure ma'am."

Moments later, I walked into a dining hall with a stage. The tables and chairs were all pushed to either side of the hall, leaving the middle wide open for everybody to sit or stand. There were about forty of us in attendance that night, plus the four-member youth band on stage, warming up.

As everyone settled in, B and Katie walked out on stage, each with a microphone, and everybody quieted down as a spotlight hit them center stage.

"Okay, is everybody here?" B asked.

As B spoke, I felt someone huddle up next to me. It was my new pal Vi, so I gave her a quick squeeze around her shoulders, which made her smile, and then we continued to pay attention to B and Katie.

"All right, are you guys ready to have some fun tonight?" Katie yelled as she tried to excite the crowd. We all responded appropriately, with whoops and whistles.

"Okay, guys, without further ado, we give you Rise Again!" Katie and B yelled, as "Eddie Junior" hit a note on his guitar and sustained it, using his whammy bar.

As the girls left the stage, Rise Again took over and played a bunch of songs, which everyone but me seemed to know. B worked her way to the front, where I stood with Vi, and took my hand as everyone rocked back and forth to the music.

After their twenty-minute set of praise and worship music, the lead singer led everyone in a quick prayer.

"Okay, guys, you know what time it is," he said.

While I was clueless, everyone around me knew exactly what was coming next and began applauding, so I followed suit and applauded along with the crowd.

"Come on, B. Get on up here!" he announced, and B shyly worked her way back to center stage.

"You're really going to like this," Vi whispered as I clapped along, still clueless.

"Well, thank you, Ryan," B said, taking her place behind the microphone. "As you all know, I never know what these guys have in store for me, so let me apologize in advance if I bomb tonight," she modestly laughed, as we applauded.

She then turned to the band, "Okay, what do you guys have for me this year?"

Kyle handed her a clipboard with sheet music and lyrics. She shook her head and giggled as she reviewed the five songs. At one point, she pulled the clipboard to her chest and looked with wide eyes at the band.

"Really, guys, *these* are the *other* two you want me to sing?" she asked.

"We told you we'd surprise you this year. You know the rules; you have to sing all of them or we get to spray you down with a hose," Ryan reminded her.

"Okay, well, I certainly don't want *that* to happen again, so I guess I'm in," B responded, making a silly face at the crowd, who applauded in encouragement.

Happen again?

Kyle placed a stool behind B, who sat down and got comfortable. The band then played the intro to "El Shaddai," an Amy Grant song.

I became completely lost in this moment as she sang, with the voice of an angel.

Amazing. Her voice is as beautiful as she is.

She followed this song with a couple of others I frankly don't remember. All I remember is they were awesome.

As we applauded, she took a sip of water and thanked us. Soon, silence filled the room as we waited for her next song to begin.

What happened next totally surprised me. The band started playing the opening chords of the song, "Sara", by Fleetwood Mac.

I can remember it like it was yesterday. The spotlight hit her just right, as she took the microphone into both hands, tilted her head slightly, allowing her ponytail to slide to the side of her face. She then closed her eyes and she sang in a beautiful and haunting voice,

> *Wait a minute baby*
> *Stay with me awhile*
> *Said you'd give me light*
> *But you never told me about the fire*

That night, it felt like she was singing directly to me, especially when she sang:

> *And he was just like a great dark wing*
> *Within the wings of a storm*
> *I think I had met my match, he was singing*

Only she replaced the words *singing* with *laughing*, and looked directly at me and smiled. Her performance was mesmerizing and I was just so proud of her.

After she finished and the applause died down, B thanked everyone, including the band. She then called Mike and Emily to the stage, where they were each presented with a gift.

"A small token of our appreciation for all you do for us," B said as Mike unwrapped his gift, which was a trophy that read: To The Best Youth Pastor Ever from the Class of 1988.

Emily's gift was a gift certificate to Macy's.

"Yay, my favorite store," she said. "And I know just WHO I'm going to spend it on," she announced, then knowingly patted her belly.

B squealed, "Really?"

Emily nodded, "Yup, we're having a baby," she announced as Mike hugged his wife. The room erupted with excitement at the wonderful news.

"I think this news deserves one more song," Mike said, gesturing to B, as we all agreed.

B held up her hands to quiet the crowd, "Okay, okay, fine. But since it's such a special occasion, I'd like to break with tradition and invite someone up here to join me . . . that is, if we can encourage him to get up here."

I feel sorry for that guy. Good luck, sucka!

With that, the crowd started applauding, and I followed suit as I looked around the room for the patsy that had to go up there and join B.

"Guys, can you please help me get my *boyfriend* up here?" she said into her microphone.

Did I just hear a needle scratch a record?

I'm sorry . . . who?

With that, Vi and Iris grabbed my arms from either side and led me to the stage. I just shook my head in defeat, took a deep breath, and joined B on stage.

B handed me Katie's microphone as I met her at center stage.

"What are you doing? I don't know these songs," I whispered as I stood there smiling.

"Oh, I think you'll know this one," she said confidently as she handed me the sheet music.

Yep, I know this one!

In fact, I think every New Yorker knows this song by heart. I just laughed and threw my hands in the air, ready to live in the moment.

And away we go.

As the piano started, I took B's hand, shut my eyes and began to sing a song I knew by heart,

Some folks like to get away,
Take a holiday from the neighborhood.
Hop a flight to Miami Beach or to Hollywood.
But I'm takin' a Greyhound on the Hudson River line.
I'm in a New York state of mind.

Before I knew it, B and I performed a duet, harmonizing as we sang the song. The youth group gave a generous round of applause and whistles as we finished.

I bowed slightly, then tried to make a quick exit. But B would have none of that, pulling me back and pointing at me, encouraging the group to applaud louder, which they did.

Is she part witch or something? She has this group in the palm of her hand!

As the applause died down, B called Mike back to the stage to close out the praise and worship service in prayer.

To this day, I'll never forget that Holy experience. It's the only way to describe it. It was beyond magical. It was truly Holy. B and I fell asleep that evening, curled up together on a couch off in a corner. As I drifted off, I felt more love in my soul than I'd ever felt in my life, and it was all thanks to the blond beauty that I held warmly and securely in my arms.

Thank you God.

43 - The Fergusen Party

The next morning, we ate more pancakes for breakfast than I thought humanly possible. Once breakfast was finished, the cleanup crew took over and we were dismissed. We all said our goodbyes, and I walked B to her car, where we made plans for me to pick her up later that evening for the Fergusen party. We agreed to stay for only an hour.

When I got home, I didn't even bother unpacking my stuff. I walked in, kissed Ma on the cheek and went directly to my room. I grabbed my B-scented pillow and crashed until two thirty that afternoon.

After a quick bite, I called Hannah to confirm what time we'd be picking her up. I then spent the rest of my afternoon lounging by the pool until it was time to get ready for the party. By six o'clock I was heading out the door, wearing one of my new polo shirts and a smile, as I reflected on the previous evening.

I made it to B's on time. She came into the kitchen wearing jean shorts, a pink top, and a light cardigan around her shoulders. She also wore a black ribbon in her hair, the rope ankle bracelet on her right ankle, a pair of pink anklet socks that matched her top, and white Keds.

We went to pick up Hannah. She was waiting for us in her driveway, also fashionably dressed. As we made our way to the party, B told Hannah all about the lock-in—including my singing debut. Hannah laughed hysterically, astounded by the fact that anyone could get me to sing on stage.

"Trust me, no one was more surprised than me," I assured her.

We pulled up to the party by seven o'clock, and the place was already packed. Cars were parked all over the place. It was like a jigsaw puzzle trying to find a parking spot. Fortunately, I found a spot near the driveway entrance, so we could easily make our escape in an hour or so.

Empty beer bottles were strewn all over the front lawn.

Classy.

Some drunken idiot stumbled past us, out the front door, and proceeded to puke in the bushes as we entered. *One hour,* I mouthed as we entered the foyer.

We were immediately greeted with "Hey, Bitch!" from Mary, shouting as she stumbled down the stairs. She was clearly on her way to another drunken adventure.

The two greeted each other first, followed by Hannah and me. I could tell already that this would be a very long hour.

Mary grabbed B by the arm and said, "Come on, there are people here looking for you." Hannah and I followed closely behind. We made our way to the kitchen, where there were two bar stations set up.

Each station had a bartender and an assortment of the finest alcohol. There was a line at each station as the bartenders took drink orders from drunken partygoers, adults and minors alike.

Across the noise, we heard a voice shout, "B! Oh, B dear, is that you?" It was an elderly woman, who shoved people out of her way to get to B.

"Hello, Nana!" B smiled widely and hugged a woman she clearly cherished.

Nana took B's hand and said, "So tell me everything, dear, and don't leave out a thing. How are your studies coming along? And tell me about all the boys you're fighting off at school. You must be fending off many. You look gorgeous!" Nana gushed.

Mary huffed out a breath and rolled her eyes. "Nana, it's still summer. We're not in school yet."

Nana waved her hand dismissively at Mary, "Oh hush, you. Why don't you go get some coffee in you? You're a worse drunk than that father of yours," she chastised as she led B away to a deck outside, overlooking a large back yard.

B looked over her shoulder and mouthed an apology as they stepped outside. I just smiled and told her not to worry about it.

Hannah slipped away as well, and I turned and found myself standing there alone with Mary.

"So what's your poison, sailor?" she joked.

"Coke."

"Wow, I didn't know you did coke. You really *are* cooler than I thought," she said with surprise in her voice.

"*What?* No! I meant to drink. I'll have *a Coke.*"

"Sweetie, this is a Fergusen party. Coke is what you *snort*, not what you drink," she cackled as she rolled her eyes at me and then stumbled away.

With that, I got in line for the bar, I looked at my watch and saw that thankfully we had only fifty minutes left.

"What'll it be, sir? We have imported beer or perhaps you'd care for a mixed drink?" the bartender asked.

"I'll have two Cokes with lemons, please," I replied.

"Well, that's refreshing," the bartender whispered to himself.

I guess he's tired of serving alcohol to minors.

There were food stands everywhere, and servers walking around with platters of hors d'oeuvres. The party was as decadent as Mary had advertised. There were champagne fountains, chocolate fountains, and an assortment of various carving stations set up throughout the place. I popped a piece of cheddar into my mouth as I made my way toward B.

She was standing there talking to Nana and an older gentleman in his mid-fifties who looked like he stepped out of an L.L. Bean catalog. He was slightly tanned, with slicked-back, salt-and-pepper hair. He wore a seersucker blazer with a white button-down shirt, a pair of khaki pants, and boat shoes.

When B saw me, she waved me over.

I handed B a Coke as she introduced me, "Nana, Mr. Fergusen—I'm sorry, I mean *Gus*—let me introduce you to my boyfriend."

Even though his first name was Oliver, I later learned that he preferred Gus, a nickname he apparently picked up at prep school.

I guess the bad apple didn't fall far from the rotten tree.

"It's a pleasure to meet you," Gus said, sniffling and fidgeting with his slightly white-powdered nostrils.

What a loser!

Nana laid a hand on my arm and gave me a pleasant smile. "Well, hello, dear! B's been telling me all about you. She says your mother is a *surgeon*, is that right?"

"Yes, ma'am, she's a pediatric surgeon. She practices locally."

"Yes, that's very nice. Very nice indeed," Gus said politely while still fidgeting with his nose.

Nana cut him off, "Oh, shut up, Oliver, and go fetch me a dirty martini, dry with one olive," she said sharply, dismissing him.

He sighed and muttered, "Yes, Mother, I'll be right back."

"Mmhmm, let's see how fast he returns with my martini. I bet he's already forgotten about it and is off searching for wife number five. You just stay away from him, young lady. I wouldn't want him sinking his claws into you," Nana warned, miming fangs and a pair of bony claws as B laughed awkwardly, grabbing my arm.

"Oh, I wouldn't worry about that, not with this one here to protect me, Nana."

"Yes, well, very good, dear. And you," she said, pointing a crooked, bony finger in my direction. "You better treat this young lady right, or you'll have me to contend with, do you understand?"

"Yes, ma'am. I will *continue* to treat her like a precious jewel," I replied as I kissed B's hand.

"Oh, I do *like* this boy, dear. I like him a *lot*," Nana said approvingly.

"So do I, Nana, so do I," B replied as she planted a kiss on my shoulder.

"Yes, very well then, why don't you two lovebirds go off and have some fun, while I track down that good-for-nothing son of mine with my martini?" She headed toward the kitchen, hollering, "Oliver! Oliver Roger Fergusen, where the hell is my damn martini?!"

"Well, that was interesting," I said.

"You don't know the half of it," she replied.

Thirty-eight more minutes to go . . .

44 - The Straw that Broke the Camel's Back

"She's actually a godsend, and so were you," B said. "Gus started hitting on me again, and in front of Nana no less. He's been doing it since I turned fifteen. He's totally disgusting, and it gets worse when he's had a few. He's always hugging me and asking when I'll be turning eighteen. It just makes my skin crawl," she said as she made a face and shivered.

What a scumbag!

We took Nana's advice and took a tour of the property, starting with the lush back yard, which seemed to stretch for a mile. It was deep and wide, with great big trees with thick trunks. I think it is part of the Old Field charm. Modern homes sitting among old-world properties.

We found a nice spot behind an old shade tree, about fifty yards away from the deck. While we could still hear the party, we were hidden in the evening shadows.

"So, mister, what's on your mind?" B asked as the moonlight reflected in her eyes.

I responded by pulling her close and kissing her softly as we slid slowly down to the grass.

I explored her beautiful mouth and slowly worked my way to the nape of her perfumed neck. She felt and smelled great. She reciprocated, using the tip of her tongue to trace a line from my ear to the base of my neck, where she began to lightly nibble on me.

As she enjoyed my neck, I reached under her shirt and felt the silken lace of her bra. I caressed her breasts as she let out a soft, approving moan, biting down a little harder on my neck.

Just then, our tender moment of bliss was shattered by a very familiar voice screaming, *"I said, leave me a-lone!"*

My senses immediately went on high alert. "B, that's Hannah. We need to go!" I said as I stood and held out my hand, helping her up.

"Of course, let's go," she said, clasping my hand as we ran back toward the house and found Hannah on the deck, trying to fend off another very familiar person.

"Oh, come on. It's just one shot. Don't be such a *baby*. Come on, little *Miss Prissy,* just one," Kyle said.

"No! Would you *please* just leave me alone?" Hannah begged. "How many times do I need to ask you to just *leave me alone*?"

"Hey, lady, this is my party. If I want to bug you all night, I will. Now *drink up,*" Kyle snarled, as he tried forcing Hannah to drink his shot of who knew what.

Hannah knocked the shot glass out of his hand, which clearly pissed him off. He reeled back to strike her, just as we ran up the steps.

I pointed and shouted, "Hey! Don't even think about it, pal!"

Kyle's hand stopped midair, and he laughed, "Oh hey, look who it is! How's it going, *A-migo?*" he scoffed, releasing Hannah, who ran over to us, visibly upset.

"Are you okay?" I whispered.

"Yes, can we just leave, please?" she asked, obviously holding back her tears.

"Yeah, absolutely, let's get the hell out of here," I said, looking at B, who agreed.

Well, that was a fast hour.

"So what were you two doing back there, Amigo?" Kyle taunted. "I'm sure it isn't anything I haven't done with that slut! So how *are* my sloppy seconds?"

"Let's go," I said, tightening up as we tried making our way inside. Unfortunately, people began to intentionally block our exit.

"Excuse us, please," B said, staying calm and civil, as we tried to glide between people, but to no avail.

Kyle, hot on our tail, kept at it, "Hey, where are you guys heading? The party's just getting started!" Kyle, who had a cigarette sticking out of his face, laughed like an idiot, as did most of the people on the deck, who I assumed were his friends. This just encouraged his behavior further.

"You aren't leaving *now* are you, *A-migo?* Come on, things were just getting interesting, right, Skank?"

When I heard that, the hair on my neck bristled and I froze in place. B and Hannah tried to push me along, as Kyle continued his tirade.

"You remember what happens later, don't you, B? You wouldn't want to miss out on the late night fun, would you?"

Just then, we heard Nana's commanding voice from inside the house, as she was heading back toward the deck, "Get out of my way, you *hooligans*. Go on, move it, move it! Kyle Gerald Fergusen! What in God's name are you doing to this fine girl and her friends?" Nana's eyes flashed with anger as she pushed her way onto the deck and examined Kyle and the rest of his moronic friends.

"This is no way to treat guests!" she chastised.

"Shut *up,* Nana!" Kyle spat, shocking everyone, but no one more than Nana. "They're not *my* guests! I didn't invite any of them, especially not that *spic*! As far as I'm concerned, he can get the hell out of here and leave *my* girlfriend behind!"

And that, folks, was his problem. He wasn't over B.

You could feel the temperature of the deck get colder as Nana glared at him through a pair of slits. That glare would have stopped a bear in its tracks, but not a stupid twenty-year-old loser who wasn't over his ex-girlfriend.

Before anyone could bring themselves to say a word, Kyle continued his onslaught, "That's right, amigo, she's *my* girlfriend, so take your wetback hands off of her! And while you're at it, why don't you go fuck yourself; you and that crappy little house of yours, and your piece-of-shit pool, and your stupid mutt!"

Wait, what did he just say?

"Yeah, that's right, you heard me, asshole! I watched you that night after the movies! I followed you to your piece-of-shit house and watched you from your back yard! I was going to take a shit in your pool too, but your damn dog started barking and ruined my surprise."

He paused for a moment, huffing from the exertion of being an asshole, and grinned at the crowd. Then he pointed his cigarette at me and continued.

"There you were, the *spic* and the *slut*, making out on your cheap-ass couch. I was hoping for a good show too, but what do you expect from the precious virgin and her spic boyfriend. You were both so pathetic! I was hoping I'd finally get to see those precious boobs of yours." He ogled B when he said that last part, mimicking someone groping breasts.

"God, you were such a fucking cock tease! *No, Kyle . . . stop it, Kyle . . . I'm not ready, Kyle!*" he mocked B. "You were so pathetic. Why'd I cheat on you, ya dumb bitch? You wouldn't give it up, that's why! So I got it somewhere else! Many times too. You think that was the first time? Hardly, ya dumb slut!"

"B!" I hissed through gritted teeth.

"Just ignore him, please. He's drunk. Let's just get out of here," she said.

With fire in my eyes, I glared at the person blocking our way. "Get. The. Fuck. Out. Of. Our. Way," I spat.

Smartly, he stepped aside, and allowed us to make our way to the front door.

"Whoa, where are you guys going?" Kyle yelled as he followed us.

"*Kyle Fergusen*, I will not tell you again," Nana warned.

"Shut *up*, Nana!"

"Hey, where are you guys going?" Mary asked as she stepped out of the bathroom, rubbing her nose and sniffing.

Like father, like daughter, I guess. Poor Mary.

"We're leaving, Mary. I'll see you next week at school," an upset B said as we exited through the front door.

Kyle was right on our heels, "Hey, don't leave. We're just starting to have some fun."

His friends followed him out front, giving him an audience.

"B," I said again.

"Just ignore him. You're better than he is; don't stoop to his level. Let's just leave and get Hannah home."

Hannah's voice, a mere whisper at this point, "Yes, please, take me home."

"Fine," I replied, taking a deep breath. "He's one lucky son of a bitch."

"Oh, come on, *amigo*! I was just *kidding.* Come back. Listen, I'm sorry. Come on, I was just kidding. Come back. Look, she's not that big a slut, *okay*? Come back! We'll do some shots of tequila and become good amigos, what do you say?" Kyle yelled as his friends all cheered and encouraged us to stay.

Directing his next comment to Hannah, "And hey there, *Princess*, if you come back, we can finish that shot you knocked out of my hand. I promise to be gentler this time!" He roared with laughter as more friends poured out the front door to witness the spectacle, adding fuel to the fire.

I was itching to retaliate, but was more concerned with getting the girls out of there, so I unlocked the passenger-side door to allow B and Hannah to get into the car. As I did, a bottle smashed against my driver's side door, with glass flying everywhere.

"*What the fuck?*" I yelled, covering the girls from any flying shrapnel.

"Aw, man! I missed! I was trying to hit that bitch in the head!" Kyle yelled. "Hell, I probably just increased the resale value of that piece-of-shit car!"

The girls and I looked at each other, all three of us shaking our heads.

Let it go, let it go, let . . . it . . . go.

"Hey, maybe I'll stop by your house later and pay your little *mamacita* a visit!" Kyle grabbed his crotch for emphasis. "I'm sure she'd like some of this. Who knows, maybe I'll shove a bottle up her ass too! I bet she'd like it! And when I'm through with her, I'll do the same thing to your fucking mutt too!"

My blood began to boil, but I had to remember my promise to B and get the girls out of there safely. So I took another deep breath—one of many I'd taken in the past few minutes—and opened the car door for the girls.

As they were getting into the car, I noticed something reflect off some light, and it was sailing straight for B's face. I quickly shoved her into the car, as a bottle blew past and missed her face by inches.

"Oh man! That was about to hit the slut right in her face, *amigo*! Why'd you do that?"

"Oh my God, B, are you okay?" I asked a clearly shaken B.

"Yes, yes, I'm okay. Let's just get out of here," she said through tears.

"Yes, let's get out of here," Hannah agreed from the back seat.

I nodded and stood cautiously, trying to survey my surroundings. With the coast seemingly clear, I walked around to the driver's side. I made it only halfway. As I got to the front of my car, a bottle hit me square in the chest with a thud, dropping me to my knees.

Fuck! That hurt!

B and Hannah immediately jumped out of the car as Kyle whooped and hollered, while his friends cheered him on.

The girls were next to me in seconds, concerned and scared. "Oh my God, are you okay?" B asked.

"Man, I nailed him right in his fucking chest! Did you see that? How'd it feel, amigo? It sure looked like it hurt real fuckin' bad!"

More laughter. More Kyle worshipping. Then he added, "Now get the fuck off my property, ya stupid wetback! And take that slut of a whore with you!"

That was when B snapped.

45 - The Fight

B stood up, and her voice shot out with a ferocity I'd never heard before. "Shut *up*, Kyle Fergusen! Just SHUT UP! Do you want to know why I broke up with you? I'll tell you why. It's because you're a *loser!*"

That put Kyle back on his heels a bit and quieted the crowd.

But she wasn't done. "It had nothing to do with you cheating on me. That just confirmed what a loser you were. So why don't you take your loser ass back inside *your* piece-of-shit house before you get hurt!"

Kyle looked around to his friends, took a drag from his cigarette, and chuckled, "Oh really, honey, and who's going to hurt me—*you*? Certainly not that spic of yours!"

Something inside of B just snapped. She threw her cardigan down as she prepared to charge him, but I stopped her. I grabbed her wrist and held her back as I stood up. While my chest still hurt, I wasn't about to let B fight this guy. Not when I was there.

I didn't care if he was older than me. I didn't care if he was stronger than me. Shit, I didn't care if we were at his house and surrounded by all his friends.

At that moment, all I cared about was B

I hated the look of rage in her beautiful eyes, as she whipped around to look at me. I hated seeing the pain and hurt in the very same eyes that mesmerized me every time I looked at them.

No, I was done. *This* was done.

"No, B. He's not worth it. I won't let you do this," I calmly said.

"But he deserves it," B said with such hatred in her voice.

"Oh c'mon, *Amigo*, let her go!" Kyle taunted.

"Yeah, I know he does, and he's going to get what he deserves, but not from you. I love you too much to let you do this. I've got it," I said, and gently brought her to my side.

I hugged her and kissed her forehead. I then bent down and picked up her sweater, handing it to her, "Here, I believe this belongs to you." Then I pointed at Kyle. "He belongs to me."

Hannah and B began to protest, but I held up my hands to stop them as I slipped off my new polo shirt, exposing the bruise on my chest where the bottle hit me. "That *asshole* made three mistakes tonight. First, he messed with Hannah, and no one messes with my family. Second, he messed with you, and no one messes with the girl I love. Third, he hit me in the chest with a bottle, and no one messes with me. So, now it's my turn," I said, clenching my fists as I spoke.

I handed B my shirt, "Here, hold this. I don't want to get his blood all over my new shirt."

"Just be careful. He knows what he's doing," B warned.

"And so do I, babe. So do I." I stalked toward my prey, full of hate and rage.

"Oh, look who's back in the game. Hey, nice bruise you got on your chest, amigo. How's it feel? You ready for some more?" He chuckled as he puffed on his cigarette, having himself a grand old time.

I felt blood flowing in my ears, and the muscles of my body tense up. It was like someone flipped a switch. I was now full of adrenaline. The mood in the yard changed—as everyone knew what was about to happen.

Kyle's guests stepped away from him as he foolishly stood his ground, smoking and grinning. That was his fourth mistake—not running back into his house to hide, not that it would have mattered.

Like a moron, he just stood there, smoking his cigarette, watching me come toward him. He squinted his eyes, shook his head, and bent down, grabbing another empty beer bottle. Laughing, he threw it at me.

But this time I saw it coming and caught it barehanded. I just threw it aside and kept stalking forward. He tried not to act like it, but I could see that surprised him.

"No more bottles and no more games, *amigo*. It's just you and me, and I'm going to kick the shit out of you!" I snarled.

His eyes grew wide as he now understood this was no longer a game. He was about to pay the piper and cash the check that his mouth had written. He looked around for support from his groupies, and found none.

As I moved toward him, I began breathing harder through my nose. My fists, forearms, biceps, and calves were all flexed, ready to roll.

This asshole almost hit my girlfriend in the face with a bottle! He tried forcing a drink down my best friend's throat! He hit me square in the chest with a fucking bottle! He even snuck into my back yard and spied on me! Enough is enough!

As I neared him, he flicked his lit cigarette at my chest. I caught it midair and just crushed it in my hand. As I crossed the Rubicon, the strangest thing occurred. A song began to play in my head. It was a song I'd heard a million times, played repeatedly in my house, as my brother banged away on his drums.

I hate to admit it, and please, no one tell my younger brother, because I'll deny it to my grave.

The song was "Tom Sawyer" by Rush, the Canadian rock band. For my first and only fistfight, Rush became my personal soundtrack.

I must have growled as I approached, because his eyes went wide, and he mouthed, "Oh shit!"

"So what were you saying, *amigo*?" I said, spitting on him a little as I spoke.

He wiped his face and held his hands up, "Hey, man, come on. We're cool, man. We're cool. Why don't you just get in your car and leave, man."

He then made his next mistake.

As I tell my children to this day: never poke an angry bear. He grabbed my shoulder as he tried to convince me to chill out.

Mis-take!

I did to him what had been done to me throughout my childhood by my older brother.

I grabbed his wrist and twisted.

He screamed in pain, which immediately brought me satisfaction.

I guess Jagger is wrong,

"Dude, what the fuck! I said we were *cool!*" Kyle yelled as I twisted a little bit more before letting go.

He grabbed his wrist, his pain turning into anger . . . but I was angrier. He took a swing at me, but missed as I bobbed my head.

I just shook my head and said, "Not tonight, amigo, not tonight." I then punched him square in the face, smashing his nose, causing blood to squirt from both nostrils.

Okay, folks, confession time . . .

Remember the guy who gave me that great advice a few chapters ago? You know, the guy who suggested I go out and buy a box of condoms, take things slow, and get to know B better? Yeah *that* sweet guy. My older brother.

So that *same* guy was also a huge Muhammad Ali fan growing up. And a bit of a sadist, to be honest. He used to wrap our hands in towels and force us to box one another when we were younger. If we whined, he'd just hit us harder.

He had age, experience, height, and weight to his advantage. He would wipe the floor with us. We'd try to hit him, but he'd just dodge out of the way and nail us in the arm, chest, or stomach, but never in the face.

He didn't want Ma to beat him for breaking our noses or giving us black eyes. He wasn't stupid, just mean. It always ended the same way, with one of us crying, usually me.

As we grew up, we boxed less and wrestled more. He'd put us into various pretzel positions, laughing as we screamed in pain. But he wasn't always a total jerk. He was also very protective—as some kids learned the hard way—and no one messed with his brothers. No one.

Unfortunately for Kyle, I was a good student, and that night he was my final exam.

Kyle stumbled backward, stunned and holding his nose as blood and tears streamed down his face. My brother taught me many things, including to look for an opponent's weaknesses.

These were actually easy to spot, if you knew what to look for. That night, I saw three and went for the first one. I came in and punched him square in the solar plexus. Now, I'd never been hit there personally, but I'd heard it was extremely painful for the recipient. By Kyle's reaction, I'd say those rumors were true.

He immediately crumpled over in pain. I then grabbed the back of his head and smashed his face into my upcoming knee, causing more blood to come squirting from his face and onto my chest. He fell flat on his ass.

He lay there writhing in pain, not knowing where to hold himself. His face hurt, the back of his head hurt from landing hard on the ground, and his chest hurt . . . but I wasn't done.

Not by a long shot, amigo. That was just my preamble. I'm just getting started.

I jumped on top of him and pinned his arms under my legs. I then sat up and came down hard, taking the air out of his lungs.

That'll teach you not to smoke, asshole!

I then started to punch him in the side of the head and face, hard and fast. *Wham-wham!*

I was full of rage. I'd punch him and then smack him as hard as I could across the face, like the bitch he was.

There was nothing he could do. He was trapped. One of his drunken friends attempted to join the fight, but I just pointed at him and stopped him in his tracks. He threw his hands up and slowly slinked away.

I then grabbed Kyle by the throat and spat through gritted teeth, "Say it!"

I pulled his head and neck up and slammed them down hard, rocking his eyes back.

"I fucking said *say it!*" I yelled into his face, turning him to face Hannah and B. "Tell them you're sorry!"

"Fine, fine, all right, just let me up," he said as blood streamed down both sides of his face from his mouth and a clearly broken nose.

"Not a chance, asshole! Say it!" I said, releasing his throat.

"Okay, okay, okay." He then sucked in some air, blood, and snot . . . and spit it square into my chest.

Oops, there he goes again—another mistake. He just isn't getting it, but he's about to.

"There's your fucking apology! Now get the fuck off of me!" he yelled as he rammed his knees into my back, causing me to wince and buckle.

Unfortunately for him, this wasn't my first rodeo. *Amigo, let me introduce you to the pretzel!*

I reached back, hooked both of his knees and locked them in under my arms. I then sat down hard on his stomach and bent forward, folding him in half. He screamed in pain as I stretched forward, bending his lower back. I learned this one from the master.

Thanks, bro!

Eventually, though, I grew tired of him screaming in my face, and getting his blood and spit on me, so I released the hold and grabbed him by the throat again.

"Are you going to say it?"

"No! That bitch doesn't deserve it!"

Jesus, this guy is delusional.

I slapped him hard across the face, "Last time, asshole, say it!"

"Fuck *you*!" he screamed.

That was it. I'd had enough. Time to earn that A-plus!

"Oh really, fuck *me*? *Fuck me?* No . . . *fuck you!*" I hissed as I reared my right fist back and prepared to punch a hole in his face, ending his very existence, consequences be damned.

That was when I felt B wrap her hands around my raised fist. "Stop it! Just stop it! Stop hitting him! That's enough!" B cried, preventing me from smashing his face in.

"Just stop it already. You've beaten him. You've won and he's lost," she cried.

"Ha! See I told you! I knew she still loved me!" Kyle yelled triumphantly.

"Wait, *what*?" I shouted in disbelief as I looked from Kyle to B.

46 - Better Call Ma

*W*ait *a minute, is he right? Has it all been some sick joke? Has she been using me to teach him a lesson or something?*

A moment later, I received my answer.

"Are you *out of your mind?*" she screamed, kicking Kyle as hard as she could, first in the ass and then in the ribs.

Oh, thank God!

"Love *you*? *Love* you? I can't *stand* you!" B yelled, kicking him a third time, this time in an extremely *sensitive* spot that rhymes with stalls.

"You're nothing but a *bully* and a *coward*, preying on your sister's friends, or some stupid skank who doesn't know any better," she yelled as she continued kicking him.

"I'm not the skank or the slut; *you* are! *You're* the *slut*! *You're* the *skank*! *You're* the *asshole*! *You're* the *loser!*"

The crowd oohed and ahhed with every kick as he writhed in pain, begging her to stop.

"I don't want *you* or your stupid *apology*! I'm certainly not in love with you, you *freak!*" Her voice hit a helluva high note on that last word as she kicked him hard in the thigh.

"I'm in love with *this* guy! And he's one hundred times the man you are and ever will be. *Him*, not *you*! If you ever talk to me again, I'll let him *finish* you. From now on, you're going to leave *me* alone, leave *my friends* alone, and especially leave *my boyfriend* alone, do you hear me? I don't want you *following* me, *looking* at me or coming anywhere *near* me."

She pointed down at him as tears flowed down her beautiful cheeks. "If you see me coming, walk in the other direction, or cross the street. I swear to God, if you come anywhere near me or my friends again, Kyle, you'll regret it!" she hissed.

She looked at me, then Hannah, and said, "Let's get out of here."

I bent over and whispered in Kyle's bloody ear, "You're one lucky son of a bitch, bub. I was just getting started. I was about to punch a hole in your face and make you swallow some of those yellow teeth of yours. After that, I was going to roll you over and twist you into another pretzel until you passed out from the *pain*. I guess I'll just have to save it for next time."

"And do yourself a favor, *asshole*, remember what she said. This way you won't have to worry about any extended hospital stays. Oh, and know this, my mom's a doctor, so I know my way around a hospital. I'll track you down and finish you, got it?" I said, shoving his bloody face in the dirt as I stood.

I then put my foot on his chest, "Don't bother getting up until we're gone. If you do, I'll come back and beat you silly."

I then turned around and walked away, putting one arm around B's shoulder while holding Hannah's hand in victory.

As we got to my car, Kyle stood up, shouting that he was going to call the cops and have me arrested for assault. He was going to sue me for damages and had plenty of witnesses.

"You just got lucky, you stupid spic! You sucker-punched me! Everyone saw it!"

When I heard that, I turned and stared at him, causing him to flinch. Fortunately, I didn't have to do anything, as someone else took over for me.

"*Ow*! *Nana*, get off me! Knock it off! *Stop it!*"

Nana Fergusen had stormed out the front door and grabbed him by one of his bloody ears.

"Oh shut *up*, Kyle! You won't be suing anyone or calling the police! You *got* what you deserved. Saying all those *nasty* things to those nice girls and that nice young man."

She dragged him into the house by his ear, adding, "And I can't believe you spoke to *me* that way, you little shit. I am *very* disappointed in you, Kyle. And you know you should *never disappoint your Nana,*" she hissed as people got out of her way.

Jesus, that guy's screwed. That's one scary broad.

"Um, B?"

"Yeah?"

"Remind me never to get on that lady's bad side."

"I told you."

We left the party and immediately drove Hannah home. She was still pretty upset and just wanted to put the whole evening behind her. As we walked her to the front door, my adrenaline started wearing off, and I winced as I flexed my right hand. B and Hannah both noticed it.

"Oh my God, are you okay?" B asked, grabbing my right hand, which looked a bit swollen and black and blue under the porch light of Hannah's front door.

Wincing again, "Ow, yes, I'm fine. Nothing an ice pack and some Tylenol won't fix."

"Here, let me see it," Hannah said, inspecting the hand. "Look, I'm no doctor, but this doesn't look good. You should have your mom check it."

"Yeah, *that's* what I need. Ma freaking out on me. Hann, it's fine, see?" I flexed my hand again, trying not to make a face.

Hannah turned to B, "Uh-huh. Please have his mother look at this."

"I will. Come on, Rocky, we better go see Ma," B said.

I was clearly outnumbered and tired of fighting, so I just nodded.

"Call me tomorrow and tell me what she says."

"I will. G'night, Hann. Sorry again about tonight,"

"It wasn't your fault. I'm just glad you were there," she said as she hugged me.

"Me too," I whispered as I hugged her back and kissed her forehead.

After we left Hannah's house, B asked if we could take a quick detour before heading to see Ma, "Can you stop at the 7-Eleven for a second? I want to grab something."

I pulled into their lot and parked right underneath their well-lit sign. B asked me to wait in the car while she walked in and went directly to the coolers full of sodas. Through the window, I watched her grab a couple of large green bottles and a bunch of napkins. After paying, she came back to the car and she asked me to step out of the car.

What she did next totally surprised me. First, she asked me to remove my polo shirt. Next, she opened the first bottle of Perrier, soaked a napkin, and began to gently wipe my face off.

Standing there under the fluorescent 7-Eleven sign, B began to gently remove Kyle's mucus, blood, and sweat, as well as some of my own, from my face, neck, and chest. People came and went as she cleaned me up.

Before we knew it, I was Kyle-free.

"Thanks B," was all I could say as she handed me my polo shirt.

"No, thank *you*. I'm so sorry about tonight," she said, as tears suddenly began welling up in her eyes.

I just held her as she began to cry. Her adrenaline was crashing as well. After a few minutes, I wiped her face using the rest of the napkins and Perrier.

As I cleaned her up, she made a face. "Ugh, that felt weird. Is that what it felt like for you?" she laughed as I nodded.

"If they only sold bottles of water," she commented as we got back into the car.

"Yeah, but who'd be dumb enough to pay for bottled water?" I asked.

Seriously, folks, I'm a moron!

A few minutes later, we pulled into my driveway and I prepared myself for Ma.

"She's going to get hysterical. You've been warned," I said to B.

"I'm sure you're over-exaggerating. Besides, you've never seen my Mamma lose it. *That's* something else altogether."

We walked into the family room and found Ma knitting and watching baseball, while Belle snored away at her side.

She looked up and smiled. "Hola, niños. ¿Cómo están?"

"Hola, señora. Soy bien, pero este aqui," B replied, gesturing to my swollen right hand.

"Ay, hijo. ¿Que te paso?" she said, putting her knitting on the couch. "Get to the kitchen. Mija, por favor, tráeme una toalla y hielo from la nevera." B nodded and retrieved a towel filled with ice from the fridge.

As I leaned against the kitchen counter, Ma inspected my hand, turning it this way and that, "Mijo, dígame. ¿Cómo hiciste esto?"

"I tripped over a bottle and landed wrong on my hand."

Ma then gave me *the look* and said, "Mija, would ju give us a moment, por favor?"

Oh crap!

"Sí, señora. Would you mind if I borrowed your phone to call home?"

Ma just nodded, never taking her eyes off me. The moment B walked away, it started.

"Ju slipped, huh?"

Smack to the back of my head.

"Mira mijo, ju may think I'm just jur mother, pero, I'm also a doctora, okay?"

Another smack to the back of the head.

My younger brother walked into the kitchen as she smacked me. "Whoa, did you get the license plate of the bus that hit you?" he marveled.

Ma frowned. "He was just about to tell me how que pasó coño?"

B walked back into the kitchen, so I seized the opportunity to change the subject.

"Did you talk to your parents?"

"Yes, they understood. I can come home whenever."

"You were saying?" my brother asked, gesturing to my hand.

God, sometimes I really hate that kid!

"Okay, fine. I got into a fight and kicked the crap out of someone. Happy now?"

Ma pressed her hand against her chest, "Ju got into a fight? ¿Con quién?"

"With no one you'd know, Ma. Look, he tried messing with Hannah and then tried messing with B, so I to put an end to it."

"¡¿Qué?! ¿Alguien trató de hacerte daño y Hannah también?" Ma asked B, whose lip began to tremble as she nodded.

"*She* understands Spanish?" my brother whispered.

"Yeah, it's a long story. She's actually speaks it better than either of us," I whispered back.

"Really? Huh, who knew?" he said, as he gave her the once-over.

Ma continued to inspect my hand. "Okay, mira, creo que es roto. Tráigame mi cartera y vamos al hospital para obtener radiografías."

"Ma, do we *really* have to go to the hospital and get x-rays? You're being a little melodramatic. It's fine, see? I can wiggle my fingers." I winced slightly as I did it.

This time it was B's turn to smack me in the back of the head.

Jesus! Everyone's jumping on the bandwagon!

"Listen to your mother (*smack*) and go get her purse (*smack*). We're *taking* you (*smack*) to the *hospital* (*smack*) and getting you *x-rays* (*smack, smack*)!"

Ma and my kid brother just looked away, trying to stifle their laughter. Belle then barked at me, adding her two cents.

Shut up, Belle!

47 - Hello, Nurse!

I t never ceased to amaze me how the good ol' boy network worked in hospitals. As an adult, I've waited in the emergency room for hours. It's not always first come, first serve. The most critical case goes first, unless . . .

You were a board member's relative, a local VIP, a celebrity, *or* a doctor's family member. If you were any of these, you went to the head of the line.

We arrived at Ma's hospital on a busy holiday weekend, and parked in the Physicians Only parking lot. The ER was very busy, but did we wait?

No.

Did Ma fill out any paperwork?

No.

Did she talk to the registration clerk?

That's a negative, Ghost Rider!

We simply walked through the ER, past the registration desk, past the various patients in need of care, and straight to the x-ray area.

Were there people ahead of us there?

Yep.

Did Ma care?

Nope.

She went straight to the head of the line. I guess with prestige came privilege, and she simply wasn't going to wait.

B and I sat in the waiting area for about two minutes while Ma talked to the x-ray technician, who was wrapping up with another patient. Moments later, he stepped out with Ma and called me in as the other patients just looked at us, like, "Hey, what the . . ."

Ma and B stood behind the protective glass as the tech put my hand in different positions and took various x-rays.

Normal people had to wait two or three days for results, but did Ma wait that long?

No.

She waited about three minutes. As she explained it, surgeons couldn't afford to wait. She needed her immediate answers, so imagine how she felt with her son.

B and I returned to the waiting area while Ma reviewed the x-rays. She thanked the tech, slipped him a twenty, and walked us into an empty exam room. She then placed the x-rays on a lit display board.

"Jur right hand is broken, pendejo, here and here," she said, pointing at the x-ray.

Twenty minutes later, we left the hospital with my hand in a cast up to my wrist. The whole visit lasted an hour, tops. Ma thanked everyone and offered to pay, but was told no. They hadn't even put me in the system, so we were on our way, free and clear.

Nice, right?

On the way home, Ma lectured me on fighting, breaking my hand, and the treatment protocol for the next six to eight weeks. I just sat there in the passenger seat, rolling my eyes and sulking, until B smacked me in the back of the head for not paying attention.

I swear to God, if someone smacks me in the back of the head one more time . . .

When we got home, I took my medicine, both literally and figuratively. B handed me a couple of Tylenol and some OJ, making sure I took it. This, of course, pleased Ma to no end. B then pulled her aside, and they began pointing at me and whispering.

Now what?

After a few head nods, B took the phone, stepped into the kitchen and called home again.

I heard her say something about staying the night, and then came back to the family room, handing the phone to Ma.

"What's going on?" I asked.

"I asked your mother if I could stay over, and she said yes, as long as it was okay with my parents. She's on with them now, so shush."

We watched Ma as she spoke to B's parents, then Ma handed B the phone. B took it, listened, grinned, nodded, responded, and hung up. She then talked to Ma some more. Based on the looks on their faces, the deal was struck.

Great, a united front. That's just fan-friggin-tastic!

"Okay, so here's the deal," B started.

I smirked, "Yeeeeesss?"

"Are you giving me *attitude,* mister?" she asked, while raising her eyebrows and her hand simultaneously, readying to smack me again.

"No," I replied as I flinched.

"Good, because I'm staying the night to watch over you. I'll need to borrow some clothes to sleep in. We'll both sleep down here on the couch, just like last night at the lock-in."

"We'll need to keep your hand elevated and make sure that you take Tylenol again in about six hours, unless you're in pain. If you're in pain, you'll take it sooner."

Sigh!

"In the morning, Ma will see how you're doing. Now, do you have any questions?" B's hands were on her hips, with Ma smiling behind her. I just shook my head no.

What'd be the point?

"Okay, good. Now go to your room and find me a pair of sweats and a T-shirt, please. You get comfortable too. I know that's one of your new polo shirts. Do you need help getting it off?"

I just nodded, causing them both to smirk.

Sigh! This is gonna be a long night!

"You're enjoying this *way* too much," I grumbled as we removed my shirt.

"Shush."

"You're lucky my mother's here," I whispered flirtatiously, which earned me another smack.

Okay, I deserved that one!

I sighed and went upstairs to my room to change and grab B a change of clothes. Ma followed close behind, grabbing sheets, blankets, and an extra pillow for B from the hall closet.

"Mira, I trust you down there tonight, so no jodienda," she said as we walked downstairs.

"Ma, do you really think I'm in the mood? Plus, you've seen her," I replied, mimicking the smacks to the back of my head.

"She *is* good at that. I like her."

Uh-huh.

I handed B her loaner jammies which included a concert T-shirt, a pair of my sweatpants, and sweat socks she could wear as booties. She kissed my cheek and headed to the bathroom to change, while Ma set up the couch.

Since it was a sectional, she was able to transform it into the approximate size of a queen size bed. I sat on the floor, watching her and petting Belle.

What a twenty-four hours I've had. At this time last night I was on stage with B, singing and praising God. Twenty-four hours later, I'm sitting here with a broken hand. This fucking sucks!

I still can't believe Ma and B's parents agreed to let her spend the night. Man, I love her. I have no idea what I did to have her in my life, but I'd do it again in a heartbeat. Even Ma likes her, and more than that, she seems to trust her, and aside from Hannah and Jean Paul, okay, Hannah really, Ma doesn't trust anyone my age.

I can't wait for school to start. We're going to have so much fun this year. Homecoming, dances, hanging out, the prom . . . heck, I'll even go with her to youth group. I had a lot of fun there. Heck, maybe I'll even go on their next mission trip.

Yeah, this whole year is gonna be a blast!

"Okay, remember to prop up jur arm. I gave B the instructions. If ju need me, I'll be in mi cuarto, okay? And again, no jodienda."

"Yeah, yeah, I know. And Ma . . . thanks for letting B stay over."

"Sí, mijo, of course. She was so worried about ju. To be honest, I don't think I could have forced her to leave jur side, even if I wanted to, right, mi rubia pequeña?" Ma said, dubbing her with the nickname "my little blonde" as B joined us, even though B was taller than Ma.

"You've got that right, señora," B said as she placed her things on the floor, next to the couch.

"'Night, Ma." I kissed her cheek.

"Good night, señora. We'll call for you if we need you."

"Good night, mija. If he gets out of line, just smack him again," she said, kissing B goodnight.

Moments later, my brother walked out of his drum room, drenched in sweat. "So you broke it, huh?"

I just wiggled my fingers, "Yep, and I have to wear this stupid thing for eight weeks."

"That sucks, but it could be worse though. At least you didn't need an operation."

"Yeah, I guess."

My brother turned to B and whispered, "Ma's actually letting you sleep over, huh?"

"Yep, she trusts me. Now him on the other hand . . . who knows what trouble he's going to get himself into tonight."

"I can *hear* you," I said as they laughed.

Sigh! Yep, it's definitely going to be a loooong night!

After he headed up to his room, I reached for B. "Alone at last."

Smack.

"You heard your mother, no jodienda. Tonight I'm your nurse, not your girlfriend."

With that, B grabbed the remote control, turned on the TV, and made herself comfortable next to me on our makeshift bed, as Belle lay at the foot of the couch.

It looks like I'll have two nurses tonight.

"So how are you feeling? Do you need anything?"

"I could use a kiss," I replied.

"Okay, but only one. We *promised* Ma." She then gave me a quick kiss on the cheek, followed by giggles.

"You suck," I grumbled.

"Gasp! How can you say that? Here I am offering to be your nurse *all* night. You should be thanking me," she said, playfully jabbing my ribs.

"Why can't I stay mad at you?"

"Because you love me."

"Yeah, yeah. By the way, you look really cute in my clothes," I said.

"You really think so?" She hopped off the couch and looked at her reflection in the sliding glass door.

Her blond hair cascaded down past her shoulders, showcasing her swanlike neck. While my T-shirt was a bit baggy on her, it was my sweatpants that I loved. They hung low on her hips, accentuating her figure.

There was something so sexy about it. And sure enough, she wore my tube socks like a pair of booties pulled up over my sweatpants.

"You don't think I look too silly in your clothes?" she asked as she checked herself from different angles.

"You're kidding me, right? I think you look amazing."

She made a funny face at herself in the reflection in the glass, "You really think so?"

"Oh God, yeah. You're gorgeous. And I *love* that you're wearing my clothes. I may never wash them."

She made another face, giggled, and came back to snuggle once more. She put her head on my chest, over my heart, and began rubbing my belly.

"Well there's no way I was leaving you tonight. Not after all you went through," she whispered.

"B, come on, I didn't do anything. I was an idiot for losing my temper. I can't believe I let that jerk get to me. I should have listened to you and left. To be honest, I'm kind of ashamed of myself."

B lifted her head and placed both hands on either side of my face, "Now you listen to me, mister. You have nothing to be ashamed of. You gave him every chance to leave us alone, but he wouldn't let it go. You were the better man tonight, in every way, and I'm proud of you."

A tear ran down her cheek when she added, "You were a hero tonight—my hero."

I smiled and grabbed some Kleenex from the end table, and gently wiped away her tears. She then stood and blew her nose. That was when I noticed something . . . *jiggle*.

"Um, B? Are uh, you, um, wearing a, you know," I stammered, gesturing to her chest.

With a raised eyebrow and a smile, she said, "Nope."

Aww . . .

I reached for her, then winced from the pain. I was sore as hell all over.

"See what happens when you're bad. Now be nice, and *maybe* I'll let you play with them when we're *sure* everyone's asleep. But not beforehand, understood?"

B grabbed a blanket from the back of the couch and covered us. Even though we had plenty of room, we spooned together and watched *The Honeymooners,* while Belle snored lightly at the foot of the couch.

Wait a minute. If she's not wearing a bra, does this mean she's not wearing underwear? I mean, I can't feel them through the sweats, but can you really feel panties through sweatpants?

"Yes, I have my underwear on, *perv*. And you *definitely* won't be playing with that tonight, so don't even think about it." She yawned.

"What? I didn't say anything."

"*What, I didn't say anything,* uh-huh," she mimicked before shutting her eyes and falling asleep.

Damnit, how'd she know?

48 - Reality Check

Throughout the evening, B periodically would reposition my arm so that it was upright. She'd roll over, sigh, and then fix my arm. Eventually we found our groove. She wound up draping her arm across my chest and snuggled up against me as we slept. At eight in the morning, Belle hopped up onto the couch and plopped herself down between us, demanding attention.

What the— C'mon, Belle!

"Aw, good morning, sweetie," B cooed. "Do you want some lovin' this morning?"

Yes, please . . . oh, you meant the dog.

Belle's tongue was hanging out as she rolled over.

"Who's a good girl? Are you a good girl, Belle? Yes, you are. You're a good girl."

I couldn't take it anymore. Let's just say I'm not a morning person. "Okay, Belle, scooch! I'll get you some breakfast then take you out back, okay?"

I then stood without realizing I was already *standing at attention*, if you get my drift. I turned and almost poked B in the eye. She quickly pulled her head back, eyes wide. I looked down, looked at her, and then looked down again.

I didn't know what to do, so I did what any red-blooded American male would do. I grabbed a throw pillow, placed it over my crotch, and ran to the bathroom.

Oh someone please . . . kill me now!

"It's okay," she laughed. "I have an older brother, remember? It's normal."

Oh, sweet Lord! Even you're against me this morning!

After peeing, the *issue* went away naturally, at least the physical one. The emotional scar was still there, but I knew I couldn't hide in the bathroom forever. Once I came out, I found B feeding Belle breakfast.

"You didn't need to do that. I would have taken care of it," I said, still a little embarrassed.

Shaking a bit, while avoiding eye contact, she shrugged, "It's no big deal. I found her food, so it was easy enough."

Why is she shaking? Is she okay? Why won't she look at me?

"B? Are you okay?"

She turned to look at me with her lips folded under her teeth and her nostrils flaring as she tried unsuccessfully not to smirk.

Oh, here we go!

"Um, it's not still *loaded,* is it?" She gestured as she snorted, then broke out into a huge burst of laughter.

Ugh!

"No, it's not still loaded. *Jesus.*" I blushed. "I can't believe that happened." This only made her laugh harder, with tears forming in her eyes.

It's a good thing I love you.

"Oh my gosh, you're so cute. Please don't be embarrassed," she said between giggles. She walked over and kissed me, while making sure not to press into me, just in case. "Good morning, by the way, mister."

"Uh-huh, good morning, missus."

I couldn't stay embarrassed around her for very long—quite the opposite actually. She had this calming effect on me. Like everything was going to be all right. To this day, I still have no idea how she did it. Today, the only one who can do that is my wife.

Over bagels and coffee, we inspected my hand. The swelling had come down some. I took my meds, helped clean up, and went to my room to grab us both a change of clothes. While I was upstairs, B called home to check in.

I changed into a pair of shorts, grabbed her a pair with drawstrings, and then went to the bathroom to brush my teeth. That was when reality hit me. I'm right-handed, and I had to brush my teeth with my left hand.

How the hell am I going to get through the next eight weeks using only my left hand? How am I going to shower and get dressed? It's not like I can wear T-shirts to school. This also means no football and no varsity letter.

*And what about senior pictures next week? That's going to look great—
me in my stupid cast. How am I going to take my SATs in October? Kyle,
you're such an asshole! You couldn't just leave us alone? You had to force my
hand? I knew we shouldn't have gone to that stupid fucking party! Damn it!*

"Hey, did you get lost up there?" B called from the bottom of the stairs,
breaking me out of my downward spiral.

"Nope, I'm coming right down."

I took another minute before coming down. I found her in the family room
playing with Belle on the floor.

"How'd the call go?"

"It went fine. Mamma was worried about you, but I told her the swelling
had started to come down. I told her I'd be home before dinner."

"Cool."

She could tell my attitude had changed. She gave me the once-over then
called me to sit next to her on the couch.

"What's the matter?" she asked.

"Nothing."

"Please don't tell me nothing. I can read it on your face."

"It's nothing. It's not a big deal, really," I said, downcast. "You're going
to think this is stupid."

"No, I won't. Please tell me. I love you, mister. You can tell me anything,
you know that."

I started getting choked up as she caressed my face. "It's just that I'm
right-handed, you know?" I held up my cast. "How am I going to do anything?
How am I going to write? How am I going to take my SATs? And forget about
getting a varsity letter in football this year." I continued down my list of things
I wouldn't do this fall. "This just really sucks, B."

The tears just started rolling down my face as I laid my head in her lap,
crying like a baby.

"Shhh, it'll be okay. We'll figure this out together." She rubbed my back
and tried to calm me down. Even after I'd finished with my crying, I just lay
there with my eyes closed.

After a while, she kissed me on the head. "Are you feeling a little better
now?"

"Yeah, I guess so."

"Listen, you're looking at this all wrong."

I sat up and listened as she wiped the tears from my face.

"Remember, you're not alone. You have a lot of friends who'll help you. More importantly, you'll have me to help you through this, and I'm not going anywhere, okay?"

God, I love this girl. She can even turn a broken hand into a positive.

49 - Blowing Some Stink Off

I handed B a change of clothes, along with a hand towel, a new toothbrush, and some toothpaste. She came out of the bathroom a few minutes later, looking refreshed. We stripped the couch and put it back to normal.

B then started a load of laundry in the washer. She threw in all her clothes from the previous evening, from undergarments to jean shorts, along with the sheets and blankets we slept on.

As she set the washing machine into its first cycle, I slowly slid my hand down her back, over her shorts to her naked legs. She leaned back, allowing me to kiss her swanlike neck from behind. I wrapped my left arm around her slender waist, pulling her close.

We just stood there surrounded by the sunlight penetrating the laundry room window. She slowly turned and wrapped one of her naked legs me around my own, and we began exploring each other's mouth as we pressed into each other.

After a few moments, I knew if I didn't stop, I wouldn't, so I reluctantly pulled away and released her.

"Mm, why'd you stop?" she whispered.

"B, trust me, if I didn't stop, I wouldn't have stopped. And I love you too much for that to happen."

She just smiled and held me in her gaze. In that moment, I finally understood what Romeo meant when he said, *"But, soft! What light through yonder window breaks? It is the east, and Juliet is the sun."*

In that moment, as the sunlight enveloped her through the window, B became my sun. All I wanted to do was to bathe in her sunlight, but I knew the consequences.

"That's why I love you," she whispered, knowing how close to the flame we'd been.

B suggested we blow some stink off and take Belle for a walk. So we grabbed Belle's leash and I gave B a tour of the neighborhood.

"You know, maybe this is God's way of telling you to explore new things this year," she said as we walked.

"Oh yeah? How so?"

"Well, you're so programmed to play football in the fall. Have you ever thought about pursuing other activities?"

Hmm . . .

"You clearly enjoy singing. What about exploring that? You're so talented and special; you could do *anything* you put your mind to."

"You really think so?"

"Of course, don't you? Now you have an opportunity to do something new and *amazing* this fall," she said with great enthusiasm. "Even if you suck, which I know you won't because I've seen you in action, I'll be there cheering you on, like your own personal cheerleader."

I grinned and said, "Huh, maybe you're right. Plus, who wouldn't love having their own hot personal cheerleader cheering him on."

"Um, I didn't say *hot*."

"Really, I thought I heard you say *hot personal cheerleader*, no? That's weird." I stroked my chin, looking up at the blue sky. "I could have sworn you said *hot personal cheerleader*, wearing short-shorts and waving her pom-poms, no?"

"Uh-huh, you're clearly starting to feel better now."

Well, she was right about one thing; I was definitely feeling better. How couldn't I with her by my side? As we walked, I told her about the conversation I had with my older brother. Well, most of it anyway.

I mentioned the parts about not knowing some of the basics about each other, like her birthday, favorite food, favorite flowers, and things like that.

She waved her hand, "Oh, that's no big deal. I can tell you all that stuff. That's the fun part of getting to know each other," she said. "I learn more things about you daily, and it makes me love you even more actually." She smiled as the sun twinkled in her eyes.

"Thanks. I feel the same way, but what about the basics?"

"So what do you want to know?"

Belle stopped abruptly to pee, and I stepped back so I wouldn't jerk her leash while she was doing her business. "Okay, I already know your favorite band and flavor of ice cream—The Rolling Stones and mint chocolate chip."

"Actually, that's not my favorite flavor," she corrected.

What?

"It's actually *lakritsglass*."

"I'm sorry, *laker glass*? What the heck is that?"

"Ha! No, not laker glass, *lak-rits-glass*. It's a Swedish ice cream I had while visiting Mamma's family one summer. It's vanilla with a hint of licorice. It's both salty and sweet all at the same time and very addicting. Kind of like you," she giggled.

Slightly blindsided by this revelation, I decided to move on. "Okay, so when's your birthday?"

"May twenty-seventh," she replied. "When's yours?"

"March seventeenth."

"Okay, that's good to know."

And this went on for the rest of the walk, the two of us going back and forth asking questions, while Belle sniffed her way around the block.

"What's your favorite flower?" I asked.

"The sunflower. There's just something so pretty about a field of wild sunflowers. They're open, following the sun, and always seem happy, you know?"

"Yeah, I think I know someone just like that," I replied with a wink as we continued our discovery session.

Yep, I definitely know someone just like that.

50 - Pleasure in the Grass

As we returned from our walk, we ran into Ma on the driveway, stepping out to run some errands. As we stepped inside, B reminded me to call Hannah. While she checked on the laundry, I grabbed the cordless phone and called Hannah to update her on my situation.

"I knew it was broken," she said.

"Yeah, yeah, congratulations. You're psychic," I replied.

I went on to explain how B slept over and helped me throughout the evening, which surprised Hannah. Not that she was helpful, but that Ma actually allowed her to sleep over.

"I know, right? But she said she didn't think B would leave my side, even if she told her to, so she said okay," I explained.

I asked her how she was doing, and that was when she got real quiet. After some prodding, she told me that she was still a bit shaken, and that she told Jean Paul about what happened, but hadn't told her parents. She begged him not to say anything, and begged me as well, which I disagreed with.

"Hann, you need to tell your mother," I replied, but she dug her heels in, so I let it go. We didn't stay on much longer, saying that she had to go, but I was still worried about it.

"I'll talk to you later," I said, before hanging up.

"How's she doing?" B asked as she joined me.

I just shook my head, "Not good. She's still a bit shaken, and won't tell her parents about it," I replied.

B took a moment, and then said, "Listen, it's her decision. While you and I don't agree with it, it's something she's going to have to deal with. All we can do now is be there for her."

"Yeah, I guess. I told her I'd call her later," I replied, still concerned.

"That's because you're a good friend," she said as she kissed my cheek. "So what do you feel like doing?"

Oh come on! You! The answer to that question will never change. You! Always, you!

We decided to round out the afternoon with a picnic in my back yard, under the trees behind the pool—pillows, blanket, food, drinks, music . . . the works.

We put the food in one of Ma's baskets, along with plastic cups and napkins. I carried the basket with my left hand, and pillows and a blanket under my right arm. B grabbed the iced tea and my box.

With everything arranged, we grabbed our pillows and lay side by side, smiling like the young lovebirds we were. It was a perfect, sunny August afternoon, so B created a makeshift bikini for herself, folding my T-shirt up beneath her breasts, and the shorts higher up her sun-kissed thighs. I couldn't help but salivate.

"How's your hand feeling?" B asked.

"It's okay. It only hurts when I try to do anything with it, I guess."

"Well I packed Tylenol just in case, so if it starts to hurt, let me know," my dutiful nurse said.

"Yes, ma'am," I teased, kissing the back of her hand softly.

She rolled over, propped up on her elbow and faced me. "So what else did you want to know about me?"

The sun coming through the leaves created an interesting shadow across her body. It was like looking at a portrait brought to life before my very eyes. The background setting, the hints of sun coming through the trees, her golden skin, toned legs, the ankle bracelet accenting her ankles, and those eyes—those beautiful blue eyes. It was like staring into the Caribbean Sea, so clear, so full of life—simply mesmerizing.

"Are you okay?" she asked.

I inched closer. "Never better."

"What are you doing, mister?" she smiled, knowing damn well what I was doing.

I didn't say a thing. I just smiled and stared into her eyes, brushing a strand of hair out of her face with my cast-covered fingers.

She tilted her head slightly and closed her eyes, which took my breath away.

Then she leaned forward and forced me onto my pillow, which still had her scent and essence from the previous evening. She lay across my chest and kissed me.

With my left hand, I caressed her back, following the line of her spine, periodically stopping at her perfectly formed bottom—just for a quick moment or two.

We lay that way for a while, wrapped in each other's love, as the music from my box serenaded us. Her very being seemed to wrap itself around me as the warm breeze cascaded across our bodies.

I was her shelter, and she was mine. I played with her ponytail, flipping it back and forth. She then released it, allowing her hair to flow freely. I dug in, running my fingers through her locks of gold.

Eventually, I worked my fingers down her back, as she dotted my chest with tender kisses. Her breathing pattern changed, and she moaned slightly as I applied soft pressure along her back and spine.

As she kissed my neck, I found myself wanting to reach into her shorts and explore her bare-naked bottom, but I didn't. I knew she wasn't ready to cross that threshold. But as she kissed her way to my jaw, her drawstrings loosened a bit, begging me to slip my hand in.

As she softly sucked my bottom lip, she whispered, "It's okay. Go ahead."

My mind and body immediately reacted to those words, "Are you sure?"

"Mmhmm," she replied as she touched the tip of my tongue with hers, before reaching down and further loosening her drawstrings.

As Phil Collins sang "Take Me Home," I reached in and felt her naked bottom for the first time. It was silky smooth yet firm at the same time.

She crawled onto my body and pressed herself against me, grinding her hips into me slowly. Then she straddled me, causing my hands to slip from the back of her shorts. So I reached under her shirt and felt her naked breast instead, teasing her erect nipple with my left thumb and forefinger.

Why are we still wearing clothes? Why aren't we naked? I love you so much. I want you so badly. I can tell you want me too, but . . . no, no . . . I won't cross that line. I can't! She's not ready yet; I'm not ready yet; we're not ready yet. I mean, we're "ready" but not ready-ready. Right?

"B, I want you so badly," I heard myself whisper.

"I want you too," she said, then hesitated before she added, "but we can't."

"I know."

But neither of us stopped what we'd been doing. It was like a mutual understanding—if we couldn't cross the Grand Canyon, at least we could peer over the edge.

Then she moaned, "*Oh*," as she bent forward, leaning on my chest, rotating her hips in slow, circular motions. I felt the muscles of her bottom flex and contract as she rode me.

My stomach and leg muscles contracted as well, as I thrust up toward her. I could feel the sweat forming on her lower back . . . and a familiar sensation building deep inside my loins.

My heart pounded in my chest as I erupted into my shorts. I thought I would pass out from its intensity. B met my zenith with her own personal crescendo, as spasms seemed to run through her entire beautiful body. While I had no idea what was happening to her, it was an incredible sight. She was clearly enjoying herself.

Moments later, she collapsed onto my chest, sweaty and breathless. I caressed her softly as she lay pressed against me. We stayed there for a while on our makeshift bed, surrounded by God's glory, holding one another, as the warmth of our bodies seemed to merge.

The birds chirped away as shadows danced across our bodies and a gentle breeze blew. Soon, she and I slowly drifted away, having crossed another threshold.

God, I love this girl.

51 - Shrimps, Grits, and Pancakes

The following day was our last day of summer break. As agreed, we would make it a special day, starting with breakfast for two.

I pulled in B's driveway at eight, and met her mom in the driveway as she took out some trash. She smiled and waved me over.

"Well, good morning. Let's see that hand of yours," she said, lifting my cast, giving it the once-over.

B popped out of the house as we chatted, "See, Mamma, I told you. It's broken."

"Yes, I see. I'm so sorry you broke your hand," B's mom said. "You be more careful now. No more tripping over things." She smiled and walked inside.

"Thank you, ma'am. I'll be more careful," I replied as she left. I turned to B. "That was sweet."

"Yeah, you seem to be growing on her."

"Yeah, like a fungus." I joked.

"Ha, you're so weird." She laughed.

"Hey, I've gotta be me."

"Yes you do, and I wouldn't have it any other way."

As we walked to the car, I basked in the sight of her. She wore a pretty off-white summer dress with matching open-toed sandals. She had on a black hairband, a matching black belt, and a light cardigan sweater around her shoulders. Wrapped around her ankle lay the rope ankle bracelet, completing her outfit.

I knew exactly where to start our day. About ten minutes later, we pulled into a very familiar parking lot in Setauket.

Hey, if it ain't broke . . .

"Does this work?" I asked.

"This is perfect," B smiled.

Our favorite waitress was working, and she smiled as we walked in.

"Welcome back. Is it just the two of you lovebirds again?" she asked as she grabbed a couple of menus and place settings.

"Yes, ma'am, just the two of us," I replied as B grabbed my arm.

She sat us at a booth and brought over some coffee and two glasses of water. "I'll give you two lovebirds a minute."

We ended up ordering the same thing: blueberry pancakes, scrambled eggs, crispy bacon and orange juice. As we waited, we talked about our future goals and dreams. Mine essentially involved getting through our senior year of high school and then figuring things out.

B, on the other hand, had very specific goals—go to Oxford, become a diplomat and help humanity, that sort of thing. Again, she totally blew my mind, but I was getting used to it. And knowing B, she'd do it all and then some.

Once our breakfast came out, we both dug in, continuing our conversation as we ate.

"Okay, quiz time," I said.

She smiled and sat up in her seat. "Okay, hit me."

"Okay, I already know your favorite food . . ." I started.

"Oh, really? I bet you don't."

"Of course I do. It's pizza."

She just grinned as I sighed in defeat.

"Let me guess. Another exotic Swedish dish that I can't pronounce?"

"Well, I wouldn't exactly call it exotic, but it's definitely something you can pronounce," she said.

"Okay, so it's not exotic, and it's not pizza, which, for a New Yorker, is a sin by the way. So, what is it?"

"You're gonna laugh."

"No I won't; spill it."

"Okay, my favorite food is homemade shrimp and grits, with a side of homemade cornbread."

Huh?

"What the heck are shrimp and grits?" I asked, making a face, because frankly it sounded horrible.

"Don't make a face. It's a Southern dish and it's delicious," she replied defensively. "I had them in South Carolina on a mission trip. We usually stay with host families on our trips, and they're usually not too well off, though they're better off than the people we're there to help.

"Anyway, one night, our sweet hostess, Mrs. Trimble, made Iris and me homemade shrimp and grits with a side of homemade cornbread and sweet tea. It was heavenly. It was warm, rich, and spicy . . . the most delicious thing I've ever tasted," she said as her eyes glazed over.

"It all just melted in my mouth. I think I had three bowls the first night. It's been my favorite food ever since."

"Wow," was all I could think to say. I wouldn't have guessed that one in a million years and, yep, she was right, I could definitely pronounce it.

We spent the next half hour eating breakfast, quizzing each other, and laughing—a lot. My brother had been right; getting to know the little things about each other was important, and fun too.

It was another sunny day, so we drove to West Meadow Beach. We left our shoes in the car, grabbed a towel from my trunk, and walked along the shore, watching as families unpacked their beach gear to enjoy one last hurrah of the summer.

The beach was packed in no time, but we didn't mind. We found a nice spot to lay the towel down and relax for a while. The sun just seemed to beam off of B. I didn't know which shone brighter.

"Can you believe by this time tomorrow we'll be in our second period class?" I sighed.

"I know. I can't wait," she said with excited anticipation. Again, she loved school.

"Although, I have enjoyed the summer, especially these past couple of weeks," she said as she snuggled up against me.

We stayed there for a while, but then we got thirsty, so we hit the 7-Eleven for some Big Gulps. Since B didn't have to be home until six o'clock, I put the car in gear and drove us to our next destination.

Like an excited child, B kept asking, "So where are we going?"

I'd just respond, "You'll see."

"Are we there yet?"

"No." It drove her nuts, which pleased me to no end.

Thirty-five minutes later, we pulled into the parking lot of our destination, Long Island's own Adventureland Amusement Park. It's a poor man's version of Six Flags, but just as fun, with its thrill rides, bumper cars, haunted house, and huge swing ride. It even had carnival games, like Ring Toss, Balloon Burst, Balloon Darts, and everyone's favorite . . . Whack-a-Mole.

"Yay, I love Adventureland!" B squealed as we parked.

I flashed some teeth. "I knew that you would."

We spent the next few hours having the time of our lives. We went on rides, played games, ate junk food, and simply had a ball. As we headed back to the car, B beamed as she carried the stuffed lion I'd won for her at the Balloon Burst. I wasn't sure which one of us had enjoyed the day more.

It was the perfect end to our perfect summer break. As I headed home after dropping B off and receiving my good night kiss, only one word crossed my mind as Van Halen sang about reaching for the golden ring . . .

Blessed!

52 - Back to School

I dragged my ass out of bed and into the bathroom the next morning at six. I showered, using a makeshift "shower cap" for my cast, brushed my teeth, and blew my hair dry as best I could. After a quick breakfast, I was off to school and at my school locker before the first bell.

As I threw my stuff into my locker, a small envelope fell out, so I tucked into my notebook and headed to my first class.

It was your typical first morning back at boarding school. You see people you haven't seen all summer. There was a lot of *hey* and *what happened to your hand* and *how are you* and *how was your summer* that morning.

Even though Jean Paul and I shared first period together, the one person I really wanted to see was nowhere to be found.

"You ready to rule this joint with me this year?" he asked.

"Don't you mean that the other way around?"

He patted me on the back. "I take second place to no one, bro."

"Mr. Michaels, I hope you're that confident after our first exam," Mr. Berry teased as the first bell of our senior year rang.

Fifty minutes later, we received our homework and moved on to chapel.

"Any sign of B this morning?" Jean Paul asked as we headed off to chapel.

"Nope, not yet, but we have chapel together, so . . ."

Jean Paul just shook his head and sighed as he anticipated the rest of the year.

As we went to chapel, I finally caught sight of B exiting another building. She looked so pretty in her back-to-school outfit. She wore a blue blazer over the blue dress we had picked out. She had on a black headband and a gold necklace accentuating her swan-like neck.

And around her ankle was the white ankle bracelet. Yep, all was right in the world. She saw me as soon as I saw her and smiled and waved. She almost ran to me as I met her halfway to chapel. People just seemed to get out of her way, like Moses parting the Red Sea.

"Hey! I missed seeing you this morning," she said as we quickly hugged. It felt so weird not to hug and kiss her hello, but PDAs—public displays of affection—were frowned upon at our school.

"God, I missed you too. You've spoiled me," I whispered softly which made her smile.

Jean Paul caught up to us, and they exchanged hellos.

I took B's hand and asked, "Are you ready to go in?"

"Yep, lead the way." She smiled as Jean Paul rolled his eyes.

Suck it, bro! We're in love!

As we walked in, people looked at us curiously, including some teachers. As we sat, I overheard things like, "Well, *that's* a new one," and "I never saw *that one* coming."

Oh bite me!

We ignored them all and sat down. The only thing I remember from that first morning was sitting there, holding her hand. I couldn't tell you who spoke or the sermon topic.

After chapel let out, we so wanted to kiss, but knew we couldn't. We couldn't even hug. All we could do was capture the affection in each other's eyes as we smiled before walking in opposite directions to our next classes.

The rest of the day went as expected. We received our books, reviewed the syllabus, received a short lesson, followed by a homework assignment. Basically, it sucked!

Hi, welcome back! Here's a crap load of homework.

The only saving grace was having the same lunch period as B. By the time it ended, it felt like half the school knew we were dating. In fact, people were more interested in my dating life than my broken hand.

One of the cons of attending a small school is that *everyone* knew your business.

It seemed the only person interested in my hand, besides B, stopped me as I walked by his classroom—Coach Connor.

"Whoa there, partner, get in here. What happened?" he asked as freshmen poured into his classroom.

"Would you believe I fell and broke it last weekend?" I asked, as he looked at my hand.

"Uh-huh, so how bad is it?"

I handed him the doctor's note from Ma.

"Ouch, eight weeks, huh?" he commented, handing back the note. "Well, that's too bad, son. What are you going to do in the meantime?"

The million-dollar question.

"No idea," I sighed.

"Listen, stop by my office after school and let's talk, okay?" he said as the bell rang.

"Yeah, okay, Coach."

After last bell, I met B at my locker.

"Hey mister, how was your first day?" B smiled.

"It was nuts. I got homework in every class. I even have to read the first three chapters of *Gatsby* tonight," I whined.

"I know, isn't it great? I missed school!" She beamed.

Oh that's right, you're one of those.

"I already read *Gatsby* and loved it," she said as I rolled my eyes. "Oh, stop whining. It's a really good book. You'll like it, you'll see. Trust me, I'm a lifeguard."

As I laughed at her joke, she looped her arm in mine, and we walked to the gymnasium.

"Have you decided what you're going to do?" she asked as I held the door for her.

"I still have no idea."

"Well, I talked to Aaron earlier, and he said he'd love for you to try out for his play this fall."

Aaron Doherty was our Fine Arts chairperson. Most of the students called him Aaron, unless you were in front of another teacher or your parents. To this day, he and Coach Connor were my favorite teachers. Thanks to social media, we're still in touch.

"Yeah, maybe," I replied as we stopped outside her locker room.

"Well, this is me," she said.

"I know," I replied, making the pouty, boo-boo face.

"Aw, don't pout. Go find Aaron, and remember, I love you."

"I love you too. Enjoy tennis tryouts. I'll call you later."

After looking around for witnesses, we kissed quickly.

"That should tide you over," she said before ducking into her locker room.

It's better than nothing.

I headed for Coach Connor's office and knocked on his door.

"Come in."

It was your typical head coach's office. There were trophies on shelves, along with books, folders, and an assortment of sports equipment.

"Hey, buddy, I'm glad you stopped in. Grab the door and have a seat," he said as I grabbed a chair.

"So you're out of commission, huh?" he asked as I nodded. "What are you going to do this fall?"

"Coach, I have no idea," I replied. My frustration with the whole subject was obvious in my tone. "I certainly wasn't planning on this."

Coach eyed me for a minute. "Did I ever tell you about my freshman year in college?"

"I don't think so, why?"

He went on to tell me how he broke his arm in a car accident, not like in a fight like me, during the middle of his freshman year.

Damn, news really does travel fast around this place.

He told me that it literally changed his life. He had a full ride to college on a football scholarship, but when he broke his arm, he lost it.

It was during that period in his life when he discovered a love for teaching. Fast-forward to the mid-'80s, and he and his young family were accepting his first teaching job at our school.

"So if I hadn't broken my arm, we'd probably not know each other, and that'd be a shame," he said with a smile.

I couldn't imagine not knowing Coach Connor, so I guess he had a point.

"Remember, you have a lot of choices in life, son, so never limit yourself. And let's be honest here. You'll never receive a full ride to college, based on your *athletic* prowess," he said.

Ouch!

"So use this as a do-over for yourself. It's your last year of high school. Go discover yourself."

"Now you sound like B," I muttered.

"Oh, do you know her?"

"Yeah, we're, um, going out . . . you know, dating."

He chuckled, "Yeah, I know. I'm not as old as you think. Well, since she's one of the smartest students in school, I'll take that as a compliment."

He then handed me a list of after-school activities to review. He also told me that Aaron has been asking him for years to talk to me about performing.

Really?
"Yep. You'll figure it out, son. I trust you," he said.
Hmmm . . .

53 - Secular Music

A s we left his office, him walking to the football field, twirling his coach's whistle, and me heading to my car, I thought about what he said. I went home and started on my homework. As B predicted, I actually enjoyed *Gatsby*. As I finished, the envelope that I'd tucked into my notebook earlier fell out. It had the scent of rosehips as I ripped it open:

Good morning, My Love!

I hope you have a great day! I know you'll do great this year!

I Love You So Much!

B

She'd left me a love note, and not only had I not even known about it, I'd left her nothing. I immediately ripped a piece of paper out of my notebook and wrote her a quick love note back.

Good morning, Daisy,

I had the best first day ever, because I got to see you!

I can't wait to spend the rest of the year with you.

I Love You Too!

Gatsby

I then folded it, placed her name on the front, kissed it, and tossed it into my backpack so I could deliver it first thing the following morning.

Having survived Ma's annual back-to-school interrogation, I went to my room and put the stereo on until seven thirty, which I proclaimed to be "B Time." I went to Ma's room and dialed her number.

Bzzt! Bzzt!

Busy signal! I tried for the next half hour, before finally getting her on the phone.

"Hey, mister, how are you?"

"I'm doing great now. I've been trying to call you for the last half hour." I replied, trying to hide my annoyance.

"Yeah, I'm sorry about that. I've been on the phone for the past hour with Mary," B said.

Oh God, why?

"I sort of avoided her today at school. Anyway, she called and wanted to apologize about the party this past weekend."

"Oh yeah, where's *my* apology?" I scoffed.

"I know, I know. Anyway, she wants to make it up to me in *her* way."

"What's her way?" I cautiously asked.

"What else? *Shopping*. She wants to take me shopping in the Hamptons on Saturday. I told her that she was being silly, that she didn't need to 'make it up to me,' but you know Mary. She insisted, so I guess I'm going to the Hamptons on Saturday morning. I hope you don't mind."

"No, I don't mind, as long as we hang out afterwards. Besides, if she wants to spend Daddy's money on you, who am I to say no?" I joked.

She giggled, "I know, right? Are you sure?"

"Yeah, absolutely. I love you, B, and if I have to share you with the world on occasion, then so be it. Go have fun shopping in the Hamptons."

"Okay, thanks. So, I'll spend the day shopping in the Hamptons with Mary, and then come home and model my new outfits for you Saturday night," she said. "Oh, and did I tell you that Mary likes to start the day shopping at upscale lingerie shops?"

Gulp!

"Um, can I come too?" I asked with a dramatically quivering voice.

"No, you perv. You'll just have to wait," she laughed. "You're so bad."

"This *no hugging and kissing you* thing is really driving me crazy, by the way. I'm just saying," I said.

"I know, but at least I still have your sweatshirt. I'm actually wearing it right now with a pair of shorts, but later . . . I'll be wearing it *with nothing at all*," she purred. "Listen, I've got to go, I love you. Good night."

Damn, she really knows where to hit a guy!

The following day I took B's and Coach's advice and tracked down Aaron. He informed me that play tryouts weren't for a few weeks, and that we'd be performing *A Midsummer Night's Dream* by Shakespeare.

He wanted me to audition for the role of Puck. Also, since I was out of commission, he encouraged me to work in the audio/video department.

"Go talk to Kevin Jenkins. He'll walk you through everything. Just tell him I sent you, in case he gives you a hard time," Aaron said, and then as an aside, "He sometimes forgets that the equipment belongs to the school, and that I'm in charge of the department."

So there you had it—problem solved. Instead of football, I'd become a theater nerd. I told B all about it at lunch, and she was thrilled.

"Well, I think that's awesome. I can't wait to see you back on stage."

"Did someone say 'back on stage'?" Hannah asked as she joined us.

"Ladies and gentlemen, you know her, you love her—Miss Hannah Michaels," I joked as I gave her a golf clap and received the finger for my troubles. "Classy," I said as some of the other students laughed. "So what's going on? Have you talked to your mom yet?"

All the eyes at the table turned to her.

"No. Can we leave it alone, please?" she replied.

"Yes, we'll leave it alone, won't we, *mister*?" B answered, shooting me *the look.*

Aw, c'mon B, not here!

"Won't we, *mister*?" she asked again, using a stern voice.

Christ.

"Yes," I sighed.

B and Hann just looked at each other and giggled as I grumbled.

We spent the rest of lunch talking about the lock-in and performing on stage together, which seemed to interest everyone at the table.

"So what song did you guys sing? You never told me," Hannah said.

I told her and she screwed up her face. "That doesn't sound like church music to me," she said.

That was when B's posture changed. She held up her finger, "Well, let me ask you, what makes one song *church music* and another one *regular music*?"

This got everyone's attention.

"Well, the song will usually have God in it, won't it?" Ben Mauro, an eighth grader at the table, commented.

"Okay, sure, what else?" B prompted in a scholarly tone.

"Usually there's a line in there about the love of Christ," said Janice Snyder, an eleventh grader.

"Okay, but what if you weren't allowed to use or say those words?" B asked the group.

"I don't know. I guess I've never thought about it before," I said as we all nodded.

B continued, "Aren't most praise and worship songs about love?"

"I guess," I shrugged.

"Well, a few years ago, my youth pastor, Mike, asked us the same question. We all threw out similar comments, like Christ, God, Bible verses," she said. "He then asked us about substituting regular secular music in place of praise and worship?"

We all sat there considering this.

B smiled and continued. "Well, no one could come up with an argument for why we couldn't. Of course, there are some songs that are clearly inappropriate. For example, if they talk about devil worship, but I'm not talking about those songs. I'm talking about more mainstream music from Fleetwood Mac, Billy Joel, Michael Jackson, and even U2."

A voice from the table behind us chimed in with, "She's right, you know." It was Dr. Andrews, our school chaplain and assistant headmaster. "We couldn't help but overhear your conversation, B," he said as everyone at his table nodded. "And I agree with you and your youth pastor. I think as long as you're offering yourself to the Lord, He'll honor your worship." He stood and placed a hand on B's shoulder. "Very good, young lady; yes, very good indeed."

God, she's so smart. What the hell is she doing with me?

We finished up lunch, and B headed to one building, while Hannah and I walked together to the same class. We talked about the usual back-to-school stuff, like what classes we had and plans for the upcoming weekend.

I told her B and I planned on attending the back-to-school dance Friday night, which made her get quiet for a moment. I also told her about B's upcoming shopping adventure with Mary on Saturday morning, which made both of us roll our eyes.

But if she wanted to spend time with Mary, then so be it. It was her life. I wasn't going to stop her. I loved her too much to put chains around her.

54 - Friday Night Dance

After a fairly uneventful rest of the week, Friday arrived, and along with it, the annual back-to-school dance. In years past, Jean Paul and I had gone stag. This year, though, I had a girlfriend.

It was raining, but nothing could dampen my spirits. I would be picking B up at seven thirty that evening, so I raced home right after school.

Ma brought home pizza that night, because she didn't feel like cooking.

"That's cool, Ma," I replied as I grabbed paper plates. "You can't go wrong with pizza."

A sentiment I share to this day.

"Y como está la B?"

"She's doing great. We have a dance tonight at school, so I don't know what time I'll be home."

"Ju mean ju will be home by midnight, right?" she corrected me, as I rolled my eyes.

"Yes, *Ma*, I'll be home by midnight," I said, then pushed, "twelve thirty at the latest."

Ma just sighed but nodded. Again, this wasn't her first rodeo. Between having a girlfriend and being a high school senior, it was highly likely that I'd be breaking the rules at least once or twice this year. I was planning on enjoying myself and pushing the envelope as much as possible.

After eating a few slices, I hit my room and went about the task of figuring out what to wear for the evening. By the time I was finished, it looked like a tornado had blown through my bedroom.

Eventually I went with cool and casual: a T-shirt and V-neck sweater vest that B helped me pick out, along with a pair of Levi's and boat shoes.

As I dressed, the weatherman on Channel 11 said it would rain throughout the evening and well into the early morning, so I grabbed my giant golf umbrella from my closet and headed over to pick up B.

As I stood at her front door, well-sheltered by my ridiculously huge umbrella, B's mom opened the door and rushed me inside. "Come in, come in, get out of that rain. You'll catch your death of cold."

I closed the umbrella, left it outside the front door, and then stepped into the house.

"How is your hand doing?" she asked as we walked up the steps to their kitchen, with Gabriel following behind us.

"It's doing okay, ma'am. Thanks for asking," I replied, taking the seat she offered me.

"Yes, of course. Maybe they will remove that cast sooner than expected."

"I hope so."

"Well, I'll go tell B you're here. I'll be right back. Gabriel, you be a nice boy while I'm away. That dog," she said, shaking her head as she left the kitchen.

Gabriel walked over, and I petted him while I waited.

"She's just finishing up. She'll be right out," her mother said when she returned to the kitchen. "Gabriel, you leave that boy alone. Go on now, go find Pappa."

That was when B walked into the kitchen.

Okay, she really didn't *walk* into the kitchen. It was more like she floated into the kitchen, using her invisible angel wings. She took my breath away.

She had her hair tossed to one side. She wore a royal blue sleeveless dress, which brought out her eyes and accentuated her figure. She also wore a matching pair of heels, which showed off the definition in her sexy tan legs.

The rope ankle bracelet looked out of place wrapped around her ankle, but she didn't seem to care. It was unconventional, just like the girl, and she wore it proudly.

She had gold studs in her ears—which I prayed I wouldn't swallow later as I nibbled on her ear—a light shade of red lipstick, and just a hint of perfume.

"So, what do you think?" she asked as she twirled in the doorway.

I blinked and whispered, "Holy crap."

She and her mom shot me a look.

"I mean, wow, you look really beautiful tonight, B."

B covered her mouth and giggled as she walked over, taking my hand.

Her mom said, "Okay, you two young people, go have fun at the dance. Remember, not too late tonight, okay? I expect to see you home by midnight, do you understand, young lady?"

B nodded, and I said, "Ma'am, I'll be sure to have her home by midnight." She smiled and waved goodbye to us as we made our escape.

Jean Paul and Hannah pulled into the parking lot just as B and I walked toward the building hosting the dance.

B said, "Why don't we go over and get them? We certainly have enough room under this tent," she joked.

So we returned to the parking lot and met them at their car. Hannah immediately got under the umbrella, while Jean Paul pursed his lips and hesitated, apparently annoyed that I didn't drive them.

"Dude, you can either join us or get wet, it's up to you. There's enough room for a family of seven under here," I joked. "It's your call, but the train is leaving the station, so decide."

Jean Paul just rolled his eyes and joined us.

"What'd you do, steal this off one of your picnic tables?" Jean Paul joked as we walked together to the dance.

"Let's just say, I got a guy," I joked.

"So it fell off the back of a truck?"

"More or less."

The girls excused themselves as we stepped inside the dining hall/makeshift dance hall, so they could dry off and powder their noses, leaving Jean Paul and me to check out the dining hall.

As we walked around, I asked why he didn't bring Iris. He told me that even though the date had gone well, they agreed to just stay friends since they went to different schools.

The girls eventually joined us as the dance started. It was your typical back-to-school dance. The music selection consisted of pop music from the late '70s through the early '80s. As the evening progressed, more and more students piled into the dining hall.

Before we knew it, we were all laughing, dancing, and having a good time. B and I danced together, while Hannah was off gossiping with her girlfriends. Jean Paul was . . . well, Jean Paul. He had this magnetism about him, I had to admit.

The girls at the dance seemed to gravitate toward him. He just picked them off one by one, never staying with one for too long. Everyone got their dance, some got two, and some even got to slow dance with the stud, but he always kept his options open.

I just rolled my eyes, shook my head, and laughed as I watched him. I caught his eye once, and he smiled like a Cheshire cat . . . about to eat a canary.

Yep, that's my boy!

B and I danced the night away, although I did dance with Hannah once.

"I promised Hann I'd dance with her; do you mind?" I asked.

"Don't be silly. I don't mind at all! Go," she said, and she pushed me toward Hannah.

I was only five feet away from B when some kid worked up the nerve to ask her to dance. I kept glancing at them as I danced with Hannah.

"You really like her, huh?" Hannah asked.

"What makes you say that?" I smiled.

"Let's call it woman's intuition. She does look very pretty tonight."

"Yeah, she sure does."

"Well, go on, lover boy. Don't let me keep you."

"Are you sure, Hann?"

"Yes, go on. Don't keep your lady waiting. Besides, if you look over at her one more time, you may wrench your neck. Go," she said, laughing as she pushed me toward B, who was now by the punch bowl.

"Finished already?" B asked as she handed me a cup of red punch.

"Yep," I replied and then drained the contents of my cup.

"You two didn't dance for very long."

"I know. She told me to come back to you," I admitted. "Apparently I was staring."

B just shut her eyes and shook her head.

"What?"

"Nothing," she said with a grin.

The DJ cued up the next song, "Faithfully" by Journey, a classic rock ballad played at every high school dance across America back in the day. We threw away our plastic cups and walked out onto the dance floor. I was finally able to hold her close in public.

As we danced, we smiled and stared deeply into each other's eyes. You could light up the entire East Coast that night with the sexual tension radiating from our bodies.

We were lost in our own world, clearly in love. I wanted so badly to kiss her right there on the dance floor. My pulse raced as we continued our slow dance.

It's funny. I still remember her pupils dilating and her nostrils flaring slightly as we moved together slowly.

I pulled her in and caressed her lower back as she pressed her lips against my neck.

"Do you want to get out of here?" she whispered.

"Oh God, do I ever."

And just like that, I grabbed her hand and we left the Friday night dance in mid-song—two teenagers madly and desperately in love. That night, two strangers fell in love again. That night, we'd share the joy of rediscovering each other. That night, I knew, without a shadow of a doubt, I was forever hers and she was mine. . .

Faithfully.

55 - Crossing Boundaries

I left my monster umbrella behind and didn't care. At that moment, all I cared about was the girl. We quickly ran downstairs to the rear exit across from the parking lot.

The rain came down in buckets, but we didn't care. All we cared about was each other and the hunger of our desire. We looked at each other, smiled, took each other's hand, and ran to my car.

B yelled at me as I held the door open for her, but again, I didn't care. Not about myself nor my cast. All I cared about, all I wanted, was the girl.

My girl!

I ran to the driver's side and jumped into the car, and we both laughed as the rain beat down on my car.

We looked like a pair of drowned rats. I reached down into my driver's side door pocket and found an ample supply of spare napkins that I kept in case of emergencies. I handed some to B and used the rest to wipe my face and neck.

As we dried ourselves, we stared at each other, and our hunger took over. I took her into my arms and kissed her, right there in our school parking lot.

To hell with the rules and to hell with detention—I needed to taste those lips. I needed to feel the warmth of her embrace. I needed to get lost in her love.

"Let's get out of here," I whispered as my pulse raced.

"Where do you want to go?" she asked with anticipation in her voice.

I grinned, "I think I know a spot."

Ten minutes later, we parked across from our favorite demi-god, Hercules. B was unbuckled before I finished parking. When I killed the engine, I immediately slid my seat as far back as I could.

B simply kicked off her wet shoes and climbed over the center console. She hiked up her dress as she mounted me. As I killed the engine, I glanced at the clock on my radio and saw that we had plenty of time.

It's only nine o'clock. We have hours! Yes! Thank you, God!

It'd been a very long week, and we were hungry for one another. *Very* hungry! She attacked me as soon as she straddled me, and we kissed passionately. Our lips parted almost immediately and we explored each other.

I could still taste the red punch on her tongue. Her lips were full and silky. Eventually, we slowed down and found our rhythm.

I reached into her dress for her breast and found lacy material, which felt both strange and interesting. Again, this was still new territory for me, for both of us really. She leaned back and slowly unzipped her dress. She looked like a circus contortionist, as I sat there marveling at the sight.

She slid her dress down to her waist, and smiled, revealing a lacy blue bra. I could see her nipples poking through, as she leaned in and began kissing me again.

I worked my way to her back and fumbled around for the clasp on her bra, but came up empty.

As I fumbled around, she giggled. "It's not back there."

She then leaned back and held me captivated in the gaze of her blue eyes.

The street lamplight and rain cast a halo around her body. She looked like a goddess, and I was unworthy to worship at her altar. She reached up to the front of her bra and slowly undid the clasp.

She was methodical, sexy, and totally in control. She raised her eyebrow, staring at me, as she started moving her hips. Biting her lower lip suggestively, she finally pulled her bra apart, revealing herself to me before playfully flicking the bra into the passenger seat. I definitely liked what I saw, and she definitely felt my reaction.

"Oh, looks like someone's happy," she murmured.

I couldn't find the words, as saliva filled my mouth and my nostrils flared. I hungered for her. I was ravenous for her. The mix of her natural and bottled scent enveloped me. It filled the car.

I leaned forward and kissed my way from her right breast to her left, as she rocked against me. My wet clothes were definitely hampering my style, so I pulled off my shirt and vest, and threw them into the back seat.

The rain provided us with background music as it fell around the car. She leaned forward and draped herself over me. She clamped down on my neck, leaving me another reminder of her love, as our hearts raced.

We went from zero to sixty in a matter of seconds.

She began grinding into me harder and deeper, and soon started letting out short puffs of air as she pushed herself against me while rotating her hips. I remembered the day on the blanket in the back yard, and I knew what was about to happen.

And it did . . . for both of us.

Well, there goes another pair of underwear.

She collapsed on my chest as our hearts beat in tandem—wild, passionate, and free.

"Oh my God, I've missed you so much," she whispered in my ear. "You have no idea how much I've wanted you this week. Every time I saw you in the halls or outside on a sidewalk, I just wanted to push you into the bushes and ravish you."

"I wanted you too, B. Every minute. Oh my God, you feel so good." I caressed her back as she nuzzled against my neck. We stayed this way for a while as the rain continued to serenade us.

After catching her breath, B slowly lifted herself off of me and smiled as we gazed deeply into each other's eyes. The love emanating inside the car was palpable. You could light up a thousand cities with it.

The streetlights and rain brought out the blond highlights of her hair. They seemed to electrify her blue eyes as she smiled at me—bright, shiny, and full of love. Her golden skin was silky smooth and rich in color.

She sat there in her flawless perfection and I just took it all in.

Just when I thought we were finished for the evening, B climbed over to the passenger seat and wiggled out of her dress. She sat there topless, in a pair of blue lace panties, with a fresh hunger in her eyes.

I gulped.

What the . . . ?

She raised her eyebrow as if to say, *Well?*

I was clueless, until she gestured toward my jeans.

Ding, ding, ding. Got it.

I struggled to remove my 505s. Since they were still wet, they seemed to become one with my body. After a lot of contortion and a bit of cursing, I eventually removed them, while B sat there shaking her head and laughing at me.

I turned to face her in my red and white striped boxers, and her eyes became slits. Her nostrils flared slightly as well as she gazed upon me with an approving but wicked smile.

Did she just growl?

She didn't make me feel uncomfortable or self-conscious. It actually turned me on. It also caused an involuntary movement in my underwear, which caused her wicked grin to grow wider as she witnessed it.

Oh God, can she see my wet spot? Does she have one too? No, that's impossible, right? Theirs doesn't work like that, does it? It must be a shadow from the streetlights.

"I see someone is coming back to life," she whispered.

I reached out for her and pulled her back over to me. When she straddled me this time, an incredible realization hit me. And by the look in her eyes, she came to the same realization at exactly the same time.

The only things now separating us were the buttons on my boxers and two very thin layers of cotton and lace. I could definitely feel her now, and she could definitely feel me.

We looked into each other's eyes and began to move in sync in every way: hips, hands, tongues. I slipped my left hand inside the back of her panties, while I kept my cast on her other hip.

She soon started sliding up and down my shaft; grinding into me as she did so.

"Oh my God, you feel so good," she whispered as she nibbled my ear.

I became more adventurous with my exploration of her backside. I wanted to respect our boundaries, but she wasn't stopping me. So I explored further.

Her underpants started to slide down, causing her to lose her rhythm, so she threw caution to the wind. She lifted her bottom and just wiggled out of them. She then pressed her bare flesh against me.

We were now down to one button and a very thin layer of cotton between us, but we just kept moving.

That was when B began to whisper into my ear, "Yes, just like that. Keep going."

I honestly didn't think I could get any harder, but then I did. I was going to pop, so I squeezed her right cheek with my left hand to stop myself from going further.

"No, don't stop. Keep going."

Wait, does she want me to keep going *keep going? There's only one way to find out.*

I removed my hand from her backside and nervously slipped it down her front, down to her most intimate of areas.

She then lifted herself off me a bit, and provided me better access. It was the first time I'd ever felt pubic hair—well, other than my own. I hesitated, not sure if this was going beyond the boundaries.

She then moaned for me to keep going and bit into my neck, sucking hard. *That one definitely left a mark.*

So I continued working my way south, past her pubic hair to a moist area. It was not just any moist area, but her most private and intimate of moist areas. We'd definitely just expanded our boundaries, which made me both nervous and excited.

She was a combination of sticky, slick, and wet, which I found both strange and arousing. I had no idea what I was doing. This was my first time, so I was *learning on the job*, so to speak. I stroked her gently, an explorer in a new land.

And based on her reaction, she definitely liked it.

"Yes, keep doing that, keep doing *that*!" She gasped as she closed her eyes, which made me nervous. Again, I was a stranger in a foreign land, and I didn't speak the language. At least I didn't think I did.

Am I doing something wrong?

"Are you okay?" I whispered.

"Oh my God. Yes! Just keep doing that, just . . . keep . . . doing . . . that." She moaned and nodded, pressing herself into my fingers as she breathed faster. She was in some kind of trance, and it was mesmerizing.

As I rocked my fingers back and forth inside her, I felt the strangest sensation: her inner muscles began convulsing around my fingers. It was an incredible, clenching sensation. It seemed to last forever.

As it came to an end, she fell against my chest, her body limp, and asked in a husky voice, "Oh, my God. Where did you learn how to do that?"

"I have no idea. I honestly have no idea what I did," I said with all sincerity.

"Mm, well, try to remember, and don't ever forget it." She snuggled into me, kissing me on the neck.

"I won't,"

I definitely won't.

56 - Our Last Round

I glanced at my watch, saw it was only quarter to eleven—plenty of time—so I held her, enjoying her warmth as she snuggled into me. The rain continued playing our love song.

When I kissed her on her forehead, she asked, "What was that for, mister?"

"Nothing, I just love you."

She shifted around so she was more on her side and began to softly scratch my belly with her nails, making gentle circles. Her belly-scratching caused yet another involuntary reaction. She pointed me toward the back seat and told me to lie back.

I did as commanded, and then I reached for her to pull her on top of me, but she shook her head.

"No. Now it's my turn to explore."

Ruh-roh.

She leaned over me, in all her naked glory, and slowly kissed her way down my body. She started at my neck and worked her way to my chest, all the while rubbing my belly, every now and again rubbing lower and lower.

As she did this, I reached down and began to play with her breast. Before I knew it, she had slowly kissed her way down to my belly button, slowly circling it with the tip of her tongue.

Then she placed her hand on my ever-expanding member, but outside of my boxers, and began to slowly stroke me. It felt amazing. I stopped playing with her breast and leaned back as she continued to kiss my belly and stroke me through my boxers.

She suddenly stopped kissing me, and I felt a tug. She was trying to pull off my boxers!

Oh my God Yes! We're going to do it! And I remembered to put the condoms in the glove compartment just like big bro told me!

Soon, however, I discovered she had something else in mind.

"Lift up, mister."

I lifted my ass, allowing her to remove my boxers, exposing my fully grown partner-in-crime to the world. She flicked my boxers onto the passenger seat.

I sat up and attempted to reach the glove compartment, but she pulled me back down.

"Where are you going?" she asked with some annoyance in her voice. "Just stay right there."

I did as I was told, and she went back to the, um, business at hand, so to speak.

I decided to just shut my eyes and become one with the moment. Her warm and soft hand felt amazing, as did her lips as she continued to kiss my belly.

What happened next was . . . well . . . I just never expected it to happen in *a million years*.

Suddenly I felt her mouth, hot and moist, tenderly sucking on the tip of my most intimate area. I gasped out loud and followed it up with a moan. The feeling was incredible.

I opened my eyes and looked down. There was B, working her magic, sending me to the infinity and beyond.

I leaned my head back and closed my eyes, lost in the moment as a familiar sensation began building inside of me.

Suddenly, my mind went into hyperdrive. I felt conflicted. I'd never done this before.

What should I do? Do I finish? I have to tell her.

"B," I said softly, licking my lips. "B. *Oh my God, B!*"

It was all I could get out. Suddenly I had dry mouth and couldn't speak. She increased her pace.

"B . . . B . . . I . . . I'm going to . . ."

I couldn't finish my sentence. I almost had a coronary as my body seized and then exploded. Seconds felt like minutes as I lay there. After I finished, I felt her softly kiss my inner thigh before working her way up my body.

"How did *that* feel, mister?"

I was speechless and exhausted. All I could do was offer a thumbs-up, which made her giggle.

"Mm, I thought so," she whispered as she reached down and caressed my now spent member.

He was unresponsive, but frankly, I think she just wanted to hold it. After a few minutes, I drifted back to reality. I softly stroked the back of her head as she lay on me.

"I see someone is back from the dead."

"Oh. My. God. B. That was amazing!" I breathlessly whispered.

"Good. I'm glad you enjoyed it as much as I did. It only seemed fair, since you made me feel, um, *amazing* earlier."

"You mean you, uh, you know?" I asked as she laughed softly.

"You're kidding me, right? Yes, you made me *you know*," she replied as she shook her head and smiled.

"Excellent," was my only response as I was still having trouble forming sentences.

B lifted her head to look at me. "Hey, can I ask you a question?"

"Sure, anything, you know that," I replied.

I figured that she was going to ask me if that was my first time.

Yeah, I figured wrong. Very wrong.

"What were you doing earlier? You know, when I pushed you back down?"

Oh shit!

"Um, what do you mean?"

"You *do* realize that I'm holding you in my hand, right?" she said, squeezing a bit to make sure I *understood* the *situation*.

"So, what were you reaching for?"

Sigh!

"Um, I was, uh . . . I was reaching for a condom." My face flushed as my skin prickled. I was completely mortified.

She gasped and released me as she sat up.

"You were reaching for a *condom*?" she yelled, smacking my chest and narrowing her eyes at me. "Since when do you keep condoms in your car? Have you been lying to me this whole time about being a *virgin*?"

"*What*? Oh my God, *no*. I swear to God, B, I didn't lie to you. I *am* a virgin! I swear to God! Why would I lie about that? Trust me, I wouldn't lie about something like that."

"Okay, well then, explain to me why you have condoms in your car."

I sighed and confessed. I told her everything, from the advice my older brother had given me to my adventure buying them. Her expression immediately changed from a scowl to a smirk to full-blown laughter.

Sigh!

"Well, you *definitely* wouldn't make up a story like *that*, and I think it's sweet that you went through all of that for us. Now listen to me, and I'm not saying this to hurt your feelings, okay?" she started. "The next time you decide to, you know *reach for condoms,* let's talk about it first, okay? I'd like to be involved in the decision," she said.

"I will B. I promise. It's just that . . ." I paused.

"It's just that what?" she asked.

Sigh!!

"It's just that this is all new to me. I've never done any of this before," I ashamedly confessed.

She lifted my face up to hers and said with a warm smile, "Do you have any idea how much I love you?"

"First, never feel ashamed or embarrassed with me, okay? Second, I love it when you're honest with me. And third, that was my first time too—*all of it*. Okay?" She confessed with a knowing smile, calming me immediately.

How do you do that?

"Yeah, okay. So what do we do now?" I asked.

"Let's just lie here for a while. We have plenty of time," she replied after looking at my watch.

We lay back and she reached back down, grabbing ahold of me, which caused an involuntary response . . . *again!*

(Man, to be a teenager again, just for one night!)

We both lay there in all our glory, softly caressing one another. Soft caresses led to light kisses. Light kisses to light touching. And light touches to . . .

We began to pleasure each other, and I became entranced in watching her as I pleasured her. The way she arched her back and closed her eyes, while slightly opening her mouth. As I continued, she simply released her hold of me and everything else.

"Yes, just like that," she whispered as I continued.

The more aroused she became, the more aroused I became.

"Yes, right there, yes! Keep doing *that*," she whispered while biting her lower lip. "Oh my God, yes, right there."

A moment later, she began to pulsate around my fingers, a wonderfully strange sensation. She lay there huffing and puffing away as she rode her climax to completion.

"Oh my God, you have no idea how good that felt," she said after catching her breath.

As she lay there, I softly caressed her side, giving her goosebumps and making her giggle. While I did this, she slowly slid her hand between my legs, grabbing hold of me again, but I stopped her.

"B, it's okay. I'm good."

"Don't you want me to?" she whispered as the rain continued to serenade us.

"Seriously, it's okay. I just enjoy being with you like this," I whispered.

She had no idea the impact she was having on me as we lay there, fully exposing ourselves to one another. Okay, maybe she had some idea.

She smiled and gently removed my hand from her wrist and took ahold of me again.

"And I enjoy being with you like this. Ever think of that?" she asked as she slowly and methodically started once again.

"Okay, you're the boss."

"That's right, and don't you forget it," she giggled as I leaned back.

She was especially rhythmic and very tender this time. As she increased her pace, my hand slid to her breast.

She then repositioned herself, allowing me to pleasure her while she pleasured me. I was further along this time than she was, however. That familiar sensation built within me, and I soon found myself involuntarily moving my hips.

I slipped my fingers from her and became one with the moment.

"B," I said with complete cotton mouth.

"Go ahead. I'm waiting for you," she whispered as I just surrendered myself to her.

And just like last time, my body seized, followed by an explosion, as she finished me. And as she kissed my inner thigh, and started her way back up my body, something inside me changed.

I don't know if it was the car full of pheromones or the fact that her exposed bottom was now pointing straight at me, but something changed and began to consume me.

I have to know.

"B, please don't move," I begged.

She didn't move her body, but she did turn her head to look at me, curiosity in her expression.

I have to know. I just have to.

I sat up and grabbed her hips, not really knowing what I was about to do.

"Um, what are you doing, mister?" she asked with concern in her voice.

I have no idea what I'm doing, but I need to know.

"I'm sorry B, but I need to know," I replied in a husky primal voice, which caused her eyes to widen a bit.

"You need to know what?" she asked cautiously as I bent forward and buried my face into her.

"*Oh!*" she responded, sounding as completely surprised as I was.

"Oh! Okay, okay, slow down, mister . . . slow down," she instructed. "Okay, yes, that's better . . . yes, just like that . . . that's much . . ."

I could hardly control myself. I buried myself deeper and deeper.

"Flip over," I said.

"What?" she asked a bit breathless.

"I said to flip over."

"Like this?"

I didn't bother answering. I just spread her legs, looked down and continued to consume my prey.

I could tell that she enjoyed this position much better, as she closed her eyes and threw her arms back against the door, arching her back and moaning.

I was very slow and methodical. I had to know her this way. I needed to know her this way. I can't explain it. It's just something I needed to do. A secret I needed to know. A mystery I needed to solve. And the answer was truly magnificent.

"Oh my God, yes . . . yes, right there."

A few minutes later she peaked, and I didn't stop until she was finished.

"Yes! Oh. Oh. Yes!" she moaned, as she collapsed and lay there for a few minutes, allowing me to sit up and gaze upon her perfection.

She slowly came to and caught me gazing at her in wonderment and awe.

"So do you like what you see?" she whispered as she leaned up on her elbows, smiling.

"My God, B. You're so beautiful."

She sat up and pushed me back, moving her naked body on top of mine, resting her blond locks on my chest.

And there we stayed, quietly, in our own world, protected from the elements. We just held and loved each other, trying to take it all in. Reflecting on the wonderful new boundary we had just crossed and what lay ahead for us as individuals and as a couple.

God I love you, B. I hope we stay like this forever.

And then my beloved angel farted.

57 - The Calm Before the Storm

"Oh my God!" she shrieked.

It was hysterical! The light of my life had just farted.

She immediately leapt up, embarrassed and mortified.

"Oh my God! I can't believe I just did that!"

I laughed my ass off.

"It's not funny!" she yelled as she smacked my chest before attempting to escape to the passenger seat.

I held her back. "B, it's okay. Everyone farts. C'mon, it's funny. It didn't even smell."

"Oh my God, I'm so embarrassed." She put her head into her hands.

"C'mon, B, it's okay. It's me. I do it all the time. Ask Jean Paul."

"That's different," she said, shaking her head, her face red.

"God, you're so funny," I said as I hugged her.

"That's because you're warped."

"This is true. Are you okay now? You don't have any more stored up there, do you?"

"Oh my God, you're such a jerk. And no, I don't. That was the only one," she replied as she playfully smacked my chest while I giggled.

I kissed her forehead, checked the time, which confirmed that we should be heading home.

We hopped into the front seat and began getting dressed. At least I did. B, on the other hand had a slight issue. She found her bra, but couldn't find her underwear.

"Well, they couldn't have just disappeared," she said.

"Hold on, let me get the lights," I said reaching for the interior light switch.

"*No! What are you doing?* What if there are people out there? Just keep looking."

B, if there are people out there, then (a) they owe us a lot of money for the show, and (b) they'd seen it all tonight anyway.

I just shook my head and kept looking around as I got dressed. As I slipped my jeans on . . . *aha!* "Found them!" I yelled.

"Oh thank goodness. Where were they?"

"Hiding inside my jeans," I said as I held them out on my index finger. "Say, remember the end of *Sixteen Candles*?"

"Sure, I love that movie, why?"

"Well, I don't suppose I can keep these, could I?" I asked as I moved them out of her grasp.

"*What*? *No*, you perv, you can't keep them. These are a set," she said, snatching them out of my hand. "You're so immature," she said as she put slipped them back on, between giggles.

"It's what you love about me."

"Uh-huh. Yeah, that's it."

We made it to B's house with two minutes to spare.

"Remember, be here tomorrow night at seven, okay?" she said as we kissed goodnight beneath the overhang at her front door, just clear of the rain, which was still coming down, but lighter now.

"And who knows, maybe after the fashion show, we'll hit that glove compartment of yours."

Oof!

"I'll be here at six thirty," I deadpanned.

She laughed and kissed me, before shoving me toward the car. "See you at seven, mister."

"I'll see you at seven. I love you."

"I love you too."

Twenty minutes later, I was home and went straight to bed with a big smile on my face. The following morning, I awoke to the sun shining in through my bedroom window. The rain had finally run its course.

I didn't want to shower, but knew I needed one. I could still smell her all over me. I actually felt a twinge of sadness as I showered her scent off of me, but then I remembered we had many more nights to look forward to. Plus, there was no getting around the need for a shower.

After breakfast, I checked in with Jean Paul, who told me he had my umbrella, which apparently came in handy for him.

"I didn't see you guys leave last night. Did you have fun?" he asked.

"Bro, I had an excellent time last night," I replied.

"What'd you guys do?"

This was a normal question and one I would have asked if our roles were reversed. Of course, I didn't provide him with any real details. Not even the fart, which still made me giggle. That detail was for us and us only.

"What? Oh, um, nothing special. You know, we, uh, just hung out."

Fortunately, he took the hint, or he was still tired—but either way, he didn't dig for additional information, which I appreciated.

"You want to hang out?" I asked.

"Yeah, come on over."

I threw on a pair of shorts and a T-shirt and headed to my best friend's house. The car still smelled of our pheromones, at least I think that was pheromones. Regardless, it put a smile on my face.

Hannah answered the front door with her hair up in a ponytail, wearing a T-shirt and pair of sweatpants.

"Oh hey, I didn't know you were coming over. Uh, Jean Paul's in his room." She looked, I don't know, embarrassed for some reason. Like I'd never seen her in a ponytail and sweats before. She quickly excused herself as I made my way to Jean Paul's room.

Jean Paul was lying on his bed, reading *Sports Illustrated*.

Me: "Yo, dude, what's up?"

Him: "Yo, bro, what's going on?"

Teen-speak. We were conversation wizards.

"Not much, what're you doing?" I asked, even though I could clearly see he was reading a magazine.

He lifted the magazine, "Nothing, just reading this." Again, wizards. "What do you feel like doing?" he asked, knowing the options were limited due to my cast.

"I don't know. What about you?"

It doesn't matter how old we are: this is how males make decisions. It's a dance. One comes over and asks what the other is doing. One then asks the other what they feel like doing. The other will reply with some noncommittal response, and it goes like this, back and forth until they mutually come up with something, or a third party interrupts them with a plan of their own.

In this case, that third party was Hannah, who barged into his room, face clearly washed and wearing different clothes.

"How many times have I told you not to come barging in here without knocking first?" Jean Paul growled at her.

She just rolled her eyes, stepped back into the hallway, kept the door open, and knocked. I just laughed at the whole thing. Hannah returned my laugh with a smirk and one-finger salute.

Yep, I'm number one!

"Come in," Jean Paul said. "There, was that so hard?"

She ignored him and asked, "So what are you guys up to today?"

I shrugged, "We haven't decided yet."

"Do you feel like hitting the mall? I want to go to the bookstore. There are a couple of new books I want to check out."

I shrugged again, "Sounds good to me." I looked at Jean Paul, who also shrugged.

"Sure," he said.

"Okay, good," Hannah said. "Let me just throw some shoes on, and we can head out."

It was at that moment, that I remembered the pheromones in my car.

Oh fuck! How do I get out of this? Hannah at least has tact, but Jean Paul will definitely say something. Idiot! You just had to say yes! You're a moron!

"Hey do you guys feel like driving? I'm running low on gas." I tried.

"Come on, dude, we're just hitting the mall. You drive. I'll even give you some cash for gas," Jean Paul replied, reaching for his wallet. I shook my head to indicate I didn't want his money.

I guess there's no way around this. Maybe my car will explode before we leave the house. C'mon, God, anything? No, nothing? How about a meteor shower? No? How about a random plane engine crashing on top of my car? Still nothing, huh? Crap! Well, tanks fer nuttin' Noonan!

We met Hannah outside and took the long walk to my car.

"Uh, dude, what's the matter with you?" Jean Paul asked as I dragged behind.

"Nothing, why?"

Hannah got in behind me, while Jean Paul rode shotgun.

Please don't say anything! Please don't say anything! Please don't say anything!

"*Dude*, what's that *smell*?" Jean Paul asked, wrinkling his nose.

"What smell?"

"What do you mean *what smell*? You don't smell that?" he asked and turned to look at Hannah.

"Oh, yeah, that. I think I ran over something last night on the way home. I checked this morning, but nothing was there."

Please, someone, kill me now!

"Do you mind if we roll down the windows?"

"Nope, I don't mind at all," I replied as we all rolled our windows down.

Once we hit the bookstore, Jean Paul and I headed straight for the comic book rack, which Hannah found juvenile. After Hannah picked out her books, we hung around the mall for a while. Before dropping the twins home, we made plans to see *Stakeout* that night after I picked up B, assuming, of course, that was what she wanted to do.

By six thirty, I was dressed and heading out the door, to pick up my girl. It's funny . . . I can still remember exactly what I wore that night—my green striped polo shirt and khaki shorts.

I arrived a few minutes early, which for me was a miracle.

Maybe she's rubbing off on me.

Her house was pitch black. There were no lights on inside or outside, which I found strange.

I knocked on the front door and heard Gabriel barking from the other side.

"Hey, buddy, go tell B I'm here, okay? Go on, buddy," I said through the door.

He just stayed put and continued barking.

Her mother will be at the door soon. His barking drives her crazy. B's probably in the shower or something. Although it is strange, since she told me to be here at seven, and it's now seven o'clock on the nose.

I knocked one more time and just sat on the steps waiting for someone to answer the door. Cars passed by the house as the minutes ticked away. By twenty after seven, I got the hint. No one was home.

I was both worried and pissed! I was worried because it was so unlike B. I was pissed, because I hate getting stood up and knew deep down it was Mary's fault. I tucked a note into the front door and left:

Hey, I came by at seven like we agreed. Call me tomorrow after you get back from church. I'm heading to the movies with the twins.

I didn't even bother signing it. My mind seemed to spin out as I drove over to the twins' house. Part of me wanted to go track her down to make sure she was okay, while another part hoped she'd read my note and feel guilty for blowing me off. I was torn.

"Dude, what are you doing here? I thought we were meeting you at the movies," Jean Paul said. "Where's B? Is she in the car?"

He was oblivious to my sour mood, but Hannah caught it right away.

"What's the matter? What happened?" she asked.

"Hann, I have no idea. I got to her house early and it was all dark. I knocked and knocked, and no one answered. Even her car was gone," I said. "She's probably still out with that bitch Mary. Whatever, I don't care. Let's just go to the movies," I said.

"I'm sorry," Hannah said as she slid into the back seat, patting me on the shoulder. "I'm sure she just lost track of time."

"Whatever, Hann. I don't want to talk about it."

"Okay. Just remember, I'm here if you need to talk about it."

"Come on, dude, forget about it. Let's head to the movies," Jean Paul said.

I just stewed as I drove to the theater, which was uncomfortable for the twins. They were used to the upbeat and chatty me, but I didn't care. I was worried and pissed.

We bought our tickets, went in, got our popcorn and soda, and found our seats. I plopped down in my seat with a scowl on my face.

Hannah said, "I'm sure she'll have a good explanation tomorrow and you'll both laugh about it."

"Whatever," I replied.

I should just drive over to that bitch Mary's house right now and get B. I know that's where she is. Mary probably came up with some bullshit excuse, and now she's trapped there. And that asshole Kyle better not have messed with her. If he did, I'll destroy him! I'll just fucking destroy him!

I actually did wind up enjoying the movie, so afterward we hit Friendly's for sundaes—which, of course, made me think of B.

"Are you doing okay over there?" Hannah asked, noticing my mood shift.

"Huh? Yeah, I'm okay. You're probably right. She probably got caught up with Mary. We'll probably laugh about it tomorrow. And knowing her, she'll feel horrible about it, so I'll try not to be a dick about it."

"Well that's good. I'm glad to see you're learning," she said with a laugh.

And then Hannah used a phrase that would ring in my ears for a very long time: "Remember . . . sometimes things are out of our control."

I dropped the twins off around eleven thirty, and I thought about driving by B's, but changed my mind. It was late, and I didn't want to get her in trouble, so I drove home.

Now, had I known what was waiting for me at home, I would have kept on driving.

58 - Shattered

I made it home by eleven forty-five, having first stopped for gas. Heat lightning lit the night sky as black clouds began forming.

I guess we're getting another storm.

As I walked to the front door, I noticed the living room lights were on, which was unusual, but I thought nothing of it.

The moment I turned the key and entered my house, my whole world *shattered.*

I should have stayed outside. I should have kept driving. I should have been anywhere else but there. But I didn't know what awaited me behind that door. I simply didn't know.

I turned the knob, opened the door, and found my family waiting for me in the foyer—my *whole* family.

There stood Ma, my kid brother *and* my older brother, home from Boston.

What's he doing home? Why didn't he tell me he was coming home? And why does everyone look so funny? Has Ma been crying? What the hell is going on?

"Uh, hey, guys," I said hesitantly as I greeted my older brother with a hug and kiss on the cheek. "What's going on? What are you doing home?" I looked around, but no one said anything. "Is everything okay?"

Ma turned her head, as if to hide her face. My older brother coughed into his fist and said, "Hey, bro, um, we need to talk. Let's go sit in here," he said as he escorted me into the living room.

Clearly, something was up, but I was completely clueless.

Ma's been crying. Why's she crying?

"Ma, are you okay?" I asked, handing her a tissue from a box in the living room.

It didn't occur to me we never kept boxes of tissues in the living room, not even when guests were over. I just wasn't picking up on the clues.

"Sí, mijo, sí. I'm okay." She wiped her eyes and gently blew her nose.

"We need to tell you something," my older brother started, "and it's going to hurt."

Did something happen to Belle? Where's Belle?

And then I heard her dog collar jingle from the other room, as she was presumably scratching herself.

"Guys, seriously, what's going on?" I asked, getting annoyed.

"First, we want you to know how very sorry we are," my older brother said as he patted my knee.

My kid brother then patted my shoulder, nodding his head. They sat on either side of me on the couch, while Ma sat across from me on the coffee table, which no one ever did. I was literally surrounded by my loved ones, and the clues kept slipping by me.

"Guys, it's just a broken hand. It's no big deal," I replied, attempting to get up, but I was held in place by my older brother. I was totally confused by their behavior.

"Mijo, it's not about your hand. I have some very bad news to share with ju. We received a call from Neil this evening."

Who the hell is Neil?

"Who's Neil?"

"He said he was B's brother."

"Oh *Nils*. Why did he call?" I asked as tears began forming in Ma's eyes.

Shit, did B get in trouble for last night. I knew we were cutting it close.

"Is B in trouble?" I asked, which triggered Ma's tears to start flowing.

I just looked at both my brothers, who sat there solemnly, and then back at Ma. I placed my hand on her knee, and she started crying harder.

"It's okay, Ma. It's okay. What did Nils want?" I asked, trying to calm her down.

"Oh, mijo, I don't know how to tell ju this."

"It's okay Ma, just tell me."

Folks, never ask a question if you're not prepared for the answer.

I was not prepared for the answer.

She grabbed another tissue, wiped her eyes, and then she handed a fresh one to me. I just took it and searched her eyes, waiting for the news.

Whatever it is, I'm sure B and I can make it right. How bad could it be?

And with four words, my world changed forever . . .

"Mijo, B died today."

~ ~ ~

"I'm sorry, *what* did you just *say*?"

"She was in a car accident y ella murió at the scene," Ma told me.

Shocked, I just looked at my brothers, who nodded somberly.

"What?" I shouted. "*That's not funny, Ma!* Seriously, *what's going on?*" I felt myself getting choked up.

"I'm sorry, mijo, I'm not joking," Ma said, her voice squeaking with emotion. "I'm so sorry, mijo, I'm so very sorry."

"Yeah, bro, we're all sorry," my older brother said, putting his arm around me.

"Yeah, man, I'm really sorry too. I really liked her," my younger brother added as tears rolled down his cheek.

What the fuck kind of sick joke is this? She's not dead! She can't be dead! I'm going to call her and straighten this out. Fuck that. I'm going over there right now and demand to know what the fuck is going on!

I shrugged my older brother's arm from me and stood up, angry, as tears fell down my face.

"Get the fuck off of me!" I shouted at them as I attempted to storm off.

My older brother stood and said, "Whoa, hold on, bro. Where are you going? Come back and sit down."

"Go fuck yourself! You go sit down! I'm going over there and straighten this out!" I yelled as I stormed toward the front door with my car keys in my hand. Both of my brothers ran after me and practically had to tackle me before reaching the front door.

"Get the *fuck* off of *me*!" I yelled. "Let me *go*! I'm going over there! She can't be dead! That's a lie! Take it back! *TAKE IT BACK*!" I struggled to escape from my brothers, using what little strength I had.

My legs turned to rubber and I just collapsed onto the living room floor. My brothers held me from both sides and eased me down as I slid to the floor. My older brother cradled my head against his shoulder and my younger brother rubbed my back. I sat on the floor and cried for a very long time as my brother held me, providing me comfort.

"I don't understand. We were together just last night. I was supposed to see her tonight, but she wasn't home," I heard myself say. "You must have misunderstood Nils, Ma," I pleaded.

"You must have. It's not possible. Not B, not her. She has to be alive. She has to. Please tell me this is a sick joke. Please tell me you're lying to me, Ma, and that I'll see her tomorrow, and she'll be all right," I pleaded.

I was nearly hysterical now, and my face felt raw from the scalding tears that wouldn't stop. Ma came over and held my face in both of her hands, looking at me with sorrow in her eyes.

"Please, Ma! *Please!*" I pleaded.

But there would be no take-backs.

Finally, my younger brother got up and got me some water, while Ma and my older brother escorted me back to the couch.

I choked out, "Ma, what happens now?"

"What do ju mean, mijo?"

"I, uh . . ." I couldn't get the words out.

"I think he's asking about funeral arrangements, Ma," my older brother said.

I just gestured toward him and nodded.

"I don't know yet, mijo. Neil told me he would call tomorrow. He said he wanted to talk to you."

"Nils," I corrected her and then thought, *oh who cares?*

"Okay, Ma." I could barely hear my own words.

I was numb from the news . . . completely numb. I suddenly wanted to be alone, alone with my thoughts, alone with my pain, alone with the darkness that had now become my world. I made my way up to my room, feeling the stares of my family on my back.

After stripping down to my underwear I flopped into bed. Every so often, someone would check in on me, but I always pretended that I was sleeping. I literally cried myself to sleep that night—my body finally shut down at around four o'clock.

Shattered.

59 - Seeds of Anger

M y older brother woke me around 8:30 a.m., "Hey, buddy. Nils is on the phone. Are you up to talking to him?"

I rubbed my eyes and felt the crustiness of dried tears on my face. I was barely lucid and still numb, but agreed to speak with him.

He handed me the phone and stepped out to give me privacy.

"Hello," I said.

"Hi, it's Nils."

We both became quiet for a moment, until I heard him sniff before clearing his throat.

"I, um, just wanted to speak with you. I know how fond you and B were of each other." *I'm not fond of her! I'm* in love *with her! And she's* in love *with me!* "We're all fond of you actually," he added.

"Nils, I'm so sorry..." I couldn't finish the sentence. "What happened, Nils?" I finally croaked.

I frankly didn't want to hear the details. If I knew the details then her death would become real, and I didn't want it to be real, not yet. Not so soon. I wanted it to be a nightmare, a really bad nightmare. I wanted B to wake me up from it, put her arms around me, and tell me that everything was okay as she held me.

"We're still trying to sort it all out," he said. "Apparently, B and Mary Fergusen . . . you know her, don't you? I believe she's one of your classmates at school."

"Yeah, I know her," I replied with a bit of anger in my voice.

"Well, they went shopping in the Hamptons yesterday. On their way back, according to witnesses, a deer ran across the highway and Mary had to swerve to miss it."

"Apparently she hit a puddle and hydroplaned off the road, right into a set of trees that lined the highway." He paused, cleared his throat again, then continued.

"The car slammed into the trees on the passenger side . . . and B died on impact," Nils choked out.

"According to the coroner at the scene, she went quickly and felt no pain. They used the 'jaws of life' to remove both of them from the car. Mary's still in a coma and on life support at Southside hospital," Nils concluded.

I seethed at the news of Mary surviving.

So that useless bitch gets to live, and my B dies! How is that fair? B was perfect! She was an angel! She had her whole life ahead of her. What about her hopes and dreams? What about her promise to always be by my side?

After that, I barely heard him giving me the details of her wake, funeral, and burial. I asked him to give the info to Ma, and he assured me that he already had, so I said goodbye and how sorry I was again for our loss. Then I hung up.

Sitting there, alone, holding the phone, staring into nothingness, my mind became a broken record of disbelief, anger, sorrow . . . I didn't know what I was feeling anymore. I was still numb from the pain.

My brother walked back in my room moments after I hung up the phone. He must have been waiting outside my bedroom door for the call to finish.

"How're you doing, buddy?" he asked.

I just looked up at him, tears returning to my eyes, and shook my head, speechless. He came over and sat with me on my bed, putting his arm around me. I just fell into him and cried as he held me, the phone still in my left hand, my heart and soul completely void and shattered.

He said, "Nils gave us all the funeral details. The wake's in a few days, on Wednesday. The funeral and burial are on Thursday. I'm gonna stay the rest of the week. I already called the office to let them know."

I nodded, barely. I could feel him watching me for a long moment, then he squeezed my shoulder, and left me alone.

I bet it was that bitch's fault! It had to be her fault. She was probably drinking and driving or talking about who-knows-what, not paying attention.

I'm gonna make that bitch pay! I don't care how much money her family has. That bitch is gonna pay! And so will her asshole brother, her scumbag father, and even her crotchety old grandmother. All of them are going pay for this!

That was the moment anger planted its destructive and wicked seed deep into my heart. Just like that, it took hold of me like some vile weed. As any homeowner will tell you, if you don't nip a weed in the bud, it'll take root, build a strong foundation, and spread.

An anger grabbed hold of me that day, an anger that would take me a *very* long time to rip out and evict from my life.

I lay back on my bed, where I stayed for the rest of the day . . . crying, as the seed of fury blossomed and spread its poisonous and evil roots throughout my heart and soul.

Vengeance will be mine!

60 - Last Exit to Montauk

The twins came over sometime that Sunday to offer their support, and Jean Paul wound up spending the night. The following day was a rough one. We made it to school, but I didn't make it past first period.

I excused myself from class and went to the men's room. I walked into a stall and broke down into a puddle of tears. Fortunately, Jean Paul wasn't far behind me, as he had also excused himself and followed me into the bathroom. What are best friends for?

He dragged me out of the stall and held me as I cried. Eventually I was able to compose myself, and after blowing my nose and washing my face in the sink, I headed to the parking lot and left campus.

I was home and back in bed about twenty minutes later. I stayed there the rest of the day. While I rested, Ma ran errands with my brothers. Apparently my older brother left home with only the clothes on his back, so he needed something to wear for the rest of the week as well as for the wake and funeral.

I stayed home the following day and was surprised to find Jean Paul at my bedroom door with bagels and coffee. His parents had allowed him to skip school and spend the day with me. We sat in my bedroom, silently watching TV and eating breakfast.

After breakfast, I dragged myself into the shower while Jean Paul went downstairs to hang out with my older brother, whom he looked up to and admired.

Once I'd dressed, I felt the need to get out of the house. I went downstairs and said to Jean Paul, "Let's get out of here, bro."

"Where are we headed?"

"I have no idea. I just need to get out of here and clear my head."

"Try to stay close," my older brother said.

I just nodded in response, grabbed my wallet and keys, and went to my car. With no particular destination in mind, I took Nesconset Highway east. I then turned left onto Nicolls Road and right onto Route 25A toward Setauket.

Before I knew it, I was driving into Old Field.

"Bro, where are we going?" Jean Paul cautiously asked.

I glanced over at him and saw the look of concern in his eyes. "I just need to see something."

Minutes later, I stopped my car and stared at B's car, still sitting in the Fergusens' driveway. Anger boiled in the pit of my stomach as hot tears began flowing from my eyes. I put the car in park and started to get out.

"Whoa, whoa, whoa," Jean Paul said, grabbing my cast.

"Let go of me! That's B's car over there, and they have no right having it in their *fucking* driveway," I snapped. "It's their fucking fault she's dead, Jean Paul! It's that fucking bitch Mary and her whole fucking family's fault!"

I tried to pull my cast from his grasp, but he wouldn't let go. "Hey, hey, you can't go out there. Not like this, not right now," he said in a soothing voice. "Come on, sit down. B wouldn't want you to do this, and you know it."

His words hit me like a bucket of ice water, and brought me immediately back to my senses. I fell back into my seat as the hot tears of anger and frustration slid down my face. And he did what any best friend would do. He leaned over and held me.

"Let it out, bro. It'll be okay. I'm here for you," he said.

We sat in front of their house for almost ten minutes, as random cars passed by, before I was able to compose myself.

Jean Paul sat back in his seat and pointed to the road. "Come on, dude. Let's get out of here before someone calls the cops on us or something."

I put the car into drive, made a U-turn and left Old Field for the last time. I wasn't ready to return home just yet though, so I took Route 25A back to Nicolls Road and took it southbound.

Jean Paul played with the radio as I drove. Subconsciously I knew exactly where I was heading, but consciously I had no idea. I was like a robot behind the wheel.

Before I knew it, I hopped onto the LIE heading eastbound.

"Now, where are we going, dude? Your brother asked us to stay close."

"Dude, I don't know. I just need to drive." I looked at him and shrugged my shoulders.

He squinted at me again with concern, but he said, "Okay."

Forty minutes later, I found myself taking Exit 70 to Hampton Bays, Route 111 South to Montauk Highway East.

Jean Paul turned slightly in his seat then, staring at me as he realized where we were going.

"Do you really think this is a good idea?"

"I have to see it, Jean Paul. I have to see it with my own eyes."

We drove silently for fifteen minutes before I found it.

To my right read a sign: *Last Exit to Montauk.*

To my left was the spot that completely shattered my world to its very core and foundation.

It was the place where my beloved B died.

61 - Our Last Goodbye

I could see the skid marks as clear as day. I could see where their car slid off the road and impacted a large tree. A good section of the tree was gone. There were still pieces from the crash scene scattered along the side of the road.

Since there were no guardrails, I illegally crossed the median and drove up to the accident site, where I parked and killed the engine.

Jean Paul didn't say a word. We just sat there and stared at the remainder of the wreckage. The whole world was impossibly silent.

I took in every detail, particularly the tree. The tree that took the love of my life from me forever.

That goddamn tree. I fucking hate that tree. I will hate that fucking tree forever!

Anger rose up inside of me once again. I wanted to get out of that car, rip that tree from its roots and smash it to pieces. I wanted to throw it into the sun and remove it from our very existence for taking away my B.

Tears rolled down my face as I exited the car; I needed a closer look. I don't know why I did it, but I just did. Like the rainy night in my car with my beloved, I had to know.

Jean Paul, God bless him, never left my side. When I stepped onto the grass and walked toward the tree, I fell to my knees and screamed in anger. I yelled at the top of my lungs until I had no air left.

Hot tears just streamed down my face, as I began to hit my cast on the ground. I needed to smash something. Jean Paul grabbed me and told me to stop—a firm, but controlled voice of reason. Somehow I heard him. I put the cast across my stomach, to protect it from myself, and bent forward, wailing, wailing, wailing.

My screams were primal. Birds took flight as I released the agony trapped deep inside my soul.

Jean Paul finally said, "Come on, let's go, buddy. Let's get out of here. Give me your keys. I'll drive us home."

I handed him my keys, knowing I was in no condition to drive. I walked out to the highway and just barely avoided getting hit by a car, but I didn't care as it drove past me, honking its horn.

Jean Paul, on the other hand, freaked out.

"Dude, *what the fuck?*" he yelled as he grabbed me.

I shrugged him off and bent down, tracing the skid marks from where they started, to the point of impact. I imagined in my mind's eye what had happened, never *really* knowing exactly what had happened that fateful afternoon.

What was B thinking about before the accident? Was she thinking of me? Was she thinking about our future? Did she think about our wedding? About our children? About the life we'd never have as the car skidded toward the tree? Did it all flash before her eyes as she passed away?

I had a million questions and zero answers.

I was in hell.

~ ~ ~

They held her wake on Wednesday at a local funeral home in Smithtown. Due to traffic, we hadn't arrived as soon as we'd planned. The place was already packed.

"Do I look okay?" I asked as we pulled up.

"Sí, mijo, ju look fine," Ma replied.

Just then, Jean Paul and Hannah walked up to our car. They were a welcome sight.

Jean Paul said, "Hey, bro, we thought we'd wait for you out here. It's starting to get packed in there. They're opening up another room to accommodate everyone. My parents saved us all seats."

I nodded and stared at the doors.

"You okay, buddy?" my older brother asked as he placed an arm around my shoulders, watching me stare at the entrance. "You're shaking a little. Why don't we wait out here a little bit?"

He then turned to Ma and our kid brother. "Hey Ma, why don't you two go inside with Hannah. Jean Paul and I will stay out here with him for a minute, okay?"

"Okay, mijo," she replied, as Hannah escorted them into the funeral home.

Suddenly my father's funeral flooded my memories. The emotions and fright of that day overwhelmed my senses and took hold of me. I was afraid to move. All I could imagine was B lying in an open casket wearing the blue dress we had purchased together; people walking up to her, touching her, commenting on how pretty she was as they offered up prayers.

I just stood there shaking a bit, with my brother and Jean Paul patiently waiting at my side, until a familiar voice broke me from my trance.

"I thought that was you," she said.

I turned and actually managed to produce a half-smile.

"Hey, Squirrel."

"You know you're the only one who's still allowed to call me that, right?" She smiled as she stood there in a black pill box hat and black dress. "Are you heading in?"

I nodded.

"Good, you can escort me in," she said, placing her arm in mine. "I think most of the youth group are here already. They'll be happy to see you."

My brother and Jean Paul glanced at each other. They had no idea who this was or how she had broken me from my state of stillness. They just shrugged their shoulders and joined us as we headed toward the door, and I introduced them to Vi.

"Oh, there's the group," she said, pointing. "Do you want to come over and say hi?"

I just said, "Yeah, okay, sure."

This was a much larger youth group than the one I met during the lock-in. It wasn't just the seniors. There were students as young as seventh grade. They took over an entire seating section. In addition to the kids, there were parents as well. I eventually saw Mike and Emily, whom I hugged hello.

I walked over and took a deep breath and blew it out, trying to hold it together while people offered their condolences. Miraculously, I was able to swallow the waterworks and control myself. It was all so surreal.

The service was about to begin, so I excused myself and found my family, who was seated with the Michaels family. Mr. and Mrs. Michaels offered me their condolences as I sat.

I took the aisle seat next to Jean Paul, which bothered Hannah, so she made him switch with her. She had a box of tissues in her lap, which I found funny for some reason.

"Are you doing okay?" she whispered, taking my hand.

"So far so good."

That was when I noticed B's closed casket adorned with a flower wreath. A blown-up picture of her sat on a stand next to her casket. Her whole family took over the first two rows. You could tell they were related. They all had different shades of blond hair and that Scandinavian look about them.

Pastor Mike stood and addressed the mourners as the organ music finished.

"For those that don't know me, I'm Reverend Michael Thompson. I was B's youth pastor. My wife Emily and I had the blessing and privilege of knowing this young lady for many years," he said as a tear rolled down his cheek.

He went on to tell a few stories about B throughout the years. The stories were funny, poignant, and serious. Mike did an excellent job. He invited the youth group to come up, and they sang a song they'd rehearsed.

Some were crying as they sang, holding tissues in their hands. I don't remember what song they sang. I just remember it sounded nice. Mike then invited people to come up and say a few words of remembrance.

People I didn't know got up and spoke about B. Iris and Katie went up together and had everyone in tears as they remembered their best friend. Others from her youth group got up as did some from church, some from her summer job, and some from her neighborhood.

A few teachers from school, including Professor Michaels and our headmaster, got up and spoke about B's many scholastic accomplishments.

"She was a remarkable young lady," they all said.

Jean Paul leaned over and asked me if I wanted to go up there, but I just shook my head no.

"I'm not there yet, bro."

Finally, B's immediate family went up one by one. Ellie got up first and tearfully shared a few words about her little sister. The moment she started speaking, the tears flowed down my face.

Nils got up next and tearfully shared additional words about his baby sister, whom he loved dearly.

Their father stood next, but was unable to say much. He was too distraught. All he was able to get out was, "She was a marvel, and the most wonderful child."

Lastly, her mother stood. She was even more upset than her husband, but she stood nonetheless. She took a deep breath and composed herself as she surveyed the room, locking eyes with me as she did so.

The moment our eyes locked, she started to cry, as I continued to do the same. In that moment, our souls seemed to connect. People seemed to look from her to me and back again, not understanding what was happening, or who I was, but she and I didn't care. I heard some murmur, "Who's he?"

But she and I understood, and at that moment, that's all that mattered.

She then composed herself again, as best she could, and spoke from her heart. She was amazing. She talked about how extraordinary *our* B was, how she was such an excellent example to all that knew and loved her, and how she held so much promise.

She finished by saying, "I will forever have a hole in my heart from *our* loss." She then looked at me with a knowing tear.

There wasn't a dry eye in the place.

Pastor Mike concluded the service with a prayer. People then began to mill about. Some walked up to the casket, knelt, and said a prayer, while others offered their condolences to B's family. Others just went to the refreshment room, which I found totally distasteful and disrespectful.

Me? I didn't move from my seat. I just sat there and stared at the casket and picture.

"Do you want to go up there and say a prayer?" Hannah asked.

I nodded.

"Okay, I'll take you," she said, as she escorted me to the back of a line of people waiting to do the same thing.

Others soon got in line behind us, including Ma, who was escorted by my brothers.

When it was finally my turn, I froze. I couldn't move.

I couldn't believe the love of my life lay inside that closed shiny wooden box. I couldn't believe the light of my life, the girl to whom I'd professed my love only days prior, was now gone forever.

The reality of the moment just cut me to my very soul. Hannah handed me a tissue as I stood there and wept.

I felt the people behind us start to get impatient. Most had no idea who I was, or why I held up the line.

"Hey, come on. People are waiting to pay their respects," some guy whispered to Hannah.

I wanted to turn around and tell him to fuck off. I wanted to tell all of them to fuck off. They didn't know her like I did.

Why hadn't anyone mentioned Oxford? How come no one mentioned her favorite flower or flavor of ice cream? Do these people even know about shrimp and grits?

Do they know she was my whole world?

Do they understand how utterly alone I feel right now?

Do they know how much I hurt?

Do they know . . . how much . . . I love her?

I knelt down, placed my hand on her casket, and bowed my head. I stayed there weeping and praying for a solid minute—waiting people be damned—before someone knelt down beside me and gently touched my elbow.

It was B's mom. She helped me to stand and gently wiped my tears and caressed my face in a very familiar way.

Wow, she has B's eyes. I never noticed that before.

She then held me. I realized at that moment she was the closest thing to B that I'd ever have again in my world, ever. I just folded into her and wept.

"I'm so sorry she's gone. I'm so sorry," I whispered as tears flowed down my cheeks. "I loved her so much."

"I know, sweetheart, I know. And she loved you too, so very much."

We just stood, people watching us, maybe wondering who I was to this beautiful girl in the picture. To this grieving family. We were soon joined by the rest of B's immediate family. Mine followed moments later, including the entire Michaels family.

We just stood there, all of us supporting each other, clinging to each other, connected by the shining soul of one very special girl.

Rest in Peace, missus. Rest in Peace.

62 - The Rest of the Story

They held a formal funeral the following morning at B's church, the place of our lock-in and those incredible memories. It was more of a sterile church service than anything else, which didn't reflect B at all. She had so much life in her, yet the service didn't really reflect that.

Maybe it was because the senior pastor presided over the service and burial ceremony, and he was older and more reserved. Who knows?

As a middle-aged adult, I'd now say it was a lovely service. But as a broken-hearted seventeen-year-old, I found it horrible at best.

At the gravesite, mourners were invited to place flowers on her casket. I made sure to place a sunflower on her casket. I made Ma stop at a florist on the way to the service to get one. Soon the gravesite service ended and everyone left.

I noticed that Nana Fergusen attended the funeral service, but left immediately afterward. I learned later that they transferred Mary to New York-Presbyterian Hospital in the city via helicopter for treatment.

She eventually woke from her coma and was released from the hospital a few weeks later, injury-free. She never returned to our school, though. I guess she felt everyone would blame her for our loss. She wouldn't have been wrong. I certainly did.

Word has it, she received her GED that spring and escaped to the West Coast soon afterwards, never to return. According to Facebook, she started in San Diego, then moved to Seattle before eventually settling in Oregon.

I have no idea what became of Kyle. I heard rumors of a drug overdose and spending most of his twenties and thirties in rehab, but I never confirmed it. I heard that their father, *Gus*, remarried a few more times before finally moving to Antigua.

According to the papers, he went there to escape federal charges. Unfortunately for him, Antigua signed an extradition treaty with the US in the late nineties, and he was brought back to the States. He wound up spending five lovely years in an Upstate New York Federal Correctional Institution.

As an adult, I feel badly for the Fergusen clan. They had so much potential. Maybe that was what B saw in Mary. Maybe she saw some diamond in the rough, stuck in the middle of this messed-up family. It's probably why, after letting go of my anger, I'm able to feel sorry for her too. Maybe.

But if anyone could see beyond the top layer and straight through to the inner person, it was B. She had the ability to see behind the façade. I guess she brought stability to Mary's life, while Mary provided B with the chaos we all sometimes need. Yin and Yang.

The weekend following the funeral, there was a knock on my front door. Belle barked as I opened the door. There stood Ellie, B's sister, with a familiar smile and a plastic grocery bag in her hand. To this day, I have no idea how she knew where I lived. It must be a family thing.

"Hey Ellie, what are you doing here?" I asked as I invited her in.

"I was gathering some laundry together, and found this in the hamper," she said, handing me the bag.

As I opened it, B's very essence escaped and filled my senses.

Oh My God!

At the top of the bag was a small box, neatly wrapped in red wrapping paper and a white bow. Beneath the box were the clothes B had borrowed from me the night she slept over.

Oh Sweet Lord!

"Thank you," I choked out as I hugged her in my foyer.

Moments later, she released me, "Okay, listen, I've got to go. Are you going to be okay?"

I could only nod.

"Okay, take care of yourself, mister," she said as she caressed my cheek in a familiar way, before turning and leaving my house.

I stood there speechless.

What'd she just say?

Coming to my senses, I ran after her and caught her in the driveway, "Ellie, wait. Back there, inside my house, what did you say?" I asked, searching her blue eyes.

"I said for you to take care of yourself, *mister.*" She grinned knowingly.

I just unabashedly threw my arms around her.

"Thanks, Ellie. I needed to hear that more than you know," I said, and kissed her on the cheek before releasing her.

I went back inside and stepped into the family room, lightly shaking the gift box.

My older brother was sitting on the couch watching TV and asked, "What's in the box?"

"Beats me," I replied as I continued to gently shake the box, putting my ear to it.

It had a homemade tag with my name written on it in familiar handwriting.

"Well, are you going to open it?" he asked.

I put the bag of clothes down between my legs, protecting it with my life.

No one is getting near these. I will kill someone if they touch these clothes.

I carefully removed the bow and the wrapping paper, intent on keeping everything intact. I then opened the box, and found a handwritten note, along with a red velvet jewelry pouch.

The note read:

Mister,

I love you so much. Remember when I told you I was getting this for someone special? Well, that someone was you. I held on to it for our first-month anniversary.

I love you so very much and can't wait to spend the rest of my life with you!

Happy One Month Anniversary!

I'll Love You Always and Forever,
Britt-Marie

Epilogue

I stared at the note and immediately knew what awaited me in the jewelry pouch. I opened it up and into my palm fell the white string bracelet B had purchased the night of our first kiss, in Port Jeff.

I just dropped to my knees and wept.

Britt-Marie, damn it, you got me again. Even after your death, you're still finding ways to get me. My God, I'm going to miss you, Britt-Marie. I'll love you always and forever too.

And that was her name:

Britt-Marie Välsignad Karlsson
May 27, 1970 - September 12, 1987
Beloved Daughter, Sister, and Friend
And Love of My Life

I immediately put the bracelet on, before heading up to my room to hide the clothes under my pillow. That night I wore my sweatshirt to sleep, enveloped by the scent of B. I didn't wind up taking the bracelet off for a very long time. I wore it well into my thirties. You can actually see it in my wedding photos if you look real close.

It was even there for the birth of my first two children. When I finally took it off for the last time, a tear formed in my eye. It was falling apart, and I was getting tired of trying to fix it. It now proudly sits on my dresser gathering dust, like so many other memories.

You're probably wondering about me and the rest of my story.

Well, the remainder of my senior year didn't go so well. I tanked my SATs that October because I lost all interest in studying. My GPA dropped from a 3.7 to a 2.1. My only saving grace was my senior project. It actually helped me get off academic probation and elevated my GPA from a 1.9 to the 2.1.

Most of my teachers couldn't understand what had happened to my brain and motivation. I mean, they knew about B, but I guess they thought I would rebound more quickly or something. I never explained myself to anyone.

Poor Ma spent many days coming to school for different academic meetings. She tried everything she could that year to get my head back in the game. She got me tutors, she threatened me, she took away my car, she took away my TV, and she even had my older brother talk to me. Nothing worked. She even sent me to a psychologist, whom I refused to talk to, so I simply stopped going. She was at her wit's end.

I never tried out for the fall play either, nor did I participate in any after-school programs the rest of the year. My enthusiasm for life was simply gone. I even kept Jean Paul and Hannah at arm's length for most of that year.

Five weeks into my recovery, I took a hammer to my cast. I was tired of the physical restraint and constant reminder, so I went out to my garage, found a mallet, and smashed it to pieces.

My mom took me for x-rays, and luckily my hand was fully healed with no damage from the hammer.

"Consider jurself very lucky, coño!" she angrily told me, and she was right. I was lucky.

Amazingly, I never turned to drugs or alcohol. Who knows where I'd be today if I had—probably six feet under, sharing a room at rehab with Kyle, or lying in some ditch somewhere in some South American country.

For weeks I'd come home from school and immediately lock myself in my room. I would lie on my bed, surrounding myself with Britt-Marie's dirty laundry.

It still had her pheromones embedded in it. It was just like my car before the scent dissipated, only better. They became my prized possessions. Eventually, the smell wore off, which was a very sad day.

Ma came home and found me crying in my room, holding onto the clothes. I'm surprised she didn't institutionalize me after that one. I eventually washed the clothes and worked them back into my rotation.

That January, I met with Mr. Chapman, the teacher who oversaw all of the senior projects. I had from January to the end of May to complete my project.

When I shared my idea for the two-term project with him, he was hesitant at first. He didn't think I could pull it off in that short amount of time. Unlike today, we didn't have access to a lot of technology.

There were no personal computers, iPads or PowerPoint. If you wanted to do anything, you had to do it manually. He told me I was putting a lot on myself.

I assured him I could do it, and he finally acquiesced. For the next five months, I spent all my free time on this project. I became obsessed with it and put everything I had into completing it by my due date—ironically, Friday, May twenty-seventh, Britt-Marie's birthday. It was also the night of our school's annual talent show.

I invited everyone I could think of, at least those who were still talking to me, which admittedly weren't many. I had apologized weeks prior to Hannah and Jean Paul for my negativity and sorry attitude, and thankfully they'd forgiven me. I reached out to Pastor Mike and asked him to reach out to the youth group as well, on my behalf.

The evening began and I spent most of it behind the scenes, helping Kevin in the audio/video booth.

Our school definitely had talent. Not many were gonged off the stage, and even when they were, it was all in good fun. The student rock band performed an Aerosmith song, which everyone went crazy over. They received a standing ovation.

"Okay, you're up. Break a leg!" Kevin said, pushing me from the booth.

The evening's MC, Hal Pilcher, called me out, and I made my way to the stage. I was terrified. I'd only been on stage once, and that was during the lock-in with Britt-Marie. This time, I didn't have her to lean on.

As the rock band left the stage, Kevin shined a lonely spotlight on me as I made my way to a piano that had been rolled out for me by the stage hands. As I mentioned earlier, we had a piano at home, and I played it periodically.

You could hear a pin drop.

As I sat down, a large movie screen lowered behind me. I closed my eyes, took a big breath in through my nose and out through my mouth. I'd rehearsed this many hours at home, which had driven my family nuts.

I said a quick prayer, looked up at the booth, swallowed, and nodded. Kevin hit a switch and a movie title filled the screen behind me:

She Was My Rainbow

"This is for Britt-Marie Karlsson," I shared.

With that, I started playing "She's a Rainbow" by The Rolling Stones.

As I sang, pictures of Britt-Marie appeared on the screen. It began with early childhood pictures that I borrowed from her parents. I included everything I could get my hands on, from vacation pictures to the classic school picture, where she was missing a front tooth.

The movie slowly transitioned from her elementary school years to her time in youth group. We got to see her blossom from an awkward seventh grader to a high schooler, including pictures from our lock-in. Someone had actually taken pictures of us singing together on stage and cuddling on the couch, laughing about something. We got to see her blossom like a sunflower, transforming before our very eyes from a beautiful young girl to a stunning young woman, full of hope and promise, guided by The Son.

During the second piano solo of the song, members of the student rock band returned to the stage and began to back me up, much to my surprise. Somehow, they'd gotten wind of the deal. Later, I found out it was Kevin's doing. A violinist from our school orchestra also joined in.

The four-minute film came off perfectly and so did the song. While I had planned to play it as a solo, God, and maybe B, had different plans for me that evening.

As a very wise girl once told me, sometimes things are out of your control.

In the fall, I went to a small college in Upstate New York, but dropped out after the second semester. I wasn't crazy about the student population and frankly had no desire to continue my education, so I put it on hold, much to Ma's chagrin. So I came home and got a full-time job working retail.

I also pursued the arts, first trying my hand at stand-up comedy. This led to theater school in the city, getting an agent, going out on auditions and getting bit parts as an extra. My last paying role was as an extra in the movie, *A Bronx Tale*, starring Robert De Niro. They shot it in the city in the summer of 1992.

My then fiancée and now wife encouraged me to take the role. I actually met De Niro between takes. If you look real close, you can see me in the background of one of the street scenes in the first hour of the film.

I transitioned from retail to computers, which I've been doing for over twenty years now. And speaking of over twenty years, my beloved wife of over twenty years, Hannah, will be getting up soon, so I better go make her some coffee. Apparently, she loves her man the way she loves her coffee: a little brown, spicy, and sweet.

Yes, I married my high school best friend. We reconnected at our ten-year high school reunion. Apparently, she had a bit of a crush on me back in high school. Who knew? One thing lead to another, and well, let's just say, we never looked back.

Before moving to Florida, I did actually make it out to Montauk Point. I took off work one summer afternoon and drove out there. I parked my car, took off my shoes, and walked toward the shoreline—with the famous lighthouse keeping watch.

I sat on the sand and put on my Walkman headset, listening to the music as the waves gently crashed onto the beach. After an hour or so, I grabbed the bouquet of sunflowers I had brought with me just for this occasion and walked to the water's edge. I tossed the bouquet into the ocean as a few tears slipped down my cheeks.

I watched for a while as the sunflowers became one with the ocean.

I guess, when all was said and done, Britt-Marie became the first person to teach me about love. Hannah took over and continued the lessons—ones that I continue to learn to this day. I couldn't be happier.

In my opinion, we have our very own personal angel watching over my family of five these days. And Lord knows we've kept her busy, especially our youngest. She's Daddy's not-so-little girl named Britt-Marie.

It was Hannah's idea. I guess B made an impression on everyone. Of course, this version has chestnut eyes and auburn hair, just like her gorgeous mother. She's also smart as a whip, just like her namesake.

Britt-Marie Karlsson, I'll always love you and know we'll meet again in heaven. I'll be the guy standing there with the bouquet of sunflowers and a crooked smile, and you'll be standing there with a creamy bowl of heavenly shrimp and grits and homemade cornbread.

Fin

Acknowledgements

I would like to thank the following individuals who provided me with encouragement, assistance, guidance, feedback, and helped make this story become a reality.

First to my wife, Jeanette, who put up with many late nights and early mornings as I pulled this book together. I love you!

To my children, William, Phillip, Michael, and Devin, whom I love with all my soul.

To my brothers, Diego and Peter, who both provided me with instrumental feedback and support.

To my friends and family, Linda, Christy, Luis, Barbara, Pepper, Carol, Mariela, Nicole, Rebecca, Suzanne, Nancy, Kara, Enio, Gene, Angela, and Karen, who also offered invaluable feedback and encouragement for the project.

I am so grateful to my the ten individuals (Mary, Krystal, Karen, Deborah, Elena, Danielle, Tracy, Christy, Jennifer, and Nancy) who were willing to review an advanced copy of the book for me. The input that came in helped me add some very important finishing touches.

And finally, to my beloved editor, publisher, friend, and confidant, Janet. All I can say is . . . You!

About the Author

I'm a husband, father, a transplanted Long Islander living in Florida, and a child of the 1970s and '80s.

When I'm not working, I spend time with my wife of twenty-three years, four sons, and two-and-a-half dogs. Okay, it's four dogs, but three out of the four are Chihuahuas while the fourth is a shepherd mix, so I say two-and-a-half.

I also enjoy going to the beach, reading, singing, performing, writing . . . and laughing.

CPSIA information can be obtained
at www.ICGtesting.com
Printed in the USA
LVOW10s0031040617

536858LV00002B/18/P